THE ACCIDENTAL GANGSTER 4

D J Keogh

Folk, Drugs and Sausage rolls

The Accidental Gangster: Part 4
David J. Keogh

Paperback Edition First Published in the United Kingdom
in 2018 by aSys Publishing

eBook Edition First Published in the United Kingdom
in 2018 by aSys Publishing

Copyright © David J Keogh

Disclaimer
This is a work of fiction. All characters and incidents are
products of the author's imagination and any resemblance to
actual people or events is coincidental or fictionalised.

ISBN: 978-1-9996931-2-1

aSys Publishing
http://www.asys-publishing.co.uk

Authors Note

I dedicate this book to my wife Abi

A Special Thanks To

Jason Ryder for all of your encouragement and genius editing and proof reading skills.

PROLOGUE

The Bog-Man

The silent black water had been flowing through the Victorian canals for nearly two hundred years, gently ebbing through countless passages and the huge lock-gates that had been pickaxed, dug and blasted to form this dark labyrinth.

The thousands who worked on the construction of these man-made rivers were known in their day as 'Navigators'. Many were content to live and die along the hundreds of miles of tow paths and water courses that criss-crossed the West Midlands like a colossal spider's web. The loss of life was, even by the standards of the day, immense but still 'an acceptable price to pay' for such a massive construction project. As long as the narrowboats, barges and water kept flowing towards the centre of Great Britain's second city and the industrial heartland that was Birmingham, all was well . . .

Unfortunately they didn't.

The arrival of the steam train followed by the motorcar and motorways made the canal transportation system with its leisurely barges and longboats seem archaic when compared to the speed of the train or the car. Waterways simply fell from grace, condemned to the annals of history. And slowly, almost without anyone noticing, the hundreds of miles of canals became overgrown, stagnant

1

and forgotten. Water flowed less easily now. Canals became filled with weeds, silt, scum, food waste, old mattresses, settees, bikes and even burnt out-cars. The black water was the resting place for unwanted puppies, kittens and even a dumping ground for abattoirs that conveniently happened to back onto the waterways.

When the new decade of the 1990s rolled into town, something unexpected happened. Suddenly, previously unfashionable Victorian design with its austerity and industrial pragmatism became 'trendy'. And so *reconstruction* became the name of the game. The gentrification of Birmingham's Gas Street Basin began in earnest and the booming multicultural population of the second city were delighted by the progress the *new*-navigators were making. It was a brave new world reconstructed from the old one.

And then the first human remains were discovered. At first the skeletons of those original 'Navies' were uncovered amongst the silt, preserved to an extent by the thick coverage of clay that seemed to cake everything with a wet, sloppy, airtight film. These 'Bog-men' as the newspapers described them, were nameless faces from the past and told a hard story of life before the 20th century's obsession with health and safety. However, not all of the bog-men discovered were Victorian . . . Some were far younger. Some remains were found to be only a few years old. To the majority of Birmingham's public this was an interesting, if rather macabre news story but to certain others, scattered around the city, it triggered the start of many a sleepless night.

One body was that of a young man. According to the coroner, he was a white male in his late twenties, early thirties. His sodden corpse had been causing a blockage in one of the overflow drains behind the back of a warehouse on Fleet Street, on the edges of the city-centre. The elderly coroner who had the unpleasant job of ascertaining the cause of death, found that the cadaver had suffered severe spinal injuries concurrent with a fall from a great height. He had therefore come to the conclusion that the victim had died from a fall before his body had been dumped into the canal. Judging by the way the body was twisted and broken, he also concluded that the remains had travelled half a mile or so down the watercourse, meaning the body had been dumped into the water somewhere along the back of Constitution Hill. Over a period of years the body had slowly been washed down by the gentle current to its final resting place in the drainage overflow system at the back of the warehouse.

The detective given the almost impossible task of finding out where the murder had taken place, came to the conclusion that the only area with a building high enough to fall from along that stretch of canal, did indeed lie behind Constitution Hill, and the only area with any real access to a canal side was the carpark at the rear of which was previously part of a nightclub premises.

The Cedar Club was one of Birmingham's most popular live music venues, owned and run by Birmingham's very own nightclub king: a certain Eddie Fewtrell.

The coroner's scrawl on the death certificate indicated that the body had wallowed in the water for approximately ten years. This gave the detective in charge of the investigation a time period to work with. He quickly came to the conclusion, based on the fact that there had been no reports from that period of a suicide or an accidental fall, that there had been foul play at work. Assuming the fallen man with his shattered spine hadn't simply picked himself up from the floor, dusted himself down and walked across the Cedar Club carpark, climbing the crumbling, red-brick wall on the way and then throwing himself into the canal, then it was indeed murder. The man had probably been pushed from some high point on the building, possibly the fire escape. The murderer wouldn't have wanted to carry the body of a fully grown man through the busy streets of Birmingham like an oversized rag-doll and so the detective also deduced that the victim, once dispatched, had been manhandled across the carpark from beneath the fire escape by one or more assailants. At this point this poor soul was added to an ever-growing list of Birmingham's unsolved murders.

Dental records later revealed the man's name to be Timothy (Tigger) Burns and next of kin, a brother, was located: one Daniel

Burns of Bethnal Green. However, this revelation only created more questions. Apart from the next of kin's name on his dead mother's council flat tenancy, there were no records of Daniel Burn's existence at all; no school reports, no doctor's registration, not even a birth certificate in the local record's office. Nothing could be ascertained about the dead man's brother. Alarm bells began to ring for our detective and calls were made to the local constabulary, asking them to visit the address to try and make contact. Even though the local police confirmed that *someone* was actually living there, they could not confirm one way or the other exactly *who* it was because they were never around when the police called. So, as a last resort, a letter was left at the Bethnal Green council flat informing Daniel Burns about the death of his relative in Birmingham. When the police returned the next day, the letter had gone and so it seemed had this elusive next of kin. It seemed that in this instance delivering news in this way had created more questions than answers. The *local* constabulary assumed that whoever it was that had read the letter didn't want to be found and had just moved on. Our Detective thought differently.

A mysterious murder victim and his vanishing brother? Call it what you will but something about this whole affair was rotten to the core and Detective John 'Dixie' Dixon knew he had some questions that had to be answered.

CHAPTER 1

Shamrocks and Sawn-offs
(1995)

The sawn-off shotgun was levelled horizontally in front of the terrified Bar-Manager's face, his field of vision filled by its deadly double barrels. Frozen in a moment of sensory overload, his frazzled brain tried to process the image in front of him. His eyes crossed ridiculously as he tried to focus on the roughly filed ends of the double-barrelled weapon. He took in the minute details: its dark gun-metal grey barrels contrasting against the bright silver of the freshly-shorn metal shards at the barrel's end. The manager's eye broke away and followed the barrel up to the gun's firing hammers. He almost passed out when he saw the ornately decorated hammers had both been pulled back into the firing position, meaning one squeeze of the gunman's finger and it would be Goodnight Irene. The manager's eye continued to follow the form of the gun unconsciously past its primed hammers, along its sawn-off wooden butt and onto the surgical rubber-gloved hand that held the weapon. He flicked his eye upwards towards the gunman's stocking-covered features and immediately wished he hadn't.

"*Don't* look at my face!"

The words were snarled slowly, deliberately, in a voice full of malevolence. A low, gritty tone that came from the grimy streets of some place in the Midlands and even though the sentence was a short one, the bar manager knew by the way he said the words, that this man had spent a lifetime doing just what he was doing here tonight. And then the robber jabbed the barrel forcefully into his top lip.

"I told you, don't look at my *fucking* face!"

The sawn-off jabbed again, only this time harder, drawing blood. The Bar-Manager yelped at the sudden shock. He lowered his eyes subserviently again.

"That's it sunshine, you keep your pork-pies pointing at the gun and you won't forget why we're here, will ya?"

The gunman paused and it was then that the Bar-Manager realised there was someone else in the room, someone out of sight, rummaging.

"Now you do know why we're here don't ya?"

The manager's brow furrowed. He raised his eyes but was forced to lower them again with another, even harder, butt of the weapon's barrel.

"Are you fucking deaf or just stupid, pal?"

The manager could feel warm blood from top lip seeping into his mouth. Its metallic coppery taste made him want to gag.

"Well, we ain't here for a pint o' the black stuff are we Paddy?" the gunman mocked, "We're here for the fucking money, ain't we? And if you know what's good for ya sunshine, you'll show us where the take for tonight's shenanigans is kept, won't ya Paddy?"

A short silence followed as a police-car's siren blared its *nee-naa* warning in the distance somewhere across the city. All three listened as the siren's wail grew quieter.

"I'm not Irish!" the reply caught the gunman by surprise.

"You what?"

The manager nodded slowly and raising his hands above his head at a snail's pace repeating, "I'm ... I'm *not* Irish!" he stuttered. "This *is* an Irish pub but I'm just the manager employed by the brewery, my name's Jamie I'm from ...!"

Bam! The gunman brought the shotgun's butt around in the blink of an eye and clouted the twenty-something hard on the cheek. The blow sent him sideways from his kneeling position to his backside. Before he could re-centre himself the gunman was in his face again.

"Are you trying to take me for some kinda *cunt . . . ?*" he screamed the last word into Jamie's face and for the first time he could see the horrific figure of the man's facial features distorted by the sheer silk stocking. Jamie watched as his white spittle seeped through the silk as the man began to vent his dominant fury in a frenzy of froth-covered insults. He felt himself physically shrink in the face of this unbridled aggression. His mind struggled to make sense of the sudden change in his circumstances, he felt as if he were watching the whole scene unfold on a TV screen inside his head as his brain invented ways to detach himself from this moment of violence.

Slap! Jamie's momentary dreamlike detachment was brought to a sudden halt as the gunman brought the back of his free hand across his face before grabbing him violently by the hair on the back of his head. Suddenly the respite of his imaginary sanctity had vanished, replaced by the gunman's curses.

"Do you wanna die tonight or what . . . ?"

Jamie felt the gunman pulling his hair, lifting him from his knees.

"What the fuck is wrong with you . . . ?" *Slap,* another back-hander across his already bloody face. "I don't give a fuck if your name is Nick-knack-Paddy-Wack. What I do care about is the money. Now get the fuck up and show us where the safe is!"

Jamie nodded subserviently, holding his open hands out in a plea for empathy.

"Ok, ok I'll show you the safe but please don't hurt me!"

The gunman dragged him to his feet where he stood swaying unsteadily. He stepped in closer to Jamie and rammed the shotgun barrels under his chin.

"Just shoot him, we'll find the safe ourselves. He's wasting our time Number two." said an unfamiliar voice.

Jamie turned his head gingerly lest the gun go off prematurely. He could see the other side of the bar counter that separated him from the main room. There he saw a man sitting on one of the bar stools. He sat leaning on the dark wooden counter holding a cardboard coffee cup, its contents steaming as if he were just another regular at the *Brazen Maiden* Irish Pub. He wasn't especially tall or broad, just a normal looking punter. That was except for the silk stocking pulled over his dark hair and the brown, knee-length lab coat also worn by his more violent associate. He wasn't drinking the coffee though. He seemed more interested in the brightly-coloured Celtic patterns that had been carved into the rim of a Bodhran drum that had been left on the musician's stage on the other side of the bar. Jamie watched as the man crossed to the stage and picked the instrument up and examined the intricate workmanship of the carved, gaily-coloured Celtic knot-work. Without turning, he said over his shoulder,

"Take the cunt down the cellar and gut him! I'll have a look for the safe myself !"

The gunman began to pull at Jamie's hair, "Come on sunshine, you heard the boss, let's go for a walk!"

"No . . . *no*!" Jamie stuttered. "*Please*, I'll show you where the cash is kept, *please*!"

Jamie's words had the desired effect and both gunman and victim waited to see what the other man would say. Jamie watched him standing in the middle of the stage, as he fingered the carved detail on the drum's wooden wall, mulling over Jamie's plea for mercy.

The helpless Bar-Manager's thoughts began to drift. Only two hours before, the *Brazen Maiden* had been packed to capacity with positive energy and now here he stood pleading for his life with this faceless killer. The man on the stage opened his mouth to talk . . .

****

The music's Celtic melody soared over the manic foot-stomping crowd in the busy Irish pub. The intricate sound of fiddle, banjo and Uilleann pipes coming together as one, swirling like an ancient spirit above the heads of the hundred and fifty or so dancers. The music bounced and coarsed around the high-walled room with its faux Irish ornaments and distressed decor. The crowd were rising and falling to the beat of the Bodhran, the large Irish drum being played manically by the sweating lead vocalist in the band. His wrist flicked the tipper-stick across the drum's taught goat-skin creating a gargantuan primeval rhythm that one felt in the stomach as much as heard in the ear.

Davey Keogh scanned the room from the twelve inch high riser that acted as a stage and smiled inwardly. He let his mind wander from the rhythm he was pounding across the drum's skin for a second and took in the eager faces of the dancing throng. Finally, he was in the right place at the right time. God knows he'd tried over the past fifteen or so years but the British independent music scene he so wished to become part of, had refused to open its doors to him and now he was in his early thirties the realisation that he'd missed his window had finally hit home. Only now had the stars aligned in the unlikely form of a Celtic Tiger. Suddenly, there was an Irish theme-pub on every corner of every street selling beers and whiskeys that most English people couldn't even pronounce the names of. However, an Irish pub is nothing without authentic entertainment. Finally, Davey could see himself getting ahead of the pack by making a living performing the *Irish* music he'd been taught as a child. Born in Ireland yet raised in Birmingham, Davey saw his Irish roots and skill-set were finally in demand *and* something to be proud of.

He blinked away the beads of sweat. The music's spirit was strong tonight, seeping into every member of the audience and band member alike. Even the bar-staff and manager had stopped serving to watch as the band reached the climax of their show. There was an old magic at work in the room, something one couldn't see or touch but it was there nevertheless, hanging over the heads of the audience as if the Greek God of music Pan himself, were dancing among them . . . Maybe that, or maybe it was just the Ecstasy tablets everyone seemed to be popping like smarties these days! Davey pondered the thought as he beat his Bodhran. Deep inside he wanted it to be the former but in his heart, Davey knew that tonight's heady shenanigans were less to do with a Greek God Pan and the power of music and more to do with the drug dealer Dan or whatever his name was, and the power of his illegal chemicals. Either way, the band's job was nearly done and this night was a one off. Or at least until tomorrow night when the band would be playing to another packed Irish pub somewhere along the M5 M6 corridor. Same shit, different flies.

The music reached its crescendo in a howl of metal, string, wind and skin. Davey screamed his trademark Celtic war-cry into the microphone announcing the end of the performance and with one last thump of his Gaelic-patterned drum he closed the show. After a short silence, the roar of approval from the drunken and drug-induced audience shook the room, vibrating the ornate glass lampshades on their distressed-metal wall stands as the crowd called for *another* encore. Davey turned to his band mates. Smiling, he gave the group of musicians a cheeky wink, indicating that their job was done before turning back to the microphone.

"Thank you!" he announced in his strange Brummie-Irish brogue. "See ya again next time . . . and if you're drink driving, make sure ya pissed!"

Davey paused as the crowd burst into laughter. He waited for a few seconds, letting the laughter calm down before delivering the well-rehearsed, closing punchline, timing it to perfection, "There's nothing worse than being in a car crash than when you're fucking sober!" A deafening mixture of cheering and laughter rose from the crowd at the irony of the comment. The gallows humour that Davey had become so well known for had found its mark.

It was as he turned back towards the band, that he saw her. The blonde girl was there again. Davey stopped and took a double take. This was the second time he'd seen the girl – the last was six months earlier at another Birmingham show. He scanned her face for a second, taking in her features. Her deep-set, bright blue eyes hidden behind her long, blonde hair. The strong cheekbones drawing Davey's eye down her jawline to her cherry red lips. She seemed to glow from within the tightly-packed crowd of rowdy friends that surrounded her.

For a few seconds Davey couldn't break his gaze, partly because of her beauty but mainly, it must be said, because she was staring directly back at him. The singer stood paralysed in her gaze like a wild hare caught in the spring moonlight, trying to work out why she looked so familiar. She smiled. The gesture broke Davey's trance. She had a broad, honest smile, as much with her eyes as her mouth. He instinctively turned to look behind him, to see who she was smiling at but there was no one there. He turned back to the girl and smiled back bashfully, suddenly feeling like a naughty school boy. Now her smile had broken and she was trying to stifle a laugh. He knew she was laughing at his bashfulness which made his cheeks suddenly glow red. Her circle of mainly male friends hadn't noticed anything and continued to talk excitedly across their tight circle as she continued to make eye contact with him.

"How could this woman be smiling at me?" he asked himself incredulously.

It was all he could do to stop himself turning once more to see if there was some tall, dark, handsome male model standing behind him, someone deserving of a beauty like this. After all why would a woman like her be interested in a man like him? He wasn't handsome or heroic. He was a *musician*, someone that walked between the raindrops who didn't get involved with other people unless it was to entertain them. He had his music to hide behind. Whereas *she,* she was the type of woman that seemed to gather people around her effortlessly like so many summer wasps. A sweet, honey-soaked being, that with a smile and a flick of her long lashes or even just a turn of the eye, could start a war or stop a heart and all done with such innocence and natural grace that she barely noticed she had left any impression on you at all.

Davey could feel his cheeks burn, making him even more uncomfortable than he already was under her gaze. He was glad to be grabbed suddenly by the arm of his shirt by a small, fat, round woman who, due to her Kilkenny black and yellow striped Gaelic football jersey, looked more like a giant bumble bee than a human being. She buzzed and flapped her arms in front of him excitedly shouting that she wanted her photo taken with him and in truth, he was happy for the distraction. He felt his surge of embarrassment pass and the burning in his cheeks subsided. This was *his* comfort zone.

He smiled at the wee woman and was a little disturbed to see a manic look in her eye. Normal was one thing, but this four foot high bundle of lust in front of him was quite another. He stepped from the stage to pose for the photograph in front of the camera being held by queen bee's friend. However, as he did so, the bee jumped as high as she could, in this case an inch or two from the ground and grabbed him around the neck. Her weight bent him in two and she took advantage of this to plant a sloppy, wet kiss on his cheek. This fifteen stone bumble bee had caught him by surprise and the two nearly toppled over into a group of drinkers sitting at one of the low tables next to the stage. The whole pub seemed to be watching and burst into a cheer of laughter. He glanced at the blonde girl. She and her friends were laughing too.

She was been joined by a dark haired man, a handsome yet mean-looking individual who came in close beside the blonde, claiming her without contact and purely by his presence. He looked directly at the singer as he raised his hand and ran his fingers along the blonde girl's cheek as if to show that this was *his* prize. The singer caught a glimpse of the man's tattooed hand. An unusual, dark blue and red swallow flying beneath a five pointed star placed between index finger and thumb. Davey took in the man's chiselled features, cloaked by a thick, dark mop of tousled hair which hung down over his piercing black eyes. Yes, this was the type she should be smiling at, a true alpha male. Far from being impressed by the man's presence, Davey noticed that the girl and the other members of the group seemed to react negatively to his arrival. They were unwelcoming, wary, as if they had been joined by a feral dog or even a wolf. The wolf seemed oblivious to this reaction and joined the others laughing at the scenario near the stage, only unlike theirs, his laughter had a touch of cruelty about it.

Davey's attention was brought back to the woman around his neck. To make matters she wouldn't let go of him and now seemed to be trying to climb up his legs, trying to meet his lips with hers. Although small in height, the woman was wide and heavy and it was all Davey could do to stay standing. Her little legs waddled and kicked in the air as she pulled her puckered lips closer to his. Davey dropped the Bodhran onto the stage in order to take her weight. The cylindrical drum rolled to the back of the platform and out of sight as Davey tried unsuccessfully to extricate himself from her vice-like grip. Suddenly, her little feet found purchase on his knees and she shuffled up his body bringing her face level with his and she wrapped her legs around his waist. She peered at him hungrily through her mole-like eyes.

He gagged as the stench of her halitosis and tobacco breath suddenly reached his nostrils. She was breaking his back. Davey reached around her, trying to counter her weight by grabbing both hands behind her back. His hands just about reached and it was all he could do to hold her there, leaning backwards in order not to be crippled. She settled into her perch, pleased with her ascent. Her eyebrows rose and fell in an attempt at sexiness. Davey watched her with a badly disguised smile which, if truth be told, was more like a horrified grimace. She leant in closer to his face. He thought she wanted another kiss and so with this in mind he closed his eyes and presented his tightly puckered lips to his adoring fan – what a professional! He held his position for a second, holding his breath, awaiting the fairytale kiss that would free him from this unravelling nightmare but nothing happened. Opening one eye her face staring back at him. Her beady, black eyes beneath their pink, semi-translucent eyelids flicking this way and that, each movement betraying her growing sexual arousal and in a voice that was at least three octaves too low and sounding as if it were coming from a six foot four, Marlborough-smoking Hell's Angel she whispered her killer pick-up line.

"*I ain't got no knickers on tonight . . . you lucky boy!*"

****

The man was standing with his back to the dance floor in the middle of the stage as Davey stepped through the *Brazen Maiden's* double doors and back into the empty pub. He was holding the bodhran Davey had returned for. Examining its design and construction, he seemed to be entranced by the instrument and, either he didn't hear Davey's entrance, or purposefully didn't react to it. Either way, he didn't turn to find out who was there. Davey had crossed the floor before he knew it. The lights of the bar were low, barely lighting the space at all. However, Davey could see the man's reflection in one of the many Irish whiskey mirrors that surrounded the stage and he could see that his facial features were somehow distorted, as if his face wasn't fully formed. At first he thought the man had been the victim of a fire but it was impossible to tell in the dim light. Davey studied the man for a few seconds before opening his mouth to speak. Just as he did, a stifled plea came from a doorway behind the bar.

"No, please there's no need for that, I can get the cash out!"

Davey recognised the voice as the Bar-Manager's. He stood frozen on the dark, empty dance floor not knowing whether he should simply ask the man for his bodhran or turn on his heel and exit the way he'd come in. The man on the stage turned his head towards the sound. He listened for a second before placing the drum down delicately on the stage. Shaking his head he stepped down from the low riser and crossed the room towards the bar entrance at the side of the long, dark-wood counter. Davey watched him leave the room and enter the small office at the rear of the bar. As the man entered the office, the bar manager began talking again, only this time his pleading had a touch of panic in it.

"Please you've got to understand, the safe's got a time lock on it. Only the head office can override it!"

Thwack!

Davey heard the sound of an open-handed slap, skin against skin, followed by a muffled whimper. Then a deeper voice spoke, this one gravely and hard without any empathy.

"You see what happens when you say something stupid, *cunt?* You get hurt don't ya!"

"Please, I can sort this, we can wait until the morning when the lock releases."

Davey turned toward his bodhran, it was only a few yards away on the stage. All he had to do was walk over pick it up and walk away without looking back, yet his feet wouldn't move. He ran the idea of leaving over in his mind. None of this was his business, after all he barely knew the Bar-Manager – he was just some bloke thrown into the pub to run it whilst the brewery found some other mug to buy the lease on the place. He stepped towards the stage but the gravelly sound of the man's voice caught his attention once more and he froze.

"Look son, we ain't a pair of fucking idiots that you can blag. You ain't talking your way out of this one ... "

Then another man's voice broke in. This voice was lighter, more refined, yet deadly serious.

"Tell me son, do you know someone called Neil Hanlon?"

Jamie's silence and surprised expression betrayed his recognition of the name.

"I know how it works sunshine ... " the man continued, " ... there might well be a time lock on the safe but we both know that you've got an override code to that time lock given to you *personally* by Mr. Hanlon!"

There was a short silence as Jamie tried to work out how the man could know this. The meeting with the brewery salesman had been a secret one, held in his office away from prying eyes. Jamie knew it was brewery policy to keep the codes secret in order to stop things like this happening and temporary landlords like himself were not meant to have them but Mr Hanlon had insisted Jamie memorised the code only a few days ago ...

Davey listened for the answer but nothing came. The silence was like a knife. A few seconds passed before the Bar-Manager spoke.

"How do you know that?"

Davey heard the refined man laugh.

"Ah, and there it is, you've been discovered haven't you son?"

"No, I eh . . . " Davey could hear the man was trying to control his panic as he looked for a way to talk himself out of the situation.

"Well?"

Davey heard a yelp of pain as Number Two struck Jamie around the face yet again.

"Open the *fucking* safe!"

The command was said in a higher tone this time. Davey heard the sound of electronic buttons being pressed then a quick trill of computerised musical notes before the sound of a metal door unlatching. The gruff man began to laugh.

"There, you've got your cash, now you can go!" Jamie begged.

"What the fuck are you so sore about, it's not your money is it? The take belongs to the fucking brewery. You could've opened that safe all along, yet here you are, covered in your own blood because of your loyalty to a bunch of millionaires and guess what? We got the cash anyway."

Another silence then a yelp of pain as the gruff man grabbed Jamie by the hair once more.

"How much is in there?" He shook the man's head. "Come on, how much?"

Jamie tried to calculate the week's take in his head, finally blurting out,

"Just over twenty-eight grand"

"Good lad," replied the more refined of the two, "ok son, bag it up and we'll be on our way!"

The words sent a tingle of panic down Davey's spine as he contemplated the prospect of being discovered by the robbers.

"Fuck this I'm out of here!" he said under his breath.

Lifting himself onto his toes he crept quickly across the dance floor, trying not to let the heels of his boots make contact with the wooden floor. He could hear shuffling inside the office as the men loaded the cash into a small, canvas, cash bag. The robbers were making small talk as Jamie sat at their feet, a broken expression on his bloody face. Reaching the stage Davey stepped up onto the wooden riser as lightly as he could and reached for the drum. Grabbing it, he tucked the instrument under his arm and turned to leave but as he shifted his weight from the dance floor to the stage, the plywood timber of the platform creaked loudly.

"Shit!"

Davey's heart nearly jumped out of his chest and he froze lest the poorly constructed riser creaked again. Even more ominous was the sudden silence from the office. The seconds seemed to slow to a halt as he waited for a movement from the room behind the bar. Davey scanned the stage for a place to hide, his eye settling on the broad chimney breast to the right of the stage. Even though the fireplace looked like the real thing, Davey knew through his conversations with the bar manager on previous gigs, that the fire basket was indeed a gas replica and would be cold to the touch. The large deep hearth was in shadow and easily overlooked.

"Did you hear something?" the refined man said in a whisper.

He stopped placing the cash in the bag and nodded to his associate. Both men rose simultaneously. Turning to the Bar-Manager who was sat on the concrete floor near the safe he whispered,

"You stay where you are, understand? Don't move a *fucking* muscle or there'll be hell to pay!"

Jamie nodded subserviently. Number two, holding the sawn off in front of him crept through the office door followed by his partner in crime and the two stepped into the relative darkness of the bar room. Number Two took up a position in the centre of the room and scanned the place with the sawn off barrels. The other man crossed the room to the front doors of the pub. He placed the cash bag on a high top table near the door and swinging one of the double doors open, he peered into the darkness outside. The city street was cold and deserted. A brisk wind blew a dust devil of litter and leaves down the gutter towards him. Apart from that, all was still. He remained in that position for a short while before pulling his head back inside the door. Number Two was waiting, gun in hand. The other man shook his head and shrugged.

"Must've been the wind?" he said, trying to hide the fact that the sound had actually spooked him more than he'd like to admit. "Come on, let's get this over and done with!"

Davey watched the scene from inside the shadowed hearth. He held his breath as best he could, desperately trying not to gasp for the air his lungs craved for. The gunman was only feet away from him and with a remarkable amount of control, Davey let the stale air escape in a low, inaudible sigh. He tried to make sense of the situation but couldn't. The drum he'd returned for was only worth about three hundred pounds and certainly wasn't worth dying for. Maybe he could explain the situation to the robbers, explain that he'd only come back for the drum and the robbery was none of his business, he'd keep his mouth shut about what he'd heard and seen. However, any idea of stepping from the darkness of the hearth's overhang and explaining himself was put to rest with the sound of the hammers on the shotgun being primed by the nervous gunman. Davey pushed himself further into the shadow, willing himself invisible.

The refined man was staring right at the stage, searching the room for the source of the sound. He crossed the room and placed his foot on the stage exactly where the singer had stood a minute before. He climbed onto the riser and the boards heaved another creak as before. Davey watched with horror as the man standing only a few feet away scanned the stage with a puzzled look on his face.

"Someone else is here!" he said without turning to his accomplice.

"What?" Number Two asked in an alarmed tone.

The other man pointed towards the rear of the stage, "The Irish drum I was looking at!"

Number Two shook his head, bewildered by the mention of the instrument, "What about it?"

The refined man turned to him and pointed at the stage. "It's gone . . . it was here a minute ago, someone's moved it!"

Davey's heart thundered, and to the hidden singer it felt almost as loud as the drum he'd played on the stage only hours before. He clutched the bodhran closer to him, as if it would somehow protect him from the thugs who were only feet away. Surely they would hear the pounding, Davey thought.

"We're gonna have to search the place top to bottom, some-one's here!"

The gunman nodded.

"Turn the lights on Number Two we'll find out who . . ."

A bleeping noise from the office interrupted him. Both men looked at each other with alarm. The office door slammed.

"Hello . . . police . . ." Jamie's voice said urgently.

Both men moved simultaneously, clearing the space between the dance floor and the office door in a blink of an eye. The gunman slammed his shoulder against the woodwork splintering the door frame, the door flying open to reveal Jamie cowering inside, the office phone held to his ear.

"You silly *cunt*!" the gunman shouted as he smashed the butt of the shotgun across the bar manager's head with such force Jamie's scalp split open like an over-ripe piece of fruit revealing the white of his skull beneath. A large flap of skin lolled across the young man's face as he fell to the floor already unconscious, the cash from the safe scattered around him.

"You *fucking* idiot!" The gunman screamed at the prostrate Bar-Manager. "We were gonna let you go, you fucking . . ."

The other man came in behind him and placed his hand on his shoulder.

"Calm it Number Two, he can't hear you!" The two men looked down on the man's body, which suddenly started to quiver.

"What the fuck is he doing De . . . ?"

The other man grabbed the gunman's arm and jerked it violently stopping him mid flow.

"Shut the fuck up, no names remember!"

The gunman nodded, "Yeah . . . sorry boss!" The refined man shook his head.

"For fuck's sake . . . " he said with a sigh and shaking his head, " . . . just get the cash from the floor!" he said as if talking to a child.

The gunman stared down at the quivering manager, "I ain't going near him, it looks like he's got a fucking disease or something."

The other man shook his head, "He ain't got a fucking disease, you smashed his skull in and now he's dying." He let the words sink in for a second, watching the gunman's reaction. "Now pick up the *fucking* cash and let's get out of here before you fuck anything else up."

The gunman instantly bent and began picking the bundles of money up from around the twitching body of the bar manager. Number One stood in the centre of the office watching him. Slowly, he raised his head and stared as best he could through the silk stocking covering his face at the small black CCTV camera on the ceiling above his head. He looked at the security device with a fresh interest for a few seconds before lowering his head to scan the room for the camera's control unit.

"What about the person that took the drum?" the gunman said, staring up at his boss from the floor.

Number One smiled to himself. "Never mind about that, just get the cash we're leaving!"

He turned and walked out into the bar. The gunman rose and stepped over the body of the manager following his boss into the bar.

Number One waved him forward, "Go get the car, I'll meet you outside.

The gunman rushed passed him grabbing the bag of cash still on the tall table by the door.

"Leave it!" Number One said sternly.

"But there's over ten grand in that bag!" the gunman protested.

Number One's eyebrows furrowed, "I said *leave* it!"

The gunman obeyed and dropped the canvas bag back on the table before disappearing through the double doors onto the street. Number One walked across to the door way. He fingered the bag, finally picking it up. He turned, his eyes flicking this way and that as he searched the shadows of the room. He turned his eye to the small black security camera in the centre of the bar's ceiling, then threw the bag into the centre of the room before turning and walking through the double doors and into the night.

Davey watched the man leave. His pounding heart began to slow as soon as he heard the sound of a car pulling up outside. Only now did he allow himself to believe he might get out of this situation without getting a good hiding or worse. He listened and heard the sound of a car door slamming before a large vehicle revved its engine and a short screech of tyres announced the departure of the car. Davey remained in his hiding place for a full ten minutes before crawling from the shadows, drum in hand. He stood there for a few seconds before plucking up courage to peek over the bar top and into the office. A shiver ran down his spine as he saw the body of the Bar-Manager lying on the floor, surrounded by a growing pool of blood. Davey walked around the bar and into the office. He bent to the man on the floor and gingerly shook him but there was no reaction. He took the phone receiver from the manager's hand and dialed the emergency number 999 and waited. A short beeping tone filled the crackly line followed by a thin voice.

"Emergency services, which service do you require?"

"Ambulance!" Davey replied trying to stifle the panic in his voice. The woman on the other end of the line began to enquire about the reason why he wanted an ambulance but he just repeated his demand.

"Look I ain't getting involved in any of this. Someone's been hurt, very badly by the look of things. You had better get someone here before it's too late!" He gave the name and address of the *Brazen Maiden* before wiping the receiver with the cuff of his shirt and placing back on its hook. He gave one last look at the man on the floor. "Sorry Jamie but it ain't gonna make any difference if I'm here or not!"

He stood above the man's body for a second. Then he shook his head at the ridiculousness of his explanation to the unconscious man. He turned and walked out of the office towards the door. As he crossed the dance floor he came upon the white cash bag. He stopped and looked at it for a second, then back at the office door. Bending, he picked up the bag and opened its narrow opening. The bundles of cash inside sent a prickle of cold sweat chasing up his spine and without thinking he dropped the bag into his bodhran and crossed to the double doors.

Turning one last time he called out to Jamie. "I've called the ambulance mate, they'll be here in a minute, I've done all I ... "

He stopped himself, shaking his head as he tried to wrestle with his conscience in the doorway. The knowledge that his Catholic guilt would come back to haunt him in the early hours of the following morning unless he drank himself into a stupor, plagued him as he stepped out onto the street and walked away through the litter-filled dust devils and into the night. Bodhran under his arm and tail firmly between his legs.

****

The small, black, security camera hung on the ornate plaster ceiling in the centre of the bar. Its brothers and sisters around the venue had all borne solemn witness to the night's events. Gaze unbroken, it sent its electrical signal to the black box recorder in the office which whirred and buzzed its inaudible digital song down the telephone line as it sent the images to the brewery's head office on the outskirts of Birmingham.

Catholic guilt wasn't going to be the only problem the singer had to worry about over the next few weeks.

CHAPTER 2

Abduction 1961

The room sparkled with anticipation as the crowd awaited the arrival of his Royal Highness: The King of Birmingham's Clubland.

The bar room and dance floor were cheerfully decorated for the Christmas season and both buzzed with the excited screams of twenty or so small children who scampered innocently in never-ending circles around the dance floor. The kids dodged in and out of the groups of men and women who stepped and swayed to the music of a local modern jazz trio. The breathy, swirling tones of the Hammond organ and brush drums fought to be heard over the delighted howls of the pack of children.

This apparent Christmas cheer was subterfuge; a thin layer of tinsel disguising the real intentions behind the party. If one took the time to peer through the clogging cigarette smoke that hung over the proceedings, you couldn't fail to pick up the undercurrent of unease hanging over the room, as hundreds of distrustful eyes watched the clandestine proceedings in one of the shady corners of the Bermuda Club.

In the gloom of the snug, a beautiful dark-haired woman was dishing out small brown envelopes to the chosen few amongst the various Birmingham crews and gangs.

Every pin-sharp wise guy in Birmingham had been invited tonight. Hazel Fewtrell hadn't omitted one name. Anyone on the rise, be they ponce, policeman, petty criminal, perverted city councilor, tough guy enforcer, bent detective, doctor, judge or anyone from whatever walk of life that could prove useful now or in the future had received an invite. She had even invited a few high class prostitutes.

Just to spice things up a little.

Guests from whatever walk of life were mingling as if it were the most natural thing in the world. Men who only days before, had been standing at the railings in one of Birmingham's criminal courts, were now happily chatting with one of the barristers or judges that had been trying to send them down on some trumped up charge. It made no difference to Hazel, she had her own reasons for inviting them to the Bermuda Club Christmas party on that freezing night of the 23rd December 1961.

Eddie Fewtrell, his seven brothers and the hundred or so strong *Whizz Mob* who stood behind him, now ran the city. Yes, there were other gangs in town but *none* of *them* had a *casino*. The other gangs were just takers, pressing money from those weaker than themselves, nothing more than an extension of teenage bullyboy gangs to be found in any comprehensive school in any city throughout England. Yes, these yob gangs could be violent, in truth *very* violent – in fact *deadly* violent but none of them had what the Whizz Mob had. All *they* could offer were threats, beatings and poverty. Whereas Eddie's gang offered good times, gambling and a glimpse of what could be. After all, the 1950s, with its post-war ration cards, de-mob suits and greasy quiffs was long gone. It was a new decade and the sixties promised a better, brighter future and by hook or by crook, the Fewtrells were going to be a part of it. That's what tonight's party was all about, moving forward, pulling people together and putting names on the payroll.

"Come on, come on . . . " Hazel said impatiently, " . . . it ain't gonna bite!"

She held an envelope up without looking at the young police-man in front of the drink-laden table. He stared at the little envelope for a few seconds, unable to bring his hand up to take the payout. Hazel raised her head and looked at the young man with a smile.

"Go on love." She shook the envelope. "It's just our way of saying thank-you."

The policeman glanced around him to see if he were being watched by any of the other men waiting their turn to be called towards the table in the corner. As he searched their faces, he was surprised to see impatience in their eyes instead of disapproval.

"For fuck's sake mate, just take the bleeding money." a coarse voice said behind him in a thick Brummie brogue.

The man turned to see a small stocky man with a mop of black curly hair. He stared up into the policeman's eyes.

"It's only money son, you ain't selling your bleeding soul!"

The younger man saw other eyes watching him now. Tough-looking men in sharp suits standing in small groups were turning their attention towards him. He felt the beginnings of a sweat as he turned back towards the beautiful young woman holding the envelope. He pondered the thought of taking the payout and crossing the line between being a straight cop and a bent one.

Hazel became serious, "Look sunshine, I gotta get through this lot." She nodded towards a shoe box full of similar brown wage slip envelopes. "It's our Christmas party and I'd like to get this over with and enjoy me-self, so if you ain't gonna take it, I'll give it to someone else if ya like and you can go home, go on . . . " She flashed him a fresh smile, " . . . treat ya mum to a nice pressie!"

The man threw another quick glance around him before snatching the wage slip. On seeing his actions the tension that had built up amongst the other men around the table suddenly dissipated. The faces of the tough guys and other policemen waiting their turn to be paid off quickly lost their scowls, turning their attention back to their conversations within the tight-ly-packed groups.

"Sign here!" Hazel prodded the ledger book in front of her. "And print your name here . . ." She picked a fountain pen from the table, " . . . and no bleeding Mickey Mouse names either." she said with a chuckle.

The man bent and signed his name before pocketing the wage slip and disappearing into the throng of people. Hazel turned to the pretty blonde girl who sat next to her.

"Sue, go get Eddie, we need to speed this up or we'll be here all bleeding night."

The girl nodded, rising from the table she drained the glass of *Baby Cham* in front of her in one gulp.

"What shall I tell him?" Hazel laughed.

"You'd better slow down on that *Babycham* Sue." The blonde girl chuckled.

"What shall I tell . . ." Sue hiccupped, " . . . t, t . . . tell him?" She stuttered.

"Tell him to get his lazy arse down here right now! He should be doing this not me!" Sue knocked the table with her knuckles.

"Good as done, Bab!"

She stepped away from the table and swayed again. Sue tried to gain her balance in her high-heeled winkle-pickers – no easy task considering the four small bottles of bubbly she had consumed in the last hour. Hazel watched her sister in-law push her way into the crowd of smartly dressed men, who as one turned to watch the sexy, blonde girl in her tight knee-length pencil skirt, sheer stockings and over exaggerated hip swing. She swayed her way through the crowd to the stairs that led to the office of the Bermuda club.

"*Next*!" Hazel shouted over the music.

****

"Look all I'm saying is that you scratch my back, I'll scratch yours!" Eddie Fewtrell said from beneath a heavy brow.

The man next to him was leaning against the banister rail at the top of a short stairwell that overlooked the main room of the club. He was watching one of the young barmaids in a mini-skirt as she collected empty glasses around the dance floor. He didn't turn to look at Eddie when he spoke.

"If you're under any impression that I'm gonna take the same payout as these small time cunts then you've got another thing coming, sunshine."

Although the words were said aggressively and the overall connotations were negative, Eddie was pleased that negotiations had finally started. He gave the man a once over. He was the same age as Eddie, although he looked a little older due to the beginnings of a bald patch. He had a gaudy gold watch on his right wrist and wore a shiny diesel- blue mohair suit that had been cut to the latest continental style. Eddie could see that there had been no expense spared on the garment, with its three buttons and small lapels, five inch side vents and four buttoned cuffs. He was impressed, not only by the suit but by the fact that a copper like DCI Ronnie Fletcher couldn't afford a set of clothes like that. *Unless,* he was on the take . . .

"So you *will* scratch my back then, it's just gonna be expensive for me when you do?" Ronnie Fletcher turned to Eddie with a spiteful smirk." All these bent coppers here tonight are just small fry mate. If you're throwing me in with them, you're making a big mistake, Fewtrell."

Eddie shrugged, "Please Ronnie, call me Eddie, I'm sure we can come to some sort of . . . "

Fletcher cut him short, "It's Detective Inspector Fletcher to you, sonny and I ain't finished talking yet!" The man's tone changed to a deadly serious one as he looked Eddie up and down.

Ronnie Fletcher hated people like Eddie Fewtrell. After all he was everything that Ronnie wasn't, smart, handsome, on the up and, to add insult to injury, he had a thick mop of blonde hair in the latest American prep style. Ronnie unconsciously ran his hand through his own thinning hair and immediately wished he hadn't, as the layer of Brylcream that coated his scalp came off in his hand. He stared at his greasy hand for a second before wiping it on a red velvet curtain that hung across the stairwell to the clubs office.

"You see Fewtrell, it seems to me that I'll be doing all the fucking backscratching, whereas *you* . . . " Ronnie shook his head with a scowl, " . . . what's a chancer like you gonna do for me? I mean, I'm the West Midland Police force's fastest rising detective, the golden boy if you like. I got more nicks this year than the Birmingham Old Bill know what to do with. So tell me *Fewtrell*, what the fuck do *I* need *you* for?"

Eddie, still smiling, shrugged and patted the other man's arm, "There's no need to be like that Ronnie, I'm only trying to smooth things out between us." Eddie swept his hand around the club, gesturing towards his seven brothers who were busy doing various jobs around the venue below. "Look, I know my family have spent more time on the wrong side of the law than the right but we're trying to keep on the straight and narrow. Tonight's party is just our way of saying thank you to everyone that's helped us along the way. I'd like it if you would work with us instead of against us."

Ronnie sniggered, "So you're trying to go on the straight-and-narrow by bribing a fucking police detective are you?"

Eddie bristled, "Bribe, *no* . . . !" Feigning an insulted look and searching for the right words he took a slug of his whisky before continuing " . . . I ain't trying to bribe anyone, as I said before *Ronnie*, I'm just saying thank you to everyone that's helped us along the . . . "

"*Bullshit* Fewtrell, we both know what these *gifts* are!" Ronnie Fletcher leant back against the banister rail, his back to the club below. "All these fuckers are in your pocket are on a small time payroll. I ain't gonna be one of em, if you want my services, you had better come back to me with a proper offer. I ain't gonna be anyone's lapdog, least of all yours. I will however, be happy to take a weekly payment from you just so you can stay on *my* good side, a ton a week should do nicely!"

Eddie's smile faded from his face, "A ton a week . . . ?" he repeated incredulously, " . . . and why the fuck would I pay you anything if you ain't gonna come on side?"

"I'll put it this way Fewtrell, if I don't get my money every week, I'm gonna make sure that you and your family end up back in that shit-house gutter you crawled of. I'll be on you cunts like a bad dose of clap and we both know how irritating a dose of clap can be, don't we Eddie?"

For once Eddie Fewtrell was speechless. He had set up the meeting with the copper in the hope of squeezing him for any information on any potential raids on the club. However his plan had gone awry and now he'd made what could prove to be a powerful enemy. Eddie knew that he'd have to get something over the detective if he didn't want to be getting his collar felt every five minutes.

"Eddie, Hazel says get your arse downstairs now!" The young blonde girl had climbed the stairwell and was standing beside him. He jumped at the sound of her grating Brummie accent.

"What?" Eddie asked, embarrassed.

The girl sighed and repeated herself, "Hazel said that you should get your arse . . . !"

Ronnie Fletcher laughed.

"Don't worry love, I fucking heard ya!" Eddie rolled his eyes."Alright Sue, tell her I'm coming."

"Ha, now we know who the real boss is." Ronnie sniggered. "You'd better get your arse down there Eddie before your Mrs. cuts ya balls off!"

Eddie opened his mouth to remonstrate but Detective Fletcher held his index finger up to stop him.

"I've heard your offer Fewtrell and you've heard mine. So I'll leave that with you until the Christmas holidays are over and then I'll be back to make my first collection in the first week of the new year!"

Fletcher turned away from Eddie and began to follow the blonde girl downstairs.

Eddie watched the man walk away with growing hatred. He knew that the negotiations had come to nothing, just as the other coppers already in his pocket had warned him it would and now he'd have descend the stairwell below not only empty handed but out of pocket too.

Fletcher stopped and turned on the stairs. Maybe it was the shadow in the stairwell or maybe one of the dance floor lights shining at a weird angle across the Detective's face but the spiteful smirk that had spread across Fletcher's features seemed even more sinister now than when they had been face to face.

"Oh!" he said sarcastically. "I didn't say thank you for inviting me, the wife and my son Daniel to your little soiree."

He laughed again, this time sweeping his hand around the room.

"We won't be staying though, son. I don't want my little lad mixing with the likes of you and your lot Eddie. After all, you've got a right bunch of villains here tonight, I can feel their eyes burning into the back of my head. If I have my way most of em will be in Winson Green nick before next Christmas, *you* and you family included." He touched his nose with his index finger. "Be seeing you very soon Eddie, if ya know what I mean!"

Eddie did know what he meant too, Ronnie Fletcher had harassed, beaten or arrested most of the party-goers below at some point over the last twelve months and now, Eddie and the rest of the Fewtrells had put themselves firmly in his cross-hairs.

****

A man stood in the shadows of the street lights beneath the tall buildings opposite the Bermuda club and adjusted a false white beard. The red Father Christmas outfit was way too big but it would do the job of hiding his real clothes and that was what mattered. He pulled the red Santa hat over a thick mop of ginger hair and stepped from the shadows towards the Bermuda Club doorway on the other side of Hill Street.

The image of a solitary child playing in a city park at dusk filled his mind's eye as he strode towards the front door. The distant memory of the tearful, blue-eyed boy sitting on the park swing back in his home town of Liverpool, sent an electric current from his brain to his groin and he quivered with a mixture of excitement, fear and power.

****

The children ran in ever decreasing circles around the small dance floor, their screams of laughter piercing the sound of chatter and live music. Their parents watched them with wide smiles on their faces as they chatted and mingled in small groups. Hazel stood with them, having finished the payouts she had started to relax a little and had joined the blonde barmaid Sue, both drinking small champagne flutes of Babycham.

Eddie joined her, handing her a vodka and tonic with a smile. Hazel took the drink but could see her husband's smile was just a front, put on for anyone that was watching, and they *were* being watched. The men and women throughout the club threw sideways glances towards their new blond-haired boss and his dark haired, very beautiful wife. A handsome couple who were quickly ascending from the poverty stricken streets of the Birmingham suburb of Aston to the dizzying heights of the city centre's clubland.

"Well, how did it go?" Hazel said under her breath.

Eddie just raised his eyebrows and sighed, "Not good Bab, he's far more stubborn than everyone made."

"Meaning?" Hazel said behind a false smile.

"Meaning, we'll have to bring him onside another way."

Hazel turned to her husband with a worried expression, "Don't do anything stupid, Ed." she said with a growing scowl.

Eddie broke into a broad grin. Hazel, registering his exaggerated smile, glanced around at the searching faces and followed his example by breaking into a smile of her own.

Eddie's tone was approving, "Don't worry Bab, it's all under control!" He put his hand around her shoulder and they turned to watch the children playing. "This time next year, we might have one of our own running around that dance floor!" Eddie laughed.

"Oh yeah, is that your idea of a chat up line?" Hazel answered cheekily.

Eddie leant over and kissed her cheek. As he did so, a loud cheer went up around the crowd. Hazel and Eddie turned towards the dance floor to see what had caused the sudden cheering.

The crowd on the dance floor parted and Eddie could see a man in a bright red Santa Claus costume pushing his way through the throng. The hard men either side of him were stepping out of his way, patting his back as he passed, big smiles spreading across their brutal faces.

Hazel turned to Eddie with a quizzical smile, "You organised this?"

Eddie just gave an uncertain smile and raised his eyebrows.

"You big softie Ed, what a lovely surprise for the kids."

She leant into his arm and squeezed his hand tightly. Eddie just kept smiling but his eyes betrayed a growing anxiety. They both watched as the man in the red suit walked into the middle of the dance floor and plonked a heavy white canvas postal sack down in front of him. In his other hand, Santa Claus had taken one of the short stools from one of the surrounding tables and had carried it with him to the centre of the dance floor. Placing the stool behind him, he sat on it and beckoned the children around him. In an instant, excited giggling kids swarmed about the man in the red suit in an ecstatic explosion of energy.

Eddie scanned the room and could see, all eyes were on Santa. One by one he saw his brothers looking towards him, some with bemused expressions, others with quizzical smiles. Eddie glanced towards Detective Fletcher, who had also turned to look directly at him. He could see the detective resting his hands on a young boy's shoulders in front of him and assumed the boy was Fletcher's son, Daniel. The little blond lad bristled with excitement beneath his father's grip. He turned to face Eddie and Hazel, his big blue eyes full of wonder and innocence.

Eddie felt Hazel squeeze his arm softly and turned to look at his wife. He could see the emotion in her face as the little boy and his wife shared a moment in each other's gaze. Eddie turned back towards the detective just in time to see Ronnie Fletcher give him a short begrudging nod before stepping onto the dance floor with his son in front of him, steering the lad by his shoulders. The policeman began to push the other children to one side or the other until his son was standing directly in front of the sitting Santa Claus. The hard men around the club watched as their own kids were pushed away from Father Christmas to allow the detective's boy to jump the queue by climbing onto Santa's knee first. Even as their smiles turned to aggressive grimaces, not one of these tough guys spoke up, knowing by doing so, they would incur the wrath of one of the most spiteful coppers to have every stalked the streets of the second city. And so they just stood there, biting their collective tongues, each of them simmering with rage.

The boy excitedly climbed onto Santa's knee.

"Ho, ho, ho and what's you name little boy?" Santa asked in the deepest voice he could muster pulling the lad into him tightly.

The little lad almost screamed his answer, "*Daniel*."

Santa Claus watched the boy's father from behind his festive disguise and leant in closely to the boy's ear and began to whisper. Ronnie Fletcher watched his son's face light up with delight as he talked in whispers to Santa Claus. Ronnie twisted his head, as if by doing so he would be able to hear the conversation between his son and Father Christmas but the band on the little stage played on, unaware that Santa Claus was holding court on the dance floor. The man in the red suit continued to whisper into the boy's ear before reaching into his sack and drawing out a small box wrapped in Christmas paper. He handed it to the boy, who snatched at it greedily. Santa pulled the present away quickly, before whispering into his ear again.

The blond haired boy suddenly calmed down. Nodding subserviently he climbed from the man's knee and took the present. Ronnie stepped forward and took his son's hand.

Santa looked up at the parent and pointed at the box, "He's not to open that until Christmas Day!" he ordered from behind his thick white beard.

Ronnie Fletcher thought he heard the hint of a Liverpool accent but couldn't be sure over the Hammond organ on the stage was now pumping loudly as its player broke into a self-indulgent solo.

Ronnie took the gift and nodded, smiling reluctantly, "Say thank-you to Father Christmas Danny!"

Father Christmas nodded, then turned from the detective and beckoned the other children towards him. Another child tried to climb onto the man's lap but was stopped with an abrupt hand. Santa reached into the sack once more and produced another box, the same size and shape as the last one. He made the child promise not to open it until Christmas Day before shoving them to one side and calling the next kid forward.

If anyone had taken the time to take notice, which they didn't by the way, indulging instead in the free glasses of cheap bubbly being handed out around the club by one of the young sexily dressed waitresses, they would have noticed that the man in the red suit suddenly seemed in a rush to leave, handing out the boxes willy-nilly to the greedy little hands . . .

Ronnie Fletcher returned to his wife and handed her Daniel's present. She took the gift and placed it in her handbag without looking at it.

"Can we go now Ronnie?"

The detective looked at his young wife with as much affection as he could muster, which wasn't a lot. His begrudging, dismissive smirk betrayed any real concern for the woman's feelings.

"Always in a rush to leave, ain't ya?" he said irritated at his wife's lack of composure. "Let me finish my bleeding drink first and then we'll leave!"

He stared at his wife for a few seconds. The woman lowered her eyes subserviently, staring at her feet under her husband's glare. Ronnie still rested his hand on his son's shoulder and threw his pint jug back and tried to drain the glass of the pale ale inside. Daniel watched the crowd of clamouring children around Santa as he rose from his chair on the dance floor. The boy couldn't contain himself anymore and sprinted back towards the other children, leaving his father to glower at his downtrodden mother.

Hazel turned to Eddie, "I can't believe you took the time to organise this for the kids!"

At that moment they were joined by Eddie's younger brother Chrissy Fewtrell.

"You can say that again Hazel!" Chrissy said laughing.

Eddie tutted looking his handsome younger sibling up and down. The powerfully built young man's face glowed with a sarcastic smile. His bright blue eyes shining beneath a mop of black hair combed immaculately into the latest fashion.

At that moment, Hazel interjected, "You can't have spent that much dosh on Santa, look he's fucking off already! He's only been here two minutes, he's left most of the kids out!" she said with annoyance in her voice, "Go and tell him to sit back down until all the kids have got a present."

The suggestion took Eddie by surprise, "Eh . . ." Eddie said flustered, " . . . nah he's . . . "

Eddie took a slug of his whisky, trying to buy time, "Eh . . . he's gotta go elsewhere! We were lucky to get him at all!"

He took another hasty drink, staring over the top of his glass to see if his words would have the desired effect: stopping the questions about the unannounced visit by Father Christmas.

Children swarmed around the man in the red suit as he began to extricate himself. Their voices were raised in shrill protest at the lack of presents being given out. Father Christmas, realising he wasn't getting out of there anytime soon held his sack over his head. He stared around him at the children searching for the blue-eyed, blond-haired boy. On seeing him amongst the gaggle of kids, he gave the boy a barely noticeable nod before spilling the contents of the sack into the group of manic children.

All eyes shifted to the children, who were now scattering en-masse after the presents, each running or sliding across the little dance floor on their hands and knees trying to snatch one of the little brightly-coloured boxes.

The man in the red suit took advantage of the distraction to step into the shadows of the club, away from the bright, flashing lights. He turned and strode quickly across the room without being accosted or even noticed by anyone. Almost everybody's attention was caught by the excited gaggle of children on the dance floor.

Stepping outside in to the crisp air, he melted into the shadows and awaited his prey.

CHAPTER 3

CCTV Star

(1995)

A black and white grainy image flickered across the screen in the small, dark office. A man sat a few feet away staring intently into the light as it danced around his face and the bare walls of the office, creating shadows that moved this way and that. He sat in silence trying to take in the detail of the events unfolding before him.

He was bored. The main image displayed a busy bar full of people who milled about below the camera in various states of drunkenness. A band performed on the stage out of shot, and the throng, unable to dance due to the packed mass, swayed in time with the music. Across the top of the screen were three smaller 'thumbnail screens' each with different views of the same location. One showed the main bar room area, another the view from behind the bar and the last one presented a much less grainy view of an office, due no doubt to the brightness of the office strip lights.

He rubbed his eyes and yawned. Glancing at the digital clock on the screen he realised he'd been watching the CCTV footage for nearly three hours. Tutting impatiently, he leaned forward and picked up the phone and placed it to his ear, balancing the receiver on his shoulder. He snatched a small diary from the desk in front of him and began searching for a telephone number, his eyes darting between the screen and the diary lest he miss something.

His fingers flicked through the pages until he came to the one he'd been searching for with its folded down corner. Holding the diary up to the light of the TV he began to press the numbers into the phone on his desk. It was an unfamiliar number. One of the new cellular telephone numbers with too many digits that always started with a zero seven. Punching in the last digit he waited for a few seconds for the call to go through. The people on the screen were clapping now, applauding some unheard song from the unseen band.

"Neil!" a voice answered abruptly.

The words were not a question, the person on the other end of the line knew who was calling. Neil Hanlon pondered for a second on how this could be, all the time watching the screen.

"How did you know it was me?"

"I've saved your number to my phone!"

The voice sounded thin on the line. Street noise in the background seeped into the call between the man's words, and it became clear that the other man was outside walking.

"Are you outside?" Hanlon asked, amazed at the novelty of having a conversation with someone on one of the new mobile cellular phones.

"Yeah I'm outside, I'm on my way to lunch."

A short silence followed as a police intruded. Hanlon listened as the wailing siren passed on its way and slowly grew quieter as the police car faded into the distance.

"Jesus, technology these days eh?"

"Never mind technology, did you watch the footage?"

Hanlon turned back to the TV screen. Yeah I've been watching it for hours and fuck all's happening!"

The man on the other end of the line sighed his reply, "The part you'll need is after closing time, make sure you erase anything before that!"

"Erase?" Hanlon said shaking his head. "You mean I've been sat here for three fucking hours watching this shit for nothing?"

The man on the other end of the line began to laugh.

"You silly fucker, you should've called me first."

Hanlon listened as the traffic noise on the line changed to the sound of people talking and cutlery. The man's voice grew softer and Hanlon realised the man on the line had arrived at his lunch destination.

"Erase anything before closing time, there might be something on there the old Bill might see . . . "

A woman's voice spoke in the background, asking if the man would like his usual seat. The sound of cutlery and chatting grew louder in the earpiece as the man walked deeper into the restaurant.

The man's voice became quieter, "As a matter of fact get rid of everything before midnight. The clip you need is right after that."

Hanlon's brow furrowed, "Why, what happens?"

"Why don't you have a look yourself, when you see it you'll understand . . . " the man sniggered. " . . . he's exactly what we been looking for mate!"

Hanlon leaned across the desk and pressed the fast forward button on the small black CCTV player in front of him. The grainy image burst into life as the swaying crowd began to speed up comically.

"Oh yeah, and what exactly *have* we been looking for?" he answered as he scanned the racing digital clock on the screen, "What was it that *Lee Harvey Oswald* called himself?"

The question threw Hanlon.

"Lee Harvey Oswald . . . " he answered incredulously. " . . . you mean the fella that shot Kennedy?"

"Yeah that's the one, he said he was a . . . "

Hanlon cut him short, "A *pasty*?"

The man on the line burst into laughter.

"Not a pasty you thicko, Oswald was a *patsy*, a stooge, someone who'll take the drop when it comes on top, we've got ourselves a *Patsy*!"

Hanlon shook his head, trying to work out the meaning behind the statement. The other man sensed Hanlon's confusion.

"Just watch the footage and you'll understand, I gotta go now, I have a lunch date."

Hanlon sensed that the conversation was coming to an end. He heard a young woman's voice in the background, well-spoken but with a tinge of a Birmingham accent. Hanlon could hear as the other man talked to the girl, a kiss as he greeted her. He caught the name 'Abi' but the rest of the greeting was out of earshot.

"One more thing . . . " Hanlon blurted before the receiver was place down. " . . . how much did you?"

The other man cut him short, almost whispering into the receiver.

"Not enough mate, but don't worry your cut's on its way to you and anyway, if our *Patsy* proves as useful as I hope he's gonna, they'll be a lot more where that came from!"

With that the line went dead. Hanlon let the receiver drop into his hand and placed it back a-top the phone on his desk. He turned his attention back to the racing image on the screen. The pub in the shot was empty now, except for three men. One sat at the bar, his features distorted and unrecognisable, the other stood on the opposite side of the counter in front of a kneeling man. He was holding a sawn-off shotgun, its barrels disappearing into the kneeling man's mouth. Hanlon smiled to himself. Spinning in his office chair he called out through the glass-paneled window of his office.

"Wendy . . . . *Wendy*!" A brunette popped her head around the door with a smile. "Hi babe, stick the kettle on will ya? Looks like I'm gonna be here a while darling!"

Without saying anything, the girl nodded and vanished.

He kept his finger on the fast-forward button as the images on the black and white screen jittered forward until he saw the images of the two gun men leaving the bar. His mind wasn't concentrating on the CCTV footage as it should have been though. The sight of his secretary, in her tight white blouse, her small firm breasts pressed tightly against its fabric had his mind now. He'd been in a clandestine relationship with the girl since his arrival at the brewery headquarters a few months ago. She was married to one of the warehouse men and Hanlon had seen on their first meeting that she was bored with her husband and in need of some *real* male attention. Of course Neil Hanlon was only too happy to indulge her needs and the pair began to work late into the night indulging in secret sexual shenanigans on Hanlon's office desk. He shook his head, trying to get his sexual urges back under control. Turning back to the screen he said to himself,

"Ok *Patsy*, let's see where you're hiding!"

He kept his finger on the fast forward button. The image of the empty pub rolled forward without any movement in the room. Then suddenly, after a few minutes, a figure appeared from the beneath the shadows of the fireplace. "*Gotcha*!" Hanlon exclaimed loudly. He took note of the digital numbers on the screen which indicated the position of the individual video frames. He highlighted the ones with the unknown figure in them and erased the frames containing the two gun men until the video only showed the lone figure emerging from the shadows and taking the little canvas bag of cash and leave. He stopped the video and pick up the phone once more. Dialling a memorised number he waited for his call to be answered,

"West Midlands Police, how can I help?" a woman's nasal voice answered. Hanlon breathed in through his nostrils deeply before answering. He was gathering his wits, for he knew that this phone call was about to start a chain of events that he wouldn't be able to stop or control once they had been started.

"I'd like to talk to a detective please!"

"Can I ask what the nature of your call is, please?"

A tingle of prickly heat ran down Hanlon's back as the realisation that he was about to cross the point of no return.

"I . . ." he stuttered, trying to control his nerves, " . . . I have information on last night's robbery at the Brazen Maiden." The woman didn't answer, instead the line buzzed as the receptionist transferred the call. The line went quiet for a few seconds. Hanlon tried to control his rising panic. For a second or two he thought about placing the receiver down and stopping the proceedings before they got started.

"Hello, Detective Inspector Chris Dixon, homicide, you say you've got information about a robbery?"

CHAPTER 4

Abduction 1961

(continued)

"*Daniel!*"

There was desperation in Ronnie Fletcher's voice as he shouted his son's name over the loud music. "Danny . . . Daaaanny!"

His initial irritation at the boy's disappearance from the gaggle of other children on the dance floor had been replaced with a feeling of dread in the bottom of his gut. His wife was already borderline hysterical as her husband began pushing and pulling the other children apart, grabbing their shoulders and shouting into their faces.

The group of hard men around the dance floor could only stand so much. Even if they were afraid of repercussions, there was no way they were going to let this spiteful, plain-clothed copper treat their kids this way. Anyone that messed with their kids, was fair game for a good hiding. The nearest group of men came forth onto the dance floor as one, grabbing the yelling policeman by the arms and pulling him forcibly. As if in a choreographed manoeuvre, the wives of these men ran in behind them and grabbed at the hands and shoulders of the crying children, dragging them away into the recesses of the club, away from the scene on the dance floor.

"Keep your fucking hands to yourself, Fletcher!", a dark-haired man in a silver mohair suit shouted into Ronnie's face. The other men gathered around the man, shouting at the copper. "I don't give a fuck who you are Fletcher . . . "

The man continued, " . . . touch my kids and I'll . . . "

Suddenly Eddie was there, pushing his way in between the man and Ronnie Fletcher, separating the pair. Fletcher's eyes were wide with rage.

"I'm looking for my son, you fucking idiot! He was with your kids and now he's gone!" Ronnie screamed into the man's face. The man seemed to be taken a-back by the reply.

"I don't give a flying fuck, you don't touch my kid, or anyone else's understand?"

"I'll fucking remember you mate." Fletcher said in a low growl. "I'm gonna make it my business to fucking ruin you." He looked the man up and down, with a look of disgust. "You jumped up fucking Teddy boy, your days are over in Birmingham . . . "

Eddie cut his outburst short.

"Alright, alright, everybody calm the fuck down!"

He pushed the two men apart. Turning to Ronnie he asked, "What's going on Ronnie?"

Fletcher glared at the man in the silver suit over Eddie's shoulder. Seeing Eddie was dealing with the situation the man shook his head, turned and walked away, reluctantly followed by the other group of men. As the men walked away Ronnie called after them,

"I'll remember this lads! You're all going in the book for a nick down the line! Your fucking life ain't' gonna be worth living!"

Eddie rolled his eyes.

"For God's sake Fletcher, why are you threatening my guests?" Right at that moment they were joined by Fletcher's tearful young wife.

"Please Ronnie, stop this and find little Danny!"

Both men turned to the woman. Eddie shook his head, even more confused.

"Can someone tell me what all the fuss is about?" Fletcher's wife burst into tears.

"He's gone!" she blurted.

"Who's gone?"

The woman opened her mouth to talk but was stopped by her husband who grabbed her shoulder roughly and began to drag her away, saying,

"Don't talk to him, he's probably the one who's taken him." Eddie's brow furrowed.

"What, taken who?" The woman spun, forcing her way back to Eddie.

"Little Daniel's gone, he's just vanished."

Eddie shook his head.

"Our little boy, he's gone!"

Eddie broke into a superficial smile.

"Nah, he's probably hiding with some of the other kids."

The woman searched his face, trying to believe his words, hanging on to the glimmer of hope.

"Yeah the little darlings are all over the club. Leave it to me love!"

Ronnie pulled the woman back towards him with some force. The woman lowered her head in subservience and took the position by her husband's side.

"You had better find him Fewtrell."

Eddie's nostrils flared.

"How's it my fault, if you can't keep an eye on your own kid?"

Eddie gave the detective a quick dismissive glance and addressed his wife.

"Okay, what's his name and what does he look like?"

Eddie listened to the woman earnestly describing her son before turning away and walking towards the low stage. When Eddie was out of earshot Ronnie Fletcher turned on his wife.

"You keep you bloody mouth shut, you silly cow!" Ronnie bent and snarled into his wife's face. "All of these cunts probably planned this from the start." The young woman looked up into her husband's face with bloodshot eyes.

"Why would they take Danny, Ronnie?" She was sobbing now. Fletcher laughed sarcastically.

"They want to get to *me* through Daniel, it's probably Fewtrell's idea because I wouldn't take his bribe."

The crackle of a microphone cut through Fletcher's barely concealed contempt,

"Ladies and gentlemen, ladies and gentlemen, can I have your attention please!"

Everyone turned towards the dimly lit stage where Chrissy Fewtrell had taken the microphone from the Hammond organ player. The band's music stopped mid flow as Chrissy spoke.

"Has anyone seen a little boy called ... " he leant down towards Eddie who was standing at the foot of the stage, the two brothers spoke, " ... *Daniel?* He has blond hair and is so high." He held his hand out flat, palm down to indicate the boy's height.

"If everyone can take a quick look around them, under the tables and the like, he's probably hiding with one of your kids."

He pointed towards the Fletchers who were standing in the middle of the dance floor, her tearful and embarrassed, him simmering with fury.

Hazel watched the lack of response from the audience for a few seconds before stepping towards the stage and taking control of the situation. Taking the microphone from Chrissy she addressed the crowd,

"Come on you lot ... " she said with a more than a little hint of impatience in her voice. " ... shift your arses, and start looking for this little lad, he's here somewhere, and the first to find him gets drinks on the house for the rest of the evening!"

Her words had the desired impact as a cheer went up around the room and the members of each of the small groups broke away from each other and began busily scouring the club. Hazel watched the local hard men in their tailored suits scurry around the space, some crawling on the hands and knees beneath tables and chairs, others dodging in and out of the crowd like excited kids as if they were on some sort of treasure hunt and if it weren't for Ronnie Fletcher and his sobbing wife in the middle of the room, the atmosphere would have been buoyant. The search went on, to no avail.

Parents started to leave the club with their own kids, keen not to 'get involved'.

Eddie stood at the bar wearing an irritated scowl. He watched the detective and his wife from a distance wondering if either of them realised how much this little charade was going to cost him in bar sales. The woman was still sobbing, which was also beginning to grind his gears as he trawled his soul for some sign of empathy. He didn't find any and so just stared at the woman as she stood fumbling with the little wrapped Christmas present given to the little lad by Santa. His eye was drawn to the little red box as it spun around and around in her hand and then the penny dropped, accompanied by a feeling a-kin to a cannonball dropping into the pit of his stomach.

He placed his glass of whisky down slowly on the countertop and sighed heavily as he realised the answer to the conundrum lay in the contents of the small Christmas present in the woman's hands.

*****

A brisk wind blew up Hill Street, bringing with it a flurry of snowflakes from the heavy grey sky. The man raised his head, hypnotized by the white crystals as they danced and swirled beneath the yellow streetlights that lined the road. He craned his neck to watch the snow descend from the sky for a few seconds but the position pulled at the elastic supporting his white Santa Claus beard cutting uncomfortably into the back of his neck. He lowered his head, freeing the elastic and as he did, he saw the young blond boy standing in front of him.

The little lad smiled despite the bitterness of the wind. Quickly, the man pulled the boy into the shadows of the shop doorway. Opposite, a group of parents hurriedly ushered their children from the club down the road towards their homes, each talking drunkenly about the scenario happening inside.

He watched them leave, all the time checking the street for other prying eyes and when he was sure he wasn't being watched he stepped into the yellow streetlight, holding the boy firmly by the hand.

"Father Christmas?" the boy asked between chattering teeth. "You told me I could ride in your sleigh."

Daniel's innocent question caught the man by surprise. He turned to look at the lad, crouching down. The boy shivered in the cold wind, blinking away the tiny snowflakes that rested on his long eye lashes. The boy's vulnerability stirred a familiar feeling deep inside the man. He returned the boy's look with a stone cold one of his own.

"My *sleigh*..." he said with a snigger in his thick Scouse accent. "...it's just parked around the corner..." He stood up and pulled the child behind him, "...and you don't need to call me Father Christmas anymore son. My name's Duncan but you can call me U*ncle Jarvis!*"

If little Daniel thought the wind was cold, it was nothing in comparison to the look in the paedophile's eye.

****

Eddie crossed the room towards the pair. His feet felt heavy as if he were walking through wet sand. The usual cocky spring in his step was gone. He crossed the room until he stood directly in front of Ronnie Fletcher's wife. She raised her red puffy eyes to look into Eddie's now ashen face. Fletcher also turned towards the club owner, his face furrowed deeply with an expression of anger, poorly disguised as worry.

"What the fuck do you want Fewtrell? Get your arse moving and find my kid!"

Eddie took no notice of the detective instead he raised his open hand towards the crying woman. She searched his face for some sort of answer and Eddie nodded towards the little box.

"May I?"

The woman looked down at the box before handing it to the club owner. Her sobbing finally stopped, replaced by a puzzled expression. Eddie took the little box and held it in the palm of his hand as if weighing it. The parcel seemed too light ... Without hesitation he began to tear the red wrapping from the Christmas present.

"What the fuck do you ... ?"

Fletcher's words halted abruptly as Eddie tore the final wrapping from the box and opened it. It was empty. The two men stared at each other for a second before Fletcher, quick as a flash left his wife's side and snatched at one of the other little boxes being held tightly in the hands of one of the other children that remained around the dance floor. The child began to cry, and the kid's angry father stepped forward, fists clenched, ready to pummel the copper.

Eddie stepped between the two, shaking his head. The man backed down instantly, mumbling his protests under his breath. Fletcher shook the box wildly before tearing it open to reveal it too was empty. On seeing the commotion, Hazel and Chrissy joined Eddie in the centre of the room, both with bemused expressions. Eddie saw them coming.

"Father Christmas!" Eddie said with disbelief. Hazel shook her head.

"Father Christmas, what about him?"

Fletcher threw the little box at Eddie's feet. Eddie looked at the box for a few seconds before calling out around the people still in the club.

"The bloke in the Santa suit, anyone know who he was?" Hazel shook her head.

"Well, you organised him Ed, you should ... ?"

Her words trailed off as she realised that Eddie had nothing to do with organising the visit by Father Christmas but he'd been more than happy to take credit for it.

Fletcher's wife wasn't so sharp.

"How can you not know who he was, you planned it for the kids?" She searched the club owner's face for an answer. "Didn't you?" she said weakly.

Eddie avoided her stare. Fletcher stepped in-between them.

"Fucking Hell Fewtrell!" he said with a snarl. "Don't tell me you didn't know who the bloke in the Santa suit was?"

Eddie's nostrils flared as he realised he'd been cornered.

"Look, I never said I'd organised Santa, you lot did, all I did was go along with it."

Hazel shook her head with disbelief.

"Bleeding hell Ed, what are you like?"

"Are you telling me some fucking nonce just walked in here off the street and took Daniel?" Eddie tried to ignore the man.

"Did anyone get a good look at the bloke?" Fletcher exploded.

"Of course no one got a good look at him, he was wearing a big white *beard* you silly cunt!"

Eddie bristled at the detective's words but stayed himself. Turning to Ronnie's wife he assured the woman he'd find her son.

Fletcher wasn't finished.

"You had better fucking find him Fewtrell, and let me tell you this, if one hair on his little head has been harmed I'm gonna hold you responsible."

Eddie turned to Chrissy and whispered in to his ear.

"Get all the brothers together, any of the Whizz Mob still here, get them too. Tell em to get out on the streets and find this pervert that's stolen the kid."

"But where do we start Ed?"

Eddie began to back away from the ranting detective, still talking to Chrissy as he did.

"Well obviously, start by rounding up anyone dressed as Father Christmas! Then round up any queers, known perverts or weirdos you might come across too and take em down the warehouse in Hockley. I'll meet you there in a couple of hours and we'll get to the bottom of this once and for all!"

"Where are you going Ed?" Hazel joined them as they walked towards the exit.

Eddie gave her a wink.

"This is it Hazel. This is what'll bring Fletcher onside."

Hazel and Chrissy stared at him in disbelief, unable to comprehend what Eddie was saying to them.

"If we find the kid . . . " Eddie continued, " . . . Ronnie Fletcher will forever be in our debt!"

"I can't believe that you're thinking like this right now!" Hazel said angrily.

"And if we don't find the kid?" Chrissy asked. Eddie raised his eyebrows and sighed, knowing that if the child wasn't found, then the full wrath of the detective would fall firmly on his shoulders. Unwilling to even contemplate the repercussions of failure, he brushed the question aside,

"I'll cross that bridge if and when. . . . "

CHAPTER 5

An Old Wound

(1995)

"*You ain't no son-o-mine!*"

Eddie screamed across the oak desk at a non-descript twenty-something standing opposite. The man physically wilted in the face of the verbal onslaught, his gangly form almost curling in on itself as if to create less surface area for the insults to take root.

"But my mum said back in 1976 you and her . . . "

The teenager's voice trailed off as his confidence evaporated under the other man's glare. The sentence ended in an embarrassed mumble, " . . . you know?" The words were meant as a statement but because of the lad's lack of backbone, it came across as a question. Eddie Fewtrell slammed his hand down on the desk top.

"No, I don't fucking know son, perhaps you can enlighten me?"

The lad shifted his weight from foot to foot and turned his attention to his shoes.

"I'm trying to Eddie, but . . . "

"It's Mr. Fewtrell to you pal!" Eddie's patience was beginning to wear thin "Well, come on then, I ain't got all bleeding day!"

The lad took a deep breath and summoned up what was left of his courage.

"My Mum said that you and her had a shag, back in the 1970s . . . " The boy blurted. "I don't know when it was exactly, but she said it was at a punk rock gig at the Cedar Club, the Sex Pistols I think she said!" Now the words came quick and fast now. "My mum was a punk rocker and you *gave* her one back stage while the band was playing"

Eddie could take no more and stopped the teenager talking with a burst of laughter.

"Stroll on sunshine!" he said between his sarcastic guffaws. "You must think my head buttons up at the back!"

Eddie's outburst had no effect on the lad, who seemed to gather confidence as he rambled on without listening to the night club owner.

"It's true Eddie, honest, that's what she told me before she died!"

Eddie stopped laughing and tilted back in his high backed office chair suddenly serious.

"Ok, let me get this straight . . . "

The lad stopped talking, looking at his shoes once more, allowing himself a quick glance at the club owner. Eddie saw how scared the teenager was and felt a sudden pang of guilt – an emotion that rarely showed itself. Eddie gestured that the lad should sit, pointing at the chair on the opposite side of the desk. The lad nodded subserviently and sat. Eddie continued,

"Your mother told you that she had an affair with me back in 1976 at a Sex Pistols gig in my club?"

The lad shook his head.

"Not an affair Eddie, *a shag*!"

Eddie sighed, "Okay, so we had a shag . . . "

The lad suddenly became animated,

"So you admit it then?" Eddie rolled his eyes.

"What? No, just shut the fuck up and let me finish what I'm saying." Eddie said impatiently. "Your mother said we had sex backstage at my club and she's told you that I'm your father?"

The lad began to nod, his broad mouth breaking into a toothy smile.

"Yes, that's what she told me, it's the truth Mr. Fewtrell honest!"

Eddie raised his eyebrows.

"Just because your mother told you this doesn't make it the truth, our kid!"

Eddie tried to give the lad a sympathetic smile but only managed a begrudged smirk. The younger man took the smile for approval and blurted.

"Do you mind if I call you *Dad*?"

Any semblance of calm in Eddie's composure fell away instantly at the mention of the word.

"No, you can't call me fucking *Dad*...!" Eddie was on his feet now. "I ain't your bleeding dad and that's a fact!"

The lad seemed unfazed by the club owner's new level of annoyance.

"How can you be sure, Dad?"

Eddie's head began to shake as a fresh level of rage began to boil inside him.

"Stop calling me fucking Dad, I ain't your bleeding father and I can prove it."

The lad also stood, leaning onto the desk with the palm of his hands facing off the older man.

"Oh yeah, how can you prove it then? The fact of the matter is you don't wanna be my Dad because you'll have to pay me a load of money!"

The mention of money brought Eddie's full rage to the fore.

"I don't owe you or your mother a fucking penny! What the fuck are you talking about? You turn up at my office door claiming to be my son and I've never heard of you or your fucking mother!" Eddie shook his head, trying to calm himself lest he say too much, after a few seconds he continued "Look I don't want to speak ill of the dead and I'm sure your mother was a nice lady but I can't remember every bird who wanted a shag. I was a very popular bloke in those days, you know. So just run it past me again son. You say she was a punk rocker?"

The lad nodded,

"Yes, Dad!"

Eddie sighed. Calming himself, he sat down again gesturing for the lad to sit too.

"Ok and was she blonde or dark haired?"

The lad seemed puzzled by the question but answered anyway.

"Well, she had purple hair, she was a punk rocker!"

Eddie laughed,

"Okay, she had purple hair. Was she white skinned?"

The lad nodded. Eddie smiled.

"Well, there you have it!"

The teenager shook his head,

"Have what?"

Eddie leant back on his chair again, a triumphant expression growing on his face.

"Your mother was a white girl."

The lad agreed,

"Yeah white!"

Eddie continued,

"And as you can see, I'm white too . . . "

Once again the teenager nodded.

"So if your mother was white, and I'm white, how can I be your father?"

The lad's brows furrowed as he tried to work out the riddle.

"Yeah so your both white, what's that got to do with anything?"

Eddie leaned forward and placed his hands on the desk, and in a low matter of fact tone said,

"Cos if you hadn't noticed, you're as black as the ace of spades nobhead!"

Eddie sat back in his chair and folded his arms, eyebrows raised watching the young black lad on the other side of the desk. However, the lad was prepared for the question and gave his answer to the riddle.

"My mum said I was a throw-back in the gene pool!"

Eddie's patience finally snapped. Leaping out of his chair again he snarled at the teenager.

"I'll drown you in that fucking gene pool if you don't fuck of out of my office, *understand . . . !*"

The lad's bravado vanished instantly and seeing his dream of an easy life evaporating in front of him, he turned his attention back to his shoes and nodded like a scolded school boy.

"Good . . . ," Eddie continued, " . . . now *fuck off.*"

Quick as a flash the lad had crossed the room to the office door and pulling it open, he stopped in the doorway. Turning towards Eddie, he thought he'd have one last shot at his con trick.

"I'll always love you, *Dad*!"

Eddie's face flushed purple as he picked up the heavy diary from his desk and threw it at the door. By the time the book had travelled the space between the desk and door the lad had vanished into the corridor outside. Eddie screaming behind him,

"You ain't no son of mine!"

****

Hazel Fewtrell pulled her dark blue Mercedes SL into the multi-storey car park above her recently-estranged husband's club on the *Five Ways* roundabout. The screech of tyres on the car park's wet surface caught the attention of the cellar men who were busy rolling heavy beer barrels down a steep wooden ramp at the rear of an old *Mitchell & Butler* brewery truck.

She was tired after the drive from her house in Bromsgrove and was relieved to have finally arrived. Turning the ignition key the engine fell silent. She slumped back into the leather driver's seat, allowing her shoulders to relax after the hour long drive along the bumper to bumper M5. Lighting a cigarette, she prodded the electric window button and inhaled deeply.

The window wound down with a soft whir and, as it did, she blew the thick smoke through it's broadening gap. A cold, refreshing breeze poured in through the window, carrying with it tiny droplets of drizzle. She closed her eyes as the droplets met her skin, enjoying the sensation in the relative serenity of her car.

The cellar men went about their work, looking like figures in a hall of mirrors through the gathering drizzle on the windscreen. The four men worked methodically in the cold. Dressed in a mixture of cheap cotton hoodies and nylon track suit bottoms, they looked frozen to the bone. With their little woollen beanies on their heads, she thought they resembled disgruntled elves going about their business in the build up to Christmas.

"Eddie's little helpers . . . " Hazel said to herself sarcastically through a cloud of exhaled cigarette smoke. She took one last drag on the white stick before flicking the half-smoked fag through the window. She followed its arc until it landed in a shallow puddle where its orange glow died instantly in the glittering rain water. Hazel breathed the last of the smoke from her lungs in a deep sigh, and drawing herself together she mentally prepared herself to meet the man she had, until recently shared her life with for the last thirty-five years. She didn't relish the prospect. He still loved her, or so he said to her face. However, as with anything Eddie said, it had to be taken with a rather large pinch of salt . . .

"I love ya Bab!"

She recalled his voice at their last meeting at the solicitors.

"We don't need to go through a messy divorce Bab!" His big blue eyes had pleaded sorrowfully, hiding their true intent. "Why don't we both sit down and sort this out as husband and wife, amicably?"

The memory of his plea sent a bolt of rage through her body. His words were always reasonable but she knew they were said for the sake of the third person who happened to be over-hearing the conversation, as if he were winning some kind of popularity contest and it worked EVERY time. The friends he'd worked his trick on had all fallen for it, so too most of their relatives, who all thought the sun shone out of his proverbial.

The solicitors, the accountants, even the fucking police thought Eddie was the voice of reason and that she was the crazy unreasonable bitch that wanted to destroy her husband. "Oh he's done his work well." she thought as she stepped from the car into the freezing drizzle on that cold December day. "He'd planted the seeds in the minds of his sycophantic followers, seeds she knew nothing about until they had already blossomed into trees of untruth, hanging heavy with the ripe poisonous fruit of lies.

Hazel stepped through the rear entrance to XL's night club and stopped at the top of the short flight of stairs just inside the doorway. As usual, she allowed her eyes to become accustomed to the dim light inside the narrow staircase. As her eyes began to take in the steep staircase, she was shocked to see a gangly mixed-race youth she didn't recognise, running upstairs toward her. Taking two steps at a time, the youth had cleared the space between them in no time, nearly knocking her over as he reached her, pushing his way past her in the fire exit. Hazel grabbed the grey metal fire exit door handle and steadied herself.

"Well, don't mind me will ya?" she shouted angrily at the lad from the doorway as he marched into the drizzle. He looked over his shoulder with an expression of spite on his dark face.

"Didn't your *Dad* ever teach you any manners?" Hazel called after him.

The words seemed to have an effect on him and he glared at her before storming away and out of view, down the car park's entrance ramp and onto the street below.

"Are yow aw-right Mrs Fewtrell?" a scrawly voice with a thick Black Country accent asked from behind her. She spun on her heel and saw an ugly looking man walking towards her.

"Who was that rude bastard?"

The man followed her gaze towards the car park ramp but the mixed-race man was already long gone.

"I dunno, he turned up here about half hour ago, Mrs. Fewtrell. Him was asking about yow husband."

Hazel rolled her eyes, "Please call me Hazel."

The man nodded, "Ahh, all-right but yow are Mrs. Fewtrell ain't yow?"

Hazel returned the question with a thin, irritated smile.

"Yes, I am Mrs. Fewtrell . . . " the answer seemed to please the man, " . . . just not for much longer if I have my way." she said under her breath.

The man's smile was replaced with a quizzical expression. "What was that you said Mrs. Fewtrell?"

Hazel shook her head, realising her comment had been louder than she'd intended. Seeing her reaction he changed tack.

"Are yow going down to see Eddie, Mrs Fewtrell?"

"What's your name our kid?" she countered.

The man in the dirty wet tracksuit pulled his woollen beanie from his head to reveal a shorn grade two haircut with large, badly-drawn Wolverhampton Wanderers club tattoo just above his right ear.

"Me name's Bob, Mrs. Fewtrell but yow can call me Jobbo, everyone calls me Jobbo!"

He held the wet beanie close to his chest and bowed as if addressing royalty. Hazel's brow furrowed. He heard her question before she'd even thought of it and answered it quickly.

"Bob-a-Jobbo. Eddie nick-named me!"

Hazel shrugged, "I ain't seen you round here before Bob-a-job!" He shook his head. "I take it you got your nickname because you work hard?"

He nodded, "Yam's right. I'll do anything for a bit o cash me . . . " he said laughing at his own joke.

He pulled the hat back over his head as a particularly sharp gust of wind washed his unshaven face with drizzle.

"Yam going to see yow husband Mrs. Fewtrell?"

Hazel raised her eyebrows, "Well, I'll tell you one thing Jobbo. I don't know how good you are at working but you ain't half a nosey beggar. Yes, I'm going to see my husband, what's it to ya?"

Jobbo seemed to physically shrink, almost bowing again,

"No, I didn't mean to pry, I'm sorry, I eh . . . !"

The other men he'd been unloading the barrels with behind began to laugh at him. Hazel gave him a cheeky wink and turned back towards the staircase.

"See ya later *Jobbo*!" she said as she let go of the fire door which slammed loudly behind her. A loud cheer of mocking laughter rose from outside, followed by Jobbo's voice,

"Fuck off yow bastards, I was just being polite!"

As Hazel stepped down the stairwell she could hear Jobbo's work colleagues making fun of him, their thick Brummie accents mocking the Black Country man. Their voices faded as she pulled the door at the bottom of the staircase open and stepped into the corridor beyond.

The narrow corridor smelt of stale beer and fags. A thin layer of cleaning product tried valiantly to disguise the aroma but failed. After thirty five years in the nightclub and casino business, the smell was a familiar one to her but in truth she had never got used to it and, in truth, she found it more and more repugnant as time went on. Making her way to Eddie's office she tried not to breathe in the concoction and was happy when she finally reached the office door. She gave a slight half-hearted knock on the door before pushing it inwards.

"I thought I'd told you to fuck ... oh ... !" Eddie's angry voice came to a sudden stop when he saw Hazel in the doorway, " ... oh it's you ... !" He rolled his eyes, " ... just what I need!" he muttered under his breath.

"Good morning to you too, dear!" Hazel retorted with just as much sarcasm.

"What do *you* want then?" Eddie said, placing his hands on the desk.

He snatched at the newspaper in front of him and perused the front page casually as he pushed himself backwards into his large leather office chair. Hazel gestured over her shoulder as she walked across the room until she reached the chair opposite Eddie's desk.

"I take it the black lad wasn't welcome?" Hazel said laughing.

Seeing Hazel hadn't come to argue, Eddie lowered the newspaper onto his desk and sighed deeply, beginning to relax a little.

"Apparently I'm his father ... " Hazel chuckled. "Yeah, can you believe the cheeky bastard?" Eddie began to lighten up, seeing the funny side of the situation. "Black as coal, saying he was my son!"

Hazel shrugged as she took up the newspaper.

"Maybe he is?" She raised her eyebrows as she examined the front page of the paper. "He might be a throw back in the ... "

Eddie finished her sentence, "Gene pool, yeah I know."

Hazel smirked, "I'm surprised you even know about gene pools."

Eddie laughed, trying to hide the fact that he hadn't got a clue what a 'gene pool' was. In fact, every time it had been mentioned, he'd pictured the Victorian swimming baths he'd visited as a child.

"I ain't stupid Haze, I know what a gene pool is."

Hazel gave a little snort and Eddie started to become impatient.

"Okay, why are you here? What have I done this time?"

Hazel took no notice of him, instead her eyes darted between the newspaper and his desk, scanning for a snippet of information that might be useful to her in the future. Eddie saw her interest in his paperwork and clumsily began pulling the bills and invoices toward him and out of sight.

"Come on, I ain't got all day!"

She pulled a cigarette from the packet in her bag and placed it in her mouth, searching for her lighter.

"Sorry Hazel, there's no smoking in here." Eddie said apologetically.

Hazel on finding the gold cigarette lighter sat back in the chair. Staring coldly at Eddie, she lit the fag and drew in deeply. She held the smoke in her lungs for a few seconds, her stare unbroken. Eventually she blew a cloud of smoke into the space between the two of them. Eddie waved his arms around, trying to dissipate the thick smoke.

"Okay, that's enough, what do you . . . ?"

Hazel cut him short, "I went to visit Abigail. You remember Abigail, don't you Eddie, you know, your daughter, the one that's the same age as your bloody girlfriend!"

Eddie rolled his eyes.

"Here we go again!" Hazel could hear the bitterness in her own voice. She hadn't come to do this, she hadn't come here to do battle. She had had enough of fighting against the inevitable tide that always seemed to flow in Eddie's favour. She had come here to talk to her husband cordially about their daughter. He *was* still her husband, even if it *was* estranged. But she just couldn't help herself. The anger she felt was still raw within her and she drew on the fag a little harder as she wrestled with herself under his disrespectful gaze. A short silence fell between them, only a few seconds long but agonising nonetheless.

"I'm sorry!" she finally said, sighing her apology in a cloud of fresh smoke. "It's been a long drive, my back's killing me and I'm tired."

He looked at her coldly, expecting that this was another of her tricks, lulling him before another attack of vitriol.

"No, *I am* . . . sorry that is." She turned and scanned the office.

"Where've you been, visiting your young lover Hodgy?" he tried to say the name without any spite in his voice, but failed dismally.

"Where's the kettle?" Hazel said trying to change the subject. Eddie drew in a breath.

"It's in the kitchen where it always is."

Hazel turned back to him and smiled sadly.

"I don't know why you're still bleating on about Hodgy Ed, he's ancient history."

"Well history has a way of repeating itself don't it?"

Hazel shook her head, amazed that her ex-husband was still so upset about one of her old lovers.

"Ancient history Eddie, that little scene with Hodgy was over ten years ago."

Eddie could barely contain himself at the ease with which Hazel talked about her affair.

"Well if I ever bump into him again I'll fucking kill . . . "

"*Good God* Ed, you appear to have a bee in your bleeding bonnet about a bloke I ain't seen since the eighties."

An uncomfortable silence fell between the pair for a few seconds before Hazel finally put them both out of their misery.

"Remember when we started out at the Bermuda Club all those years ago, that shitty little office we had then?"

Eddie shrugged.

"That was a long time ago Haze, thirty-five years. I can barely remember what I had for breakfast these days. Anyway, that wasn't an office, it was a kitchen that we *used* as an office, two very different things Bab."

Now Hazel rolled her eyes,

"You were never very good at taking a hint were ya?" Eddie's brow furrowed. "I'm *hinting* that I want a cup of tea!" she said.

He laughed, "Why don't you just ask for one then instead of beating around the bush?"

Eddie reached across his desk and pressed a button on the large phone in front of him. A girl's voice answered. She began to talk but Eddie cut her short before she could say a word.

"Bring in two cups of tea Beck, you know how I like mine, Hazel will have it strong and sweet, two sugars."

Hazel nodded, impressed that he still knew how she liked it.

He lifted his finger from the button and sat back, "So tell me, why *are* you here?"

"I told ya, I'm reporting in that Abi has met a new fella."

Eddie perked up, "Oh god, how much is it gonna cost me this time?"

Hazel ignored him, nodding she replied, "Yeah, she's infatuated with him,."

Eddie scowled, "Infatuated, well that won't last too long, you know what she's like, very fickle."

Hazel nodded again, "Yeah, mind you, he's a handsome bastard, tall, dark, handsome *and* charming!"

Eddie could see Hazel was impressed by the man.

"How old is he?" he enquired.

Hazel shrugged, "Late twenties, early thirties, I dunno?"

Eddie's expression became quizzical and he began asking more questions, "What does he do?"

Hazel shook her head, "Dunno that either, he doesn't seem to do anything, not a day job anyway, he seems to have plenty of cash though, got a flash car, nice clothes and all that."

"So he hasn't got a job but he's got a nice car, clobber and plenty of cash?"

"And a lovely new flat too, overlooking the city, you can even see Gas Street Basin from his lounge window in the distance, must be worth a small fortune."

Eddie leaned forward on his chair, "Gas Street Basin, that's a shit-hole Haze?"

Hazel shook her head tutting, "Not anymore Ed, you gotta keep up with the times, the whole Gas Street Basin area is being gentrified."

"Gentrified?"

Hazel sighed her reply through a cloud of cigarette smoke,

"Brought up to date, you know cleaned up, properties down that part of town are premium prices these days."

Eddie mulled her words over for a few seconds, trying to work out why anyone would choose to live in the Gas Street Basin. He brought the conversation back to his daughter's new boyfriend.

"Well, it doesn't seem strange to you that he doesn't work but he's loaded?"

Hazel shrugged, "You're getting too suspicious in your old age, Ed. We know a hundred people like that, almost all our friends kids do fuck all apart from drive around in flash cars buying new clobber. Mom and Dad do the business and the kids act like *they've* earned it."

Eddie laughed, "True Haze true but those kids we know, we know their parents too, and how they made their money, this guy . . ."

He held his hand out as if the man's name was on the tip of his tongue.

"Dez!" Hazel said matter of factually.

"*Dez*?" Eddie repeated. "What kind of name is that?"

Hazel shrugged again, "Dez, it's short for Derrick I think?"

"Derrick, I fucking hate that name, it's a ponce's name."

Hazel laughed, Well, presumably that's why he calls himself Dez then ain't it?"

At that moment they were joined by a short round girl carrying two mugs of tea. She rushed across the office and almost dropped the mugs onto the desktop.

"*Ow . . .*!" she squealed in a high-pitched Brummie accent. "f . . . f . . . fucking *hot*! Is that all Eddie?"

The girl turned and with a quick dismissive glance towards Hazel, she crossed the room and pulled the office door open.

"Here Bec . . ." Eddie called after her. " . . . when was the last time you talked to our Abigail?"

The girl froze in the office doorway and without turning she answered in a bored tone,

"I ain't seen her in . . ."

She left the words hanging for a millisecond, then, when no reply came from Eddie, she stepped into the corridor and vanished, letting the heavy door slam behind her. Hazel and Eddie sat in silence for a few seconds, both of them watching the door as if the girl would re-enter and finish her sentence at any moment.

Hazel spoke, "She's very . . ." she said searching for the right word, finally settling on, " . . . efficient!"

Eddie bristled at her sarcasm.

"Who, Becs?" he answered brightly. "Nah she's alright, she looks after the office Haze, she's very good at typing!"

Hazel looked at the steaming dark brown liquid in the dirty mug in front of her and wondered what the girl had done to make the tea appear so dark.

"I hope she's better at typing than she is at making bleeding tea!"

She smirked as she picked the mug up. Her eye was drawn to the photo of a curvy, scantily clad woman that had been printed on the side of the mug of tea, with the words *Zig Zag Gentleman's club* written above it in a bright yellow font. She glanced at Eddie. He sat back in his chair and raised his eyebrows, pleased with himself about something. Hazel stared at him, a bemused expression growing on her face. Eddie raised his eyebrows again, this time gesturing towards the mug with a nod of the head. Hazel turned her attention back towards the steaming ceramic cup. She looked at the picture and was about to burst into laughter at its tackiness just as the picture on the mug began to change before her eyes. Her expression changed from one of disdain to disbelief as the day glo pink bikini on the woman in the picture slowly began to vanish, leaving the woman totally naked in an obscene pose that left nothing to the imagination. Hazel's look of horror was lost on Eddie, who beamed excitedly from the other side of the desk like some sort of demented naughty school boy.

"Great ain't it?" he said breaking the silence with a boyish giggle. "She gets bollock naked if you look long enough, you can see her *Bristols and everything!*"

Hazel turned her attention away from the mug towards her estranged husband then back to the mug again. She opened her mouth to respond but words failed her. Eddie slapped the table and burst into laughter.

"It's been printed with magic ink, when the temperature changes on the surface of the mug, she strips off . . . !"

He beamed his broad smile. Hazel shifted her gaze from the mug to Eddie and back to the mug again, her mouth wide, speechless. "I've ordered a thousand of em as give aways for the Zig Zag punters, they only cost fifty pence apiece," He picked his mug up and examined it closely. Eddie's mug had the same girl on it only in a different, even more obscene pose.

"Every time you have a cup-o-tea, you get to see her *giblets!*"

Hazel placed the mug back on the desk and looked at her husband. He sat opposite her, enthralled by the vanishing bikini on the porno model on his mug. Hazel sighed to herself as the realisation dawned on her that the divorce she so desperately wanted wasn't going to be either easy or quick.

The phone rang out loudly, breaking Hazel's melancholy. The girl's high-pitched Brummie accent on the other end of the line announced the arrival of another visitor. Just as Eddie reached across for the handset the door to the office burst open. Hazel turned in her chair towards the entrance and saw a handsome man in his late fifties standing in the doorway. On seeing her the man smiled. His cheeky white-toothed grin filled his face, his dark, mischievous eyes sparkling from beneath his short, salt and pepper, greying hair. She stood to greet him, but was beaten to it by Eddie who had come from behind his desk and crossed the floor at a surprising pace, his hand held out in front of him in a friendly gesture.

"Detective *Inspector* Chris Dixon!" Eddie said cheerfully. Dixie took Eddie's hand and shook it firmly. He felt the club owner's tight grip and he suddenly remembered how competitive his old friend was. Dixie stepped past Eddie and smiled at Hazel. She sat in the office chair, watching her soon to be ex-husband's greeting with her big hazel eyes, a smile growing across her face.

"Hazel!" Dixie crossed to her chair, bent and kissed her softly on the cheek. "How are ya Babs? I ain't seen you in an age!"

Hazel returned his kiss with one of her own and hugged him. The two held each other, eyes closed and genuinely pleased to see each other after such a long time.

"All right you pair . . ." Eddie said, returning to his side of the desk, " . . . break it up or you'll have to get a bleeding room!" Hazel and Dixie broke apart, suddenly embarrassed by their mutual show of affection.

"Well, it's been a bloody long time Ed!" Dixie said, patting Hazel's shoulder as Eddie pulled another office chair from the corner of the room over to the desk.

"There-ya-go, park your arse there our kid!"

Eddie slapped his old friend's shoulder and Dixie sat, turning his chair to face bothof them. Eddie told the receptionist to bring in more tea for the trio and as they waited, they chatted as if no time had passed whatsoever. The old stories just rolled off the tongues of the three friends, and any animosity Hazel held towards her estranged husband was temporarily forgotten as they spoke. Funny, tall stories began to be told, tales of old faces about town who had got lucky through business, gambling or both, and those that hadn't been so lucky and had either gone down the pan through bad business practice, divorce, mental illness or in some cases, all three. Dixie informed them of their old Whizz Mob associates who were currently serving time at Her Majesty's pleasure, ironically with some help from Dixie it must be said. Even though the conversation was sometimes about serious subjects, it remained light hearted throughout, even when they ran through the names of those that had popped their clogs in some way or another, there were still the obligatory jokes. That was until the talk came around to the painful memory of *that* Christmas in 1961. The image of the bogus Father Christmas and the missing little boy Daniel haunted all of their memories with a mixture of shame and anger. If truth be told, Daniel was exactly the reason Dixie had paid Eddie a visit.

"Asking questions?" Hazel said after hearing the information from the detective, a puzzled expression spreading across her face. Dixie raised his eyebrows and shrugged, barely able to understand it himself.

"Yeah, someone has been asking around about a body we found in the canal at the back of Fleet Street."

Eddie scowled from behind his desk, "A body?"

Dixie gave an uncertain smile.

"Yeah, at least that's what I've been told by the boys in the station but that's not the interesting thing. Whoever it was asking the questions about the body and I can only assume it's the victims next of kin, they've also been asking about the night Ronnie Fletcher's kid went missing."

"But he's been missing nearly thirty-five year now, why wait till now to ask about him . . . ?" Hazel muttered under her breath, still digesting the information. "No-one's seen head nor hair of him since that night."

She looked between the two men opposite, her puzzlement replaced by a look of sadness.

"It's funny, I haven't thought about that night for years until now."

"There's no reason to think about it either." Eddie interjected, "It's all in the past now and you know what they say, best leave sleeping dogs and all that."

"No-one's talked about it, apart from Fletcher of course!" Hazel whispered "I mean he never shut up about it after it happened but I suppose you can't blame him for that though can you?"

The melancholy had truly settled over Hazel now and Eddie saw the beginnings of a tear in her eye.

"His wife never recovered from it either you know, she took an overdose soon after didn't she?"

She glanced at Dixie for confirmation. Dixie nodded.

"Yeah, she killed herself on her son's birthday the year after. So in the end Ronnie Fletcher lost everything."

"It's no wonder he was such an arsehole to everyone!" she said with a sad smile.

"Fuck Ronnie Fletcher!" Eddie said abruptly.

Dixie sighed. He had forgotten the intensity of ill feeling between the old detective and the night club owner.

"Well, rightly or wrongly, Fletcher never forgave you for that night Eddie, that's why he was on your back all those years . . . "

Eddie and Hazel stared back at Dixie with expectant expressions but the detective didn't finish his sentence. Instead he just sat back in the office chair and supped his tea, looking at the semi-naked girl on the mug of tea in his hand, a bemused look on his face.

"Ronnie Fletcher's dead and gone ain't he? Last I heard from him was back in the eighties when he was trying to set *me* up for a fall and drink *himself* to death, something I truly hoped he's achieved!" Eddie could barely hide his hatred towards his old nemesis. Finally controlling his temper he continued. "So who's asking the questions then Dixie?"

"Oh sorry Ed but I ain't got a bleeding clue who he is, he didn't leave a name. The only description the sergeant gave me was that he was a gaunt looking bloke in a nice suit if that makes any sense to ya? I just thought I'd better let you know as soon as possible."

"Let *me* know, why? What exactly has he been asking about?" Eddie said, his voice now deadly serious.

"You Ed, he's been asking about *you*."

The words caught Eddie by surprise.

"*Me!*" he said astounded by the statement, " . . . what the fuck is he asking about *me* for?"

Hazel saw her ex-husband's discomfort and however uncomfortable her own memories of that night so long ago, she couldn't help but smirk.

"Maybe he thinks *you're* his father?"

"Oh here we go again, another bastard after a few quid."

Dixie glanced toward Hazel, puzzled by the outburst. Hazel just returned the glance with a knowing smile.

Eddie hadn't finished, "I just got rid of one scrounger right before you pair arrived. Black as the ace of spades he was, trying to pull the wool over me eyes, saying I'd shagged his mother at a punk rock gig at the Cedar Club back in 1976."

Hazel snorted, "Well, it sounds plausible to me, Ed!"

"Oh don't you start for fuck's sake, how can he be mine, he's *black*!"

Dixie raised his eyebrows, "He might be a throwback in the . . ."

Eddie finished his sentence, "Gene pool, do me a favour, the bloke looked like he'd never seen a bath never mind a gene pool."

Dixie burst out laughing but Eddie hadn't finished.

"Anyway, never mind the bleeding gene pool, why has this character been asking about *me*?"

Dixie's laugh trailed off and he shifted uncomfortably in his seat trying to work out what to say next.

"You *and* Ronnie Fletcher!"

CHAPTER 6

Cutthroats, Canal Boats

1995

Davey awoke with a start. The yapping of a small dog on the dockside overhead had shaken him from his alcohol-induced slumber. After the initial shock of the dog's bark had subsided, he lay in his bed for a few seconds staring blankly at the small porthole in the wall at the foot of his bed, feeling the rock of the boat on the water.

The gentle rolling of the narrowboat on which he lived was usually relaxing. However, this morning the action made him nauseous and as he tried to blink away the fuzziness in his brain. The hangover kicked in almost immediately with a vengeance. Davey winched at the pain in his head as images from the previous night's drunken debauchery came flooding back to him with the morning light that streamed through the porthole. His salutation to the new day was a little less than poetic,

"*Oh . . . Jesus!*"

Living on a narrow boat in the Gas Street Basin was a romantic lifestyle Davey had embraced willingly. He was an instant hit with the small community of boat-dwellers that clung to the tall, stone walls on the dockside, rising and falling with each opening and closing of the distant lock gates. The Basin housed an eclectic mix of down on their luck, borderline alcoholic singles, romantic water-gypsies and fanatical waterborne adventurers and Davey's talent for rabble-rousing Irish folk singing made him a perfect neighbour to whomever chose to moor alongside his canalboat, *Hideaway*.

However, no one had told him about the nonstop city noise that accompanied living on the water. True, there was no council tax or big energy bills to pay, so it was cheap, and it also had an element of anonymity when compared to living in a house but on days like today, hangover days, and there seemed to be more and more of them these days, it was literally a pain in the neck.

He snuggled beneath the thick quilt and sighed. His breath hung in the air above his head for a few seconds and for the first time Davey felt the cold of the air in the boat. He let out another deep breath of air and watched as it floated above his face like a ghost. Slowly the vapour spirit dissipated into the freezing air and he blew again, trying to measure exactly how cold it was by the time it took his breath to vanish.

"F . . . f . . . fucking freezing!"

The only consolation to the coldness inside the canal boat was that it seemed to help him shake off his hangover. In a burst of energy Davey threw back the quilt and swung his legs over the side of the bed. The initial pain in his head was quickly forgotten as his naked body became obscured beneath a rash of goosebumps. Dragging the quilt over his shoulders, he walked down the corridor that led to the small living area with its battered log burning stove.

He crouched down in front of the stove and grabbed at a bundle of kindling. Pulling the stove's door open he threw the bundle inside followed by a one of the small white firelighters he kept beside the kindling before striking a match and lighting the fire. The fire-lighter caught immediately and Davey watched as the first flickers of flame danced around the spaces in between the small pieces of wood.

Davey knelt in front of the fire watching the flames take hold through the smokey glass panel at the front of the log burner. Pulling the handle on the air intake at the bottom of the fire until it was wide open. He listened to the crackle as the flames grew in intensity as it sucked air in through the small gap beneath the stove as the fire caught light to the larger logs. He sat back on his haunches pleased with the results and lifted himself onto the long bench settee behind him. Pulling the quilt around him tighter he watched the flames dance within the small stove and he shivered. He always enjoyed Monday mornings whether he had a hangover or not, however, if truth be told, he couldn't remember a Monday morning when he *hadn't* had a hangover in a very long time.

Davey sat watching the fire as the air around him grew warmer. He listened to the city of Birmingham come to life in the distance and pondered his weekend shenanigans before, during and after his musical performances.

The memories of the previous few days and nights came in no particular order, and it took some concentration to put the hedonistic mischief he'd got up to in some sort of order of events. The three day drinking binge always spread a thick layer of fog over his memory but this Monday's recollections were different. These memories brought a feeling of dread with them. A feeling that he'd done something stupid, gotten himself involved in a situation that he had no doubt was going to come back and haunt him at some point in the future. He glanced at the small antique pine trunk that sat beside the log burner. He recalled his antics on Friday night, his drunken stumbling down the gangplank arm in arm with some drunken faceless woman he'd already forgotten the name of.

Davey also remembered the little white canvas bag he'd been holding onto. He recalled peeking inside it and seeing money, but that could've been one of his drunken dreams. He did have a clear recollection of hiding the bag inside the pine trunk, just before he was sidelined by the pretty girl with no name who took him by the hand to his bed. He hadn't thought about the bag since then. He hadn't forgotten about it, he'd just pushed the little sack to the back of his mind whilst his attention was given to the girl in hand. However, the weekend was over now and without a look over her shoulder the girl had vanished in the early hours of that winter's morning.

Yet like some dirty secret which of course it was, the little white canvas bag remained.

He stood, pulling the quilt around himself and he returned to the bedroom and dressed himself in jeans and t-shirt before making the bed and folding it back into the space where it was stored when not in use. The heat from the fire had taken the chill from the air and Davey walked back through to the living room area of the boat. A small kitchenette lay on the left hand side and Davey stepped into it and picked the kettle from the top of the small gas cooker and shook it. The splashing of water inside assured him it was half full and he placed it back on the burner and lit the ring on the cooker.

He stepped into the corridor again and looked at the little pine trunk. The memory of the Bar Manager lying in a pool of his own blood on the office floor of the *Brazen Maiden* jumped into his mind's eye, accompanied by another hollow feeling of dread in the pit of his stomach and he winced again.

Friday night's gig seemed a very long time ago now. Three days of heavy drinking had made sure of that and as the alcoholic fuzz from the weekend's drinking dissipated and his antics became clearer, the price of his actions and what he'd seen on the previous Friday night still remained as murky as the brown water outside the portholes of the little narrowboat *Hideaway*.

The sudden shrill whistle of the kettle broke his melancholy and he turned his attention back to tea. Grabbing the box of *Barry's Irish tea* he'd picked up after his last gig in Dublin a few week's before, he made a brick red brew and returned to the living room, mug in hand. He sat cross-legged in front of the pine box and took a sip of the sweet tea. The taste was familiar and reassured him things weren't as bad as he thought.

Placing the mug to one side he lifted the lid on the box and peered inside it. There it was, the item that was filling him with dread. A small white canvas bag, crumpled yet obviously full of something. He reached for the mug and took another sup of tea before reaching inside the box and lifting the bag out. It was heavier that he'd realised. The weight brought back the hollow feeling the tea had chased out. He plonked the bag in front of him and took another large sup of the sweet tea, as if it would steady his nerves. Then placing the cup down once more he reached to the bag and opened it. The sight inside caught him by surprise and sent a charge of cold sweat running up his spine, a mixture of excitement and dread in equal measure. He reached inside the bag, as if he didn't trust his eyes. His fingers were met with bundles of counted cash . . .

He touched the money as if it were something diseased and dirty, picking each bundle between forefinger and thumb and laying them out in front of himself on the raw oak floor of the boat.

One, two, three, he counted it out in an arc around him, twelve bundles. Davey took another sip from the steaming tea as his conscience battled with feelings of exhilaration, greed and regret. He picked up one of the bundles and flicked the notes through his fingers. Davey estimated that it must be a thousand pounds wrapped in the thin elastic band. He dropped it back with the others.

"Twelve grand!"

Picking up the tea he sat back against the footboard of the bench settee and stared at the money, thinking of the ways he could spend it. But as his imagination began to create images of holidays, cars and guitars, so too came the image of the Bar Manager in the pool of blood on the cheap linoleum flooring of the office. He shook his head, as if doing so would chase away the image, yet there it remained.

"*Fuck*!"

The realisation that the blood money would have to be returned finally dawned on him.

"Maybe I could have half of it, a quarter, just a couple of grand . . ." he thought, " . . . as a reward?"

He tried to convince himself that it was a fair enough idea. After all he'd return the rest of the cash and maybe they wouldn't know how much had been taken from the safe at all. The two gun men could've taken any amount of cash. Davey wrestled with the opposing emotions of guilt and greed until his tea had gone cold. Finally he gathered the bundles up and threw them back into the bag. Dropping it back in the pine box he returned to the bedroom and began to get himself ready to go out. There would be only one way to decide whether he should keep the cash or not and that was to return to the *Brazen Maiden* and see how the Bar Manager was and how the land lay. He could always explain his way out of it and return the cash bag by saying he'd been drunk when he'd taken it. Surely, then if the old Bill were involved, which he was sure they would be, they would understand.

After dressing himself properly, he pulled on an old, brown leather peacoat and stepped out into the Monday morning chill of Birmingham city. Davey stood on the rear deck of the little boat for a second and took in the view. The day was bitterly cold but clear and the winter sun glimmered on the grey-brown water of Birmingham's docks.

The scene had a grimy charm that captivated him whenever he saw it. Nothing had really changed here for the last 200 hundred or so years. *Yes,* the developers had started to move in, cleaning up the scruffy edges of the basin, gentrifying the area in order to attract the first-time buyers to the over-priced apartments that had started to spring up here and there. However, in doing so, they had already planted the seeds to end the area's charm. Davey wondered how long it would be before the old authentic Victorian buildings that surrounded his boat, would be ripped down only to be replaced by modernised, sanitised versions of the real thing in order to satisfy people with plenty of cash and no taste.

The sight of the waterway, with its canal boats and watercraft moored along the huge stone quaysides, took his mind away from the little bag of blood money he had inside his coat for a moment. The sound of an engine caught his attention as it rattled into earshot. Davey turned to see a yellow canal boat drawing closer as it made its way along the waterway around the city-centre carrying a full load of tourists. He automatically stepped to the side of the boat and waved towards it. The yellow boat instantly changed direction, heading towards him across the open space of the basin.

Anticipating the backwash from the dockside wall Davey held onto the handrail of his boat as the tourist boat came in close to his narrowboat in a flurry of small waves, rocking the stationary vessel violently. The tourist boats weren't meant to stop anywhere along the docks unless it was an authorised docking space but the skippers of the little yellow fleet always made a point of looking after the local canal-dwellers, much to the annoyance of the Monday morning sightseers.

Slowing, but without stopping, the skipper closed in on the port side of the canal boat and skimming the side of Davey's narrowboat, Davey and the skipper timed things perfectly. Davey stepped onto the deck of the yellow boat and grabbed another handrail. He could feel the eyes of the irritated men and women burning into his back as he climbed down into the cab's seating area. However, instead of joining the rest of the passengers, Davey walked through the cabin towards the wheelhouse at the rear of the boat.

Recognising the skipper of the boat, he wrapped his knuckles against the glass of the little compartment. The girl glanced down at him and smiling beckoned him up on to her risen area in front of the tiller, acknowledging him with a nod and smile before pushing a long chrome leaver forward. Her action caused the diesel engine to roar, driving the boat forward through the dark brown water.

"Thanks for stopping." he said over the din.

The girl just nodded again, concentrating on the boat's acceleration.

"Where do you want to be dropped?" she finally said, once the difficult manoeuvre of clearing the moored boats was over and the boat was back midstream. The question caught him by surprise. She turned to him, whilst keeping one hand on the tiller of the boat and her other on the throttle.

"Where are you heading and I'll get you as close as I can?"

"I'm heading down towards Digbeth but you don't have to go out of your way."

He turned to look at the faces of the tourists, they all looked thoroughly miserable. Several of them were staring directly at him. The skipper turned to see what he was looking at.

"I think this lot will lynch us if we delay 'em any more than we have already." He said laughing.

"Ah, don't mind these bunch of wankers, they always look like that, miserable bastards. I'll drop you under Benny's bridge, at the back of Digbeth there's an old set of steps there no one uses anymore, it'll bring you up right behind the High street."

Davey smiled and nodded.

"Thank you, really appreciate it, I owe you one."

Without turning the girl just shrugged her shoulders.

****

The transvestite sat in the window of the pub and rubbed the bristle on his chin. The weekend had been fun just like every other weekend since he'd made the 'transition' from man to woman. However at forty-six, his age was catching up with him and he really should have gone home to his wife and kids on Saturday night, instead of snorting himself into a nerve-tingling, heart-attack stupor.

Now it was Monday morning and worse than that, it was daylight. He felt like an ageing vampire that had over stayed its welcome, numb, naked and foolish in his short length 1960's style mini-dress, stockings and high heels. His cheap, platinum-blonde wig was too bright to be seen in during daylight hours and he was terrified of the prospect of anyone from the car dealership where he worked in his *normal* life, seeing him in all his finery.

Well, finery wasn't really the right word . . . On Friday night, with the help of his *understanding* wife, he had transformed into a life on the tiles slut, a city she-cat, singing, drinking and showing her flesh to all and sundry in a hedonistic celebration of womanhood. The butterfly who had been jailed all week in a two button suit, had once more escaped its chrysalis and was flying high as a ketamine kite above the heads of Birmingham's flamboyant, gay and dandy.

However, that was Friday night, forty-eight hours had passed since then and the transformation had now began to reverse. Now a fully-grown man was blooming from the young girl and the butterfly was plummeting down to the ground with all the grace of an over-fed caterpillar. He sat in the small bay window of the *Old Fox* pub and watched the traffic buzz by on Hurst Street outside, wondering how he'd explain himself, *again*. He supped on a gin and tonic as if by doing so he could squeeze every last drop of fun from the weekend and stave off the inevitable comedown from the coke and ketamine and the 'once and for all' roasting he'd received from his *ever*-understanding, yet tearful wife on his one and only phone call home to her that weekend.

"No Geoff, this has to end, God knows I've tried my best to understand, but enough is enough!"

He ran through the tearful conversation in his mind.

"Don't think I don't know what you get up to with your *queer* friends!" She had been bawling, and from what he could hear in the background, so had his three young children,

"It's over, I don't want you to come home until you're the man I married!"

It didn't help that he'd burst into laughter when she'd said it. He hadn't really been listening. He'd been watching some of the pornographic antics of the other punters in the *Old Fox* and with the help of too many G&Ts and a very good wrap of cocaine, just couldn't help himself from laughing at the absurdity of it all. He too had cried, only his tears were ones of laughter, well, they were to begin with. However, as the weekend wore on, the almost pure cocaine, had turned from an uplifting experience, to one of anxiety with every snort he'd taken and so he'd moved onto the horse tranquilliser, ketamine which had lifted his spirits for a short while.

She was wrong about one thing though. He wasn't part of the gay scene. He never had been. He wasn't gay, well, he'd tried a few things with different people over the years but that didn't mean he was gay. He enjoyed the company of like-minded people is all. The sex only went as far as the other transvestites. He loved women, that's why he dressed as one. If there was any sex involved it was with a strapping six-footer in fishnets and high heels, *hardly gay*!

As the weekend had wore on, he'd sat at the same table and entertained the old faces of the Brummie gay scene as if he were a Parisian mistress. Flamboyance was the name of the game and *Kylie,* his alter ego, had it by the bucketful. The newly permitted 24-hour licensing laws now made it possible to live in a pub for the whole weekend and that's exactly what Kylie liked to do. As the crowds came and went, she stayed in her usual seat, smoking drinking and snorting her time away until the wee hours when things quietened down somewhat and gave her time for reflection on Geoff's life. *Not* an enjoyable experience it must be said and one to be avoided at all costs.

And so, it came as a great relief to see a commotion in the street outside the little Irish bar, late on Friday night, Saturday morning. Geoff had occupied his time since then by watching the police buzzing around the Irish bar, coming and going in a swirl of blue flashing lights. Something serious had happened in the *Brazen Maiden* and as time had gone on, curiosity had got the better of him.

Saturday and Sunday were given over to watching the scene unfold on Hurst Street, until by early Monday morning, he had no choice but to high-heel it down the street to chat up the young copper standing guard beside the blue and white police tape that stretched across the front door to the pub. As well as finding out any gossip, he'd tell the young Bobby about the two suspicious looking men in long, brown overalls and nylon-covered faces he'd seen racing away from the pub in a black BMW in the early hours of Saturday morning whilst enjoying a fag on the doorstep of the pub. He'd seen one of their faces too, clear as day. Thinking the street had been empty, the man had pulled the nylon stocking over his head as he'd stepped up to the side of the car, revealing his face. Kylie had got a good look at him. However, the man suddenly froze as he spotted Kylie staring from the shadows of the doorway and the two had had a moment, their eyes locked together for a few seconds and in a chilling moment Kylie thought the man was going to cross the road and come and get *her*. However, the man had thought better of it and, after a long menacing stare, the two gunmen sped away into the night.

On Monday morning, *Kylie*, the rapidly-waning butterfly crossed the street and was greeted by a horrified young policemen.

"Good morning officer, what's happened here then?" he said in his highest most feminine voice.

The young Bobby shrivelled under the salacious gaze of the transvestite.

"Come on now, darlin . . . " he stuttered as the transvestite got closer. Kylie's 5-o clock shadow became apparent and the policeman checked himself, over-emphasising his embarrassment lest his fellow officers catch him talking to such a 'freak' " . . . look, just fuck off mate, I ain't got time for the likes of you!"

Kylie held her handbag in front of her large false breasts as if it were a shield, protecting her from the officer's harsh words.

"Well, there's no need to be like that is there?" She let her voice drop to its normal tone, that of a forty-something man, "I was only trying to help mate. I drink in here and know the landlord. I was watching from over . . . "

The policeman shrugged.

"No-one's interested in what you know or don't know, you weirdo. Now you heard me, fuck off back to that poof's palace across the street and leave me alone, you ain't my type!"

Kylie rolled her eyes.

"Charming little twat aren't you? Well, let me tell you, you shouldn't flatter yourself darling. You couldn't handle a girl like me."

"Go on piss off, before I arrest you for being ugly in broad daylight!" The officer smirked at his little joke and he continued. "This is a murder investigation sunshine not a bleeding beauty pageant!" He waved his hand towards Kylie as if wafting away a bad smell. "Go on . . . fuck off!"

The last words came as a command. Kylie gave a pantomime huff, rolling her eyes once more and turning on her heel. She crossed the road back towards the pub doorway whence she came.

"Who was that?" Dixie asked.

The young policeman turned to find DCI Dixon standing in the doorway of the Brazen Maiden.

"I..ehh!" the policeman stuttered. "Ehh, he's just a queer sir, he was nosing around trying to find out what's going on!"

Dixie looked the young man over with some disdain.

"I heard what you said to him son, you told him to fuck off didn't you!"

The young man tried to think of a way out of the situation but nothing came to mind.

"Don't go trying to think up an excuse, I heard what you said, son!"

The policeman shuffled like a guilty school boy. Dixie stepped closer to the man and placed his hand on his shoulder. The action caught the bobby by surprise.

"That ain't how you do police work, our kid. You don't tell a potential witness to *fuck off*, just because they're queer."

The policeman tried to answer.

"No sir, he was just nosing about . . . "

"You don't know that do ya? You didn't give him a chance to talk. No you just told him to fuck off and insulted the bloke."

"Yeah b . . . but he's a . . . a freak sir!" the young man stuttered. Dixie laughed.

"Well if your gonna be offended by freaks, then you're in the wrong fucking job sunshine, because when you signed up to this, you signed up to protect these *freaks!*" He emphasised the word, as if it were an insult to the young man.

"From my experience, and I've seen my fair share of *freaks* over the years, its people like that who are willing to step into the limelight, many times at their own risk by the way, and help you do your job." Dixie let the words sink in for a few seconds. "So when we're finished here, you can trot across the road and apologise to that gentleman . . . " He stopped himself and rephrased, " . . . or woman or whatever and politely ask if they could come over here and talk to me about whatever it was they trying to talk to you about before you told them to *fuck off.*"

The young policeman looked into the old detective's eyes. The bobby shrank under Dixie's stare. He could see the anger simmering just below the surface in the old man's stare and he knew that the detective was barely keeping a lid on his temper. He lowered his eyes to his shiny boots.

"Yes, sir . . . " the young man muttered.

"Good, because unless you wanna be stood outside every fucking crime scene for the rest of your career instead of being inside, where the good stuff happens, then I would wake-the-fuck-up and start acting like a member of the West Midlands fucking police force!"

With that Dixie turned and stepped back inside the pub, leaving the young Bobby still shuffling his feet and feeling very stupid indeed.

****

As Kylie watched the altercation between the two policeman through the dirty panes of blown glass in the otherwise empty street outside, her eye was drawn to a young blonde man on the opposite side of the street walking towards the *Brazen Maiden*.

The man had the collar of his thick, leather peacoat turned upwards almost covering his face as he approached the pub and Kylie wondered whether that was due to the coldness of the day or so as not to be recognised. She followed as the blonde man approached the policeman and watched them talking for a short time. Kylie bristled at the sight of the two men talking in a friendly manner, the policeman all smiles and conversation now. He seemed to be going into great detail with the blonde man and the transvestite wondered why the copper hadn't taken the time to talk to her in that way.

At that moment Kylie caught sight of her distorted reflection in the twisted blown glass of the little bay window and suddenly understood the policeman's reaction to the sight of her. The reflection caught her by surprise. Her dark blue eyes were surrounded by black mascara, the make-up running in dark lines down her cheeks and onto her jowls making her look like some sort of ghoul in the morning light. As if that wasn't bad enough, her chin was lined with a dark shadow of stubble that a macho truck driver would've been proud of. The realisation that she looked ghastly finally hit her and the butterfly crashed completely.

Kylie was vanishing before her eyes and Geoff was reclaiming his body in all its hairy glory.

The blonde man turned away from the policeman and was now walking back down the street towards the Old Fox. He looked pale, as if he'd just heard something awful from the rude policeman and Kylie, in a last pang of curiosity threw herself at the opportunity to find out more. Rising from her chair she crossed to the front door to the empty pub and pulled the heavy door open.

"Here, handsome!" she called as the man drew near.

The blonde man didn't react, as if in a world of his own.

"Oi blondie, over here!" she said in a higher pitched voice.

Davey turned at the sound of the *Monty Python*esque woman's voice. The sight of the six foot woman with the 5-o'clock stubble stopped him in his tracks and he stood in the middle of the road staring at the transvestite for a few seconds before answering.

"I'm sorry luv, are ye talking to me?"

The man's Irish accent caught her by surprise and both were caught in a moment of speechlessness. Kylie could see the man's mind was elsewhere but was encouraged by the way he'd addressed her as *love*.

"You look like you need a drink, handsome?"

Davey stared blankly at Kylie for a second, wondering what the time was.

"Is it open?" he nodded towards the gay pub.

Kylie shrugged, "It is for us darling, come on in here and I'll buy you a drink."

Davey turned towards the policeman who was watching the little scene with a smirk, then he turned back to the transvestite.

"You're right luv, sure after what he's just told me . . . " he gestured towards the policeman, " . . . I could do with a large one."

Kylie gave a well-rehearsed sexy giggle.

"We are talking about the size of your drink now aren't we?"

Davey laughed.

"*Saucy mare*!" he said as he stepped into the doorway of the pub.

Davey followed the transvestite inside to the bar area where Kylie pointed at the table by the window and told him to sit, while she went behind the bar and poured herself another drink.

"What'll it be handsome?"

Davey watched her with a mixture of amusement and distrust.

"I'll have a whiskey please, my love!" he said turning towards the window and viewing the scene across the road. "Irish whiskey that is, none of that Scottish rough stuff!"

Kylie had already grabbed a bottle of *Jameson's* whiskey from a shelf over the bar and began to pour the golden liquid into a small glass.

"Shame, I like a bit of Scottish rough stuff myself, you know the Sean Connery type."

"Look bird, just to get one thing straight, I ain't gay!" Davey said sternly. "I don't care if you are but I ain't, you asked me if I wanted a drink and I . . . "

Kylie interrupted, this time in his normal voice.

"Don't worry mate, I ain't gay either . . . " he said as he crossed back to the window seat with two large drinks, " . . . well not in the way you're thinking anyway. I just like dressing like a lady."

Davey looked the transvestite up and down, taking in the mini dress, high heels and clearly visible stocking tops and laughed.

"Jesus girl, you don't look like any of the ladies I've ever met!"

Geoff plonked himself on the other side of the table and sniggered.

"I know mate, look at me, what a fucking state I am now. I looked a treat when I was leaving the house on Friday. Mind you, I had a right snorty weekend if you know what I mean."

He held one finger up to his right nostril and sniffed, raising his eyebrows as he did. Davey understood the gesture.

"Sounds like you had a wild one."

Geoff gave a wink.

"I did, *fucking* wild!" He tried to give his sexy giggle again but the weekend's chains smoking had taken its toll on his throat and the giggle turned into a spluttering cough. He took a sip of his drink and the coughing bout subsided.

"Even if it did cost me my marriage." he sighed.

Davey took his glass of whiskey from the table.

"Slante!"

His brow furrowed.

"You're *married*?"

Geoff shrugged as if it didn't matter. However, Davey could see the first tinges of regret in the man's bloodshot eyes. Not wanting to get into the transvestite's life story Davey changed the subject.

"Well, at least your weekend was better than his." he gestured towards the Brazen Maiden.

Geoff shook his head.

"I know, a bloody murder investigation!"

Geoff spoke as if he knew more than he actually did.

Davey scowled.

"*Murder*?"

Geoff looked disappointed and confused at the same time.

"Well, you probably know more about it than I do, after all me and Bobby McGee over there didn't exactly hit it off but you pair were having a right old chin wag."

Geoff's tone sounded as if he were jealous of Davey's conversation with the policeman.

"Him . . . ?" Davey gestured to the policeman standing at the threshold to the Irish theme pub door, " . . . no, no you got it wrong love."

Davey took another sip, enjoying the bitterness of the whisky on his palette so early in the morning. "I'm in an Irish band and I played there on Friday night . . . .did you say murder investigation?"

Geoff nodded.

"Well, that's what he said to me, they were conducting a murder investigation." The colour in Davey face drained to a sickly white. "Are you alright mate? Looks like you've seen a ghost?"

"So he died!" Davey said under his breath.

"Who died?" Geoff's words brought Davey back to the moment.

"Who died?" Geoff repeated.

"Jamie!" Davey said as if the transvestite would recognise the name. However, Geoff just shook his head. On seeing the man's bemused expression Davey continued.

"The landlord of the Brazen Maiden. He's . . . *dead*!"

Davey took another swig of the whiskey as if it would calm his nerves – it didn't. He held the liquid in his mouth, swilling it softly around his tongue as he tried to think what his next move should be. Geoff on the other hand suddenly became animated. Davey's attention was drawn to Geoff, and he watched the man for a few seconds, taking in the change in the transvestite's demeanour.

He finally asked in a soft voice, "You know something don't ye?"

Geoff began to fumble with his cigarette packet, unable to meet the Irishman's stare.

"Come on love, I ain't gonna say anything, you can tell me!"
Geoff shook his head.

"I ain't getting involved mate, those blokes looked fucking dangerous!"

Davey's brow furrowed.

"Sounds to me like you already *are* involved!" Davey said, raising his eyebrows in a questioning manner. "You saw them too?"

Geoff stopped fumbling, almost too frightened to answer, finally blurting.

"Yeah, I saw one of them, I had a good look at him too but more's to the point, he saw *me*, I thought he was gonna come and get me."

Davey smiled, nodding slowly.

"I can't see there's anything to smile about blondie. That bloke could come and get me if he thinks I can recognise him!"

Davey placed his glass down and rested his hands on the table. He pointed at one of the large, antique, pub mirrors that lined the room.

"Go take a look at yourself!"

Geoff didn't move. Davey continued.

"That bloke didn't see *you*, he saw ... " Davey looked for the right words, " ... This, he saw your alter ego, *Kylie* or whatever you call yourself, if you want my advice, I'd put her to bed for a while until this thing blows over."

Davey's words seemed to have the right effect, and Geoff seemed to calm down somewhat. Davey sighed.

"That's my advice anyway!" He took another swig of his whiskey, this time draining the glass.

Geoff spoke up.

"So how are you involved?"

The question caught Davey by surprise. Suddenly feeling self-conscious he reached inside his leather coat. His fingertips touched the bundle of cash in the canvas bag he had secreted under his arm. He could have sworn the sack had become heavier at the sound of Geoff's question. He tried to shrug it off, still unsure exactly how he would answer, or what he should do now he knew Jamie the landlord was dead. There was suddenly too many things to take on board. However, if Geoff's question made him feel uneasy, the transvestite's next words hit him like a slap around the face.

"Those two men weren't the only ones I saw that night. I saw *you* there too!"

Geoff's face seemed to suddenly flush as the scene from the previous Friday night came back to him through the fog of cocaine and alcohol.

"It *was* you wasn't it. You left the *Brazen Maiden* right after those two men in the black BMW. I didn't recognise you at first but now I do. You're the bloody singer in the band, ain't you?"

Davey's face, already pale from the shock of hearing of the death of the landlord, went an even whiter shade as Geoff's recollections flooded from his mouth. He stared at the ridiculous looking man in his platinum blonde wig, false tits and mini dress and tried to find a way to explain himself but nothing came to mind except escape. Suddenly, he felt cornered. His mind ran over his options that only milliseconds before had been a swirl of muddy ideas yet now appeared in his mind's eye, as clear as spring-water. His plan of handing the cash in to the old Bill and just explaining his way out of the situation as being drunken foolishness had now gone past its sell-by-date.

"A *murder* had taken place." Davey thought to himself, the finality of the word suddenly sinking in, *murder*! And now, this stubbled-chinned transformer had just placed him at the scene of the crime. Not only that but if the old Bill were to pick him up now, this little bag of cash was all the evidence they'd need to charge him with the crime, never mind his drunken, garbled phonecall for an ambulance after the event ...

"Yeah, it was you!" Geoff said, this time with some alarm in his voice. "How do I know it wasn't you that killed the landlord?"

Geoff moved closer to the front door of the pub as if to make a dash for it, Davey realised his intentions and rose quickly from his stool, blocking his escape.

"Sit down!" Davey ordered.

Geoff didn't move.

"Sit the fuck down *now*!" This time with a growl of desperation in his voice.

Geoff did as he was told and Davey stood over him and tried to control his temper.

"You're jumping to conclusions, mate!" He breathed deeply, controlling the volume of his voice. "*Yes, I was there* on Friday night but I didn't *kill* anyone!" Davey plonked himself back on his stool. "I saw the two blokes you saw, they were robbing the place. I walked in halfway through the robbery, they didn't even know I was there. If they had, maybe they would've killed me too!"

Geoff's expression of confused distrust didn't change as he listened to the Irishman's explanation.

"Listen Miss Marple, don't go getting any stupid ideas of running over there and telling the copper that you've caught the culprit and solved the fucking crime, cos you ain't. Besides, what reason would I have to kill Jamie?"

Davey reached over and patted Geoff's shoulder. The transvsestite flinched at the touch and suddenly rose from his chair, pushing Davey's arm away from him as he did. Without warning, the white canvas, cash bag fell from beneath Davey's armpit. It landed on the sticky pub carpet with a dull thud spilling a couple of bundles of cash as it did. Both men stood in a shocked silence looking down at the money. Davey was the first to move and dropping to his knees he began to bundle the cash into the small bag.

"I'd say that little lot is a good enough reason to kill anyone!" screeched Geoff.

Davey stopped grabbing at the bundles and sitting back on his haunches he looked up at the transvestite with a guilty expression.

"It ain't what you think."

"Ain't it? Well let's see what the old Bill think!"

Geoff stepped across the strewn money making his way towards the door of the pub. Davey sprung to his feet with surprising speed and held his hand out towards the cross-dresser, blocking his path.

"You can have some if you like!"

Geoff stopped in his tracks. With a flinch, Davey pressed a bundle of cash in the direction of Geoff's padded bra.

"No, I can't let you go out there and tell that copper a load of bullshit. You've put two and two together and come up with twenty."

Geoff glared at Davey's hand.

"Move it, *now!*"

"Hear me out before you do something that you won't be able to undo!"

Geoff blinked his red eyes, his nostrils flaring with anger as he thought over the words of the Irishman.

"Seriously . . . " Davey continued, " . . . I didn't kill anyone, I was just in the wrong place at the wrong time."

Geoff turned towards the hand holding the bundle of cash and snatched it. He waved the bundle in Davey's face.

"Well, some people wouldn't see it like that, would they? Some people would think that you were in *exactly* the right place."

"That might well be the case but it doesn't make it true does it?" Davey glanced at the bundle. "There's a grand there, it's yours if you keep you mouth shut until I can work out who those two blokes were."

Geoff raised his carefully shaped eyebrows.

"I dunno . . . " the transvestite's eyelashes fluttered nervously, " . . . this whole thing gives me the creeps. This isn't a game I want to get involved in."

Davey cut him short.

"You already are involved mate and if you walk over there and start blabbing your mouth off, things might get even more creepy than they already are. Whether you like it or not, we're both involved in the game. I'm trying to make sure we both don't end up being the jackpot."

Geoff stared at Davey for a few seconds before taking the cash and stuffing it inside his bra beneath his low cut blouse.

Davey nodded, happy that the other man had taken the cash.

"Right . . . " he said with a relieved sigh. " . . . I'm gonna lay low for a few days, I suggest you do the same, in case those blokes come sniffing around looking for you. After all, you and I are the only people that saw them and you are the only person that can identify one of them." Davey's words sent a shiver through the cross-dresser's spine. He nodded towards the man's false breasts.

"Now take that cash and get yourself something nice to wear and whatever you do, stay away from here for a few weeks!"

Geoff nodded.

"What about you?"

Davey laughed.

"Don't worry about me mate. I'm getting out of town for a few days, until I've had time to think this through properly."

"But when will we meet up again?" Geoff asked.

Davey looked at the man with a bemused expression.

"Why would we need to meet up again?"

"You know, to solve the crime." Geoff said with a thin, uncertain smile.

"Don't get carried away mate, we ain't *Starsky* and bleeding *Hutch*. I've seen these guys in action and if you go doing a Scooby-Do, you're gonna end up dead."

He let his words sink in before continuing in a sharper tone.

"Look, it's been a bit of good fortune that we've bumped into each other cos now I know that I've got a witness to testify about the robbery if it comes on top with the old Bill."

Geoff nodded.

"But until that happens, if indeed it does happen, I think it's best if we steer clear of each other."

Geoff seemed disappointed so Davey smiled and patted the transvestite's shoulder.

"Don't fret love, it'll all blow over, I'm sure of it. Oh and . . . " He pointed at the bundle of cash which protruded through the man's blouse, " . . . don't go snorting that lot up your nose either!"

Geoff shrugged innocently and Davey turned and walked towards the front door to the pub. As he opened the door to the street, he turned in the doorway.

"That's the problem with coke, it makes you yap too much, the less people know about this little mess, the better."

Davey tapped his nose with his forefinger before vanishing into the street.

Geoff stood in silence for a second, listening to the sound of the city coming to life outside. The Irishman was right, he thought, cocaine did make a user *yap* too much. However, at that precise moment in time, Geoff was running his coke dealer's telephone number through his mind and wondering how much he could score for a grand ...

CHAPTER 7

1995

A Growing Feeling of Dread

Hazel swung her Mercedes into the empty drive of the expansive house in the leafy suburb of Edgbaston. The mansion had once been a place of happiness, yet now as she sat in her stationary car staring at the house, she was filled with unease and regret.

The seven-bedroomed status symbol which had perfectly reflected the Fewtrell family's rise from rags to riches, now felt like a millstone around all of their necks. The garden parties for Brum's high and mighty had been fun back in the 1980's but things had changed. Along with success and money – and there was lots of money, came the green-eyed monsters of jealousy, distrust and ultimately, crippling paranoia. Piece by piece the intricate tapestry of their lives unravelled in front of their very eyes and nothing and no one could do anything to stop it.

She stepped from the car and crossed to the house. Pushing the large, unlocked oak door she stepped into the hallway and threw her designer handbag across the hall onto the cream leather chaise-long that rested against the banister rail of the elegant sweeping staircase.

She stared up at the Swiss-crystal chandelier which hung from the hall ceiling, twenty feet above her head. The palatial space irritated her. The sweeping elm staircase irritated her, even the unlocked front door irritated her and she bristled as she heard Eddie's voice in her head explaining that there was no reason to lock the front door, because no one in the right mind would *dare* to rob Eddie Fewtrell's house.

Yes, it was such a fine house, lots of space, too much space if she were honest with herself. Too easy for the family to avoid each other, which they did when possible on every occasion. Only crossing each other's path when going from kitchen to bedroom whenever that might be. Eddie and Hazel always slept separately these days. His early hours drunken home-comings had become irritating to the point where she wanted to throttle him whenever he awoke her from her valium or painkiller-induced sleep.

Where once the place had been full of mischievous children's laughter now the house seemed to echo with emptiness. The *kids*, well they just came and went as they wanted. Even her youngest seemed to have a social life she knew nothing about, although she knew he would always show up when he needed something or other or had fallen foul of someone around town and needed her wing to cower under. Abi, her second child had blossomed into a young woman and moved her life to another part of Birmingham. Hazel felt as if she had had to become a private eye just to find out what Abi was up to these days and as the birds flew the coop, Hazel felt the years closing in on her. Her heady days of long nights on the town were over. These days she lay in bed till midday listening to the other people in the house going about their business as she mulled over her regrets and times of happiness and contentment they had shared in the big house.

However, on reflection, she wasn't one hundred percent sure that those times had actually existed at all. Eddie and her had always struggled, that's what had once made them strong and unstoppable. Every day a new insurmountable challenge threatened to bring them down, and without fail they had fought against those challenges, never giving up, fighting back to back, shoulder to shoulder with Eddie's other brothers against each new challenge. Gangsters, corrupt police, vicious gossip and sexual affairs, none of these things had broken their family apart as quickly as success had. Nothing had wormed its way into their lives with more self-serving destruction than contentment.

She didn't even recognise her husband these days, mind you, she rarely saw him for more than a few minutes a week anyway. The marriage was over, everyone knew it, well, everyone except her husband that is. He refused to accept it and even though the money kept rolling in and life *was* good. Money *wasn't* everything and life could be so much better if they just went their separate ways once and for all. Hazel couldn't listen to Eddie's ever exaggerated coffee-table stories anymore. She'd heard them way too many times. The only enjoyable thing about them these days was Eddie's ability to expand on his last telling of a particular tale which always seemed to have him firmly at the middle of the action, always the hero, always the victim.

Maybe it was her. Maybe *she* was changing in the way women seem to change when they reach her age. Maybe life *was* good, money *was* everything and Eddie was right and she just couldn't see it. Either way, Hazel felt a deep inescapable feeling of dread settling over her compounded by the conversation with Eddie and her old friend Dixie. It was as if his fresh information about the abduction of the little boy from the Bermuda back in 1961, had re-opened a wound that she thought had healed years before. But now, that old scar had suddenly been pulled open and found to be infected. And she knew with all her heart that, at some point in the not too distant future, something horrible would come of it all.

CHAPTER 8

Ain Sionnach Rua

1995

(The Red Fox)

"*Tiocfaidh ar la*" Declan O'Dwyer said passionately as he raised his shot glass to the door man with a wink. The burley bouncer raised his own glass and touched it against Declan's. The cut-crystal glasses clinked against each other with a musical note that hung in the air of the empty bar for a second or two before being drowned out by the traffic noise from the busy high-street outside.

"*Our day will come!*" The doorman translated the Gaelic phrase, so popular amongst Irish Republicans, with just as much passion as the Irishman's. Both men downed the Irish whiskey in one movement before placing the delicate glasses back on the bar counter. They stood in silence, enjoying the warmth of the whiskey on their chests, each lost in their own thoughts as they listened to the sounds of the busy Monday morning rush hour traffic rolling passed the windows of the *Dublin Barrel* Irish pub in Birmingham's Irish quarter, known locally as *County Digbeth*.

Declan poured another shot for each of them. His huge rough hands suddenly as delicate as a child's as he handled the wafer-thin Waterford cut-glass.

The doorman turned and stared blankly at the world outside as the pedestrians, bent beneath their umbrellas and hoods, hurried this way and that in the freezing drizzle, scurrying between the stationary traffic caught in the bottle neck that was the Bull Ring one way system.

He scanned the line of grime covered Victorian buildings across the wide street with distaste. The Kebab shops, Balti takeaways and massage parlours stretched down the litter-ridden street, and he pondered on how much the place had changed since his childhood and how the Irish were hanging on to the area by the skin of their teeth, as the new *Asian* immigrants slowly took over.

His eye was drawn along the street until it came to a pub's green frontage with an Irish tricolour flag hanging above its front door. The sight of the green white and orange flag sent a tingle of pride running through him, an emotion he couldn't really explain. He certainly didn't get it when he saw the Union Jack, or the 'Butcher's apron' as he and his circle of friends liked to call it. He didn't really bare any malice to the English, well, not the Brummies anyway. He had been born in Birmingham so was technically English himself and therefore his allegiance should have been with the red white and blue flag of the United Kingdom. However, his parents were both staunch Irish, and he and his siblings had been brought up within the huge Irish community of Birmingham. Along with the fact that most of his childhood holidays had been spent 'Back home in Ireland' which in-itself was a contradiction in terms, as his home was actually in Kings Heath, Birmingham, he now considered himself as Irish as the huge Dublin bar owner who stood on the opposite side of the counter.

"So what ya got for me, Sonny?" Declan said, his broken nose emphasising his thick Dublin accent.

The words broke the doorman's daydream and turning back to the bar, he heaved a small, black, shoulder bag onto the counter, its size belaying its weight. Declan leaned across the bar and pulled the bag towards him, pushing the refilled whiskey glass towards the young doorman as he did. Unzipping the bag Declan peered through the opening. His broad, brutal face breaking into a yellow-toothed smile when he saw the pressed bundles of cash inside.

"Looks like our day *has* come!" he said with a snigger as he lifted one of the bundles from the bag. He handed it to the young man. "Well done Sonny, treat ya ma to something nice!"

The doorman took the bundle with a contained smile.

"Thanks boss!" he said nodding towards the bag. "Things are looking up for the *cause*."

Declan laughed.

"Fuck that, all that shit's over now, the cause is dead. McGuinness and Paisley are best pals these days so the war's over as far as I'm concerned."

The young doorman shook his head with a growing confusion.

"Well, what's that lot for if it ain't for the cause?"

Declan leaned across the counter and shook another bundle of cash in the doorman's face.

"It's for keeping your fucking trap shut, Sonny!" He pushed another, smaller bundle into the doorman's top pocket. "Yeah, the IRA will want some of it, well, most of it to be sure but now's a time to start feathering our own nests. *Yes*, we'll keep collecting but obviously the 'collections for the cause' will not be as profitable as they once were, now that we have peace in the six counties in the North."

The doorman shrugged.

"My old fella says he never thought he'd see peace in Northern Ireland in his lifetime!"

Declan took his glass and slugged the golden liquid. He blinked a few times as if by doing so it would dissipate its strength on his palette.

"Peace?" he coughed. "Fuck peace! There's more money in war!"

"There's more money in *pubs*!" the doorman countered with a thin smile.

The big Dubliner laughed.

"You can say that again me lad."

He pulled the cork from the bottle of *Tullamore Dew* whiskey and poured two glasses. Handing the glass to the other man he raised his own and made a toast.

"Here's to Irish theme pubs and the plastic Paddies that drink in em!"

The bouncer laughed and chinked his glass once more.

"Careful Declan, I *am* one of those plastic Paddies."

The Dubliner shook his head.

"Nah, Sonny McBride, you're an Irish thoroughbred!"

"But I was born in Brum?"

Declan threw his drink to the back of his throat.

"Yeah but your parents are Irish so as far as I'm concerned, that makes you Irish. Trust me boy, if your folks had been Chinese or Pakistani, then no one would doubt your nationality."

The doorman nodded, pleased with the Irishman's explanation on his claim on Irish nationality.

"You might have been born here but now you're a foot soldier for the cause!"

"I thought you said the cause was dead?"

"It *is* dead, as dead as dead can be!" Declan said with a wry smile. "That was the old cause, I'm talking about the *new* cause!"

The doorman raised his eyebrows.

"Oh yeah and which cause would that be then?"

"The cause that's gonna make me, you and all of our crew very rich men Sonny, that cause."

The other man laughed.

"You mean we're gonna skim off the IRA? You don't need me to tell ya, that's a very dangerous business!"

Declan became animated.

"Look outside Sonny. There is an Irish pub on every fucking corner these days, some of em are owned by breweries, some are owned by the landlords who run em, and some, as you know, are funded by the IRA or organisations connected with the 'Ra' and used as money laundering operations. *We*, or should I say *you*, collect that money on behalf of the Belfast boys who, up until recently, spent that money on the *cause*. The thing is, now we have peace in Northern Ireland, they are spending it on, shall we say less patriotic causes . . . " The Dublin man touched his nose and sniffed before continuing " . . . if you know what I mean. Now that the I.R.A. as an organised military force are becoming obsolete and the infrastructure within the chain of command is imploding. There's going to be a power struggle between the I.R.A. patriots and the criminal elements within the movement. It's already started to happening in the U.D.A. and the Ulster Defence Force on the protestant side. There's gonna be another turf war, only this one won't be about religion and civil rights, it'll be about *drugs and protection*."

He let the bouncer think about his words for a few seconds before continuing.

"I say, whilst all this shit is going down in Northern Ireland, we take this opportunity to fill our pockets!"

"And how exactly are we gonna do that, boss?"

Declan smiled at the doorman's naivety.

"I'll tell ya how son. We skim the take from the 'Ra' pubs *and* we do a protection racket on the Irish theme pubs too."

"Protection racket?"

"Yeah, an old school protection racket. We tell the landlords that we're the I.R.A. and if they don't pay up they'll get trouble with a capital T, simple."

The doorman wasn't convinced.

"What about if they go to the old Bill?"

Declan burst out laughing.

"Nah, I doubt they'll do that me lad. Not when they meet the fucking nutter I'll be sending out to spread the message!"

The doorman suddenly perked up.

"Oh, I thought you were sending me?"

Declan shook his head.

"You're a good lad Sonny McBride and you will still be going on the collections for the 'Ra' but we need someone with a bit of . . . " he searched for the right words, finally settling for, " . . . imagination *and* a thick Irish accent, if we're gonna convince these Brit landlords that we mean business. We tell them we're working on behalf of the I.R.A. which or course we are, just not in those particular circumstances. We press em for a small amount every month, nothing too much, just a few hundred quid or something and with so many Irish theme pubs to hit all over the U.K., it'll amount to thousands of pounds every month. As long as the I.R.A. get their monthly payments, they won't suspect a thing and we won't have to look over our shoulders for some fucker in a balaclava."

Sonny gave a nod of approval.

"It's a good plan boss but who you got in mind to spread the word?"

Declan O'Dwyer's brutal face suddenly lost its usual expression of self-belief.

"*Ain sionnach rua*!" he said with some uncertainty.

The doorman placed the shot of whiskey down on the bar top.

"*The Red Fox?*" he said with mild amusement. "Who the fuck is the red fox? A fucking super hero?"

Declan seemed surprised that the bouncer hadn't heard of the man.

"The *Red Fox . . .* !" the Dubliner left the words hanging, as if by doing so the younger man would suddenly recognise the name. He didn't . . . " . . . the fucking *Red fox*! You know one of Martin Cahill's crew?" Declan stared at the doorman with astonishment,

"You do know who Martin Cahill is, don't you?"

Sonny shrugged and shook his head. Declan walked around the bar and stood next to the young doorman.

"Jesus boy, you really are a plastic Paddy, Martin Cahill is known in Ireland as the 'General'. He's infamous throughout the whole of Ireland." Declan stopped himself. "Sorry, I'll rephrase that, he *was* infamous throughout the whole of Ireland.

Sonny McBride screwed his face up in a puzzled expression.

"Sorry boss you're not making any sense, the *Red Fox*, the *General*, I've never heard of either of em?"

Declan, who was slightly light-headed after polishing off almost half a bottle of whiskey so early in the day, sighed and drawing the bottle to his side of the bar and pouring them both another shot, began to explain.

"Martin Cahill was until recently *the* most notorious gangster in Ireland. He was responsible for flooding Dublin with grade-A heroin as well as robbing almost every bank in the capital. He became a folk hero to the scallywags back home!"

Sonny smirked.

"Sounds like a decent fella."

Declan shrugged.

"Yeah, well he was, if you were in his crew, if you weren't, then you were fair game to be ripped off or worse. He didn't give a fuck about anyone or anything, not the Garda, nor the Special branch who were set up to catch him, not even the high courts. He didn't give a fuck about the *Provos* either who he pissed off several times but always managed to talk his way out of it. Anyone that went against him, ran into his crew which at the time was headed by . . . the Red Fox, a right nasty bollocks if ever there was one."

"Why was he called the Red Fox?"

Declan raised his eyebrows and laughed.

"Ha, well you know how we Dubliners are whores for a good nick-name, most people have one in Dub but few truly deserve it as much as the Fox. He got his nick-name from the fact that he has a mop of bright red hair on his head and was once an apprentice butcher in the Dublin meat market until Cahill saw his talent with a razor-sharp, filleting knife. You know the type of thing, very thin long sharp blade?"

Declan drew the outline of the knife between his fingers. Sonny nodded as Declan continued his explanation.

"Anyway, Cahill, got the lad hooked on the smack he was supplying throughout Dublin until after a few months, old Foxy had a very expensive habit. Of course by this point, the Fox was well and truly in the General's pocket and if the General gave the order, the little Red Fox would make very short work at gutting which ever unfortunate bastard had fallen from the General's grace and from what I've heard, he does it with such skill and speed, that the poor fucker being gutted, doesn't even know its happened until he's handed his own intestines in a plastic carrier bag."

Declan stared at Sonny's expression of horror.

"And you're bringing that nutter over here to work with *us?*"

Declan sighed his reply.

"Sure, I haven't got a lot of choice in it, Sonny!"

"You're not in with the General are you Dec?"

The Irishman shook his head.

"Nah, thankfully, it's a bit too late to be in with the General!"

Sonny's brow furrowed.

"How so?"

"Martin Cahill's dead!"

The bouncer shrugged.

"Ah, well that's what happens to all drug dealers ain't it? You're the top dog until another, bigger dog turns up and bites your balls off."

Declan laughed.

"You're right there me-lad!" Declan took another swig of whisky, and as he threw the shot back, he knew the rest of the day would have to be written off as he had a taste for the drink now. He swayed slightly at the bar and had to steady himself before continuing his story.

"He pissed off the I.R.A. one too many times and was executed in his car whilst on the school run!" Sonny watched the big man's rough face flush red with the strength of the liquor. "Anyway, the cut and short of it is this. The I.R.A. don't want Cahill's old crew wandering around Dublin getting up to any mischief that interrupts with their own fund raising, *hence*, the Fox is now our problem until the Provo's high command say he can return to Dublin."

"What about his smack habit?"

Declan shrugged.

"I dunno, maybe he's kicked it, maybe he ain't, either way he's arriving tonight and you are gonna have to get used to him!"

"But won't he go telling the 'Ra' about our shenanigans?"

Declan shook his head.

"I doubt that the man has any love for the I.R.A., so as long as he's taking his fair share of the cash and we supply his habit, if he still has one. I don't think we've got anything to worry about. These fucking Brit landlords ain't gonna know what's hit em when this lad turns up!"

Sonny McBride seemed less convinced.

"But boss, we can't have this nutter just going around filleting fucking landlords willy-nilly, can we? It'll bring the old Bill on top!"

Declan patted the young man's shoulder.

"Well, that's where you come in. You're gonna have to keep this little red fox on a very short leash Sonny. He's a loose cannon so he is but like any cannon, if he's aimed in the right direction he'll do plenty of damage. It's gonna be your job to aim this cannon at *our* targets. If anyone gets in the way of our theme pub take, then we'll let the Fox off his leash, he'll do the filleting . . . "

Sonny nodded slowly.

Declan sniggered, " . . . whilst you get to hold the plastic carrier bag!"

CHAPTER 9

Serendipity

Davey eased off the throttle on the *Hideaway* as he
approached the overgrown mooring near the little village of Lapworth on the old Stratford-upon-Avon canal.
The heavy roar of the old Listor engine dropped to a slow steady
throb as the engine began to idle and the longboat slowed to
a glide as it drifted through the low morning mist that always
seemed to lie heavy on the river at this point.

Davey cut the engine completely, enjoying the sudden silence.
He pulled and pushed the long, heavy brass tiller which controlled the boat's rudder, bringing the canal boat slowly into the
mooring he'd chosen for its isolated location. He followed the
tree line, partially obscured by the thick mist, constantly checking
the bank of the river on his right for an old rotted mooring post
indicating that he'd arrived at his chosen spot.

The journey had taken almost four hours by canal to what
felt like the middle of nowhere – much further away from Gas
Street Basin and the murder at the Brazen Maiden than it actually
was. If truth be told, it could be reached by road in less than an
hour from the City Centre but that wasn't the point, it *felt* safe,
isolated and even on this grey misty winter's day, the countryside around the mooring was beautiful, or at least it would be

when the white veil had lifted. More importantly than that, the mooring was in walking distance to a decent pub. Only a few hundred yards away, along the overgrown canal tow-path, was a 16th century riverside inn called *The Boot* which served a good pint and a ridiculously good game pie.

Davey had been here before, on summer days mainly, when the water in Birmingham docks had become too smelly, or the area around the docks had become too busy with tourists poking their collective noses through the windows of his boat to take photos of the 'quaint river gypsies.' He'd literally had to throw out a party of Japanese snappers who thought that his home was some sort of water-bound theme park attraction and thus crowded down inside his canal boat, whilst he lay in a semi-conscious hangover in his bed. He awoke to the sound of snapping cameras and nonsensical yapping as they discussed this real life version of the painting of the *Death of Chatterton.* The look on the Japanese faces when the naked Pre-Raphaelite leapt off his bed screaming *"Get the fuck off my boat!"* was a picture!

Sometimes after a heavy weekend of gigs and drinking, he would head here for some relative peace and quiet, to clear his head, or maybe to impress a girl with a country bonfire under a starlit sky and a bottle of wine on a blanket in a yellow field of rapeseed. However, this time he was here for far less romantic reasons. The shit-storm surrounding the killing at the Irish pub had deteriorated after his visit to the transvestite. The local paper had covered the story with huge headlines screaming *Bloody Murder* across its front page. After that blind panic had subsided only to be replaced with a good dose of Catholic guilt and Davey decided that a few days in the countryside would give him time to think about what he should do with the cash he'd taken. He couldn't return it that was for sure. The police would fall on him quicker than he could shout *pig*. He knew that the old Bill were like water, they always sought the quickest, easiest route. If he turned up with his little canvas bag of stolen money and a dodgy story of drunkenness, they would simply nick him and throw away the key.

"Not in this life." Davey thought, as he tied the thick ropes to the mooring posts. He stood on the tow path and stared as best he could into the mist either side of the canal boat. The narrow path ran off into the distance and he could only see around fifty feet along the riverside due to the thick white fog. Either side of the river were what seemed like endless rolling fields which during the summer were covered with bright yellow rapeseed flowers but were now just fields of brown waterlogged mud, reminiscent of the old photos he'd seen of World War One. He knew that beyond those fields were people, roads, cars, houses and police. He was happy to forget about them this morning, nestled in his secret spot, hidden within the mist on the river.

A dull white disk hung in the sky, and Davey knew it was just a matter of time before the weak winter sun burnt off the veil, probably around midday. However, by that time, he'd be three hundred yards down the tow path, tucking into a game pie and a pint in front of a crackling fire at the Boot Inn where nobody knew him or his business. He stepped back aboard the boat and climbed down the small steps to the galley where he turned the gas hob on and prepared himself a cup of tea.

****

The tyres of the black BMW tore up the loose gravel of the pub carpark as it took the turn from the tarmac road onto the gravel carpark a little too enthusiastically.

"Here we are!" shouted Dez.

The sudden change in direction caught his passenger by surprise, throwing her sideways towards the driver with some force. Only her seat belt stopped her from being thrown into the driver's lap completely.

"For God's sake Dez, do you have to drive so bloody fast? It makes me wanna throw up!"

The driver sniggered spitefully before pressing his foot down on the accelerator even harder, pushing the car at breakneck speed across the long narrow carpark straight towards the pub at the far end. A plume of loose gravel sprayed in the air behind its rear wheels as the BMW accelerated.

Dez steered directly towards a small thigh-high stone wall that separated the carpark from a deserted outdoor seating area. To Abi in the passenger seat, it looked as if he were going to crash the car straight into the wall and she stretched her arms out in front of her, placing them on the dashboard above the glove compartment, as if by doing so it would protect her from the inevitable impact. She screamed wide-eyed, unconsciously preparing herself for the crash. However, just as the car was about to hit, Dez pulled the steering wheel to his right, whilst simultaneously pulling hard on the handbrake. The sports coupe spun sideways with a loud screech of tyres and came to a halt at a perfect ninety degrees to the wall.

Dez turned the key as the cars momentum stopped, killing the engine and leaving Abi sitting in shocked, open-mouthed silence. She slowly turned her head towards the obstructing wall, still in shock. The wall was now only twelve inches from her side of the car. She raised her shocked stare towards the old pub where she saw three scowling faces staring back at her through the small bow window.

She turned to Dez, finally losing her normal coolness.

"Just what the hell do you think you're playing at?"

The driver began to laugh as he pulled on the driver's door latch.

"We could've crashed into that wall you idiot!"

Dez ignored the girl, climbing from the car he dusted down his new expensive leather coat and grabbed the large mobile phone from the centre console.

"Are you gonna moan all fucking day?" he said without looking at the girl.

"Oh, you're a real gentleman aren't you?" she said sarcastically.

"Look . . . " he said, unable to control his impatience, " . . . you said you fancied a meal in a country pub. Well here we are, a country pub. What's the problem?"

Abi Fewtrell's nostrils flared with anger.

"The problem?" she incredulously, "*Yes* I wanted a meal in a country pub but I didn't want to show up here like a bloody rally driver did I? It's embarrassing!"

She glanced towards the faces in the windows, still scowling.

"Jesus, nothing is good enough for *daddy's* little girl." Dez said, extracting himself from the car and slamming his door.

Abi undid her seatbelt and pulled on the lever of the passenger door. As she pushed the door outwards it slammed against the low wall which was only twelve inches away, leaving her no room to climb out of the car. Dez, who was standing in front of the motor, turned at the sound of the door hitting the rough stonework.

"*For fuck's sake Abi!*" he shouted, his arms raised in horror at the sight of the chipped paintwork. Abi sat back in the black leather seat and scowled at him through the windscreen.

"Well, what did you expect Dez? Look how close you've parked against the wall! What do you want me to do, climb out the bloody window?"

The tall, dark-haired man rolled his eyes and tutted his disproval.

"Spoiled little rich girl!" he muttered as he turned and walked into the pub, leaving the blonde girl to clumsily climb across the driver's seat on her own and out of the driver's door.

****

The log-burning stove had gone out by the time Davey had awoken from his unplanned sleep and dressed himself. His panicked departure from the Gas Street Basin had been an exhausting haul along the Stratford-upon-Avon canal, through a various set of locks, no easy task it must be said. The image of the dead Bar Manager and the bag of blood-money refused to leave his troubled mind throughout the journey and his troublesome disturbed four hour nap.

The dribble of water that fell from the shower-nozzle in the narrowboat was weak and barely lukewarm but still felt refreshing as he tried to wash away the grogginess of his midday sleep. He pulled on some Levi's and a t-shirt and threw a thick knitted woollen jumper over the top before striking out to the Boot Inn for lunch. He didn't bother locking the canal boat, no one ever came along this stretch of canal, especially at this time of year and *especially* when these winter mists blanketed the area as soon as the winter sun sank anywhere near the horizon.

He stood on the river bank for a short time wondering how, if the fog came back, he would find the boat again in the pitch-black evening, especially after a few pints. Stepping onto the short prow of the boat, he opened a small compartment and he took an old hurricane oil lamp from it. He spat on the filthy glass, cleaning it as best he could, before shaking it. The dull splash of oil inside indicated that it could be used. He took a disposable lighter from the compartment and lifted the lamp's glass. Striking the lighter he lit the short wick of the lamp, which instantly began to flair. He replaced the glass and drew the wick into the lamp by turning the little handle, until the lamp gave off a small but bright flicker of flame. He placed the rusty old lamp on the forward and highest most part of the prow, hoping it would be bright enough to find again if the fog returned that night.

By the time Davey reached the Old Boot Inn, the tranquil atmosphere that normally rested over the 16th century hostel, had been replaced by the sounds of a furious row between two young lovers in the midst of a serious tiff.

Davey stepped up to the bar with a sarcastic smile, the landlord raised his eyebrows with a resigned sigh.

"Afternoon sir, what'll it be?"

Davey reached across the bar and tapped the Guinness tap.

"I'll have a pint of black stuff please boss!" On hearing the man's Irish accent, the landlord broke into a smile of recognition.

"Oh it's the Irishman . . . " he said with a laugh, " . . . have you got your guitar with you this time?"

Davey returned the chubby man's smile, realising that the landlord was referring to a previous summer drinking session that had turned into a spontaneous drunken sing-along in the bar. Davey chuckled.

"Nah, no sing-songs this time I'm afraid, just a pint and one of your game pies, please."

"Well, the last time you were here was a bloody good laugh, our locals loved it!"

"Aye, it certainly was a night to remember!" Davey said with a broad grin, trying to hide the fact that he couldn't remember any of it due to the fact he'd been so drunk he hadn't even made it back to his boat. Instead he had wandered off into the night, guitar in hand and ended up sleeping off the booze in one of the surrounding rapeseed fields until the first drops of dew had woken him at sunrise. The landlord opened his mouth to answer but a man's raised voice from the rear of the bar interrupted the conversation.

"Just eat your bleeding food and stop your moaning!"

The landlord rolled his eyes and sighed again. Davey's brow furrowed and he stepped towards the edge of the bar and delicately peered around the corner of one of the upright posts of the bar, into the dimly-lit small rear room that acted as the inn's restaurant seating area.

"My God Dez, just who do you think you're talking to?"

This time a shocked female voice, " . . . I'm sorry about your car door but I didn't know it was gonna bash against the wall did I? Anyway, if you hadn't been driving like a lunatic it wouldn't have happened would it?"

Davey tried to see into the gloom of the room, which, even though only 1pm, was only dimly lit by candles, partly for effect and partly due because the 16th century room had tiny heavy-leaded windows which allowed virtually none of the mid-winter daylight into the room.

"There's nothing wrong with my driving . . . " The insult about the man's driving had obviously hit the mark. " . . . maybe you're just not happy unless your in your Dad's Rolls Royce. You're just a spoilt little rich girl, that's what you are!"

The few other people that were eating in the room were so embarrassed by the couple's outburst, they had begun to pretend that the couple weren't there at all and just ate their food, eyes down and in silence.

"Well, you don't call me that when you're busy trying to get in with my family though do you?"

The woman's words obviously pressed a button because the man suddenly stood up and made as if to leave, grabbing his leather coat from the back of his chair. The woman, obscured by the standing man, seemed shocked by the sudden movement.

"Oh sit down Dez, you're being dramatic, it's embarrassing!"

"That's eight quid sir!"

The landlord's voice brought Davey's attention back to the moment. He turned back to the landlord, who had a long-suffering smirk across his chubby red face.

"Would sir like a table in our restaurant room?" He gestured towards the sound of the argument, "or would sir prefer to eat in here?"

Davey laughed.

"Oh here's just fine." He dragged a high barstool towards him and plonked himself down on it, his arms on the counter. "I'll eat here at the bar if that's ok?"

The landlord nodded. He glanced at the packed shelf behind the landlord, his eye drawn to the tall black bottle of Scotch whisky, its neck covered in dust.

"That looks interesting!" The landlord turned and scanned the shelf. "The black bottle, the old one with the dust all over it!"

"Ah, you have a good eye for a fine Scotch."

He took the bottle of *Loch Dhu* delicately from the shelf and blew away the thick coating of dust. "This is *Loch Dhu*." The man said as if sharing a secret. "It was barrelled seventy-five years ago, it's *expensive!*" the chubby man said with a raised eyebrow.

"Hence the dust!" Davey laughed.

He felt the fold of stolen cash in his pocket and gestured that the landlord should pour him a glass. The big man seemed impressed that the Irishman hadn't asked the price. He reached under the counter and drew out a small cut glass and placing it down in front of his customer, he pulled the cork from the bottle top and reverently poured the golden liquid into the cut-crystal glass.

"Are you sure you wouldn't like a table in *there* sir? We have entertainment.' he said with a laugh of his own.

"Ha, screw that, it's like an episode of Eastenders in there. Nah, I'm good here thanks boss!"

With that the landlord re-corked the bottle and turned to place the bottle back on the shelf but Davey stopped him.

"No, leave the bottle, I'm feeling flush tonight, feel like treating meself!"

The landlord turned smiling, shrugged and disappeared into the kitchen area behind the bar. Davey watched his Guinness settle under the tap whilst eavesdropping on the argument in the other room. He stared at the old whisky for a few seconds, enjoying the candlelight as it danced around the saffron liquid inside the whisky glass. He lifted it to his lips but stopped at the sound of another loud outburst in the backroom.

"You're just a spoiled brat Abi, nothing's good enough for you!" the man said loud enough for everyone in the little pub to hear.

"Spoiled and how do you work that out then Derrick?"

There was a short silence whilst the man sat again, composing himself before snapping.

"Yeah spoiled. I bring you out here to a nice restaurant and all you do is moan!"

At that moment another voice spoke up, this time a man's voice with a soft West-country accent.

"The only person I can here *moaning* around here is you matey!"

Dez spun to the sound of the voice.

"What did you say?"

The man spoke again.

"Oh, I think you heard me and if you hadn't noticed, there are other people in here trying to have a nice peaceful meal and all we can here is you bullying this girl!"

Davey heard the sound of footsteps on the flagstone floor in the restaurant as Dez crossed the space between his table and the other man's. Then the sound of a chair being pushed back.

"If I were you old man, I'd keep my gob shut before I shove that fucking meal down your throat!"

Suddenly, there was the sound of a scuffle as the older local man tried to stand. Davey watched as the landlord re-entered the bar and rushed around to the restaurant area an alarmed look on his face. Davey followed the chubby man as he stepped between the two arguing men.

"Alright mate, that's it, time to go!"

The landlord placed his hand on Dez's shoulder.

Dez stopped instantly and stared at the landlords' hand.

"Get your fat fucking hand off me *now* or I swear to God I'll break your arm!"

The landlord's face suddenly lost its rosy glow as he snatched his hand away from the man.

"Look, we don't want any trouble but you pair have to leave!"

He pointed towards the girl who was sitting open-mouthed with shock at the speed at which events had escalated.

Dez sniggered.

"Trouble?" his sinister smile turning to a violent grimace. "You ain't got a fucking clue about the kind of trouble I can bring down upon your head *fatty*."

"I'll . . . I'll call the police if you don't go *now*!"

The landlord stuttered, trying to sound unfazed by the other man's aggression but failing.

"You'd be better off calling a fucking ambulance by the time I'm finished with you. You're gonna need one!"

Davey left his stool and stood at the end of the bar. He could feel the build up to the inevitable fight even if the landlord couldn't. He'd seen it before, at his gigs in the rough Irish pubs he'd been playing over the years, a bit of argy-bargy, then a punch would be thrown, maybe a glass used as a weapon and it would end up all blue flashing lights, coppers and ambulances. He stepped into one of the shadows created by the wall-lights along the raw stone walls of the eating area, ready to jump in at the first sign of a fist being drawn back. At that moment the girl spoke up.

"Dez, for God's sake stop it! What are you doing? These people have done nothing wrong!"

Without turning to her, Dez answered.

"You shut you're fucking mouth, posh girl. I'll deal with you later!"

The girl stood and began to cross the room to where the three men were facing each other off. As she stepped into the circle, Davey recognised her as the beautiful blonde girl from the gig at the Brazen Maiden. He stepped from his shadowed position beneath the lamp just as Dez drew his arm back with lightning speed and punched the old man in the jaw. The man, who must have been in his seventies, fell under the blow instantly, crumpling beneath the table, where his horrified wife and family watched in shocked silence. Dez stomped his heel into the old man's face a couple of times and when he was happy with the result of his work, he turned his attention to the chubby landlord. The landlord's reaction came too slow and before he could raise his own fist to the young man, Dez had punched him and was already following through from the first punch with a second from his stronger right arm. It caught the large publican square on the end of his nose which burst as easily as a child's balloon. A shower of thick crimson sprayed all over the seated diners before the big man sprawled across the table, sending the plates of food and glasses everywhere.

Davey stepped from under the light just as the girl came behind Dez.

"*Stop* it Dez! What the hell are you do . . . .?"

The girl didn't finish her sentence. Dez brought his elbow up and shoved it into the girl's face, hitting her square in the mouth and bursting her bottom lip. She too went sprawling backwards into the dining table she'd just left.

On seeing this, Davey crossed the space between himself and the aggressor in two strides. He didn't consider himself a fighter although he knew how to throw a good punch, a skill he'd unwittingly learned after years of entertaining drunken revellers in some of the roughest pubs and bars in the world. He raised his fists in front of his face, intending to give as good as he got. Dez turned to see Abi just before she fell into one of the chairs surrounding the low table, dazed by the blow.

"Fuck!" he said loudly, before instinctively turning back towards the two men he'd just put down. He began to point at the old man's family, ready to give them all a warning, however, instead of finding subservient victims staring back at him, he found the Irishman's fist aiming straight into his face with what should have been a powerful sucker punch. For a split second he froze, unable to comprehend where the man had come from. He was sure there had been no one else in the room but this man had just appeared from nowhere with a well-aimed punch. Dez let his instincts take over. A quick twist of his neck and the Irishman's fist flew past his face harmlessly, swinging into thin air, unbalancing Davey as it did. Dez lost no time in grabbing him by the collar of his thick knitted jumper and bringing his head back in order to deliver a headbutt to his nose. Davey was caught, his outstretched arm trapped beneath Dez's right arm, his other fist uselessly drawn back behind him. However, just as Dez was about to smash his forehead into Davey's nose, he froze. Davey braced himself, half-closing his eyes waiting for the inevitable headbutt that was sure to do to *his* nose what Dez's punch had done to the landlord's. The milliseconds ticked by with every heartbeat as the Irishman waited for the crunch of bone against bone.

But the knockout never came. Instead Davey opened his eyes to find Dez stepping back from him, a look of puzzled recognition on his face. Davey, unbalanced dropped to floor on his knees.

"It's *you*!" Dez said, letting go of the Irishman. "What the fuck are you doing here?" he blurted in astonishment. Davey suddenly recognised the handsome man as the blonde girl's boyfriend from the gig on the previous Friday. The look of shock on the dark-haired man's face was puzzling to say the least but anything was better than a broken nose so Davey let the man step backwards, a surprised expression slowly spreading across his dark handsome features.

Dez pointed at him with his tattooed hand as he stood speechless. Finally, he turned and glanced at Abi who was slowly starting to recover from the initial shock of the blow to her face and was now starting to feel the pain of her split lip which had started to bleed. Dez stood in front of her for a second or two not knowing what to do. Realising his uncontrolled aggression had probably scuppered his plans to get his feet under the Fewtrell's table, he reached into his pocket and pulled out a twenty pound note and he shrugged as he threw the money towards the quivering girl.

"There you go, you can get a fucking taxi. I'm out of here!"

Without hesitation he made to leave but as he crossed the flagstone floor he stopped and stood directly in front of Davey. For a heartbeat, Dez didn't move and the Irishman was convinced that this was probably going to be the moment he was going to get a good hiding from the powerfully-built thug. Davey started to raise his head to look into the man's eyes.

"Don't you fucking look at me, you Irish cunt!" Dez ordered.

Davey lowered his head.

"Ok, ok . . ." he held his open hands out in front of him in a gesture of peace, " . . . you've made your point, just go!" He allowed himself a quick peek in the man's direction and as he did, he could see a touch of panic in the dark-haired man's eyes . . .

****

By the time the police showed up at the Boot Inn, the winter sun had fallen below the horizon. The white mist had climbed once more over the river banks and blanketed the area with a thick pea-soup fog that was almost impenetrable to the eye.

Just like the fog outside, the heavy atmosphere created by the little drama *inside* the pub, had hung in the air even after Dez had left the pub. Davey had helped the old man and the landlord regain their feet before turning his attention to the blonde girl, who was now slumped over the table sobbing.

He had remonstrated with a member of the bar-staff when he'd found out they had called the police, knowing that the old Bill would be taking names and addresses when they arrived. That was the last thing he needed and so he decided to leave right away. However, just as he was about to extract himself from the proceedings, he caught sight of the distraught girl. Maybe it was an attack of that oh so famous Catholic guilt or because there was something about the girl that seemed so familiar to him, he decided to stay and comfort her by pushing the glass of the expensive whisky under her nose to steady her nerves. He decided to take the risk that the old Bill wouldn't be arriving anytime soon due to the fog outside.

"Here, take a swig of this!"

Abi turned to the Irishman's voice with tears in her eyes and she stared at him for a few seconds, trying to work out where she'd seen him before and then finally, with a wide-eyed expression of recognition she blurted out.

"You're . . . you're that *Irish* singer!"

It wasn't a question. Davey smiled as he held the glass of golden liquid to the girl. She took the glass without looking at it and took a large gulp. The strong whisky took her by surprise and she spluttered as the liquor hit the back of her throat. Davey tried to stifle a laugh as the blonde girl's face flushed bright red.

"S . . . shit . . . " she said in between a sudden fit of coughing, " . . . that's disgusting!"

Davey patted her back softly.

"Well, it's an *acquired* taste I'll give you that but at least it's stopped the tears, eh?"

She shook her head.

"He's a bastard!" she said, changing the subject and gesturing towards the front door of the pub where Dez had made his dramatic exit.

Davey raised his eyebrows.

"Well, I'd have to agree with you there. I thought the gobshite was gonna knock me out!"

Abi nodded. She pushed the drink back towards the Irish man who took the glass with a bemused smile.

"I'm not a whisky girl."

Davey shrugged.

"Well, it seems a shame to waste such a nice whisky!"

Abi put her finger under the glass and steered it towards the singer's mouth.

"Go on . . . " She said, breaking into a tearful smile, " . . . before you start slavoluring!"

Davey laughed, raising his eyebrows in fake surprise.

"Well, ain't you the smooth talker!"

He threw the drink back into his mouth, closing his eyes, savouring the instant warmth brought on by the whisky. Abi watched him with bright eyes. The question as to why the Irishman was here suddenly coming to the fore in her mind. The moment was broken as the other customers and staff began to chatter with a little more confidence, making their protests now that the bully responsible had left the building, instead pointing their fingers at the blonde girl who had accompanied the man, trying to lay some blame for the events firmly at her feet. Davey, raised his eyebrows as the accusing eyes began to burn into his back.

"I think it's time to leave!"

"I'll have to call a taxi!" Abi answered softly.

Davey shook his head.

"Nah, I don't think so, not on a night like tonight!"

Abi, who had already become comfortable in the man's presence even though she had only just met him, looked up at him with a puzzled expression.

"What do you mean a night like tonight?"

"You'll see when you get outside!"

Abi's seemed even more confused.

"Outside?"

Davey nodded towards the group on the other table, who were already starting to remonstrate with the landlord about the amount of time the police were taking to get there.

"Yeah outside, they've called the old Bill, so it's time to go!"

"But what about a taxi?" she enquired, still trying to work out how she could get back to Birmingham city centre if indeed the Irishman was right.

"Like I said, you'll understand when you get outside . . . "

He smiled at her, trying to reassure the girl that his intentions were honourable.

"Don't worry . . . " he said, " . . . I'll make sure you're safe."

Abi stared into the man's face, trying to work out whether he was a good samaritan or someone on the make as was customary when it came to the Fewtrell family. The chatter from the other table had become more animated now, raised voices and accusations aimed towards her.

"Come on, I ain't a bleeding serial killer, if that's what you were thinking. I just don't wanna be around when the coppers turn up and I don't think you will want to either cos this lot will stitch you up and the blame firmly at your feet. You'll end up answering a load of stupid questions down the local cop-shop about your gob-shite of a boyfriend if you're not careful."

He held his hand out towards the girl, she stared at it for a second, then turning her bright blue eyes upwards, she searched Davey's face for a few seconds more, then, throwing caution to the wind she took his hand and pulled herself from the chair.

Without turning or looking at the other customers, they made their way to the exit. Davey grabbed the almost full bottle of *Loch Dhu* and slapped a fifty pound note down on the counter as he passed. The pair stepped into the early evening darkness where, arm in arm, the couple were instantly swallowed up by the deep blanket of freezing, white fog.

Davey led the girl through the mist down the tow path towards the mooring where his canal boat was tied up. They walked blindly in the pitch blackness around the rear of the pub before a security light with an infra-red sensor detected the pair and turned on, its blinding halogen creating a dazzling pool of white light in the dense fog. They walked like this for a short time until

Davey spotted the old hurricane oil lamp he'd left on the prow of the boat earlier that evening.

The white mist dissipated the lamp's light, making it seems as if the glow was far larger than it actually was and from a distance it looked like a phantom, fidgeting and dancing in the still fog. Abi didn't hide her surprise at the sudden appearance of the boat in the darkness, its bow protruding from the white veil. She hadn't even questioned the Irishman as he led her along the path, thinking he was taking her to one of the small hotels or bed and breakfasts that could be found in this part of the country.

The freezing fog and the isolation of the mooring made the interior of the boat seem all the more cosy to the girl as she stepped down into the dimly lit narrowboat.

Davey soon had the small log burning stove crackling, the warmth of the fire making the boat seem both safe and secret. He poured her a glass of red wine and for the first time in a long time Abi found herself relaxing, *really* relaxing. Not just in the intimate atmosphere of the little canal boat but in the man's company too. Feeling as if for the first time in her life, she was out of view from the ever-present hangers-on that seemed to follow the ups, downs and fortunes of her infamous family.

The two talked for hours, their tongues loosened by the wine and whisky. Abi asking about Davey's Irish roots, he asking about the soft Birmingham tinge hidden within her accent. It was the mention of Abi's infamous family name that finally brought about the sudden realisation as to why they had such strong feelings of recognition toward each other. After some discussion they discovered that they had met before, in Birmingham many years ago back in the 1980s. She a live music loving fifteen year old pretending to be a woman, all hair lacquer, lipstick and fishnets. He, the twenty year old frontman of an underground indie band taking his first fumbling steps towards an ultimately unobtainable stardom. Two innocents in a world of hurt. Their paths converging through their need to escape a brutally violent skinhead riot at an illegal Birmingham cellar bar, at one of Davey's gigs.

The intention of the skinhead gang had been to kidnap Abi in order to get to her father Eddie Fewtrell. However, after a life and death chase through the deserted streets of the second city, Davey had led the girl to safety at one of her father's clubs. Expecting a thank-you, if not a free pint and pat on the back from her father, Davey had been surprised to find a less than welcome "*Fuck off cowboy!*" from one of the two burly doormen who grabbed Abi from the street, dragging her through the venues doors into her father's bar and safety, leaving Davey, still in his western style fringed jacket he wore as stage clothes, to get a bloody good hiding from the skinhead gang and never to see Abi again.

That is until now.

Realising the serendipity of the moment, she, with the sparkle of a happy tear in her eye, threw her arms around the Irishman as if he were an old friend. He had proven his trustworthiness to her all those years ago. Putting himself in harm's way to save her from the gang without question and thanks to her father, she had never thanked him properly. Davey was surprised by her sudden reaction, the last time he had seen her she had been little more than a young teenage girl, yet here she was, now a fully grown beautiful woman. He squeezed her, enjoying the reunion. Abi sat back on the long bench settee, a wide smile across her face. For the first time she actually looked at the man with her. She had found him charismatic when watching him performing on stage the week before at the Irish pub, yet now she saw he wasn't a pretty boy like Dez or the other boyfriends she had dated. Davey had strong characterful features, scarred, flawed but strong.

"Gabriel Oak!" she said under her breath.

"Pardon?" Davey asked as he refilled her wine glass.

"Gabriel Oak, he's a character in my favourite book."

Davey shrugged.

"Never heard of him!"

"Far from the Madding Crowd!" Abi said, incredulously.

Davey shook his head.

"Really?" she asked. "It's a really famous book, a classic."

"I'm not really into the classics."

"Well, Gabriel Oak is a character from *Far from the Madding Crowd!*"

Davey took a sip of his whisky, trying to figure out where this conversation was going.

"He's my favourite character . . . " she continued, " . . . you remind me of him!"

Davey laughed.

"Oh, he's a handsome devil then!"

"No . . . !" Abi chuckled, " . . . he's *dependable!*"

Davey almost spat his whisky out with laughter. He managed to swallow before answering.

"*Dependable*, Jesus, no one's ever called me that before and I've been called plenty of things in my time, I can tell ya!"

Abi joined his laughter.

She left the words hanging for a second or two before adding, " . . . *and* he's quite handsome too!" she said with a mischievous smile.

"Really?" Davey laughed, " . . . well, none of that sounds like me!"

The pair talked and laughed into the night. Whether it was warmth of the fire, or the strength of the liquor that made them feel so comfortable in each other's company, it was hard to tell. But one thing was for sure. As the reunited friends recalled the dangerous adventure that had brought them together all those years ago, both taking turns to explain everything that had happened in their lives since that time, a new connection was forged. Not a quick flash in the pan bond, like so many others in their lives but a real fondness for each other. A friendship that would prove as solid and unbending as any oak.

The two of them sat and talked intimately, against the backdrop of the crackling fire, and the still mid-tide river which lapped gently against the boat's hull.

Neither of them noticed the dark-haired man hidden in the white shroud of the tow path. He watched the illuminated scene inside the boat as it played itself out, and from his hidden position on the mist covered path, he watched undisturbed for hours and saw everything, the talking, the drinking, the laughing, even the first passionate kiss.

As he watched in the freezing fog, his piercing blue eyes betrayed his jealousy and contempt. He planned a revenge that was even darker and colder than the black river that ran along the bank on which he stood.

CHAPTER 10

A Loose Canon

It had been over a week since Declan O'Dwyer had searched the sky from his vantage point at one of the huge windows in the arrivals' lounge at Birmingham airport. He'd watched the planes coming and going through the cloudy grey sky, waiting for the first glimpse of the green livery of the Aer Lingus flight with its large shamrock emblem announcing the arrival of one of Dublin's most notorious enforcers.

Declan had thought about sending the young doorman McBride to meet him but decided against it so that he could weigh the fellow up himself before unleashing him on the Birmingham publicans. They say first impressions are everything and so Declan was singularly unimpressed when he saw the painfully thin, chain-smoking red-headed man stepping from the stairs of the airplane onto the Birmingham tarmac.

A spiteful grimace was the only greeting the man gave as he was welcomed to England by the publican. Declan knew that if this man had run with Martin Cahill's Dublin crew, then there must be more to this scruffy bag of bones than met the eye. Anyway, Declan's thoughts about the man's appearance were irrelevant. The IRA had ordered him to accept the man and put him to work collecting for the cause, saying all he needed was a little food, drink, fags and speed. Any kind of amphetamine would do, the rougher the better; pure amphetamine sulphate, blues, dexedrine, black bombers, anything that would take him 'up' and keep him there for days on end until he crashed.

This was usually after three or four days when he'd hit the sack for twenty-four hours straight before starting the whole manic process again. If speed wasn't available, he'd accept the weaker more refined rush of cocaine which he could freebase in order to get the same effect as the stronger rougher rush of the speed. Either way, this heady cocktail was one that Declan intended to supply on a twenty-four-seven basis in order to keep the man in line, besides anything was better than having a smackhead about the place. If the 'Red Fox' needed speed to keep himself off the smack, then Declan was more than happy to make it available on tap.

All that was seven days ago now and Declan's opinion of the thin man had changed dramatically after watching him 'work'. After only an hour of his arrival, a quick fry-up and a line of sulphate, the pock-faced Fox was out and about extorting money from the unsuspecting landlords on Digbeth High street. Declan and McBride had accompanied him on that first day, stood in the shadows like two guilty school boys as the Fox quickly displayed the prowess with the filleting knife that had given him his nick name.

Within five days, every Irish pub in the city limits, be they theme pubs or the real thing had been pressed into upping their weekly 'donation' to the cause. Either that or terrorised into handing over a small amount of cash with a promise to continue the weekly payments under the guise of 'entertainment costs' to a bogus Irish band named *The Rigga-Doos*. All of this was agreed under pain of death and the promise of another visit from the Fox if the payments stopped or the police were called. The operation worked especially well on the Birmingham based Irish landlords, who if they had not heard of Ain Sionnach Rua himself, had certainly heard of the IRA and knew that things would get very difficult for their families 'back home' if they didn't pay up.

Seven days and twenty four pubs later, McBride made the first of his collections from the Fox's new clients. The theme pubs and Irish drinking dens all paid up without any fuss whatsoever. Even the Irish theme pubs owned by the national breweries paid up. The managers offsetting the missing £300 to the *Rigga-Doos* Irish band and as a smiling Declan O'Dwyer counted out the cash of that first collection on one of the long tables of the *Dublin-Barrel,* he had trouble containing his elation at the thought of this 'not so little' windfall landing on his lap every month.

McBride who was helping count the cash, was watching the Fox with a distrustful stare. The Dublin gangster seemed to have no interest in the piles of money. Instead he was happily tucking into *another* greasy fry-up, declaring the slop to be a masterpiece of culinary delight, in between loudly supping on brick-red tea followed by another white line of whatever sort of speed that had been served up by Declan in the one of little paper wraps that seemed to be everywhere over the past week. In truth, McBride and the Fox didn't like each other from the start. The Brummie doorman taking umbrage to the Dublin man's constant barrage of anti-Brummie-Irish insults that seemed to spew from his mouth in a never-ending river of inane babble, due no doubt to the amount of speed he consumed in ever-larger quantities.

Declan gave a crafty wink towards the young doorman. He gestured towards the Dublin enforcer, who was bending over another line of the amphetamine and sniggered.

"Looks like it's going to be a white Christmas!"

SNORT . . .

The Fox sat back in his chair and coughed, as the bitter taste of the speed hit the back of his throat. He threw back what was left of the tea and gargled it loudly before swallowing.

"Now that's what I call a fucking breakfast!" he said in his thick Dublin brogue, before coughing again.

McBride watched the man with a disdain he could barely hide as the Fox drew up a mouthful of phlegm from the back of his throat and spat the green blob onto the remains of his breakfast. McBride gagged at the sight. The man laughed as he saw the disgust in the younger man's face. He pushed the plate towards the bouncer.

"Here ya go sonny, you can finish it off if ya like."

Declan watched the two with a look of mild amusement as he wound a thin elastic band around the last of the bundles of notes.

"There ya go, that's the last of em!"

The Fox turned his attention to the publican.

"How much boss?"

Declan took the first bundle from the table and pushed it towards the man.

"That's yours pal, well done for getting things moving so fast!"

The man's smile faded.

"Hold on there boss, this ain't your cash to be handing out!" He stared at the publican, suddenly totally serious. "This cash belongs to the high command."

Declan shook his head with a forced smile.

"Nah," he said sliding the bundle across the table, "I've been ordered to reward your hard work whenever I see fit." he lied. "And let me tell ya, Foxy . . . " He stopped himself, " . . . what is your real name? I can't keep calling ya Ain Sionnach Rua for the rest of your stay here, can I?"

The redhead eyed the publican up and down.

It's the Red Fox or you can call me *Foxy*, if you must. There's no point in having a fucking nickname if no one every bleeding uses it, is there?"

Declan's face flushed with embarrassment.

"I only meant that . . . "

"You only meant to find out my true identity, you mean!" the Fox sniggered sarcastically. "The point in the fucking nickname is to hide my identity ain't it? So if I told you my name was Doolan, Malone, O'Roark or fuck knows what, then there would be no point in me being called the fucking Red Fox would there?"

Declan felt a wave of nausea wash over him as he looked into the eyes of the thin man across the table. In those blank eyes he saw a killer staring back at him. He decided to change the subject quickly.

"Anyway, whatever your name is . . . " he said, attempting to hide his nervousness,

" . . . you've done a fucking good job at scaring the shite out of the landlords here scan, and this is just the beginning."

The Fox stood up, his expression unchanged.

"You ain't counted the take properly, boss." he said taking the bundle and handing it back to Declan. "There's one collection missing!"

Declan grimaced, a look of puzzlement replacing his nervous smirk.

"Missing? What do you mean? It's all here. I've ticked off the pubs and it tallies up perfectly."

The man shook his head, his stringy, red, greasy hair swaying across his face.

"The Irish Centre . . . " he said coldly, " . . . they haven't paid." Declan leaned back on his chair and sighed with relief.

"Oh no, we never take from the Irish Centre, that's out of bounds!"

"Out of bounds and why would that be?" Fox said with an even colder tone to his voice.

"The Irish Centre is only a hundred yards up the road, almost all the Irish businessmen who've made anything of themselves over the last fifty years drink in there and every Paddy fresh off the boat uses the place to pick up work. It's a family place, it always has been."

The Fox shrugged.

"So?" he said nonchalantly. "It's still got a bar, a fucking big bar too. They must take a fucking fortune in that place. We could take them for a few quid every week and they wouldn't even miss it."

"No . . . " Declan said sternly, " . . . it's out of bounds and that's that!"

"But why? Give me a good reason cos the lads in *Dub* won't give a fuck about these Brummie-Irish businessmen."

"And *I* don't give a flying fuck about the Dublin lads. They don't live here do they? I fucking do and I say squeezing the Irish

Centre for cash is tantamount to shitting on your own doorstep. If we lose the support of the Irish in Brum we're screwed. I mean we ain't the only gang in town you know."

McBride couldn't help smirking as he watched Declan put the Fox in his place.

"So you don't go near the Irish Centre under any circumstances. *Understand*?" Fox broke into a sarcastic smile.

"Ok, Ok, keep ya fucking syrup on! It was only a suggestion. I'm meant to be here to open new ground and that's all I'm doing."

"Yeah, well not at the fucking Irish Centre you're not, got it?"

Fox nodded, embarrassed but unable to leave the table without having the last word.

"Well, I recon you lads have gone soft here in England. The easy life has turned you into a pair of Royalist pussies."

McBride rose from his chair.

"Watch ya mouth pal! You ain't in Dublin anymore, no one here gives a fuck about who you ran with back there. If you keep mouthing off, someone's gonna lay you out!"

The Dublin gangster turned on him with surprising speed.

"Oh the Plastic *Paddies* awake!" he answered mockingly.

McBride crossed the space between them, bringing his clenched fist up in front of the Dublin man's face. However, the Fox was too fast and only too happy to illustrate to the doorman how he got his nick name and as McBride stepped in close, the long blade appeared from nowhere. McBride felt the sharp prick of the man's filleting knife at his throat.

"Oh yeah, Plastic Paddy and just what are ye hoping to do with that fist of yours?"

McBride snarled.

"I'm gonna ram it in your fucking face if ya keep pressing my button pal!"

The Fox pressed the blade a little harder into the man's throat, drawing a little bead of dark red blood which dribbled down the long blade.

"Oh really and when are ye gonna do this terrible thing *Plastic?* Would now be a good time? It's good for me!" he sniggered.

"You ain't always gonna have that knife on ya and one night you'll get caught off guard and then . . . "

" . . . and then what?"

"I'll . . . !"

" . . . *You'll do fucking nothing* . . . " Declan bawled.

He stepped in between the two, pushing each man roughly away, taking control of the moment. McBride raised his finger and pointed at the Fox.

"You may be some big name in Dublin but you're fuck all here mate . . . !" Declan slapped his arm down.

The redhead nodded.

"Yeah I heard you the first time you said it."

"Shut the fuck up McBride!" Declan said sternly.

The Fox burst into laughter and Declan turned on him.

"And you can shut the fuck up as well!"

His words seemed to have the required effect and both men stepped away from each other. McBride simmering silently, the Fox seeming to have lost interest in the argument altogether, instead he was examining the trickle of McBride's blood on his blade with a wry smile on his face.

"In case you pair of gobshites hadn't noticed, this is a business and I'm the fucking boss. So if I say jump, you pair of cunts say 'how high?', understand?"

Neither man moved.

"*Understand?*" Declan shouted.

This time both men nodded.

"Good, now I ain't asking you to be friends or suck each other's cocks but *I am* asking you to work together. It's only gonna be for a few months until the I.R.A. say you can go back to Dublin, then you pair will never have to see each other again."

He left the words hanging, "*Understand?*" Both men nodded again. Declan took two bundles of cash from the pile on the table and threw one to each of the men.

"Good, now get the fuck out of here so I can get this cash where it needs to go and open the bar!"

CHAPTER 11

Abduction 1961

(Continued)

The wee hours of Christmas Eve 1961 were not a good time to be dressed as Father Christmas in Birmingham. Being the big man himself, one of his elves or any other kind of festive character for that matter, virtually guaranteed you a visit to the Whizz Mob's warehouse in Hockley.

Well, warehouse was pushing it a little, it was more like a storage room. The room was packed almost to the ceiling with a plethora of household goods; fridges, cookers, saucepan sets for the kitchen, hoovers, ironing boards, nylons for the ladies and shirts and ties for the gents. The place was a virtual Aladdin's cave of knocked-off goods.

Well, knocked-off wasn't really the correct term either because none of the goods were actually stolen but 'long-firmed'. Which, if one wants to be pedantic about such things *is* stealing but with the owner's unknowing consent. Anyway, this storage room was located in the Georgian back streets of Hockley, an area known around Brum as the Jewellery Quarter and was the HQ for a very successful long-firming scam that had been set up between members of Birmingham's Whizz Mob and various London post-war black market racketeers.

If one had been a young child on that night before Christmas and able to view the place incognito from across the street, one would have sworn that it was Santa's secret grotto, hidden away in the dark streets of the second city. Because one by one, drunken Father Christmasses, elves and flamboyant homosexuals were delivered by the van load to the hidden doorway of the property in the wee hours of Christmas Eve 1961. Each van load of men pushed through the doorway under threat of a good hiding by a Whizz Mob member as the search for the paedophile Santa Claus who had stolen Ronnie Fletcher's little lad Daniel began in earnest.

****

By the time Duncan Jarvis had reached the Market Tavern, Daniel had sobbed himself to sleep. Jarvis, who still wore the Santa outfit, carried the little boy in his arms, cradling him delicately lest he awaken. What with the oncoming snow and cold wind, the streets were deserted except for the odd car or van, all of which he'd managed to avoid by walking through the alleyways between the buildings that led to his destination and the home turf of his gang, the Meat Market Mob.

He knew the passing cars were out looking for him, Ford Zephyrs and Zodiacs full of smartly-dressed men, their brutal faces peering through steamed-up car windows out to the snow-covered streets, which is why he was happy to finally see the pub's signage. He stepped into the pool of light that was cast through the large glass windows onto the white pavement outside. As he did, he saw a small group of the same hard men he'd seen passing in one of the cars, arguing with another group of scruffier men inside. No one in either group was looking in his direction and he took the opportunity to cross the illuminated space quickly stepping into the shadowed cellar doorway further up the street.

He pushed the thick door into the dimly-lit concrete corridor which acted as a cellar to the pub. The aluminium barrels lined one side of the room opposite a long line of coat hangers. Jarvis carried the lad inside and pulled several coats from the rail. He quickly threw the winter coats into a bundle on the floor and lay the still sleeping lad down on top of the pile. He then pulled another coat from the hangers and lay it over the lad, covering him completely. Sweating now, he stripped off the Santa Claus outfit and stuffed it behind one of the barrels on the other side of the room.

A door at the end of the corridor opened to a small, filthy toilet and Jarvis stepped inside and looked into the mirror. His thin, pain-lined face stared back at him. He searched his own eyes for any sign of pity for the boy but found none. His sexual appetites had driven any empathy from him many years ago and, as he turned to look at the little bundle of clothes containing the boy, the sight sent a shiver of sexual excitement through him.

The shouting from the bar became more animated and it brought Jarvis's attention back to the moment in hand. He turned back to the mirror and drew his hands through his hair, reforming the greasy quiff before walking through to the bar via the door behind the bar. No one noticed the man enter and he took his place at one of the booths in the corner of the room. He watched as his best friend and the vicious leader of the Meat Market Mob, Toddy Burns argued with one of the smartly-dressed men.

"I don't give a flying fuck who's kid it was! He *ain't* here!" he bellowed in his thick Birmingham accent.

The man he was speaking to made it obvious he wasn't convinced and laughed sarcastically.

"Fuck off Toddy! Who do you think you're kidding? We've all heard about your queer pal and what he gets up to with the foster kids in your care and how he does it all with *your* help."

Toddy Burns, who had been standing with his foot on one of the low bar stools and his weight resting on his knee, stood to his full height of six foot six. The action had the desired effect and the Whizz Mob men knew they were out of their depth with the big man.

"Oh yeah and what have you heard then pal?" Toddy snarled the words in a low guttural tone, his breath a mix of fags, alcohol and a bad case of halitosis.

"He's a fucking kiddy-fiddler, ain't he?"

"Yeah, I've heard he's a proper nonce and by all accounts you are too!" another Whizz mob man said angrily from the back of the four.

Toddy stepped amongst them, pushing his way to the back of the group to the man who had just spoken. He grabbed the man's jacket lapel and pulled him close. On seeing this the other men in the pub stepped forward and surrounded the four Whizz Mob men.

"Did you just call me a nonce?" Toddy lifted the man from the floor with his huge hands by the lapel of his jacket.

"Well, anyone t . . . t . . . that fiddles with kids is a nonce!" the man stuttered with far less certainty than his first statement.

Toddy slapped the man with the palm of his hand around the face before turning on the other men.

"Just get one thing straight, I ain't no fucking kiddy-fiddler!"

"Well, your ginger pal is . . ." One of the other men said more confidently, " . . . what's his name?"

"*Jarvis,* Duncan Jarvis, that's his name!" Jarvis called from the dark corner of the pub. The man's scouse accent caught everyone by surprise. He stood and crossed the room towards the little scene in the middle of the bar.

"Exactly what is it you lads want with me?"

The sight of the lean redhead emerging from the shadows seemed to take the wind out of the Whizz Mob men's sails, all of whom turned to look at each other with uncertain expressions. Toddy Burns tried to hide his surprise at the sight of his sidekick. He'd been wondering where the man had been all night and now without any warning, here he was.

"A little boy's been taken from the Bermuda club and . . ."

Jarvis cut him short.

"The Bermuda club, that's that new place owned by the Fewtrell Brothers, ain't it?"

The man nodded. Jarvis crossed the room until he was in the centre of the group. He addressed the leader of the four men.

"Yeah I've been meaning to get up there at some point and see what it's like."

"Bollocks, you were there tonight, dressed as Father Christmas." the man said, feeling very foolish as soon as the words left his mouth.

A short silence was followed by a burst of laughter from the men around the bar. The Whizz Mob man looked at the men surrounding him. They were a motley crew of scruffy market workers who by the look of their clothes seemed to be trapped in the Teddy Boy days of the 1950s.

"Don't tell me you still believe in Father-fucking-Christmas boys?" Jarvis said mockingly.

"No I meant that . . . "

Toddy, who was the only person *not* laughing interrupted him.

"You Whizz Mob boys have made a big fucking mistake coming here tonight." His voice deadly serious. "This is Meat Market turf and you cunts are trespassing."

"Aww don't be nasty Toddy, they're looking for Father Christmas!" Jarvis sniggered.

"I don't give a fuck if they're looking for their fairy fucking godmother. The only thing they're gonna find is a bleeding good hiding!"

With no more warning than that, Toddy swung a haymaker punch that knocked the Whizz Mob leader off his feet, smashing the man's nose to a pulp in one blow. The man absorbed the punch as best he could, sprawling backwards onto the filthy beer-stained carpet. Without any delay, the other members of the Meat Market Mob were on the outsiders, showering them with punches and kicks without mercy.

The Whizz Mob men didn't stand a chance against such a brute-force animalistic attack and it was all they could do to hold their own and fight their way back to back as the attack came from all around them. Slowly, they made their way towards the front door of the pub and onto the street. Even then the attackers didn't let up, showering the small group with whatever came to hand as the men limped and stumbled up the street. By the time they had extracted themselves from the fight, the Whizz Mob men didn't look so smart. With bloody heads and faces, tattered suits and even more damaged pride, they retreated along the street away from the Market Tavern as fast as they could, their tails firmly between their legs and no wiser than when they'd arrived.

CHAPTER 12

Parade Day
March 11th 1995

Thousands thronged the pavements of Birmingham's Irish quarter dressed in every shade of green known to man or animal. Shamrocks, Irish tricolour flags and all manner of Celtic knots were painted on the cheeks of the young, old, black white and Asian alike. Thousands of hands waved miniature Irish flags and plastic shillelaghs, along the lines of railings that stretched one mile either side of Digbeth High Street.

Waist-high railings separated the pavement from the main road and the hundred or so Irish-themed floats that trundled along the street on the back of seven tonne lorries donated by various local Irish owned builders and scaffolding companies. Each of the floats had a different theme, be it a traditional Irish cottage, built in miniature from plywood and cardboard, a famous Irish pub from the auld country or one of the local Gaelic football teams promoting their club, or an Irish dance team dancing out a sixteen-hand reel as the lorries trundled along at a snail's pace.

The one thing they all had in common was the music, for each of the elaborately decorated wagons had chosen to have loud music blaring from sets of speakers on the back of the flatbed.

Some just played Irish CDs, others had live music, solos, duos or five or six piece musical groups pumping their Celtic tunes over the heads of the beaming, cheering onlookers. The sound of fiddles, guitars, mandolins and whistles, were mixed with the drone of ten or so Highland pipe bands who marched in perfect order in-between the lorries, all dressed smartly in saffron or tartan kilts and regalia made for a glorious cacophony of sound that brought a smile to the hardest of faces and gave the Birmingham Irish a reason to be proud of their Celtic heritage making this the biggest Irish parade outside of Manhattan.

However, not everyone was there to celebrate and the two men dressed in the same long brown lab coats pushing their way through the packed crowds weren't smiling Even if they were, no one would have noticed, for each wore a cheap plastic leprechaun mask over his face. No one took any notice of the pair as almost everyone wore something similar. They even got the odd laugh or pat on the back from a fellow reveller as they threaded their way through the crowds towards their goal and the epicentre of the festival, the Birmingham Irish Centre.

Located right in the centre of the Irish Quarter, the building acted as a start and finish line for the parade and so was the most crowded area and always had the busiest bars. Two thousand-plus partygoers packed the main ballroom called the Leinster Suite, and between six and eight hundred drinkers huddled in the smaller Connaught Bar at the front of the building. The perfect venue for a long weekend of Irish-themed shenanigans ending traditionally on the Sunday before St. Patrick's day with this behemoth of a parade. Whichever way you looked at it, and both men had looked at it from every possible angle, the take from Birmingham's biggest Irish venue was going to be gargantuan by anyone's standards and thanks to the chaos of the St. Patrick's day festival, it was going to be easy pickings.

Both men carried a large white carrier bag in their left hands, each containing two hundred or so identical leprechaun masks to the ones they wore. They stopped outside the front entrance to the venue and took a second to scout the entrance out. Both men stood in the river of brightly-clad pedestrians watching two huge bearded doormen, one Asian one Italian, as they checked the ID's of the younger punters entering the building.

"See you inside Number One!" the burliest of the two men said from beneath his leprechaun mask.

The other man nodded as they turned from each other and parted, stepping towards the entrance independently. As they did so, both men dug in their bags and pulling out several masks at a time began handing the plastic masks to the revellers entering the club.

"Go on, they're free, have one!" the burley man said in a fake Irish accent to a group of young people.

One of the group took a look at the man wearing the same mask and took one. He pulled the thin elastic over the back of his head and placed the comical mask upon his face. His friends began to laugh at the ridiculous, freckled-faced leprechaun, topped off with a small plastic top hat. Instantly, several eager hands snatched at the freebies, until all the young men in the group were sporting the cheap masks. Cheering and laughing, they entered under the doormen's amused gaze and into the club, followed closely by the two men in the brown lab coats. As Number One passed the doormen, he handed the Italian-looking bouncer a mask. The man took one with a snigger and placed it on his head before waving the two men inside.

"What do ya reckon Haroom? Do I look like a twat?"

The huge Asian man rolled his eyes at his associate's tomfoolery.

"You don't need a mask to look like a twat, Mario!" he answered shaking his head. "We're meant to be working if you hadn't noticed!"

The Italian pulled the mask from his face with a scowl.

"I was only having a laugh. You need to lighten up our kid, it's parade day."

He reached forward and grabbed Number One by the shoulder of his lab coat. The man turned with a start.

"Here ya go mate, I'm not allowed to have any fun today . . . " he gestured with his head towards Haroom, " . . . so you may as well ave it back!"

Number One took the mask and nodded, smiling beneath his own mask that his plan was working. As he did, something caught his eye as he glanced over the doorman's shoulder. It was a poster for the Irish club's entertainment for the day and as he read the poster his smile transformed from one of amused confidence to a calculating smirk as he realised, the *pasty* was exactly where he should be.

Davey Keogh
and the
Wylde Green Band.

The poster announced, in its colourful celtic style. Number One inwardly congratulated himself for having planned this job down to the finest detail. The whole thing was so simple he was sure it couldn't fail. Not only that but he'd even managed to lay the seeds of blame at someone else's feet. His heart picked up pace as he stepped into the smaller of the two bars.

If the crowds were manic outside on the High street, then the Connaught Bar was a pandemonium of revellers, ten deep trying to get served at the long bar and others heckling an elderly Irish musical duo who were busy murdering song after song from the stage. Both men began pushing their way through the crowd until they reached the door to the main room. Once again, both were shocked at just how busy it was inside. Number One scanned the excited crowd, tricolour flags, Guinness hats and face-painted children were everywhere and the crush at the bar was as busy here as it had been at the other bar. This room seemed to be handling the crush with a little more ease due no doubt to the manager of the venue organising the bar staff as if he were some sort of ship's captain.

Number One watched the bespectacled manager for a few seconds. This was the man that would later be getting the brunt of his attention but for now there was work to do. As Number One turned to his companion a loud cheer went up around the hall as the band took the stage. He watched the blonde-haired singer walk to the middle of the stage and address the audience.

"*Hello!*" the singer shouted into the microphone. The cheer was deafening. "No, no no, that's no good, you can do better than that! *Hello!*"

This time the audience roared their reply.

"*Helloooooo!*" they screamed back.

"Are you ready to party *Birmingham?*" the singer shouted over the cheering.

Once again the audience burst into deafening applause. Number One tapped his associate's shoulder.

"Remember why we're here. You do that lot . . ." he nodded to the far side of the room, " . . . I'll do the area in front of the stage."

"What about him?" Number Two nodded towards the lead singer.

"I'll deal with him. As soon as you're finished, meet me over there by that door at the end of the bar!"

The other man nodded before turning and disappearing into the throng. Number One began to push his way towards the stage. As he did he reached into the plastic bag and pulled out a handful of masks. He began to hand them out to anyone that crossed his path. He glanced around the room as he threaded his way through the audience and caught a glimpse of his associate doing the same on the far side of the dance floor. Slowly, he could see people begin to don the identical, cheap, plastic, leprechaun masks. Number One reached the edge of the stage just as the band finished their first song. He beckoned the singer over to him.

Davey Keogh saw the man in the mask holding a white plastic bag towards him. The man was saying something but he couldn't make out anything over the din of the crowd and the man's muffled voice from behind his plastic mask. Davey would normally have just pressed on with a song but the man seemed insistent. The singer stepped forward and crouched down, bringing himself closer to the masked man.

"Here you are mate, some free masks." the man shouted up at the singer, "Throw em out to the crowd if ya like."

Davey gave a bemused smile, he could hear the touch of a fake Irish accent. He nodded before looking inside the bag.

"What? Are you just gonna give em away?" he asked.

The man nodded and Davey took the bag.

"Nice one fella!"

It was at that point that Davey noticed the man was wearing surgical gloves. Thinking this was a tad strange he peered back at the man's face and found himself looking into his eyes which glinted from behind the mask. Suddenly, the leprechaun mask lost its comical qualities, and seemed to change in to something threatening. Davey glanced down at the gloved hand once more and this time the man's hand was illuminated by one of the neon stage lights. Under the bright beam of purple neon Davey could easily see through the surgical glove and a dark outline of a small swallow and five-pointed star tattoo between index finger and thumb. He recognised the tattoo but with the chaos of the gig, he couldn't work out where he'd seen it before. The man saw the singer's look of recognition and snatched his hand away.

Dez turned and forced his way back through the packed crowd not knowing if he'd been recognised or not. As he threaded through the audience he turned to see the singer holding up one of the masks. He turned back towards his destination and as he did so he came face to face with Abi Fewtrell who had joined the throng at the front of the stage. Dez froze, momentarily forgetting that his face was covered by the mask. He felt a wave of panic wash over him and his face flush red beneath the plastic. He stood in front of the blonde girl for a second, unable to move. She glanced up at him and smiled.

He realised with some relief that she didn't recognise him at all. How could she? He'd gone to some lengths to ensure he wouldn't be recognised by anyone. From the stage Davey followed his slow progress through the throng. He watched him stop in front of Abi for a second before finally losing sight of the man completely. Abi was smiling at him and he returned her smile with a cheeky wink and as he returned to his microphone. The image of the tattoo on the man's hand wouldn't leave his mind though and he suddenly remembered where he'd seen it before but this was neither the place nor the time and as the band behind him began to grow impatient, he knew the show must go on.

"Does anyone want a *freebee*?" Davey said into the mic as he pulled a few masks from the bag, holding them up to the crowd.

Hundreds of hands shot up into the air simultaneously and without hesitation he threw the masks into the throng where they were snatched at by numerous eager hands. On seeing this he did it again. Again the masks vanished in a mass of hands before reappearing a few seconds later on various partygoer's faces. Eager to get on with the next song, Davey pulled a handful of masks from the bag and threw them into the crowd. The audience became a mass of smiling excited faces and waving hands as they each grabbed for the masks snatching them away here and there. The singer threw again and again until the bag was empty as the band began the opening chords of their next song One by one the audience watching the show began wearing the masks until finally, hundreds of the same ridiculous, cheeky, freckled leprechaun faces were staring back at the band in a bizarre display of Irish kitsch.

Dez spotted Number Two as he worked his way through the crowd towards their pre- appointed meeting place at the door at the far end of the bar. The sight of his accomplice spurred him on and he also began to push his way towards the door as arranged.

****

Shaun sat in his tiny office between the two bars of the Irish Centre. Although everyone called it his office, it was really nothing more than an eight foot by three foot plywood construction that barely fitted his small office desk and the huge Victorian safe which in itself took up almost a third of the space. However, although the office was minute, Shaun had made the best of the tiny space whilst rejuvenating Birmingham's biggest Irish club, personally dragging the place out of its mismanaged 1960's committee, money-haemorrhaging chaos and turning the place into one of the most successful live music and boxing venues in the second city.

Fuelled by Red-Bull and vodka, chain-smoked fags and the occasional bacon butty, Shaun had been awake for nearly forty-eight hours on this particular shift. The long hours were nothing unusual for Shaun but the manic atmosphere that surrounded the festival had worn him down. After seven days of dealing with the various Irish county committees involved in the parade, complaining musicians and the never-ending problems with bar staff, Shaun had totally had enough of the St. Patrick's Irish parade. He was beginning to lag and it was only 4pm. He knew he had another twelve hours to go before they kicked out the last of the drunken revellers onto Digbeth High Street to become someone else's problem and no longer his.

He sighed as he drew deeply on the cigarette that hung from the corner of his mouth. The smoke drifted up into his eyes as he counted out *another* pile of cash into hundreds and then thousand pound bundles. He wrapped a thin elastic band around the bundle, noted it in a little book and stacked it on top of another bundle before starting again on another pile of notes. The novelty of counting so much money had worn off after the first few months of taking the job twelve years ago. He kept counting until the pile was ten bundles high and then he wrapped them in another, thicker elastic band and placing the bundle inside a transparent ziplock bag, he stuffed it inside the safe. He knelt in front of the antique safe and forced the bag into the ever-decreasing space left at the top of the pile of other similar ziplock bags, each containing ten thousand pound bundles of cash.

He'd been doing this all week, virtually nonstop and by his accounts, the safe contained just over one hundred and thirty thousand pounds give or take the odd hundred still in the tills and the busiest day of the week still had another six hours of cash-till time to go. Shaun estimated that he would probably do at least another twenty grand before kick-out time came and he could retire to his small apartment on the top floor of the venue and finally get some sleep.

Returning to the desk he picked up a can of Red-Bull and shook it to see if it contained any of the energy-inducing liquid.

It didn't, picking another, then another he did the same until on the fifth attempt he found one that was half full and took a slug from the can wondering how long he could keep this up. The drink had long lost its energy-providing effects. He yawned, removed his glasses and rubbed his tired eyes and reclined in the high backed-office chair, closing his eyes and taking a few seconds to gather himself together. He listened to the cheering audience as the band in the main hall finished the second song.

The sleep came over Shaun imperceptibly and without him noticing it crept upon him and placed its irresistible weight on his eyelids and slowly closed them. He fell deeply into a powerful sleep and the dreams came quick and fast. However, after less than a minute his exhausted head lolled to one side. The action caused him to wake from his nap with a little yelp. He sat there feeling as if he'd been asleep for hours, and thinking he had, he wondered if he'd been missed by the bar staff. His glasses still lay on the desk top in front of him and blinking, at the blurred images around him, he shook his head trying to dislodge the sleepiness that still threatened to overwhelm him. As he did, he noticed two figures standing to his side. He yawned as he reached for his glasses, embarrassed in case he'd been caught napping on such a busy day.

"W ... what's happened now ... " he stuttered in his dirty Brummie brogue, "I ... I was just resting me eyes. Don't tell me we've had a till go down again. I've only just ... !"

As he pulled his glasses on hurriedly he turned to look at the two figures he'd mistaken for staff members. His first reaction was one of bafflement. The two men stood in the tiny office in their long, brown lab coats. Shaun's eyes began to focus properly and he sat in his chair looking blankly at the two six-foot leprechauns standing in front of him. His mouth dropped open as if to say something but for once in his life Shaun was speechless.

"Just stay in the seat sunshine!" the bigger of the two men ordered.

Shaun's eyes screwed up as his wits began to return.

"What the fuck are you two doing in here? This is my private office, the punters stay out there!"

He pointed in the direction of the doorway that stood at the end of the long bar and obviously the way both men had entered the office.

"Go on! Out ya go lads! If you're looking for the toilets they're on the other side of the ... "

BAM! The punch came without warning. It was hard and powerful, smashing into Shaun's nose and forcing his head back into the chair violently, catching him totally by surprise. Inside Shaun's head a shower of sparks exploded in a blinding display until the inevitable blackness of unconsciousness overwhelmed him.

Dez stepped in close to the seated manager's face and started to slap the man's cheek as he waited for the manager to come to. After a few seconds, Shaun's eyes rolled in his head as he became conscious again.

"W ... what ... !" Shaun stuttered.

The metallic taste of his blood filled his mouth as the crimson liquid dribbled from his broken nose onto his top lip and into his open mouth.

"I was only having a kip ... !" Shaun's befuddled punch-drunk mind tried to make sense of what had just happened and he began to babble inanely. "I only shut me eyes for a minute. Have you got a fag?"

Dez reached across the manager and picked up the cigarette pack from the desk and pulling one out he placed it in Shaun's mouth.

"There ya go sunshine, you just rest your pretty head and we'll go about our business."

Shawn drew on the fag deeply, his mind having difficulty coming back to full consciousness. He watched as the two leprechauns produced two, folded, green canvas bags from beneath their coats. Number Two pushed the manager's chair out of the way and knelt down in front of the safe. Shaun watched him, a bemused expression growing across his face. The blood had started to clot around his nose and he began to prod it with his finger. Dez took a tissue from a small box on the desk and handed it to him. Shaun took it, puzzled by the gesture. He dabbed the painful area around his nose and was surprised to see it was covered in blood when he examined the tissue. Dez saw Shaun's bewilderment and knew his mind had gone. He'd seen things like this before, at other robberies where the victims of his or his accomplice's violence had been unable to accept their current circumstances and so had suffered from sensory overload. Dez guessed that was exactly what was happening to the manager right now. He also knew from experience that given a chance, Shaun's brain would, for a short time at least, accept any explanation to its current, confused situation.

"You've had an accident mate, that's why you're bleeding."

Number Two turned around and gave Dez a quizzical look from beneath the mask, Dez returned the gesture with a short nod indicating that he should start filling the bags and turned his attention back to the seated manager.

"We've been sent by the bank mate . . ." He patted Shaun's shoulder, " . . . they said we should collect the cash bags and deliver them to the bank for you as you've had an accident."

Dez's voice was friendly and reassuring. Shaun nodded, still holding the tissue to his nose. However, the initial shock of the punch had already began to wear off and Shaun began to wonder why these men from the bank were wearing the leprechaun masks. He took another tissue from the desk and dabbed at his bloody nose.

"What kind of accident did I have?"

Dez bent and looked into the manager's dilated eyes.

"Car crash mate, you crashed your motor into another car!"

Shaun's face scrunched into a puzzled expression.

"But I can't drive!"

"Well, there ya go then, that's why you had the crash, ain't it?" Number Two said with a snigger.

Dez glared at his accomplice.

"Get on with it Number Two and keep your trap shut!"

"If you're from the bank, why are you wearing leprechaun masks?" Shawn's question signalled that his sensory overload was quickly drawing to an end.

Without thinking Number Two answered.

"It's the St. Patrick's day parade, everyone's wearing em!"

As if by the click of a hypnotist's finger, the mention of the parade brought Shaun back to the moment as if he were being brought out of a deep trance by a hypnotist. He tried to stand but as he did Dez pushed him back into his chair.

"No mate, if you know what's good for you you'll stay where you are!"

Shaun tried to rise again. Dez raised his hand and slapped Shaun around the face. The open handed slap across his cheek had the desired effect and the manager slumped back into the chair, his hand raised to his face for protection. Dez glanced at the kneeling man by the safe.

"Come on Number Two, we ain't got long!"

As the last words were said, Number Two stood up. He threw the small, fully packed duffle bag over the top of the manager's head. Dez caught the bag easily but was surprised by its weight. He looked at the open door to the safe and smiled as he saw that, apart from a few rolls of coins at the bottom of the safe, Number Two had completely emptied it of its contents. He watched his accomplice throw the other bag over one shoulder. Dez copied him before bending once more and pointing his finger into Shaun's face.

"Now we both know what's gone down here, don't we? You ain't been in no accident, have you?" Shaun, who was now fully compos mentis, glared back at the man in the mask.

"Look, this ain't your cash mate! You're just a manger here, so it ain't worth dying for, is it? Just sit there like a good lad and keep your fucking fingers away from that phone!" He patted Shawn's head, "Understand?"

Shawn's expression didn't change. Dez stood again. He looked over Number Two. The burly man stood opposite him in his mask, brown lab coat, surgical gloves and the canvas bag slung across his shoulder.

"Let's go!" Number Two nodded without saying a word.

He pushed his way past the office chair and opened the door to the main hall. As the office door was opened all three men were hit by the wall of sound coming from the main stage. The Irish uileann pipes were playing a reel at breakneck speed, accompanied by the lead singer on the bodhran drum, who drove the tune along with its primeval rhythm. Both men stood in the doorway for a second, caught by the music's hypnotic power over the audience. To Dez's amusement, many of the crowd still wore the leprechaun masks. He turned to the dazed bar manager behind him and nodded before shutting the office door with slam.

Shaun sat in his chair for a few seconds not knowing what to do. He spun in his office chair towards the safe. As he caught sight of the empty safe, he felt as if a lead weight had somehow been dropped into his stomach and it made him feel nauseous. He leant forward in his chair and held his head in his hands. As he did so a fresh dribble of blood flowed from his nose onto his grey flannel suit-trousers, the sight of which brought him out of his melancholy like a slap around the face. He spun once more in his chair back towards his desk and grabbed at a small black walkie-talkie. The little wireless handset buzzed with white noise for a few seconds before Shaun flicked one of the switches on the top of the handset and connected it to the other six handsets used by the door staff.

"Mario . . . Mario . . . " Shaun let go of the little button on the side of the walkie-talkie. It crackled with white noise, " . . . Mario . . . *Mario,* come in!" Again he let go the button. However Mario the huge Italian Irish bouncer who managed the door staff didn't answer. Shaun continued in earnest. "Mario, answer your fucking . . . "

"What's up boss?" a cheerful voice came from somewhere on the other side of the venue.

Shaun could hear music through the little speaker on the little two way radio and assumed the man was in his usual position at the front doors of the venue.

"Mario ..." he stopped for a second, not really know what to say, " ... we've been fuck ... "

"Hello?" Mario's voice crackled through the radio again. Shaun realised he hadn't depressed the button on the walkie-talkie and the Italian hadn't heard his words. He gripped the radio tightly in his right hand and pressed the button. The mistake had given him a chance to gather his thoughts.

"Mario, we've been fucking robbed. They've taken the lot, over a hundred and thirty grand ..."

There was a short silence whilst Mario took the information in.

"What is this a fucking joke or something boss? Cos it ain't funny if it is!"

"No, it's not a *fucking* joke! Two fuckers just came in my office attacked me and robbed the safe!"

He let the words sink in whilst he thought about what his next step should be. The idea that the club would ever be robbed was unthinkable, what with its connections to Birmingham's most powerful Irish families. The prospect of the Irish Centre becoming the victim of a heist was something that nobody had ever prepared for.

"Shut the fucking club down *now!* No one comes in, no one goes out!"

Mario looked around him at the river of people flowing to and fro through the main doors like so much Irish-themed flotsam and jetsam.

"Eh? Did you say shut the club down?"

"Yes, *yes* shut the fucking doors now! They're still in here." Mario's heart sank at the thought of trying to stop the hundreds of revellers trying to get in and out the pub and how much trouble it would cause.

"I don't think you understand what it like out here, Shaun!" Shaun shivered with anger on the other end of the line.

"I don't think you know what it's like in *here* Mario. I'm sitting next to an empty fucking safe and if we don't catch these fuckers we'll all be for the high jump!"

Mario could hear the anger in his manager's voice, the sound of which kicked him into action.

"Ok, Shaun calm down and . . . "

The manager exploded.

"Calm down? Calm fucking down? We've just been fucked by two six foot fucking leprechauns!"

Mario pulled the radio away from his ear and stared at it for a second. Haroom crossed the space between the doors and listened to the manager venting his spleen.

"Leprechauns? Have you had a blow to the head, boss?"

"Who's that laughing?" Mario and Haroom stared at each other. They had never heard Shaun so animated. "Does this sound like it's fucking funny to you, Haroom?Like a joke? Cos I ain't fucking laughing, am I?"

Haroom's smile dropped as Shaun continued his rant, "They had leprechaun masks on. Just stop anyone with a leprechaun mask on. There can't be that many of them, for fuck's sake!"

"Leprechaun mask? What type of leprechaun mask?" Now it was Shawn's turn to look at the radio in disbelief.

"A *fucking leprechaun mask*. A smiling leprechaun with freckles and a little green top hat on his head with a . . . "

Mario finished his sentence for him,

" . . . golden shamrock on the front of it?"

Shaun gasped.

"Yes, that's it exactly Mario! Can you see em?"

Ignoring the musical duo performing to the packed crowd, the doorman climbed onto the edge of the small stage that stood next to the main exit in the Connaught bar where he scanned the room quickly. As he did he pressed the button on the two way radio.

"Yeah, I can see em!" he said flatly.

"Where are they?" Shaun said, trying to hide the panic in his voice. Mario shook his head as he looked at the hundreds of green faces staring towards him.

"They're everywhere boss!"

"What do you mean they're everywhere?" Shaun's voice started to tremble as the shock of what had just happened to him began to come to the surface of his emotions.

"There was only two of em!" he continued.

Mario laughed sarcastically.

"Well, there's more than two of em now . . ."

The doorman tried to count the amount of faces looking back at him who were also wearing the leprechaun masks. He stopped at fifty but estimated that there was well over one hundred. He turned to the duo on the stage and was shocked to see that even the guitarist on the stage was wearing one of the cheap plastic masks.

"What? You're not making any sense, Mario." Shaun's voice crackled over the music.

Mario stepped down from the stage and crossed to the other doorman with the hand held radio still at his ear.

"You had better come out and see for yourself, boss!"

Shaun dropped the radio unceremoniously onto his desk and stood from his chair. The room spun slightly as he stood, due no doubt to the punch on his nose. He held on to the edge of his desk until the motion sickness had passed and stepped through the door of his little office and out into the main hall.

The sight made his heart sink.

For there in the main hall were thousands of people drinking, dancing and singing along to the band. Scattered throughout the thousands of revellers were hundreds of the same, cheap, leprechaun masks that had been worn by the two criminals who had committed the heist. Shaun sighed deeply as he scanned each of the masks, trying desperately to recognise any of the figures in the crowd who wore them but it was impossible to differentiate between one or the other. All of them stared back at him blankly and the masks had suddenly lost all comical value.

Shaun felt sick to the pit of his stomach.

CHAPTER 14

Abduction 1961
(Continued)

J arvis lifted the edge of the coat delicately from the sleeping boy. The little boy had curled himself into a foetal position for warmth and was still sleeping, his blond mop of hair ruffled around his tiny face. The paedophile's eye roamed over the boy, lingering on the area of skin between the high socks and the bottom of the boy's grey flannel shorts and Jarvis felt a familiar feeling of arousal around his groin. Jarvis turned to the other man looking over his shoulder and raised his eyebrows in a mischievous sexual manner.

"What the fuck have you done, Jarvis?" Toddy Burns snarled as he caught sight of the boy.

Jarvis raised his finger to his lips.

"Shh, you'll wake him up!" he said softly, letting the coat drape back over the boy again.

He gestured that they should step further along the cellar corridor to talk.

"He's beautiful ain't he?"

Toddy's face flushed with rage.

"You fucking idiot! What the fuck were you thinking?"

Jarvis just shrugged his shoulders and did his best to look sorry for himself.

"It's a Christmas treat, I couldn't help myself Toddy!"

The big man turned away from the paedophile and ran his thick fingers through his mop of black, greasy hair. As he did, he caught sight of the red Father Christmas costume hanging beneath another coat. He stepped towards the costume and flung the coat that covered it to the floor. He grabbed the red suit and held it towards the red-haired man.

"Couldn't help yourself . . . " he said incredulously, " . . . what the fuck are you talking about?"

Jarvis raised his finger to his lips again.

"Shh, we don't want him waking up do we Toddy?"

Toddy's fury threatened to explode and Jarvis knew it. The giant stepped into Jarvis's face, still holding the red suit. He grabbed the paedophile's shirt and pulled him close.

"I should stuff this thing down your fucking throat, you sick cunt!"

Toddy kept his voice down as best he could. He knew Jarvis was correct about that. The last thing he wanted was for the boy to start crying and the other members of the Meat Market Mob to start nosing around especially after the earlier run in with the lads from the Whizz Mob.

"Don't try that innocent shit with me, Jarvis! You set out to lure some kid into your trap tonight and did just that, you're a fucking wrong-un mate!"

"I'm just different is all Toddy, there's no need to insult me, I've got feelings you know, anyway, you've always known I've had a weakness for young boys."

"Young boys?" Toddy repeated, astounded by the man's description of his victim.

"Young boys are twelve, thirteen or fourteen, this . . . " He pointed towards the pile of coats on the concrete floor, " . . . this is a child, a little child, I mean, how old is he, seven . . . eight?"

Jarvis had never seen Toddy Burns so angry but far from being upset by his friend's fury the sight of such a hard man as Toddy

Burns losing his temper and being the target of such venom, was to Jarvis a powerful sexual turn-on. You see, Duncan Jarvis enjoyed pain, not just inflicting it but receiving it too. He stared into the other man's face expectantly. Toddy's features resembled that of a huge grizzly bear rather than that of a man. He'd seen Toddy at his meanest and the sight of the gang leader's ultra-violence never ceased to turn him on. He waited for Toddy's hand to slap him or maybe a punch. Just the thought of this sent a tremor through his loins, creating an erection that pressed hard against the inside of his trousers. However, Toddy was too sharp to waste his time on beating someone that enjoyed such things. He was already addressing the practicality of the problem at hand.

"Well, what do you intend to do with him?" Now it was Jarvis's turn to look shocked.

"What do you think I'm gonna . . . ?"

"No, you ain't gonna touch him! He's going back where you found him Jarvis!"

The red haired man scowled and Toddy grabbed his throat, pulling him close again he squeezed it tightly, stopping the other man's breath mid-flow. Jarvis spluttered, his eyes closing into thin watery slits.

"Now, I don't wanna fall out about this Jarvis but I will if I have to and if that happens we both know how it'll end don't we and it won't be good for you!"

He let the words sink in for a few seconds. Jarvis listened to the hubbub of the crowd in the bar starting to grow quieter and he knew that he was starting to pass out. Toddy saw the man's eyes roll in his head and released his grip slightly.

"Now my *perverted* friend, you're gonna pick him up and take him back up the Bermuda club where you found him!"

Jarvis shook his head, which was still trapped in Toddy's grip.

"I . . . I can't!" Jarvis stuttered. Toddy let go completely. Jarvis fell to his knees gasping for air.

"What do you mean, *you can't?* Of course you can?" Jarvis knelt in front of the big man, his face only inches from the other man's groin and even in his state of breathlessness, he was aroused by his position.

"The boy, he belongs to R . . . Ronnie Fletcher!"

Toddy looked down at the kneeling man open-mouthed.

"Ronnie Fletcher?" he said, as if trying to comprehend the gravity of the name. Jarvis nodded. "*Detective* Ronnie Fletcher?" Jarvis coughing, nodded again.

"I can't take him back now! If Fletcher finds out it's me that took his son, he'll bang me up and throw away the fucking key!"

Toddy fell to his knees, the wind well and truly taken out of his sails.

"You abducted Ronnie Fletcher's boy? What the fuck were you thinking Jarvis?"

The paedophile just shrugged.

"I couldn't help myself boss. I didn't set out to take *him*, Ronnie Fletcher gave him to me and I just . . . "

"You just couldn't help yourself, yeah, you said before." Toddy sat back on his haunches. "Fuck!" he said under his breath. He looked at his old friend and knew that he would stick by him no matter how sick he was and whatever level of shit-storm this would cause around the town.

"Those lads from the Whizz Mob were just the first you know!"

Jarvis nodded. "They'll be back again, so will the old Bill, you've got a record Jarvis and people know you're a . . . " He searched for the right words, finally settling on, " . . . pervert. Most of us Meat Market lads couldn't care less when it comes to a teenager or something but a little kid, well that's a different thing!"

Jarvis nodded again, this time with an emotion coming to the surface, stifling the erection in his trousers. It was an emotion he couldn't explain or had never felt before in his life but to any other human being it was called guilt. This guilt wasn't about anything he had planned for the boy, the feeling, for what it was worth, was stemmed from the fact that he'd let his protector Toddy Burns down in some way or other. Toddy continued.

"We'll have to get rid of him sharpish!" Jarvis looked disappointed.

"Couldn't I ... you know ... before we ... "

"*No,* you fucking can't!"

Toddy tried to think but the noise from the bar was getting louder. He could hear people asking the landlord where he was and he knew it was just a matter of time before someone came through and discovered the two of them with the little lad in the cellar, then the cat would truly be out of the bag.

"He's just a little puppy!" Jarvis said unexpectedly.

Toddy shook his head.

"What?"

"He's just a little puppy!" Jarvis repeated.

"What the fuck are you talking about?"

"What do you do with an un-wanted puppy?"

Toddy, who was still sat on his haunches looked at the other man with a puzzled expression and Jarvis waited for his words to make sense.

"An un-wanted puppy ... ?' Toddy said repeating the other man's words. As he said the words toddy saw the beginnings of a thin smile spread across the paedophile's face. Jarvis turned and looked at the bundle, he watched the slow rise and fall of the pile of coats as little Daniel breathed in and out softly in his sleep, turning back to the huge gang leader he said softly.

"You put the puppy in a weighted sack, take it down the canal, throw it in the cut, and simply walk away!"

CHAPTER 13

Empty Safe, Saving Face
1995

"So what exactly am I looking at?" Dixie said to the Irish Centre manger. The two men were huddled together in front of the tiny black and white CCTV monitor in Shaun's tiny office.

"There!" Shaun pointed at the screen with his left hand. His other hand was rolling pieces of tissue into small balls. Removing the bloody white handkerchief from his still bleeding broken nose, he stuffed his nostrils with the tissue bungs where they instantly began to soak up his blood. Talking hurt him, so he was determined to keep his communication with the detective to a minimum.

"Dat's dem!" he said in a blocked nasal comical Brummie brogue.

The image on the screen displayed two men in identical, knee-length lab coats, both of whom were wearing the same leprechaun masks. The CCTV camera had captured the pair entering the building minutes before the robbery. Dixie tutted. He'd been working the streets of Birmingham for nearly fifty years, clipping the green buds of crime before they could spring into blossoming money trees. The West Midlands police had changed over the years and Dixie had seen them all come and go and he was still here. The hard-nosed by the book police inspectors, the trendy liberals politically correct arse-lickers and the down-right horrible bastards like Dixie's personal nemesis, Detective Constable Ronnie Fletcher had all had their day. No matter, they had fallen by the wayside and still he remained. Slowly climbing his way from the streets through all the shit until now he was one of the most respected officers on the force from the young constables just joining up to the top brass.

That wasn't to say *he* wasn't bent, of course he'd taken a few backhanders over the years. If truth be told, it'd been more than a just few but he'd always kept his feet on the ground. However, he knew things were changing. A new breed of criminal was coming to town. Clever, educated fuckers, stealing with mobile phones, computers and telephone scripts instead of shotguns and cudgels like the old days, like these pair on the screen. Personally, he preferred the latter. He'd seen off the London gangsters back in the 1960s, standing shoulder to shoulder with Birmingham's very own godfather Eddie Fewtrell and his seven brothers. The I.R.A., Pakistani drug lords and interracial tribal football hooliganism had all had a go, each new challenger taking their toll on him, each new on-comer furrowing another line into his already crisscrossed brow, and yet he had stood amongst the carnage and dealt with the bloody chaos and still he remained. Actually he'd done better than just remain. Just like a flea on a mangy dog, over the years Dixie had virtually thrived from the second city's crime wave, and he knew that however strong Eddie Fewtrell's iron grip on the town, it was nothing without the help of the long arm of the law.

But like the words of the song, 'times they were a-changing.'

Dixie watched the black and white images. Shaun held his finger on the screen indicating the two figures in question.

"Keep your eyes on deese pair!" Shaun said painfully. Dixie watched as the men crossed through the Connaught bar but lost them as they each made their way deeper into the crowd, unable to decipher the details in the grainy picture.

"Fucking hell, how old is this CCTV system?" he said with a sarcastic laugh.

Shaun took no notice, instead he leaned across and pressed a button on a small plastic control board. The picture changed to one of the Leinster suite. This picture was much clearer *and* in colour.

"Oh and as if by magic we have a proper picture at last." Dixie sniggered.

Shaun gave him a cold look.

"I don't think this is a laughing matter, do you?"

Dixie raised his eyebrows.

"Well, you know what they say about leprechauns, don't ya?"

Shaun rolled his eyes and sighed. Dixie continued.

"Once you take your eye off em, you never see em again!"

Shaun lost his cool.

"I'm glad this is all so fucking funny to you but can I remind you that I've just had . . . " he mulled over the amount stolen in the heist and realising that this could be an opportunity to make up on some monetary losses he'd suffered in over the last twelve months, whilst simultaneously making a few quid for himself on top, before answering and upping the amount taken. " . . . over one hundred and fifty grand stolen from that safe!"

The outburst took Dixie by surprise. He turned to the bar manager with a reassuring smile.

"Ok son, keep your hair on."

He raised his hand and placed it on Shaun's shoulder, his smile broadening as he did.

"I've been doing this a long time son, longer than you've been alive but I *can't* guarantee, that we'll get these pair. Now, you're lucky to have got me instead of one of my younger pimple-faced colleagues instead. This crime is right up my street. A proper old school heist, no computers, no conmen, this is a real robbery carried out by two professionals. They might even ex-military."

Shaun stared at the detective with a bemused expression.

"See how they move, both working independently of each other . . . of course that's only an assumption."

"It sounds like you admire them?"

Dixie shrugged.

"I do son, I do. Proper old school criminals, what's not to like?"

"For fuck's sake!" Shaun said angrily.

Dixie gave him a rehearsed smile.

"Anyway, let's keep this friendly at this stage, after all, don't forget, we're both on the same side here."

Dixie turned back to the TV monitor.

"Now why don't you go and get us both a cup of tea and we'll pick through this footage for something that'll giveaway the identity of our leprechauns."

Shaun just stared at the back of the man's head before turning his attention to the small TV screen.

"Well, good luck with that Detective! I've been through that footage three times and couldn't find anything to differentiate the robbers from everyone else wearing the masks."

Dixie just kept watching the screen.

"Don't worry, as I said, this is old school, people don't do this stuff anymore and there's a reason for that!"

Dixie left the words hanging, prompting a reply from Shaun.

"What reason?" Shaun complied.

Dixie's smile grew into a reassuring grin.

"Criminals don't do this type of crime anymore because it's too unpredictable. You'll see, somewhere along the line they'll have made a mistake, they always do!"

Shaun shook his head.

"What type of mistake?"

Dixie sighed. Turning again he smiled, trying to hide his growing irritation with the manager's questions.

"One sugar with mine please son!"

He just stared at the manger with his stupid grin, until Shaun got the message and left, heading off to the kitchen, his nostrils stuffed with bloody tissues.

Dixie turned back to the screen, his grin still in place. He watched the picture of the main hall, the two men in the masks came into view of the CCTV camera. He noticed both held white plastic carrier bags, and knew that was how he would track them through the club as the grainy video rolled on.

By the time Shaun returned to his office with the tea, the detective had gone.

****

Dixie took the video tape and left Shaun's office in a hurry. The Irish Centre manager noticed that the officer's former sense of humour had suddenly vanished, replaced instead with a worried scowl.

The detective climbed into the unmarked police car and drove the Ford Sierra Cosworth as fast as was possible through the Monday morning rush hour. He flicked a switch on the dashboard and the police car's blue lights, hidden beneath the cars grill, began to flash. The action had the desired effect and as if by magic, the traffic jam in front of him began to melt away. Dixie knew that the blue lights weren't strictly allowed unless he was either in pursuit or on an emergency call. However, after what he'd just seen on the CCTV footage in the Irish Centre, the detective wasn't in the mood for hanging around. Anyway, who was going do anything about it, the local coppers? Nah.

He glanced at the Steel-House Lane police station as he passed it, and could see the odd policeman's head peering over the frosted glass in the reception trying to break up the monotony of the their office duty. Dixie took no notice. He had to get across town to Eddie Fewtrell's office and show him what he'd found.

****

Declan slammed the table with his fist. The action made the glasses jump, spilling their contents onto the dark brown surface to be soaked up by the old beer mats.

"I fucking told ya didn't I? The Irish Centre is out-o-fuck-ing-bounds!" He snarled at the men across the table. McBride shrivelled beneath the aggression but the Fox just stared back at him with an uncaring eye. McBride tried to answer.

"Bu . . . but!" He stuttered. "But we didn't . . . "

"Don't give me that shit . . ." Declan leaned across the table and pointed his finger at the Fox. " . . . this cunt was talking about doing the place over it and now he's gone and done it and from what I hear, he wasn't alone either!"

Declan turned his glare on the doorman. McBride opened his mouth but shut it again quickly when he saw the depth of Declan's fury. The Irish landlord drew on his cigarette before pointing at the Fox again.

"I'm gonna talk to the Dublin lads and tell em that they had better get you the fuck out of my town before I . . ."

"Before you what boss?"

The thin man's expression hadn't changed. He stared back at the red-faced landlord and I.R.A. collector with a look of total disdain.

"Before you do fuck all that's what. There's two things you should know about me *boss* . . ." the Fox turned and addressed the doorman too, " . . . and you had better listen up as well Plastic Paddy." McBride bristled. "Firstly . . ." the Fox's voice dropped to almost a whisper, making the words that followed even more threatening, " . . . don't *ever* fucking threaten me, or I won't be able to answer for the consequences."

Declan sniggered, trying to hide the feeling of self-doubt rising inside himself. The Fox saw his amusement and continued talking.

"Yeah, that's what they all do, give a little nervous laugh, right before my knife finds their throat!"

Declan exploded. Standing he leant across the table and snarled at the sitting man opposite. The Fox just laughed in his face.

"I ain't told you the second thing yet, boss!" he said, unruffled by the landlord's aggression. The Fox's words had the desired effect. "The second thing is that I'm gonna start pulling the strings from now on, you and this gob-shite . . ." he nodded towards the doorman, " . . . had better start listening up!"

Declan O'Dwyer couldn't take anymore, he stood again, shaking with anger.

"Don't you go getting too big for ya boots sonny or I'll pick the phone up to the Dublin lads and I'll tell em . . . !"

"Go on then!" The Fox said the words with such confidence that it stopped the landlord in his tracks.

Declan blustered a few obscenities under his breath.

"No, seriously boss . . . " he continued, " . . . call em, they want a few words with you anyway. The boys in Dublin have been concerned about your operation in Birmingham for a while now, hence my presence here!"

The landlord sat again, shocked by the sudden eloquence of the hitman. The Fox had been in Birmingham for weeks now and this was the most he'd said in all that time. Their first impressions of the man as a mindless druggy, had been pure subterfuge. Now Declan and Mc Bride could see the man was far more intelligent and powerful that they had first thought, and as if to drive the now obvious point home, the Fox continued.

"The Dublin firm have noticed that the I.R.A. take has been getting lighter and lighter over the last twelve months. So they've asked me to come and find out what's going on."

He looked at the two shocked faces in front of him and sniggered.

"What, you thought you were in charge of druggy old me?" He raised his eyebrows and shook his head with another chuckle. "No *boss* . . . " he said sarcastically, " . . . you don't get to run with someone like the General by being a mug . . . " He made the sign of a cross on his forehead, " . . . may he rest in peace."

He stopped for a second, as if remembering his old Dublin gangster boss before standing and leaning into Declan's face.

"Anyway, yeah, I like a bit of speed every now and then but you had better believe that I follow my orders to the *T*, without question and I'll do whatever I have to get this Birmingham racket back on track . . . "

The Fox pulled the knife from his waistband of his trousers with such speed it caught both seated men off guard. He waved the knife around, pointing towards the other men threateningly.

"So go and make your calls to Dublin if you like. As a matter of fact, I insist you call Dublin and confirm what I'm saying is true, then perhaps you'll understand exactly how thin the ice is under your fucking feet!"

The Fox returned to his chair and all three sat in silence for a short time listening to the busy Monday morning traffic on Digbeth High Street outside the large pane glass windows. The awkward silence was broken by a police siren coming towards them through the drizzle. The high-pitched siren piecing the background rumble of traffic with its shrill alarm. All three stood and looked through the bar windows, watching the silver unmarked Ford Sierra Cosworth forcing its way through the morning traffic bottle-neck towards the city centre with its hidden blue lights flashing from beneath its front grill.

As the car disappeared up Digbeth High Street, towards St. Martin's cathedral, the Dublin hitman took the opportunity to speak again, only this time in a more conciliatory tone.

"Ok boys, now what's going on here has sunk in, let's get down to business."

He nodded to the other men with what he considered a smile, but was more like a broken-toothed grimace. "Let's start off with the business at hand, the Irish Centre was robbed yesterday." He glanced at Declan and raised his eyebrows in a judgmental manner, "and not by me it must be said. Nevertheless, it *was* robbed and seeing as you pair have been telling anyone that'll listen, that the place is out of bounds, that's a bit strange, don't you think? So, taking into account the fact that most of the Birmingham Irish don't want to get on the wrong side of you or the I.R.A. I'd say the place was turned over by someone on the outside, someone not connected."

He left the words hanging for a second. Declan nodded reluctantly followed by McBride.

"Yeah, well that makes sense to me." McBride said, agreeing with the hitman.

"Yeah, it does, doesn't it?" The Fox replied. "And guess what a little birdie told me?"

Both men shuffled uncomfortably as if the off-the-cuff remark was aimed at them.

The hitman continued, "The little birdie said that these lads were wearing leprechaun masks when they committed the heist."

Declan realised with some relief, that it wasn't aimed at him, just shrugged.

"Well, they weren't gonna just rob the place bare-arsed, were they?" The Fox stared blankly at him, his pock-marked features not showing any emotion at all.

"You're missing the point *boss*." he said the last word as if it were a challenge, which it was, a challenge that the landlord wouldn't be taking up anytime soon. "You see according to my man on the inside, almost *everyone* was wearing those same leprechaun masks and our two robbers made their escape knowing that they wouldn't be spotted if everyone had the same mask on."

Declan shook his head.

"So, everyone was wearing the same mask, someone must've been selling 'em on one of the festival stalls outside."

The Fox shook his head.

"No, you're wrong on both counts."

The answer seemed to confuse the other men even more than they already were.

"*A*, they didn't buy the masks, they were given them, and *B*, they were given the masks inside the club not outside. You see there were more than just two robbers, they had someone helping them from inside. Someone important to the day's events, *someone* who was handing out the masks in order to cover the robbers' escape."

The Fox began to turn the razor-sharp knife over through his fingers, juggling it delicately between his knuckles.

"My little birdie told me that the singer from the band on the main stage was giving the masks out to the crowd. He said he'd seen the singer talking to one of the robbers from the stage on the CCTV footage just before the heist. Then the singer had begun to hand out masks by the handful to the audience."

Declan and McBride perked up at the explanation. The landlord turned to the young bouncer.

"Who was playing their yesterday?"

McBride thought for a second.

"Davey Keogh and the Wylde Green band!"

Declan seemed shocked.

"He's played here a few times!"

McBride nodded.

"I know, he's all right too, a good lad as far as I remember!"

Now it was the Fox's turn to perk up.

"And when he played here, did he have access to the office?"

Declan nodded.

"Yeah, that's where we pay the bands, why?"

The Fox raised his eyebrows.

"The office where you pay him, where you keep all the cash?"

Declan broke into an uncertain smile.

"The crafty bastard!" he said finally getting the point. The Dublin hitman nodded.

McBride was still none the wiser.

"So he had access to the office, so what?"

"Don't you get it?" Declan said happy that the emphasis to the conversation had drifted away from him for the time being, happy to lay some blame at someone else's feet for the moment. "If he had access to *our* office, then he's had access to the Irish Centre's office and anyone that's been in the office there, knows that there's a big old safe in there, a safe that would've been stuffed full of cash after the busiest week in the Irish calendar."

The Fox smiled his black-toothed smile again.

"There ya go, you ain't so stupid after all, are ye?" Now, there's also the point of the other Irish Pub robbery at the Brazen Maiden that happened and guess what?" He searched the faces of the men opposite but found nothing but more confusion, "This singer was playing at that venue on the night *it* was robbed too!"

He took a small note book from his jacket pocket, taking an old bookie's pencil from the breast pocket of his jacket he began to write a name in the scruffy little notepad.

He said the name as he wrote the words. "*Davey ... K.e.o.g.h ...*"

He drew a line under the name before putting the pencil away, laying the pad on the table and taking the knife from his belt once more. He began to juggle the weapon between his fingers before finally stabbing it into the scribbled name on the page.

"Well, as you know better than anyone, we are charging money for protection on these pubs and the I.R.A. can't be seen to be failing its duties by allowing some fucking singer to rob the places we're protecting. So let's find out where this singer is, bring him in and we'll see if we ..."

The Fox broke into a grin, " ... can't make him ... *sing!*"

CHAPTER 15

Loose Ends

1995

Dez sat across from his brother in the little office. Neil sat on the other side of the desk, a greedy self-assured smirk on his face. The two brothers sat in silence looking at the three separate piles of cash on the table.

"Not bad little bruv . . . " he finally said raising his eyebrows, pleased that his scheme had finally come to fruition, " . . . not bad at all!"

"Thirty-eight grand each Neil . . . !" Dez said as he drew on a cigarette, "Taking Number Two's share into account.

Neil's smile dropped from his face.

"What, you ain't gonna give that bonehead you work with the same share as us, are ya?"

Dez shrugged, nodding that that was exactly his intention.

"Yeah, he takes the same risks as I do so why shouldn't he get the same payout as us?"

Neil laughed sarcastically.

"Cos he ain't one of *us* that's why!"

Dez rolled his eyes.

"I owe him Neil, you know that!"

Neil leant forward and placed his hand on his desk.

"You owe him for what?"

"You know for what, if it hadn't been for him I'd have never survived in prison, he looked after me, watched my back ...!" His voice quivered with emotion. "Anyway I owe him ... "

"Yeah *you* owe him, I fucking don't ... " Neil's voice became firmer. "And how much longer is this debt going to last bruv, forever?"

Dez sighed.

"Nah it ain't like that."

Neil interrupted.

"And exactly what is it like Dez, shall I tell ya what it's like?" Neil snarled. "It's like this, that bald cunt you call *Number Two* is gonna keep holding that debt over your head for the rest of your fucking life, and if you don't wise up, he'll fuck it up for both of us."

"Nah he won't he's ... "

Neil stood up behind his desk and leant across it, his normally passive personality replaced by one of impatient fury.

"Wake the fuck up bruv, the cunt's using you. Don't you see, he's got us both over a barrel!"

Dez scrunched his handsome face up into an expression of puzzlement.

"Over a barrel, how so?"

Neil sat again, trying gather himself together and control his temper. He glanced at the girl in the other office to make sure she couldn't hear him before continuing.

"He's an old blag, ain't he?" he said, with a more sympathetic tone. "I mean he's spent most of his life either in prison and before that, when he was a kid, probably in borstal, he's forty odd years old and boasts that he spent most of those years behind bars, he's a fucking liability Dez."

Dez shook his head.

"Yeah he's spent a while in the nick, so what?"

"I'll tell ya so what, once a mug like that's on the loose, it's just a matter of time before he gets nicked again, it means nothing to him if he gets banged up. As a matter of fact, an arsehole like *Number Two* feels more comfortable *inside* than outside. So it's just a matter of time before it comes on top for him. I mean look what he did at the Brazen Maiden, he turned a small time heist into a fucking murder inquiry . . . "

Neil noticed his voice growing louder and tried to control himself again. He reached across the desk and took the third pile of cash and split it in two. Placing each on the bundles of cash on top of the other piles he sat back.

"Just for that alone he don't deserve to be paid.

"What!" Dez said astounded. "We ain't gonna pay him anything at all, he ain't gonna be too happy about that, is he?"

Neil chuckled.

"He ain't gonna be in a position to moan about it though, is he!" Dez shook his head.

"Oh, he'll moan about it alright."

Neil shook *his* head.

"Nah, not where he's going he won't!" Dez looked his older brother over and the two became silent for a while, Dez thought over the meaning of his brother's words, until Neil spoke again. "If you ain't got the guts Dez, I'll do it for ya!" Neil knew the barbed comment would press the right button and when Dez answered angrily it confirmed his suspicion.

"What, you think I couldn't do it?"

Neil sighed.

"Look, neither of us wanted this but that bonehead has brought it on himself when he killed the kid at the Irish pub, I mean, what if he does it again?"

His brother's words made sense.

"I know, I know you're right of course!" Dez had begun to resign himself to the inevitable. The commanding bravado he displayed so violently in public, quickly dissipated in the glare of his brother's alpha dog charisma.

"Yeah, you know I am, now bruv, you brought him in, you've gotta get him out. Thank God you had that stooge to take the blame, what's happening with that by the way?"

Dez's mind was elsewhere. He knew that Number Two wasn't exactly the type of man that could be talked to or reasoned with, especially when there was cash on the table, *his* cash. Number Two wasn't gonna take a hiding and walk away from it either. He would *have* to have payback, it'd be a matter of pride for him and so with a lack of alternatives available, that could only mean there was one way to handle it and so Birmingham's long list of unsolved murders would have to grow a little longer.

"Dez! Dez are you listening to me?" The question seemed to wake his younger brother from his dark thoughts. "I said, what's happening about the . . ." He tried to remember what his brother had said in their first phone call about the robbery at the Brazen Maiden.

"The Patsy . . ." Dez replied sharply, " . . . yeah I heard ya."

Neil raised his eyebrows at his brother irritable reply.

"Well?"

"Well, nothing, you've talked to the copper involved, you showed him the CCTV footage so you probably know more about it than I do. I did my bit by handing the masks to that *bastard* onstage and leaving the bag of cash at the Irish pub!"

Neil sat back in his chair a bemused expression growing across his face. He knew his brother, and he knew that Dez's little outburst wasn't just impatience towards him. He could see Dez not only had a real dislike towards the man they had chosen to take the fall for the robberies but there was something else troubling him too, something that he didn't want to talk about. He decided to broach the subject.

"You don't like this patsy do ya our kid?"

Dez's face flushed, embarrassed that his brother had easily seen through his angry smoke screen. He shrugged nonchalantly, trying to hide his real feelings.

"He's nothing to me."

Neil laughed.

"Is this something to do with your little project of trying to get into the knickers of that Fewtrell girl, what's her name?"

Dez was shocked that his brother was so close to the mark.

"Abi, Abi Fewtrell, yeah, well, she seems to have hit it off with our Irish stooge."

"What the *singer*?" Neil said incredulously. Dez nodded.

"Yeah, the fucker snaked me over the girl!"

Neil shrugged.

"Well, that's an easy fix our kid!"

A mischievous smile broke across Neil's face. "After the old Bill have questioned and released him, we'll do the bastard, do you know where he lives?"

Dez smiled, remembering the secluded canal-side retreat that would be perfect for some payback. His mind ran over the image of the two young lovers inside the canal boat in the soft, yellow candle-glow, as he watched from his hidden vantage point on the dark, misty tow path just outside the narrowboat's windows. He allowed his twisted mind to wallow in the feelings of jealousy, until a visible shiver of rage ran through him. Neil saw his younger brother's anger and decided to take advantage of it – channel it into their project.

"There's something else isn't there Dez, something you're not telling me!"

Dez smiled, trying to disguise his shock at his brother's insight. However, his dark eyes betrayed his inwardly feelings of doubt as the shifted from side to side, as if searching for a way to answer his older sibling.

"It's . . . " he stuttered, "It's nothing!"

"It's something, I can read you like a cheap paperback our kid, so come on fess up!" An uncomfortable silence fell between the two until Neil spoke. "Come on, it can't be that bad can it?"

Dez sighed.

"I can't be sure but if think the singer saw my tattoo through my surgical glove. There was a light over the stage and it made the rubber virtually transparent."

Dez held his hand up to his brother, showing him the swallow and five-pointed star tattooed in dark blue ink. He shook the hand, as if the tattoo would somehow fall off his skin before planting it in the pocket of his trousers. Neil watched him with a concerned glare.

"There's something else!" Dez continued. "The Brazen Maiden!"

Neil already alarmed, visibly perked up, his concerned look now replaced by a more urgent one.

"What about it?"

"I was seen!" Neil shook his head.

"But you pair were wearing the nylons over your faces?"

"No, when I was outside getting in the car, a tart . . . "

"*What* you took the fucking nylon *off*?"

Dez shrugged.

"I was getting in the car the job was done, it was dark, I didn't think anyone was around did I?"

"But there *was* someone around, wasn't there?" Neil asked sarcastically.

Dez nodded. "Who?"

"Like I said a . . . " Dez tried to find a way to describe the transvestite he'd seen in the doorway that night. "A tranny or whatever it is you call em?"

Dez's description was inadequate, so he decided to explain the whole chain of events that led to him being seen without his disguise by the transvestite. Neil sat back in his chair and listened to the story with a look of disbelief, finally interrupting his younger brother.

"Well, he, she . . . whoever . . . or . . . whatever it was that saw you ain't been to the old Bill to tell em anything yet, so it shouldn't be a problem should it?"

Dez raised his eyebrows.

"It's easy to say that when it ain't your mug that's been spotted is it. If this queer fucker goes to the old Bill, they'll know that there was someone else there the night of the robbery. Never mind when the old Bill interviews the singer."

Dez began to pace up and down the small office. Neil spoke up.

"There's only one thing for it!" he said after some thought. Dez raised his hands.

"Whoa, whoa hold your horses, let's not get ahead of ourselves here. We ain't murderers!"

"And we ain't common thieves either bruv." Neil said sternly. "We're *businessmen*, and that's the difference. May I remind you, that this little nest egg we're busy putting together from the pub robberies, is gonna set us both up for the rest of our days!" He let the words sink in before continuing. "Now if that means we gotta tie up some loose ends along the way, then so be it, Number Two, this Irish singer, the transvestite and whoever else gets in our way, *including* your Fewtrell girl if needs must. They have to be taken out of the equation in whatever way we deem necessary, understand?"

Dez nodded reluctantly.

"So you had better harden the fuck up our kid and go take care of our first little problem."

"Which is what?" Dez asked.

Neil smirked and held up two fingers silently mouthing the words.

"Number Two."

CHAPTER 16

A Familiar Face

1995

"You are joking Jobbo, tell me you're fucking joking!"

Eddie Fewtrell was busy giving the Black country cellar man a dose of emotional blackmail he wasn't going to forget in a hurry.

"I mean, I took a chance on employing you when no one else would, and *now* you're telling me you want the weekend off?"

The skinny cellar man stared at his feet, unable to return Eddie's glare.

"It's just that ..." he stuttered, " ... I'm."

Eddie cut him short.

"You're a lazy cunt, that's what you are son. What am I meant to do this weekend?"

Eddie glanced around the room, to make sure his bullying wasn't being overheard. He lowered his voice a little.

"Shall I just tell the punters to stay at home, just because you want the fucking weekend off?"

Jobbo shook his head.

"No Mr Fewtrell, I ... I"

Eddie didn't give him a chance.

"I ... I ... I'm a cunt. That's what you should be saying son!"

Jobbo swallowed the growing lump in his throat and plucked up his courage.

"I did tell you I needed this Saturday off Mr. Fewtrell!"

The words brought Eddie's rant to a standstill. He knew the man had said something but he hadn't taken any notice of him and he wouldn't have cared even if he had.

"Call me Eddie son, not Mr Fewtrell, that's me old man's name, god bless his soul."

Eddie's hot and cold manic change of mood caught most people by surprise, and Jobbo the cellar man fell for it straight away.

"Ok Eddie, I told you two weeks ago that I was . . ."

"I don't really give a fuck what you said son. I'm the boss and I say . . ."

Now it was Jobbo's turn to interrupt.

" . . . but I'm getting *married* on Saturday, Eddie!" the cellar man blurted.

"Oh congratulations . . ." Eddie replied without missing a heartbeat. "Eh . . . what's your name again?"

"Bob, Eddie but everyone calls me Jobbo!"

Eddie smiled,

"Bob-a job?" Eddie's smile vanished as he searched for a silver lining to this particular cloud. "What time are you getting married son?"

Jobbo's face broke into a nervous smile.

"Twelve thirty Eddie, you can come to the wedding if you . . ."

"So you're getting married at twelve thirty . . ." Jobbo nodded, " . . . so what's the problem with you working on Saturday night then?" Jobbo's smile sank into a frown.

"But it's my wedding night Eddie!" his words were said with a little too much impatience. However, Eddie just smiled catching the man off-guard again.

"Bring the Mrs. down to the club, after you've finished your work in the cellar, you can have the V.I.P. treatment. I'll even give you and the wife some free bubbly and take you home in me rolla at the end of the night, treat you like a couple of film stars!"

Jobbo pretended to think it over.

"But what about our wedding guests?"

Eddie's ears perked up.

"Guests?"

"Yeah, guests, we got over one hundred and fifty guests coming to our reception in the function room at O'Neill's pub on Broad Street, Eddie."

In the time it took to answer, Eddie had performed a lighting fast mental calculation, and knew he couldn't miss the opportunity of having so many people drinking in his night club, and thus decided to go above and beyond to make sure the scruffy little cellar man wouldn't have any choice but to bring his guests to XL's nightclub, instead of some pub five hundred yards down the road.

"Of course son, I understand." he said, his tone now conciliatory. "It's all been planned months in advance by your fiancée, I suppose."

Jobbo nodded.

"They've given us the top room for our party and thrown in some food."

Eddie gave him his most charming smile.

"That's very nice of em. Well look, if anything changes, you know you've always got my offer to fall back on. I'll look after all your guests and you and your Mrs. as if you were all pop stars."

Eddie patted the man's shoulder.

"And, of course you can have the night off, Jobbo."

A broad white-toothed smile broke Eddie's face, returned by a toothless one from the cellar man.

"Thank you, Eddie!"

"No problem son, no problem"

Eddie turned as if to leave but stopped after a step or two.

"By the way . . . " he said trying to hide a wry smile, " . . . where did you say you're having the reception again?"

****

Dixie found Eddie in his office halfway through what appeared to be a passionate telephone conversation.

"I told ya, it won't be happening anymore!" Eddie snarled into the receiver.

On seeing Dixie, Eddie gestured with a smile that the detective should sit. Dixie stepped into the space as quietly as possible and plonked himself into the office chair.

"Look, do you know who you're talking to, son?"

Dixie could hear the tinny sound of the other man's voice on the far end of the line. Eddie kept interrupting the man he was talking to.

"Well, I'll tell ya sonny, this is Eddie Fewtrell here!"

Eddie's smile fell from his face, "Never heard of me, well, you'll fucking hear of me in a minute dickhead. Now if I say the wedding party's off, then it's off, understand?"

Eddie winked at Dixie who stared back with a puzzled expression.

"Look I ain't got all bleeding day so I'll explain this in a way you'll understand!" Eddie said, exasperated. "We can do this one of two ways sunshine, either you can call the wedding party and tell em you've had to cancel their reception in your pub and we won't say anything more about it or I can come down there with my crew and I can stuff that fucking telephone up your arse sideways and then *you* can call the wedding party and tell em it's off. Either way, the fucking party's off."

Eddie rolled his eyes towards Dixie.

Placing his hand over the receiver he whispered, "I'll be with you in a minute Dix, I've just gotta educate this twat as to the way things run in Brum!"

The tinny sound of the other man's voice became louder as he reacted predictably to Eddie's words, warning Eddie that he would call the police. Eddie burst out laughing.

"You're threatening to call old Bill, are ya?" Eddie winked at Dixie again. "Tell ya what, I'll save ya the hassle."

Eddie leant across the desk and handed the receiver to Dixie. "Eh-ar Dixie, have a word with this twat will ya? He seems to be hard of hearing!"

Dixie took the receiver with a resigned smile, placing it to his ear he listened to the man on the other end venting his spleen. He waited until the shower of expletives began to slow down before speaking.

"Hello, this is Detective Inspector John Dixon here, who am I talking to?"

The line went quiet.

"Hello?" Dixie asked again.

The bar manager on the other end of the line spoke again, only this time without the so much fire in his voice.

"Who is this?" he asked.

"As I said . . ." Dixie repeated. "This is Detective inspector John Dixon here, who am I talking to?"

"Ehh . . . how do I know you're the police?" the man replied.

Dixie's voice became serious, tinted with an official tone.

"You'll know soon enough sunshine, when I come down there with my friends from the council and shut the fucking place down!"

The Bar Manager's voice became cocky again.

"Oh yeah? How are ya gonna do that then?"

"However I fucking like pal!" Dixie snapped. "You ain't from round here are ya?"

The other man laughed.

"What's that got to do with anything?"

"It's got everything to do with it mate and to be honest, I don't really give a fuck where you're from, the point is, that you're *here*, in *Birmingham*, and this town belongs to two people, me and Eddie Fewtrell, and if Eddie says the weddings off, then it's off, end of, and if you continue to go against his wishes, well, that's where I get involved and that is the last thing you want cos I'll have the council boys all over your arse until it just won't be worth you opening at all. *Now* do you understand?"

The line was silent.

"Now, make the fucking call and cancel the fucking wedding party if you know what's good for ya!"

Eddie held his hand out and Dixie passed him the receiver back.

"I'll give you an hour to cancel it. If I haven't heard back by then, I'll be coming down to have a word with you face to face. Alright? *Tarah*!"

Eddie slammed the phone down.

"What the fuck was that all about Eddie?" Dixie asked.

Eddie just shrugged.

"Business is business Dix, I gotta get the punters in somehow. There's pubs, bars and nightclubs popping up all over the bleeding shop these days.

"Yeah but is it worth the hassle?" Dixie said, trying to understand why Eddie would go to so much trouble to grab a few customers from another venue.

"Probably not but what am I meant to do? Just sit back and let these fuckers take all my business away?" He sat back in his large office chair and began to rock back and forth slowly. "To be honest, I'm worried Dix, the city ain't what it used to be. My clubs are half empty most of the time and I'm haemorrhaging money left, right and bleeding centre. It's like the young people want to do other things these days. The fuckers would rather dance all weekend in an old, piss-stinking warehouse listening to some amateur DJ on a shit sound system, than come to one of *my* clubs. I don't know what the nightclub scene is coming to Dix, I really don't!"

The detective watched his old friend with a passive eye from the other side of the desk. He had seen Eddie upset plenty of times before but never with such a manic look of desperation in his eye and Dixie thought he might be witnessing the first tremors of a nervous breakdown that would come to fruition somewhere further down the road.

"Anyway . . ." Eddie continued, " . . . another visit so soon, that's twice in ten years Dixie, what's going on?"

Dixie became serious.

"There's something you need to see, Eddie."

Without warning Dixie rose and crossed to a bank of small CCTV monitors that sat on a shelf to the side of Eddie's desk. He found the video player that fed the screens and pressed the eject button. Eddie watched him with a bemused expression as the detective pulled a video cassette from his raincoat pocket and pressed it into the slot at the front of the machine.

"What ya got there Dix, porn?" Eddie said with a laugh.

Dixie ignored him, pushing in the cassette, the machine came to life with a whirr of plastic cogs and electronic beeps. The little screen next to the player came to life in a flash of white noise and crackly images, before finally settling into the image of a stage with a band playing on it. The CCTV camera was positioned high above the stage and its small lens captured the heads of the audience as they danced and rocked along to the band. Dixie sat on the bench next to the monitor and turned to look at Eddie. Without looking at the screen he pointed at the images.

"Recognise anyone, Ed?"

Eddie looked from the detective to the screen with a fresh grimace.

"Who am I looking for?"

"Don't worry you'll know who it is when you see em!" Dixie said seriously watching Eddie's baffled expression change to one of concern. "There ya go Ed, you've spotted her!"

"It's our Abi, what's she doing?"

"She's watching a band, Ed!"

Eddie nodded.

"Yeah I can see that, what's the problem?"

Dixie sighed.

"If it were just that then there wouldn't be a problem, it's what happens at the end of the show that's the problem!"

Eddie watched his daughter dancing at the front of the stage, he could see she was enthralled with the blond vocalist. Dixie, leant across the monitor and pressed the fast-forward button. The screen exploded into a scribble of white lines and images moving way too fast, making them seem comical as if it were an early keystone cops drama from the early 1900s. Taking his finger from the button the video slowed to normal speed. Now the concert was over, the crowd were dancing to a DJ's music and the band were busy clearing the stage, the singer and Eddie's daughter no longer in view. Dixie pointed to a shadow at the side of the large stage.

"Here!"

Eddie scrunched his eyes together, trying to make out what Dixie was pointing at.

"What's she doing?"

Dixie smirked.

"She snogging someone!"

Eddie shook his head.

"So what, what's the big deal?"

"Kissing someone ain't no big deal Ed, the big deal is *who* she's kissing!"

Eddie leant forward trying to make out who the man in the image was. Dixie stopped the tape.

"His name is Davey Keogh, he's the singer in an Irish band called *Wylde Green* !

"*Wild Green* ?" Eddie said trying to understand the choice in band names.

Dixie shrugged.

"Wylde with a Y . . . Fuck knows Ed. anyway the point is, that during this gig at the Irish Centre, the place was robbed to the value of one hundred and fifty grand, by two blokes wearing leprechaun masks."

Eddie became more confused.

"Leprechauns?" he said trying to stifle a laugh. "Is this what the West Midlands Police do now Dixie? Chase fucking leprechauns around? I'm looking forward to seeing this re-enacted on *Crimewatch U.K.* I'll tell ya!" he said sarcastically. "But what the fuck has this got to do with Abi and that bloke?"

"I'll tell ya Ed, your daughter Abi, is knocking around with our one and only suspect for the heist and by the look of things . . . " he tapped the small screen with its frozen image of the two young people in a passionate embrace, " . . . I'd say they know each other pretty well, wouldn't you?"

"*Suspect*?" Eddie asked.

Dixie nodded.

"I ain't saying he's involved but another pub was robbed earlier this month and guess who was playing at that pub too.

"Wylde Green?"

Dixie nodded.

"Wylde Green. Now I've watched this video several times and he does make contact with one of the robbers but it may have been coincidental."

Eddie shrugged.

"So it's possible he's not involved at all?"

Dixie shook his head and sighed.

"You're missing the point, Eddie."

"Am I? Well perhaps you'd like to share the *point* with me?" Eddie said, growing tired of the detective's tact.

"The I.R.A. is the point Ed!"

Eddie scrunched his face into a confused expression.

"I.R.A.? all that shit's over and done with now!"

Dixie nodded.

"Yeah, but they're still around, still doing the collections around all the Irish Pubs. Trust me, they ain't gone anywhere!"

"Sorry you've lost me Dix, who are we talking about now? The singer, the robber's or the I.R.A.?"

"All of em, Eddie." Dixie said with a scowl. "Look, the Irish Centre is one of the *only* Irish run venue that the I.R.A. don't take a cut from and there's a very good reason for that. After the 1970's pub bombings in town, the Birmingham Irish community was brought to its knees. Something that, quite rightly was never forgotten *or* forgiven by the Brummie Irish and the I.R.A., or whoever planted those bombs know that. Hence, the Irish Centre has always been out of bounds to any collections for the *cause* and then out of the blue, these two leprechauns rob the place on the busiest week of the year. We can't identify the men in the masks but we can identify the only other person that makes contact with them during the heist." Dixie tapped the small screen with his finger. "The singer."

He left Eddie to do the calculations. Eddie sat looking between the detective and the screen with a blank expression on his face. Dixie sighed once more and continued his explanation.

"If this singer *is* involved with the robbery, then he and our two leprechauns are gonna be at the top of the I.R.A. hit-list and if your daughter Abi is involved with the singer, then it brings things a little too close to home, don't you think? I'm telling you now Eddie, it won't be long before this singer gets a visit from the boys of the old Brigade and if Abi is around him at the time it could be dangerous for her!"

The penny dropped.

"I know loads of *duck eggs*, everyone in Brum knows that Eddie Fewtrell is a friend of the Birmingham Irish."

Dixie shook his head.

"These cunts ain't ya normal Paddies, Ed. We've had a report from the Irish special branch that one of Dublin's meanest hitmen is on Brummie soil and taking control of all the I.R.A. collections. If this Davey Keogh is involved, we need to know."

"And if he ain't?" Eddie asked.

"Then we need to explain to him just how thin the ice beneath his feet is!"

****

The Fox and McBride slowly walked the canal side of Gas Street Basin searching for signs of the Irish singer. They knew he lived in one of the fifty or so boats that lined the waterway that ran under Broad Street.

McBride hadn't been down this part of town for years and was surprised by the amount of construction work going on along the old Victorian canals. There was something about the water that made the place feel exotic to him, like walking on to a film set. He glanced at the Fox to see if the scene was having the same effect on him but one look at the scrawny hitman told him that he had his mind on the job at hand.

After a midnight visit, Shaun had told them everything he knew about the two men in the masks, which in all honesty wasn't a great deal. With some prodding from the Fox however, he had eventually managed to drag out more detail and what Shaun didn't find out he simply made up. During this conversation he unwittingly confirmed the identity of the Irish performer who had been onstage at the time. It wasn't exactly a secret amongst the small community of Birmingham landlords that the *Brazen Maiden* had been robbed and this same Irish singer had been performing there too. It all added up to either a huge coincidence or the conclusion as Declan O'Dwyer put it that '*the fucker's involved'* which was why the pair were now trudging the cobbles along the stretch of canal leading to the Gas Street Basin.

Two swans drifted along on the gentle flow of the waterway, their majestic whiteness contrasted dramatically with the filthy black water on which they floated. The morning sun was still rising and the men walked in the shadow of a high, red-brick wall along the bank of the canal, following the steady progress of the swans. The Fox's thin red eyes searched every nook and cranny along every boat they came across searching for something that would give the whereabouts of the singer's narrowboat away.

The uneven cobbles were wet with the morning dew and McBride's leather-soled shoes had already slipped a couple of times, nearly sending him sprawling into the water, much to the Fox's delight, who laughed spitefully at the burly doorman whenever it happened. The Irish man reached down to the fallen bouncer and pulled him to his feet. The doorman reluctantly took the other man's hand and righted himself. He dusted down the dirt from his black jeans, trying not to catch the Fox's eye, knowing that if he did he'd have to show his appreciation. As he did so McBride caught sight of a celtic shamrock window decoration on one of the narrowboats. The Irish design on the faux stained-glass window ornament drew his attention. He recognised the ornament as the same ones sold by John Fitzgerald in the shop at the Irish Centre and so he scanned the rest of the boat for something similar. There were other telltale signs that whoever owned this particular canal boat had some Irish connection.

The canalboat's name, *Hideaway,* was written in a Celtic font and there was a tiny Irish tricolour flag poking out of a potted plant on the rear deck area and suddenly McBride knew that this boat belonged to the man they were after. Turning to the Fox he pointed towards the narrowboat.

"Get ready to be happy, Foxy!"

The Dublin man's eye followed the bouncer's finger until it came to rest on the boat. He turned back to the doorman and patted his broad shoulders. The action caught the young bouncer by surprise.

"Well done Scan, you've just got yourself in me good books."

The Fox turned away and began to walkaway down the tow path towards the boat's small rear deck area.

"You stay here and watch the front of the boat!" he called over his shoulder.

McBride watched him leave, happy with the Dublin man's approval. The thin man stepped onto the deck of the boat, which shifted its centre of gravity in the water under his weight. McBride walked to the front of the boat and continued to watch with fresh interest. The Dublin man leant down and tried the boat's small rear door but found them locked with a small padlock from the outside. He stood up and looked at McBride, shaking his head, pointing towards a small bench he said.

"He's not home, I think we should wait for him over there." he said pointing towards a small bench along the canal side.

They sat on the bench and began their vigil just as the sun rose high over the red-bricked buildings, the bright orb's rays changing the black canal water into a light brown soup. The little community of boats began to stir as the men watched and the city around the peaceful enclave began to hum once more as another day started above the sunken waterway. The sun rose higher and still there was no sign of the man they were after. The unlikely pair sat on an old bench and watched the scene come to life around them. McBride yawned, already bored by the proceedings, he was exhausted from the previous night's work keeping a beady eye on the dancing Brummie Irish drunks and travellers from his post at the door of the Dublin Barrel.

"This is bullshit mate!" he suddenly exclaimed. "He ain't coming, is he? We're wasting our fucking time sitting here on this bench like a couple of rent boys!"

The Fox gave him a sideways glance.

"Rent boys? That's a laugh, who would want to rent a pair of cunts like us?"

McBride laughed, surprised at the quick wit of the other man.

"Yeah, fuck this for a game of soldiers!" McBride answered. "We'll have to come back another time, catch the cunt off-guard!"

He turned to look at the other man and instead of the sarcastic Dublin hitman, he saw someone who was tired. Not just physically tired but mentally worn out. A sorrowful melancholy seemed to have fallen over the hard man as if a dark cloud had passed overhead. His normally red eyes were now a watery blue as the depression of a sulphate come-down had begun to settle into the Dubliner's bones.

McBride saw for the first time that *this* was the real man that had been hiding beneath the amphetamines all this time. The sharp-tongued knifeman who had dominated the last few days was simply a facade put up in order to survive the dog eat dog, I.R.A., underworld back in Dublin. In reality, McBride could see that this man was caught in a trap of his own making, a trap that would tighten around his throat and strangle the life from him without a moment's notice if he showed any kind of weakness, humanity or mercy to his fellow man. What he would do with this new insight into the hit-man's personality, he wasn't quite sure yet but he'd seen the killer's weakness plain as day and the bouncer knew that at some point in the not too distant future, he might be glad of that.

"Fancy a fry up?" McBride said pointing to the bridge overhead as nonchalantly as possible. "The rendezvous cafe is just up there on Broad Street?"

The Fox's moment of self-doubt vanished in an instant and turning to the doorman with his blue-grey watery eyes, he scanned the other man's brutal face. In it he saw a fresh confidence, something the doorman had never displayed around him before. The Fox considered whether the seeds of a friendship might have spouted. However, in the back of his mind he also knew that McBride had just seen behind the veil he'd draped about himself for protection and as far as the Fox was concerned, from that moment on, the doorman's days were numbered.

"Fucking right I do, I'm starving."

****

"Abi, it's ya dad!" Eddie said sternly.

The girl's answer was slow to come, she could hear a hint of aggression in her father's voice. It had taken only thirty or so minutes of phone calls to track the whereabouts of his daughter down to the *Edgbaston Palace Hotel* on the old Hagley Road.

"Oh hello, Dad." she knew Eddie Fewtrell's business voice only too well and although she wasn't too shocked about her father knowing where she'd spent the night, the tone of his voice meant one of two things; money or trouble and she wasn't expecting any money.

"What's up?" she said trying to hide anything that might betray the growing uneasy feeling in her stomach.

"Where are ya, Abs?" the question seemed a strange one.

"You know where I am Dad. I'm . . . "

His question was left unanswered as Abigail realised her answer might not be the right one. Eddie left the line silent. He already knew why the answer was slow to come and so decided to oil the wheels a little.

"You need to come into the office, our kid."

He looked across his desk at Dixie who was busy examining another of Eddie's magic tea mugs. This one had a blonde *Baywatch* babe in a red bikini. As soon as the hot tea had warmed the porcelain, the *babe* slowly became naked as her bikini magically vanished.

"Straight away if you can Abs, it's very important." Eddie continued, a softer tone to his voice now.

Abi picked up on the change of tone and knew everything was going to be all right. It was getting increasingly difficult to know the difference between her father's emotions these days. Anyway his previous urgency, if indeed it was urgency, seemed to have passed and she turned to look at the blonde Irishman laying in the bed next to her and smiled nervously.

"Ok Dad, I'll be there in about an hour!"

"Perfect Abi." Eddie's voice suddenly cheerful, "Oh and by the way, bring that singer with you, will ya? I'd like to meet him. Tarah, bab!"

With that the phone line went dead. Abi's heart skipped a beat. The hollow feeling she'd felt earlier, now suddenly returned with a vengeance.

"*Shit*!"

Davey stroked the soft skin on her naked shoulder.

"What's wrong?" he said sleepily.

"It's my Dad!" she said earnestly. "He wants me to come into his office . . . " she turned to look at her lover, " . . . and he wants you to come in with me!"

Davey shook his head, puzzled.

"How did he know I was here?"

Abi slung her long legs over the edge of the bed, sitting with her back to him and sighed softly.

"My Dad seems to know everything that happens in Birmingham!"

"But how did he . . . ?"

"Oh he's got eyes everywhere, doormen, barmen, taxi drivers, coppers, so on, so on and so on. It's been the same all my life. I can't go out with anyone without my father getting involved."

Davey watched the girl's shoulders slump slightly and he could feel her sadness. He pulled himself to the side of the bed and the two sat beside each other naked. He put his arm around her shoulder and she nestled into the space beneath his neck.

"It'll be ok, kiddo."

Abi pressed her head a little closer.

"You don't understand, if my Dad doesn't like you, then it's over between us!"

There was a finality in her words that left no doubt in the Irishman's mind that there was a touch of fear in the love she held towards her father.

"Well, surely you have some choice in who you see?"

Abi shook her head.

"No, I've had it my whole life, if he doesn't like my friends, he'll either mug you off or pay you off!"

Davey laughed.

"Well, the latter sounds better to me!"

Abi tutted, nudging him in the ribs with her elbow.

"I'm being *serious*!" she said, laughing herself now.

"Oh, so am I!" Davey said, feigning pain from her blow. He rolled onto the floor holding his side.

"Oh my God, you don't half take after your father. Look at me, I'm being beaten up by Eddie Fewtrell's daughter, violence must run in the family!"

She reached down towards him.

"Come on, stop messing around, Dad's gonna be waiting for us!"

He grabbed the girl's arm and pulled her onto the floor. She fell on top of him her legs astride his waist, her soft blonde hair hanging over both their faces. He pulled her down towards him and kissed her passionately.

"Let him wait!"

CHAPTER 17

Coffee and Cakes

1995

Dez found Number Two in the smoky back-street cafe behind Digbeth high street. He could just make out his accomplice's bald head and brutal features through the steamy windows as he sat opposite another bald man, the two of them talking earnestly over their cups of frothy coffee.

Dez opened the door and stepped into the cafe. The smell of cigarette smoke and old grease enveloped him instantly almost making him gag. The sound of nattering, blue-rinsed, old women mingled with the tinny sound of Radio 1 pop songs blasted from a radio somewhere behind the glass-topped counter. A twenty-something, heavily made-up woman stood behind the counter looking, for all intents and purposes, like she had been steaming her face over the deep-fat fryer, her shiny face slick with grease, acknowledged his entrance with a short nod and a far from sexy false eye-lashed wink. He crossed the space between the door and the counter, squeezing himself between the chairs and old women. He glanced at Number Two's table. Neither man had noticed his entrance.

"Coffee, please love."

The girl flickered her eyelashes at him.

"Sugar?"

Dez nodded blankly. He took the cup of brown froth, slapped two pound coins on the counter.

"Keep the change, love."

He turned towards the table on the far wall. The girl placed her hand on the note, a look of disappointment on her face.

"Thanks, big spender!" she said sarcastically but the man was already out of earshot.

As he approached the table he could hear his accomplice telling the other man about the robbery at the Brazen Maiden.

"Are you two planing your wedding or what?"

Dez addressed the two men, who were talking almost head to head across the table. Number two and the other man turned simultaneously to see the younger man standing at the table's edge, cupping his coffee in both hands. He smiled innocently as he dragged a chair from another table, the feet squealing on the linoleum flooring as he did so, the sound adding to the cacophony inside the small cafe. He placed it at the end of the table and plonked himself down on it unceremoniously.

"Well, whatever it is you're talking about, my ears are burning!"

The statement and sudden unannounced appearance caught both men by surprise. They looked at each other like guilty schoolboys caught smoking a crafty fag behind the proverbial bike sheds.

"Eh Dez, I err, . . . " Number Two stumbled over his words trying to establish whether the young man had heard any of the conversation he'd been having with his old jail mate opposite. Dez raised his eyebrows.

"Mind if I join ya?"

The question was a rhetorical one, as he'd already pulled his chair into the table and was resting his elbows on the red-checkered, vinyl-covered table with his coffee cup still in hand. The bald man looked at the man opposite before nodding.

"Eh? Yeah, yeah of course you can join us, boss!"

Dez gave Number Two a weak smile before turning his attention to the other man.

"I take it this is a pal of yours from nick?" he said with a nod of the head.

Number Two suddenly seemed embarrassed and didn't answer. The other man just stared back at Dez with a well-rehearsed prison glare that was meant to unsettle whoever it was aimed at. It didn't work, Dez knew that due to his surprise arrival he had the upper hand in the situation and returned the brutal stare with a sarcastic smile.

"And I suppose that you've been telling your pal here about our little scheme?" He turned to look at Number Two, his smile suddenly dropping from his face.

"Eh? Nah, we was just talking about old times, Dez!"

Dez's smile returned.

"Old times, in nick?" He said with a laugh. "What? Like who was shagging who in the showers!"

Number Two gave a nervous chuckle.

"Nah, we ain't queers, Dez!"

Dez placed his coffee on the table.

"What, you've been in prison most of your life and you ain't dabbled in a bit of buggery? Fuck off, you two *must* be a pair of bum boys."

He said the words as spitefully as he could, trying to get a reaction from either of the men. It worked.

"We *ain't* queers!" the other man spat vehemently.

Dez shrugged.

"Of course you ain't sunshine. Anyway, it don't count if you're in the nick, does it?"

For the first time the other man began to lose his cool.

"I fucking told ya! We ain't' bent and even if we were what the fuck's it got to do with you!"

"Look, if you pair shared a cell together and were balls deep in each other's arseholes every night, that's got fuck all to do with me, has it? I mean that's no one's business but your own, right? I mean, I don't give a fuck if you're the Village fucking People. If you can find love in a man's hairy arse that's your business, not mine!"

The other man's nostrils flared as he began his retort.

"Yeah, that's right it ain't any of your fucking business! So why don't you just f . . ."

Dez cut him short.

" . . . I'll tell ya what is my business though . . ." the words stopped the man in his tracks, " . . . what you pair were yapping about when I arrived!"

He placed the coffee cup down and placed his hands flat on the table and addressed Number Two.

"When I walk in here and find you talking openly to this fucker about *my* fucking business, alarm bells start to go off in my head." He turned to look at the other man.

"Those alarm bells make me think that maybe I've made a mistake in trusting you Number Two. That maybe the reason you've spent so long inside is because you've got a big fucking mouth that you can't keep shut!"

Number Two shook his head.

"No boss, it ain't like that. Bull here has just got out the nick and needs a start. I've been filling him in on what we're doing. I thought maybe he could work with us!"

"You thought? You ain't here to do any thinking sunshine. You're the fucking muscle in the operation, not the brains."

He turned to look at the other man's meaty pock-marked, tattooed face, trying to weigh him up. He was older than Number Two by about five or six years and he had a look of desperation about him that made him seem fearful and pathetic in equal measure. The tattoos on his face and neck were mostly homemade blue-ink jobs, done on the inside by the look of it and mainly through boredom rather than any aesthetic or political agendas. The realisation that Number Two had already told the man too much began to dawn on him and so Dez changed tack.

"So you need a job?"

The other man suddenly became ridiculously subservient and if he'd worn a hat, Dez was sure he would've tipped it to him as if he'd been some sort of lord.

"Oh yes boss, I do. Me old pal here says you got a number going on robbing pubs!"

The words sent a tingle of panic up Dez's spine.

"Shhh ... shut the fuck up!" he whispered.

Number Two laughed.

"These old bags can't hear us, Dez. All they're interested in is fucking knitting!"

Dez leant forward into Number Two's face.

"And that's the reason why you've spent most of your life in fucking jail. You've got a big fucking mouth Number Two!"

The other man nodded.

"He's right, you have, *Number Two,* a fucking big mouth, you always did have!" He said spitefully.

Dez turned to look at the older man with a new respect.

"What's ya name?"

"They call me Bull, boss!"

Dez's mind began to create a silver lining from this cloud.

"Ok, Bull, you've got the job, now, me, you and Number Two have got to track down someone that could be a problem for us, someone that could recognise me." He pointed at the older man. "*You'll* have to take care of that problem as a sort of ... " he searched for the right word, something to give the Bull the impression he was entering an exclusive club, " ... *initiation,* into our little group if ya like. Can you do that?"

"I can do that, boss. I can do *anyone* you put in front of me as long as there's a picture of the Queen's head at the end of it!"

"Oh your money worries will be over Bull. *After* you've taken this person out of the equation, you'll get your reward. I guarantee it!"

CHAPTER 18

Abduction 1961

(continued)

After a change of heart, Toddy decided that the little blond puppy would never find itself drowning in a bag in the murky-brown water of the local cut. He was far too valuable for that. Toddy could see a day in the not too distant future when the kid would come in useful, especially if Ronnie Fletcher or any other members of the West Midlands Police were to come down hard on the Meat Market Mob. Yes, little Daniel Fletcher was Toddy Burns' very own get-out-of jail card.

Now, at first glance this seemed to have been a lucky turn of events for the little boy. However, a quick death by drowning in a canal would soon prove to be far more preferable a fate than the lifetime of physical, sexual and mental abuse the lad would suffer over the next thirty odd years, initially by Duncan Jarvis, then later, but no less painfully, at the hands of his older step brother, Tigger Burns.

The boy was snatched up, still wrapped in the coat and smuggled back to Toddy's council flat, where he was dumped unceremoniously with Toddy's downtrodden subservient wife, until such a time as Toddy would need to pull this blond trump card from his pocket. Only two people knew the true identity of little Daniel and thanks to the untimely death of Jarvis a few months after the abduction, the secret remained solely with Toddy Burns and would have stayed that way if karma hadn't come a-calling in the form of a gunshot to the head and a powerful heroin overdose.

Tigger Burns never forgot the horrific sight and smell of his father's dead body. After all, by the time Toddy's cadaver was discovered, he had been sitting in his favourite armchair for weeks, slowly decomposing in his bloodstained, silver mohair suit. The rats had had a field day, beginning with his wide, smack eyes, followed closely by his nose, ears then the rest of his face until all that remained was a black-holed skull with a mop of black, curly hair. The image and gag-inducing odour was burned into Tigger's mind and if Jarvis's sexual abuse hadn't tipped the fragile minded 12-year old over the mental precipice, then this horrific scene certainly did.

Soon after these tragic events Toddy's widow decided to relocate her flock of scarred, ugly ducklings to London. She never mentioned her husband's name again and Tigger unconsciously blocked any thoughts of his father from his mind. Instead he recreated the torture perpetrated by Jarvis, on this strange little boy who had just turned up one night, out of the blue. As is often the case in situations like this, abuse follows abuse. Passed down from father to son, from son to stepson, stepson to . . . , like a family heirloom the rot crept through the generations until it finally destroyed any self-esteem the abducted little boy had possessed. After two decades when Tigger had had his fill of Daniel he decided to return to Birmingham to address some unanswered questions of his own. Unfortunately, for him the only answer Tigger found was a deadly fall from a fire escape at the rear of a nightclub and a watery grave in a canal drainage system behind a scruffy Victorian warehouse on Fleet Street.

This left Daniel all alone in his soon to be dead stepmother's council flat on a south London estate for the next ten years, with no contact with the outside world and no idea who he really was. After his stepmothers passing, and for the first time in his life. Daniel found himself a master of his own destiny, finally free to ask those unanswered questions he'd always had in his mind. The ones he'd buried where Tigger's brutality couldn't find them. They had lain there unanswered for years, irritating him, as if some sort of malicious spider that had crawled into his ear when he'd slept and now took great delight in torturing him by crawling across the surface of his brain with its spindly hairy legs, scratching and scraping for hours on end, driving him out of his mind. He sat about the flat for days on end, trying to shake the spider from one ear or the other, rocking back and forth desperately trying to stop the spider's never-ending crawling. As he did, he mulled these questions over and over until slowly they drove him to despair.

Daniel's sudden freedom of mind and body had the effect of creating a 'Stockholm Syndrome' impact in the young man's fragile mind. He longed for the only person who had meant anything to him. *Yes*, Tigger meant cruelty but in the void that was Daniel's life, at least cruelty was something real. Therefore, driven more by twisted instinct rather than any sort of deliberation, the six foot, lean, blond man was driven to go and find out what happened to his step brother Tigger in the far off town of Birmingham.

CHAPTER 19

Suited, Booted & Blind

February 1995

D aniel opened the wrapper on the sandwich with shaking hands, filled with nervousness from the unfamiliar surroundings on the London to Birmingham train. The grey flaccid slice of meat hung from between the two pieces of stale bread like some sick dog's tongue, the sight made him gag and the nervous tick he'd suffered since a child, returned to his left eye.

He tipped the contents on to the small table and began to pull the sandwich apart with his index finger, as if he were dissecting a lab-rat. The businessman in the opposite chair watched him from over the top of his newspaper with a mixture of confusion and suspicion. He leant over the food and began to separate the individual pieces that made up the deli-ham and cheese sandwich. He could feel the other man's stare bearing into him but he carried on with the process of separation regardless of the other commuter's prying eyes. The trembling index finger pushed the grey ham to one side, sliding the old meat along the table top until it lay in a sickly pile at the end of a trail of dull, yellow mustard. Next was the plastic-like Edam cheese, finger picked from its bed of bread with surgical delicacy, as if the trembling man was a doctor taking the skin from a burn's victim.

He held it before him between fore finger and thumb and examined it for a few seconds before laying it next to the ham on the table. He sat back in his chair with quizzical look on his face, his eyes scanning each piece of food intensely, as if by doing so, he would find the answer to an unknown question that had been troubling his mind for most of his life. The businessman dropped his newspaper slightly in order to view the mess laid out on the table that separated the two train seats. He tutted sharply, Daniel's attention. Daniel didn't react. He just continued to stare at the mangled food on the table with the same pained expression.

"*Excuse* me!" the commuter said angrily over the top of his copy of the Telegraph, rustling the broadsheet to add emphasis to his words "You may not have noticed but there are other people sharing this carriage with you and some of us don't appreciate the bloody mess you're making."

This time the words had more effect. The commuter met the Daniel's gaze. His critical eye running over Daniel's handsome yet gaunt features. The look Daniel returned was so empty of any kind of emotion, that it stopped the business alpha male dead in his tracks. Daniel shook his head to his left, the spider was on the move again. The man broke his stare and looked uncomfortably around the carriage for some sort of back up from the other travellers. However, the carriage was empty apart from the two men opposite each other, the other passengers having departed at the various stations on the long haul from London.

The businessman shrank behind his newspaper for a minute before folding it in two and standing. He glanced down at Daniel and the mess on the table and was disgusted to see him collecting the individual items that made up the sandwich together and rolling them into a messy ball. As the businessman looked down his long nose at the scene, Daniel picked up the ball of food and turning his head towards the other commuter, popped the sloppy ball into his mouth and started to chew it. Daniel's stare became intense as he summoned up all his own disgust and aimed it at the smartly-dressed businessman.

The man turned on his heel and marched along the aisle of the carriage until he got to the toilet. He glanced back at Daniel and was alarmed to see he was still staring at him. He pressed the large button on the right of the toilet entrance and the sliding door to the toilet vanished inside the compartment wall. Stepping inside, he bolted the heavy electronic door and instantly felt a wave of relief washing over him. He bent over the sink and ran the tap. Cupping his hands under the dribble of water he splashed it on his face, careful not to get his shirt wet. He felt the train slowing and he watched the pool of water in the sink slosh to the front of the basin.

The train will be arriving at Birmingham New Street in five minutes.

A raspy voice announced through the tannoy speaker above his head.

Thank God, he thought to himself. The incident with the oddball had spooked him far more than he'd like to admit. Although the man was obviously mentally disturbed in some way or other, he looked formidable in a lean, mean sort of way. Yes, he thought, this guy was the type of nutter that could take punch after punch and it not even register in his mangled brain, someone best avoided at all costs. Then there was the sandwich. The image of the dollop of mush slowly churning over and over inside the man's mouth. The thought of it made him want to gag, especially when he caught sight of himself in the toilet mirror. His pristine suit, his white shirt and old school tie.

The train lurched as it came into its final destination, slowing to a snail's pace. He reached for a paper towel and wiped off the spattering of water still on his face. He threw the towel into the bin and adjusted his tie one last time before turning to the sliding, electric toilet door. He pressed the button nonchalantly and turned his attention to his shoes. They were beaded with droplets of water from the sink. He examined the expensive black lace-ups, wondering whether he should take a toilet tissue to them and wipe the moisture off. He couldn't be bothered so he turned his attention back to the opening door.

And so, he came face to face with Daniel, arms stretched out either side of the entrance blocking his way, his hands resting on the frames on the door. There was a moment of silence between the two as the businessman tried to workout what was happening and Daniel stared at the smartly-dressed man, open-mouthed chewing the slop of food, around and around. The sight of the gloop and the close proximity of the strange man made the commuter step back into the toilet compartment in shock.

"What the hell do you think you're . . . ?"

Without warning Daniel spat the ball of slop at the man. The gloop exploded squarely in the centre of the man's face, most of it spattering inside the businessmen's open mouth. He gagged, his face screwed into a ball of disgust as he tried to wretch the mass of saliva and slop from his mouth. The food particles had sprayed in to his eyes too and he tried to blink away the gloop in his eyes, as the silhouette of the other man in the doorway, stepped across the threshold of the toilet compartment to join the startled businessman in the cramped space.

The first punch came from nowhere. A mean, terrible blow that had a lifetime of oppression behind it. The blow caught the businessman square in the jaw, shattering a tooth as it did so. The businessman's head swung behind him and smashed into the stainless steel mirror above the metal sink. He went down, semi-conscious. The train was slowing to a halt now. Daniel raised his head and peered out of the window as the city suburbs came into view.

He didn't have long.

Bending he began to undress the man. The prostrate businessman tried to put up a half-hearted struggle but a hammered fist to the bridge of the man's nose brought any resistance to a sudden halt. Daniel took everything from the poor fellow; jacket, trousers, shirt, shoes and underwear. He stood in the compartment dressed in the fine suit of clothing, looking more or less like a blonde-haired version of the man who had walked in there five minutes before. He caught sight of himself in the blood-stained mirror and was shocked at the reflection. For staring back at him was another man, one he'd never seen before. This fellow with his expensive suit, shirt and old school tie was a confident being. Someone who could control, instead of being controlled.

He smiled at the man in the mirror and the man in the reflection smiled back and Daniel was more than pleased with what he saw. He glanced down at the wretch on the floor, who was slowly coming around. He was lying in a pool of his own bloody vomit. Daniel bent and patted the man's shoulder. The businessman stared through his fuzzy vision, searching for a glimmer of empathy but there was none, only a cold, smartly-dressed psychopath staring back at him.

The train began to lurch as it slowed towards its final destination of New Street Station. Daniel felt the train's movements and quickly straddled the man. The spider vibrated with pleasure beneath Daniels skull and placing his thumbs into the business man's eye sockets he pressed as hard and as quickly as he could. The pain was instant and the man jolted and bucked beneath Daniel, at the shock of his eyeballs being crushed into his head. Daniel clenched his thighs tight around the man's flanks and pressed harder until he felt the pop of an eyeball inside the man's skull.

The train's brakes began a long, deafening screech along the metal tracks announcing its arrival, simultaneously drowning out the businessman's screams of pain, confusion and horror, as the other eyeball burst with a sickening 'pop' beneath its eyelid.

Daniel stood and looked down at his handy work, a thin smile drawing across his face. Like a rotten pustule lying dormant beneath the skin, the years of abuse had finally come to a head spilling hatred all over this poor victim, leaving him to swim in a world of blackness, thrashing around like a landed fish on the piss-sticking, vinyl flooring.

As Daniel turned to leave, he caught sight of the businessman's briefcase and snatched it up. Pressing the button for the door, he waited as it slid into the partition wall and stepped out into the empty carriage before finally stepping from the train itself and on to the platform of Birmingham New Street station in his new suit of clothes and a sense of self-confidence he'd hadn't felt since he'd been a child.

Although he didn't know it at that moment in time, he had unconsciously stepped out of the past and into the present.

Daniel had finally come home.

CHAPTER 20

Blood at the Mop

1995

Kylie sat at her normal chair in the window of the Old Fox pub watching the never-ending traffic flowing through the one way system along Hurst Street. The panic she had initially felt when handed the thousand pounds by Davey a few weeks ago, had now subsided and been replaced with the usual foggy hangover and acidic, cynical mood.

Nothing had come of her worrying, no police questions or villains' fists. Even the newspapers seemed to have overlooked the murder in the Irish pub across the road and if *they* didn't care, why should she give a toss? The grand she'd been given had bought the best part of an ounce of good cocaine, so good in fact that she still had over half of the white powder stashed away back at the house she shared with her wife, two kids and alter-ego Geoff.

The wife hadn't kicked him out *yet* but he knew it was only a matter of time before her indoors was going to get sick of Kylie and demand that her husband Geoff return to her without the mini-skirts and make-up. The end of the relationship was inevitable. *He* could see it even if his ever-faithful wife in their council maisonette back in the leafy suburb of Kings Norton couldn't.

As a matter of fact, the window seat of the Old Fox was probably the only place that, he ... she, felt comfortable these days. It was like a no-man's land for emotions. A place where she could be whoever he or she would like to be without anyone else's involvement or opinion. Yes, every now and then there was a sarcastic comment from one of the straights that drank in the pub, usually aimed at her outrageous transexual outfits but they were nothing that couldn't be dismissed by one of her sulphuric retorts which usually left the *piss-taker* being the laughing stock of the bar. No, the Old Fox was a place where no one seemed to care and that's exactly what Geoff wanted these days, for no one to care.

Of course this could have been the cocaine talking, making him become ever more paranoid. Geoff had his wife's possessiveness to deal with and now to add insult to injury, the bastards at the car showroom had fired him for turning up to work high as a kite (something he'd omitted telling his wife). Then there were the bouts of crippling self-loathing which had begun to creep into his daily routine. Long term use of cocaine always seemed to have the same effect on its addicts; dizzying champagne highs to begin with, then, as the drug takes hold a toxic mix of self-doubt, delusions of grandeur and schizophrenic paranoia, work their way beneath the skin until the victim is a self-deluded bag of bones.

Geoff was more than halfway there, only Kylie was keeping things together for him now, and the longer he spent in her company, the more comfortable he felt travelling down the rabbit-hole of self-destruction.

The juke box interrupted his melancholy with a song about sunshine. He'd seen the video to the tune on some TV somewhere and for a few minutes it had made him happy. A twenty-something blonde girl in leather trousers on a beach somewhere in Ibiza, arms held in the air in a celebration of MDMA and life as she sang earnestly over the heavy, rave beat.

'*Sunshine on a rainy day, makes my soul, makes my soul, drift, drift drift away.*'

Geoff wanted to be her, Kylie wanted to be her, the girl in the sunshine on a rainy day in Ibiza. The music lifted his heart somewhat and he took another cigarette from the packet on the table and placed it in his mouth. Just as he was about to pick up his lighter, a hand came from out of view and held an already-lit match out in front of him. The action caught Geoff by surprise.

"Oh, cheers pal!" he said in a deep, gravelly voice.

The sound of his own voice seemed to take him by surprise. It was impossible to keep in character all weekend. Kylie was a hard act to perform and sometimes he let his mask slip and this was one of those moments. Catching himself, Geoff raised the tone of his voice to a more feminine one and repeated the words.

"Oh, thank-you darling!"

In the blink of an eye, Geoff and his gravelly voice vanished to be replaced by the tart with a heart, Kylie.

"You're so kind, nice to see there's still some gentlemen left in the world!"

She turned to see a stout, bald man smiling at her. He held the tip of the lit match against the end of the cigarette before shaking it and dropping it in the ashtray on the table.

"Ha, gentleman!" she said breaking into a short breathed laugh.

"Nah, you must have the wrong person, love!"

Kylie smiled, trying to hide her disappointment at the man's British bulldog appearance.

"Well, thank you anyway." she said, giving it her best her best Diana Doors. "You might not be a night in shining armour love but you're a gentlemen to me!"

"Can I get you a drink?" the man asked, breaking into a smile that betrayed the fact his teeth only had a casual relationship with his toothbrush.

Kylie's eye ran over the tattoos on the man's neck, face and hands. He didn't look the type to be in here, not one of the regulars anyway. As a matter of fact, she hadn't even seen him arrive, and she saw everyone come and go. Maybe he'd come through from the other bar, anyway, it didn't matter, he was paying her some attention and who was she to turn down a drink even if it was from someone that appeared to have more in common with a silverback gorilla than a human.

"That would be lovely darling, I'll have a G&T!"

"Would you like ice and lemon in that, my dear?"

Kylie was taken aback by the question. This inked-up nean-derthal really *was* a gentleman. Kylie flickered her eyelashes.

"That would be lovely darling!"

She watched as the man turned and left her to go to the bar. Her eye followed the back of the man's bald head with its thick roll of fat at the bottom of the back of his neck. The shaven head was covered in lines, scars left there in the not too distant past by some bottle, glass or knife. The back of the man's neck was also tattooed but the roll of fat obscured most of the tattoos and she could only make out four letters. "'A. C. A. B. All coppers are bastards."

She said to herself. "Well, he's certainly got that right!"

As she watched him push his way to the bar, she caught sight of two men sitting at the other end of the lounge. One was bald and looked like a rougher, less-tattooed, version of the silverback, the other had his back towards her but she could see he was younger, with a full head of dark hair and a chiseled jawline. She hadn't seen this pair come in either. Maybe she'd been caught in her melancholy for longer than she'd realised. Kylie watched the two men for a second. Call it what you will, second sight, cocaine paranoia or a transvestite's ability to spot trouble coming from a distance. Whatever it was, a prickle of panic ran up Geoff's spine at the sight of the pair. Something wasn't right about them. Even though the bald man looked the more violent of the pair, it was the dark-haired man that set her alarm bells ringing. Even though she couldn't see his face, Geoff knew he had seen him before.

He turned away, lest he caught their attention and as he did, he caught sight of the pair in one of the pub mirrors, it was then that Geoff saw the bald man's eye glance his way. It was only for a split second but it was enough to give the game away. They were watching him speaking under their breath about him. All aspirations of female imitation fell away now. Geoff suddenly felt ridiculous in his sparkly, transvestite get-up, naked and vulnerable in the company of wolves. He turned back to the window for a second, trying to work out why the sight of the dark-haired man filled him with dread. Geoff spun his head towards the wall mirror once more. Again he caught the bald man's eye upon him, only for a split second this time but there nevertheless, and there was no doubt that he was looking at Geoff, and this time the dark haired man glanced his way too. An uncomfortable sensation of cold sweat ran down Geoff's spine as a fresh panic gripped him. For, although it was only a quick glance, or maybe *because* it was only that, Geoff's memory recreated the exact moment outside the Brazen Maiden weeks before, when he'd caught sight of the dark-haired gunman removing his nylon stocking mask as he'd gotten into the black BMW.

It was the same man.

A wave of adrenalin washed over the transvestite as if he were coming up on a thick line of cocaine, only far from being a pleasurable, uplifting experience as it was on the white flaked powder. This was a stifling feeling of suffocation, a nauseating head spin that made him want to gag. The room became too hot, his forehead was suddenly beaded with sweat and he knew there was no hiding the fact that something was wrong.

Geoff gathered his things and threw them into the small bag on his arm and drawing a deep breath he tried his best to pull himself together and stood up. He grabbed the table to steady himself. He forced a smile and turned towards the bar. He could feel the men's eyes on him as he crossed to the tattooed silverback who was still waiting to be served and tapped his shoulder. The man spun around with a start.

"I'm just going to powder my nose darling." Geoff said, trying his best to slip back into his Kylie persona. "I'll be back in two shakes of a lamb's tail, wait for me at the table lovey."

The stout man seemed at a loss of what to say and without giving him a chance to answer, Geoff turned and walked across the bar and through a door marked *Ladies*. The distance to the doorway was only a few meters but it was the longest walk Geoff had ever known. He could feel their eyes burning into his back and he swore at that moment, that if he got out of this situation, he would happily never don a woman's clothing again. He would bury Kylie and all her trappings for good as the Irishman told him he should. Suddenly, the thought of his faithful wife and their scruffy little maisonette in Kings Norton seemed like a distant sanctuary.

The three men watched the transvestite vanish through the door to the women's toilets with some confusion. Bull returned to the table where Number Two and Dez sat speechless at the actions of the crossdresser.

"What do we do now, boss?" Bull said under his breath.

Dez thought for a second before answering.

"Go stand by that door!"

He pointed at Number Two, " And don't let anyone in or out of there!"

Turning to Bull he stood and tapped the burly man's shoulder.

"You come with me!"

The other customers in the pub began to notice the sudden movements of the three men standing from the table and pay attention.

Dez turned and smiled falsely towards them and at his companions.

"Not too fast . . . " he muttered under his breath, " . . . we don't want any unwanted attention, do we?"

He ordered the other two men to finish their drinks and they threw the drinks back in one fast gulp, draining the pint glasses in just a few seconds. On seeing this Dez just took one small sip and left his glass down on the table before crossing to the side door of the pub and stepping out onto the street followed closely behind by Bull.

As soon as they were outside, Dez grabbed Bull's arm and ordered the man to go around the back of the pub to the right of the building.

"There's bound to be an alleyway at the rear of the building where the draymen load in the barrels. If the queer bastard's trying to escape, it'll be round there!" The two men split, each breaking into a sprint along the pavement surrounding the pub.

By the time they had reached the alleyway, Geoff was already half way out of the window of the women's toilets. Geoff's legs dangled ridiculously from the little window as his legs splayed in mid-air, the six-inch platform shoes making his hairless legs look as if they were too long for his body. Dez and Bull charged towards the figure hanging from the window, only to be stopped by several aluminium beer barrels that had just been delivered and stacked against the wall of the narrow alleyway.

Bull reached the blockage first and tried to squeeze through the space between barrel and masonry but the gap was too small for his thick-set build. He pushed himself further into the tight gap, forcing the full beer barrels towards the opposite wall as far as he could with both hands but the space was too small. Dez looked past Bull to the crossdresser who had, by now, climbed out of the window and was now trying to unhitch his dress which had snagged on the latch. Their eyes met for a second. Dez's furious glare, burning his hatred into the panicked expression in Geoff's eyes.

On seeing this Geoff just let go of the window sill and dropped to the floor, the dress ripping along its hem line, tearing the fabric up to the waist. He dropped his handbag and climbed to his feet and half-stumbling, half-running continued down the alleyway. He glanced behind him at the bag but saw the two men struggling to get through the gap between the barrels and wall and decided to leave it behind. He could see the dark-haired man was busy pulling the bald man backwards and out of the way as he swore obscenities at the crossdresser. Geoff was horrified by the level of aggression the men had towards him and for a split second he wanted to approach them and try and reason with the pair but a fresh shower of vulgar obscenities sent a surge of uncontrollable panic ripping through him and he turned and fled down the tight alleyway and onto the busy high street.

He stumbled onto the pavement with far too much momentum and nearly fell under the wheels of a black-cab that was about to pull into a taxi rank opposite the Hippodrome theatre. Without thinking he grabbed the door handle and pulled the heavy, side-door open. As he stepped into the still-moving cab, he could hear the sound of the aluminium barrels in the alleyway crashing the ground as the two pursuers cleared the way towards him. The Pakistani taxi-driver turned to the sound of the rear door opening, a concerned look on his face.

"Get me the fuck out of here!" Geoff ordered in a deep growl, any idea of female impersonation long forgotten as he climbed into the rear of the cab and threw himself onto the rear seats.

The cab ground to a halt, the little Pakistani man peering over the back of his seat, through the scratched plexiglass at the man sprawled across his back seat.

"No, no no, you get out of my bladdy cab!" the man ordered.

Geoff pulled himself into a sitting position and looked through the rear window towards the alleyway. The dark-haired man appeared at the opening, his head turning left and right as he searched the busy road.

"Get out of my cab, bladdy poof boy!" the driver snapped.

Geoff didn't answer. He watched the dark-haired man who was still searching the busy street. Suddenly, he was joined by the silverback who emerged from the alleyway and, to Geoff's horror, the man was holding his handbag. Geoff's eye rested on the handbag for a split second before turning back to see what the dark-haired man was doing. Geoff's heart stopped as he realised that he was staring directly back at him. He watched as his hand rose toward him and pointed at the taxi and without hesitation, both men began to walk towards the black cab, sinister smiles breaking across their faces.

Geoff turned to the taxi driver who was still spouting homophobic bile.

You *get out now* poofing, bum boy!"

His accent made his angry comment almost comical but *no one* was laughing. Geoff leapt across the small space between seat and bulkhead and reached through the money hole in the plexiglass. He grabbed the unsuspecting driver by the collar of his coat.

"Please, please, just drive, those two bastards are gonna kill me!"

The driver continued to stare at the transvestite as if he were an alien and didn't move.

"I'll pay you *double*, just fucking *drive*!" The words had an instant effect and the driver turned and threw the cab into gear. With a rapid screech of tyres the cab sped away down Hurst Street, leaving its passenger to sprawl on the black vinyl seat once again.

The two men chased in its wake the along the busy street, screaming blue murder.

****

The Mop Fair had been coming to Kings Norton village since King James had granted permission in 1616. Since then, little had changed on the leafy village green, even some of the old black and white wattle and daub buildings from that era remained. The houses, shops and pubs nestled snugly alongside each other around the tree-lined triangle shaped village green in a display of architecture through the ages, with examples from Tudor to Victorian. Only the imposing redbrick 1930's cinema known locally as 'The Flea Pit' to the west of the green and the Victorian gothic church to the North, broke up the triangle of quaintness.

However, the place wasn't so peaceful when the Mop Fair came to town with its brightly coloured stalls, flashing pontoon lighting, music and screaming fairgoers, and anyone wandering through the tightly-packed sideshows and rides. It gave the space beneath the trees an almost medieval atmosphere which was palpable, and if it wasn't for the large groups of tribal chain-smoking school kids, one would have thought they had stepped into the pages of Chaucer's 'Canterbury Tales'.

The taxi screeched to a halt at the northern end of the village green, much to Geoff's relief. He was back on his own turf now. The old church spire that poked its black tiled spike high above the trees, had been a welcome sight as the taxi driver had tried his best to lose the black BMW that had tailed them from Hurst Street. The other car hadn't been able to catch them due to the little Pakistani driver's knowledge of the area, and the mouse had managed to stay ahead of the cat by four or five hundred meters along the six mile journey through the suburbs to Kings Norton.

As they approached the village green, Geoff realised that if the taxi continued to his house, then the BMW wouldn't be too far behind and so he ordered the driver to pull up at the green and let him out. Geoff had forgotten the Mop Fair was in town, and when he saw throngs of families, school kids and fairgoers his heart rose. Generally, he steered clear of crowds whilst in his cross-dresser clothes – the aggravation and catcalling was something that he went out of his way to avoid. However, on this occasion, the mass of people on the usually deserted village green was a welcome sight. He could cross the space to his house on the far side of the green directly behind the cinema, hidden within the crowds and no one would be the any the wiser as to where he'd gone. He checked behind him in the cab's rear window to see if he could spot the BMW. He couldn't.

"Okay pal!" he said without turning. "I think we've lost 'em. When I get out you had better fuck off pretty sharpish before they spot the cab and realise I'm not in it."

He reached inside his blouse and pulled a bundle of notes from the padded bra. He looked at the taxi meter, £11.00. Geoff pushed two, twenty-pound notes through the hole in the plexi-glass with a short nod. The little man grabbed the money and without looking at it, shoved it in the top pocket of his scruffy jacket. He went to say thank him but Geoff had already climbed out of the cab and vanished into the crowds who streamed into the narrow gap between two stalls on the border of the fair.

The taxi-driver searched for any sign of the cross-dresser but saw nothing, he then noticed the man had left the rear door to the cab open as he'd left. He climbed from his driver's compartment and walked around the black cab. He scanned the immediate area of the pavement, to see if anyone needed his services before slamming the door. As he stepped back onto the road behind the taxi, the black BMW drew up behind him. He froze in the headlights as the car came to a halt only inches from his legs. A thick-set man jumped from the front passenger seat and walked towards him with a scowl and grabbed the frayed collar of the Pakistani man's jacket.

"Alright Punjab . . . " Bull said aggressively, " . . . where's the poof?"

The wide-eyed taxi-driver just pointed towards the fairground.

"There, there!" Bull's eye followed the man's finger and saw the throngs coming and going under the soft glow of the pontoon lighting beneath the canopy of trees. He dropped the little man, who without hesitation scampered back into his taxi and locked the doors. Bull returned to the car. The passenger window slowly wound down and the big man leaned on the sill with both of his hands.

"He's in there somewhere, boss." Dez looked behind the burly man at the crowd of fairgoers.

"Ok, you pair get in there and try and find him!"

He nodded to Number Two in the back seat. "Come on, come on, get the fuck out and find that queer!"

The big man climbed from the back seat and stood next to his old prison associate. Dez leaned nearer the open window.

"A six foot transvestite can't be that hard to spot!" he said without any humour in his steely voice.

"What do we do once we've found him?"

"You know what to do with him, Bull!"

Bull's face lost it colour. Number Two leant over Bull's shoulder.

"Where are you going then, boss?"

Dez looked at the handbag on the passenger seat with a smile and patted it.

"Never mind where I'm going! You just concentrate on catching the queer." He leant over and opened the glove compartment and pulled out a large mobile phone, handing it to Bull he said. "Take this, you answer it by pressing the green button, I'll call you from the car phone."

The big man's brutal face scrunched up into a childish smile.

"This is one of them new types of phones ain't it?" he questioned, examining the phone with its long black antennae protruding from the top.

"Yeah a fucking phone, press the green button when it rings and just talk, it'll light up when I'm calling you."

Bull examined the phone for a second or two, watched by Number Two, who was trying to hide the fact that he was upset over being usurped by his old prison pal into the number three position within the gang.

"It's a mobile phone, as in it's mobile, as in you can walk around with it!" Dez's sarcasm was lost on the pair of old blags at the window. "So fuck off and find him then!" Dez shouted. "If that fucker gets to the old Bill and talks, we're all fucked!" There was a short silence before Dez revved the cars engine impatiently. "Well, go on then, *fuck off*."

Bull stood upright and turned towards his associate and shook the mobile phone in his friend's face. He gestured with the phone antenna towards the fairground and both men turned and disappeared into the throng of fairgoers.

Geoff hadn't been to the fair since he was a teenager. He was surprised just how much things had changed since he'd last visited. The twee, hand-painted, hook-a -duck and coconut stalls he remembered as a child had all been replaced by more modern but tackier versions of the same thing. Miserable-looking showmen in cheap, oil-stained, body-warmers stood in front of their market stalls scowling at the passersby. The stalls themselves looked cheap, each covered in ridiculously large cuddly toys hanging from every nook and cranny, prizes for the gullible. The showmen and women half-heartedly calling mugs to take a shot at the target for a fiver in the off-chance they could win one of the cheap, Chinese, cuddly toys which were only worth a pound or two at the most. Their voices were barely audible over the blaring rave music spilling from a plethora of old speaker cabinets, each pumping out a different tune creating a cacophony that would give a deaf man a migraine.

Much to Geoff's relief, people paid him no attention at all, even in his ridiculously over-the-top glittery outfit he just sank into the background of bright colourful pontoon lights and noise. He assumed that they thought he was something to do with fair and thus he passed through the crowds of youngsters without as much as a wolf-whistle. Inside the fairground the air hung with a mixture of roasting meat, wood smoke and the sweet smell of candy-floss and of course the deafening noise. Screams of joy and horror fought above the racket of a hundred different pop songs all playing at once from the loudspeakers on the rickety rides. The voices rang shrill from the throats of young and old, enjoying the *Waltzers* or the *House of Horror*. The sounds amplified beneath the thick layer of diesel and woodsmoke that hung in a smog mid way between the heads of the fair goers and the green canopy of the trees above. Geoff suddenly felt safe.

The chance of them catching him in here would be like finding a needle in a haystack. He slowed from his panicked trot to a walk before finally stopping at the far end of the village green on the corner of the cinema. He stood panting softly as he peered back around the edge of the red brick building into the chaos of the fairground. He stood like that for a few minutes scanning the heads of the crowds illuminated by the flashing lights of the Mop fair.

Slowly, he began to allow himself to relax. He'd lost them, only just but he'd done it. Now he could go home to his wife and kids and just vanish into the ether. He ran his hand down his glittery frock. The life and death shock of the last hour had scared any notions of Kylie out of him for good. He unconsciously stepped into the shadow of the building as he felt the nakedness of his transvestitism. Still watching the heads of the crowds he began to run over the conversation he would be having with his wife in a few minutes. How he'd be happy to apologise profusely and she'd be happy to accept his apology. "This whole Kylie thing . . . " he said under his breath, rehearsing the future apology, " . . . had just been a faze . . . "

He didn't finish his sentence.

Suddenly, there were two bald heads coming towards him through the throng of people, the shiny skin scalps reflecting the bright lights of the fair around them. He watched as they walked through the crowds, taking no notice of the stalls and vendors, each pushing his way through the mass of people towards the cinema, along the narrow thoroughfare between the stalls and rides until finally they stood on the edge of the fairground free of the tightly packed mass, both of them staring in his direction. He noticed that one of the men, the silverback was holding something to his ear, like a walkie talkie type of thing, its long aerial sticking up above his head.

"Maybe they're the police?" Geoff tried to reason with himself but he knew these men were killers. He shrank back into the shadows a little more and watched as the pair began to cross the fifty yards between the edge of the fair and the cinema steps where he hid.

"How can they know I'm here?" he said aloud.

Suddenly, he was illuminated by the bright lights of a car's headlamps. He spun towards the lights, panic gripping him again. He wanted to run but his feet wouldn't move and he stood motionless like a moon-crazed hare in the headlights of the BMW. Geoff raised his hand to shield his eyes from the blinding light and as he did he saw the silhouette of a man emerge from the car and stand in the centre of the beam. He could hear shouting coming from behind him now and glanced over his shoulder to see the bald men running across the space towards him. "I . . . I . . ." he said pathetically, unable to think of anything to say. His mind awash with the sensory overload of too many questions. In the end he just burst into tears.

"Please don't hurt me . . . " he pleaded. "I don't know what you want from me, I didn't do anything wrong!" his voice trailing off as the panic took away any notion of escape.

"But you did do something wrong, didn't you Geoff?" the silhouette said spitefully.

The mention of his name completed his panic and a trickle of warm urine ran down his leg beneath his glittery frock, puddling at his feet. Geoff stared down at the wet patch and began to blubber.

"How do you know my name? I didn't do any thing, honestly . . . " his cheeks suddenly shiny with tears, " . . . please, please don't hurt me, I won't say anything to anyone, honest!" Geoff now saw clearly that the man in front of him was the dark-haired man he'd seen on the night of the murder at the Brazen Maiden.

"I won't tell anyone, honestly I won't!"

Dez ignored his pleas.

"Stand up straight Geoff!" Dez said as he crossed towards the cowering transvestite. He stopped only a foot or two from his face. "For once in your life, try to act like a man!" Geoff could hear the other two men approaching from behind and he turned to see their arrival. Both men panting from their short run across the green, Bull still holding the phone on which Dez had guided them into the hiding place of their prey.

"How did you now he'd be here boss?" Bull asked.

"Geoff, here left his handbag in the alleyway and in it was this!" Dez threw a woman's purse onto the floor "You made it all very easy for us Geoff, you left your driving licence in the purse with your address on and if I'm right your house is right about there!" Dez pointed towards a block of council maisonettes in the distance. "All I had to do was wait for you to come to me and with the help of my two blood hounds here . . . " he nodded towards the other men, " . . . you did exactly that and so here I am and here you are *Geoff*."

The transvestite flinched at the mention of his name, turning his head back towards Dez and as he did, he saw the silhouette of the dark-haired man's hand fly across his field of vision in a sweeping arc. As it did, he felt a strange sensation across his bare neck. There was no pain. The contact was more like something feather-like brushing against the soft skin of his throat in a lightning-fast slash. The sensation caught Geoff by surprise and he looked into the mean spiteful features of the handsome man in front of him with a confused expression on his face, as a warm thick gooey liquid began to drool down his neck and onto his hairless chest, pooling in the wired bra beneath his gown.

"Wha . . . !" he gurgled falling forward onto Dez's shoulder as he tried to speak.

There were no words there. Kylie's normally acidic tongue was suddenly silent. Dez stepped backwards and Geoff fell forward onto his knees holding his neck, the dark red liquid trickling between his fingers. Dez crossed to Bull and leant in close towards him. Number Two came closer but a quick vicious glance from Dez stopped him in his tracks. Bull looked at Number Two then at the choking transvestite. He could see that the man was badly wounded and would no doubt bleed out if left untreated. However, he could also see that the man had no intention of being left untreated, in fact he was climbing to his feet as they spoke. Bull nodded and crossed to the transvestite and lifted him from the gravel.

"Come on then darling, up you get, we're going on a date to the fair!" he said with a snigger.

"Well, don't just stand there . . . " Dez ordered, " . . . go fucking help him!"

Number Two jumped at Dez's words.

"Yes boss, what are we doing with him?"

Dez sniggered.

"You heard Bull, you're all going on a date to the fair."

Number Two came alongside the transvestite and helped his old prison friend lift the dead weight of the bleeding man. Pulling Geoff's arms over their shoulders they frog-marched the man back towards the fairground. As they did, Dez stepped alongside Number Two and delicately dropped Geoff's purse into his trench coat pocket, careful not to bring attention to himself.

The three men walked across the dark space back towards the fair, watched from the shadows of the cinema by Dez, who climbed back into his car and lit a cigarette his mind already on other things. The crowds had grown denser in the narrow thoroughfares as the Mop fair reached its peak. However, Bull had no intention of joining them, instead he and Number Two half dragged the semiconscious man around the rear of the fair rides to a space where the sound of music and cheering wasn't so loud and where only the pump and grind of gears and turbines could be heard, where the smell of roasting pork and candy floss couldn't penetrate the thick, diesel fumes which pumped from the generators which supplied the electrical power to the fair rides and lighting.

The pair of thugs half carried the transvestite into the shadows until Bull was sure they couldn't be seen from the thoroughfare beyond. Number Two looked above him at a massive platform which rose and fell at breakneck speed. He saw the platform above was covered with flashing lights, brightly-painted panels and members of the public, who screamed their delight as the platform rose and fell through a 360 degree motion. From the front of the ride, the movement was a seamless motion but behind, in the darkness and noise, it was a violent mass of hydraulics and metal. The space was protected by a small pair of metal railings which was meant to stop any members of the paying public from accidentally or drunkenly straying into the danger zone.

Bull pulled the barrier out of his way and stepped through the small gap. The noise of the machinery seemed to revive the dying man and Geoff, one hand on his slit throat, began to struggle against the men. Number Two pushed the cross-dresser through the gap and the pair of thugs dragged the man to the edge of the spinning machinery until all three stood silent in front of the powerful gyrating hydraulic arms, each man enthralled by the gargantuan machinery spinning at dizzying speed, each rotation forcing the incredible weight of thirty people above it high into the air. The grinding cogs and gears spun against each other perfectly in some kind of metallic apocalyptic ballet and slowly it dawned on Geoff why the men had frog-marched him here.

"Oh my god no, *no . . .* " Geoff screamed in a bloody gurgle, his head spinning this way and that to the men either side of him, finding his voice again he continued to plead. " *. . . please*, you don't need to do this, I won't say a word honestly I . . . "

Geoff's words couldn't be heard over the deafening sound of the fair ride and even if they could have, no one was listening. Without warning, Bull grabbed the transvestite by the hair and pulled. Geoff's wig unexpectedly came off in Bull's hand. The bald man stared at it for a second before turning to the cross-dresser, unable to comprehend what had just happened. Number Two, who was watching on burst into laughter, quickly joined by Bull. Their brutal faces gurning into hideous tattooed masks in the semi darkness of the multicoloured pontoon lighting.

"Ha!" Bull shouted above the machinery, " . . . you really got me there, I thought it was your real hair mate. Don't worry pal, the boss said we're only meant to scare ya!" On hearing Bull's words, relief washed over Geoff like a warm shower, instantly reviving him with glimmer of hope.

"Oh my God . . . " he gurgled, breaking into another burst of tears, " . . . scare me?" he screamed over the top of the noise.

Bull patted his shoulder again. As he did the fair ride above came to a halt, bringing the huge hydraulics to a standstill. The noise abated as the old passengers got off, and new thrill-seekers climbed aboard. Bull smiled and placed his arm around Geoff's shoulder.

"To be honest mate, I don't even know what it is you're meant to have done. My mate here probably does but I ain't got a bleeding clue." he said with what sounded to Geoff like a drunken laugh. Geoff still holding the bleeding gash on his throat with his hand, nevertheless sighed his relief.

"Oh thank you, thank you, thank . . . "

Suddenly, Bull grabbed Geoff's arm and with his other arm around the man's neck, he spun him forward towards the stationary machinery. The transvestite lost his balance at the sudden movement. His platform shoes unbalancing him he stumbled towards the hydraulics. Geoff caught himself on one of the long arms and tried to right himself but Bull was in behind him with a kick to the rear of his knee. The kick made Geoff collapse against the machinery and as he did, Bull came behind him and grabbed both of his legs at the ankle and lifted the man over the first hydraulic arm and pushed. He glanced over his shoulder at Number Two.

"Come on you lazy cunt, help me!" he ordered.

Number Two sprung to his side and began to smash Geoff's hands with his fists. Under the shower of punches the cross dresser let go of the stainless steel hydraulic bar he held onto for balance and fell into a small space in the midst of the huge cogs and gears. Bull stood back from the scene and stared into the shadows beneath the ride where Geoff had begun to gather himself together in a tight ball. He could see the transvestite trapped in the mass of machinery. Geoff's eyes wide with panic met Bull's and the two shared a moment of triumph and terror.

Number Two stood next to the outermost hydraulic arms in case the trapped man tried to free himself. Bull looked above himself, to the rear of the attraction and could see the showman crossing the ride, checking the thrill seekers were correctly strapped in. The punters chatted and laughed nervously with anticipation, totally unaware of the horror about to take place beneath their feet. Suddenly the music from above became louder as the fair ride came to life. The hydraulic arms began to spin slowly this way and that, driven along by the mass of steel cogs. Geoff curled into a tight foetal position lest his arms and legs become tangled in the moving parts of the fair ride. Bull scowled at the transvestite's quick thinking and began to mull over what to do about it, he could hardly stand here all night waiting for the man to get tired. He looked at Number Two and considered asking him for suggestions but the man was a meathead – barely able to construct a sentence never mind anything else.

The arms were rotating faster now as the ride accelerated. Inside the machine, Geoff still curled in his ball of safety untouched by the cogs that spun and ground away against each other only millimetres from his skin. As he watched, Bull's eye was drawn to the blonde wig on the grass at his feet. He bent and picked it up with a sinister smile spreading across his face. Bull then threw the wig just in front of the swinging arms, right at Number Two's feet. Bull tapped his associate's shoulder and pointing at the wig he mouthed the words,

"Pick it up!" over the deafening noise of the ride.

Without thinking Number Two bent and grabbed the platinum blonde wig from the oil-stained grass. As he did, Bull raised his foot and placed his Doc Martin boot on the other man's buttocks and pushed. Number Two fell head-first between the two opposing hydraulic arms. The machine didn't even register the man's body. Instead it chewed, churned and ripped him apart as if he were nothing more than a child's balloon full of red offal, bone and shit. The big man never knew what had hit him as he was instantly turned into a cloud of red mist that hung in the shit-stinking air for few a seconds before showering Bull in tiny, red droplets.

"Fucking hell!" Bull screamed his astonishment, wide-eyed and covered in his friend's blood, brain matter and gristle, he began to laugh like a mischievous school child.

"Did you see that fucker explode?" he screamed his excitement to Geoff beneath the ride. Geoff sobbed as he too was showered with Number Two's intestines and he instinctively shuffled away from the gore-ridden arms of the machine. As he did, he could suddenly hear the sound of ripping material mixing with the grind of the machinery around him. He raised his head and to his horror he saw the end of his glittery frock becoming snagged in one of the enormous, spinning cogs. The material began to rip along its hem line until it reached the zipper at the rear of the gown. Suddenly, Geoff felt himself being dragged towards one of the spinning cogs, he uncurled himself slightly and reached for the zipper and began to pull it towards him, trying to free it, trying to win the tug of war between the man and machine. He didn't have a chance. Instead of freeing the zipper, he simply slid across the metal girder he lay on towards the cog until the metal grabbed him by the ankle and yanked his leg into the mass of gears. This time the machine did notice. The minute space between the cogs didn't have space for the bones and it slowed slightly but didn't stop.

Instead it slowly dragged the transvestite into its mass, crushing him to death, inch by inch . . .

Bull watched fascinated by the macabre spectacle happening in front of him. The tattooed man had seen plenty of torture in his years in prison but never in his life had he heard a noise like this and so he stood transfixed, his blood-spattered grinning face gleaming in the fairground lights, listening to Geoff's blood-curdling, white-light, pain-ridden screams as they drifted away on the candy-floss breeze of the Mop Fair.

CHAPTER 21

The Visitor

1995

The old man sat in his wheelchair watching his reflection on the blank screen on the dead television. Ronnie Fletcher spent most of his days doing the same thing. The empty, rectangular screen gave him something to focus his hatred on, a canvas to paint the images of his bitter past.

He rose every morning at first light, shaved as best he could, then dressed himself in the same manner before descending the stairs at a snail's pace to the wheelchair he had left at the foot of the stairs the night before. The grey days were all the same for the retired detective. He hated the wheelchair but these days it was a necessary evil. He *could* walk, if only a short distance but it was a sweat-inducing, lung-bursting effort to cover only a few steps these days. The desperate state of his health meant that any kind of exertion forced him back into the national health wheelchair he hated so vehemently.

Years as a functioning alcoholic had caused the liver damage that crippled him now. He liked to think the stress of his police-work on the streets of Birmingham had forced him into the bottle but that wasn't really the case and he knew it deep down in what was left of his soul. Back in the day, when he'd been a young man and champion of the West Midlands police force, he hadn't felt the need to drink. Why would he? He was the golden boy, the maverick with a mean streak. D.C.I. Fletcher couldn't be bought off or bribed like some of the others coppers had and the top brass knew it, or at least they thought they did. He was their man on the street, well that was until Chris Dixon had shown up all smiles and backhanders. Dixon was the first of many chinks in Ronnie's armour and now there were too many to mention. As a matter of fact, by the time D.C.I. Ronnie Fletcher had retired, there were so many chinks in his armour, it resembled a threadbare chainmail patchwork of mistakes, regrets and envy.

Every day he simmered over these thoughts in his chair. Spilling his silent hatred into the blank screen, replaying everything that had brought him to this, a crippled, bitter old man that could barely breathe. The downward spiral had begun far earlier than anyone knew, including Fletcher himself. The cruel twist of fate that had seen his darling little boy Daniel vanish from under his nose had started his descent all those years ago. He had hidden his heartbreak behind a policeman's professional stiff upper lip. However, behind the scenes, back at the Fletcher household, all pretence of control simply fell away from the detective. The shame of the golden boy's inability to protect his own son from some faceless pervert was more than he could bear, and so, he passed that shame onto his young wife in the form of mental and physical abuse. Helped along by his new fondness of cheap liquor, it began with verbal abuse. Cruel words so cutting that they reduced the poor former mother to a crumpled wreck, bound into a foetal ball by her clasped hands, hiding within the folds of her own body from the razor sharp rantings of her drunken husband. Then a few short weeks after the abduction came the thumps and kicks. The policeman cried whilst he beat her. The tears of frustration at his own incompetence were the only clue he was willing to give to the world that he felt in anyway responsible for the missing boy. Instead he aimed his uncontrollable rage at the young wife curled into a ball on the bedroom floor before once more finding the solace of drunkenness at the bottom of another bottle of Scotch.

If the Birmingham underworld were wary of Ronnie Fletcher before little Daniel went missing, then afterwards he was seen as nothing less than a pariah by both villain and cop alike.

You just couldn't work with Fletcher, be it legally *or* illegally. Fletcher couldn't see the change taking place himself. The process of transformation had been too subtle to notice, especially when he was drunk, which he was most of the time. From where he stood, it looked as he was the one standing still and the whole world which spun around him was filling with corruption and perversion and he at its epicentre, incorruptible, the last true knight in a shadow world of deceit. Of course on the outside of DCI Fletcher's mind, in the normal world, things looked far less dark. Where others saw opportunity, Ronnie Fletcher saw criminality. Where the punters of Birmingham's blooming nightlife saw fun and good times, Fletcher saw depravity and perversion in a new concrete Gomorrah and all of it headed by his nemesis, Edward Fewtrell.

He'd done his best to put a stop to the rise of the Fewtrells over the years by twisting the truth and planting evidence here and there, just as he'd done with the those poor bastards known as the Birmingham Six after the pub bombings of 1974. Stitched 'em up good and proper he had. It didn't matter if they were guilty or not, in DCI Fletcher's mind they were all guilty. So what difference did it make if they actually did the crime or not. If the truth needed to be stretched here and there, or an incriminating item planted at the crime scene, then that was just a means to an end.

His sudden rise to the top of the West Midlands Serious Crime Squad after the Birmingham pub bombers were thrown in jail, came to an abrupt halt after questions began to be asked in certain circles. Questions about how Fletcher had gone about securing the confessions from the six men. However, Ronnie and his tight gang of sycophantic coppers had been a little too zealous in their interrogation skills. The mug shots of the six with their black eyes and broken noses were leaked to the papers, causing raised eyebrows in all the wrong places and suddenly the confessional statements were being read and re-read, with questions asked as to why they were all written in broken-fingered scrawls. This was the beginning of the end for DCI Fletcher's ascendance to the dizzying heights of the head of the West Midlands Serious Crime Squad. Instead he fell like a corrupt Icarus into a sea of distrust and slow-burning madness.

Bing . . .

The doorbell broke the old man's melancholy and blinking his crusty eyes, he resurfaced from his bitter imagination and back to the real world like a man brought back from the brink of death.

Bing . . . Bong . . . .

There it was again, another intruder into his own private purgatory. He glanced at the wall clock. 11.20 am. He sat listening to the bell tone as it faded in the hallway.

Bing, bong, bing, bong . . .

It was too early for the carer to bring his food.

Bing, bong, bing, bong . . .

"Alright, alright, I'm fucking coming!" He spun the wheelchair towards the sound.

Bing Bong Bing Bong Bing Bing Binggggggg . . .

The sound floated around the empty house like a memory as the caller left their finger on the bell's push button.

"I'm fucking *coming,* stop wringing the bleeding bell!"

The effort of his words left him breathless and he hadn't even stood to answer the door yet. Rolling into the wooden floored hallway he pushed himself towards the front door where he could see the distorted silhouette of a man through the blown glass. He saw the silhouette raise his hand to press the doorbell again.

"Hold ya fucking horses! I'm coming as fast as I can!"

The shadow beyond the glass lowered its arm to its side. Fletcher rolled across the floor until the wheelchair was stopped by a dirty Persian rug at the foot of the door. He looked up at the black figure through the glass. He couldn't make out any distinguishing features due to the thick blown glass. The silhouette pressed his head against the window and shaded his eyes with his hands. The sight of the man trying to peer through the glass front door made Fletcher bristle with anger.

"Cheeky cunt!" he said under his breath.

The obscenity seemed to give the old detective a new lease of life. A tiny flame re-lit somewhere deep in the old man's psyche and for a few seconds he felt his old twisted self again. That was until he tried to stand. With a Herculean effort he pushed his dead weight from the wheelchair and stood unsteadily, one hand resting on the arm of the wheelchair. He stood as straight as possible and shuffled across the Persian rug until his hand rested on the latch to the door. He looked at the man's face peering through the glass only inches from his own. The features of the man were distorted beyond recognition but somehow, maybe it was a sixth sense or just his old detective skills coming to the fore, Ronnie Fletcher knew this visitor was somehow special. Maybe if he'd been a younger man, when he'd been in the prime of life and had more of his razor sharp wits about him, he would've thought twice before opening that door.

Click. He unlatched the door and drew it open slowly. The silhouette pulled his head away from the glass and stood back. Ronnie was surprised to see it was a nice day outside. The leafy street was green behind the silhouette of the visitor framed in the doorway. A blue sky filled in the background. A waft of fresh air blew into the hallway and for the first time in a year or two, Ronnie could smell the world beyond his self-imposed prison of bitterness and regret.

"Are you Detective Fletcher?"

The man at the door asked the question as if he wasn't really interested in the answer. Ronnie was taken aback, he hadn't been addressed in that way for a long time and at first didn't know what to say. Drawing himself together he looked the visitor up and down, buying time before answering the stranger.

"I might be, depends on who's asking?"

The gaunt man's face remained expressionless.

"Daniel."

There was a short silence as Fletcher ran through the thinning list of names from his past. He shook his head, eager to get back to his television.

"Nah, mate you must have the wrong address. I don't know any Daniels!"

"You *are* Detective Ronnie Fletcher though?"

Fletcher reluctantly nodded.

"As I said, I might be. What do you want?"

"Well, either you are or you're not. You can't might be." the stranger said with a touch of aggression. The tone made the old man bristle once more.

"Look, if you're one of them fuckers from the newspapers about the Birmingham Six, then you can fuck off! That's all water under the bridge as far as I'm concerned."

"Newspaper?" the blonde man replied, still expressionless.

Ronnie nodded.

"Yeah, fucking newspaper, you bastards won't give me five minute's peace. Now fuck off!"

"I'm not from a newspaper, I'm Daniel!"

The last word was said in a slightly higher tone, as if by doing so it would explain his presence. Ronnie didn't pick up on it but the spider in Daniel's ear did and once more it danced around his brain, buzzing and vibrating. He imagined the spider beneath his skull laying its eggs in the mass of Daniel's cobwebbed-infested brain matter.

"Yeah, you said Daniel, and I said I don't know any fucking Dan . . . "

"Daniel F..F..Fletcher!" the man stuttered the surname as if uttering something blasphemous. "Daniel F . . . Fletcher!" he repeated, trying to get used to the name he'd unknowingly been christened with. This time he said it with a little more confidence.

The old man's face grew purple with rage.

"I fucking told you I don't know any . . . " Ronnie stopped mid-sentence, all these years he had steadfastly refused to say the boy's name since his son's abduction over thirty years before and now by doing so, he had unwittingly opened the floodgates to the memories and emotions he'd pushed to the back of his mind,

"Daniel Flet . . . cher" his words trailed off as he saw the resemblance to his deceased wife. "D . . . Daniel?" he said softly, unable to comprehend the enormity of the moment.

As he focussed on the stranger's features, the blood drained from the old man's face as the shock of recognition set in. His puffy red eyes stared from beneath his low brows as the man claiming to be his long lost son, stood emotionless in the doorway. Ronnie opened his mouth to speak but all that came out was a rasp of breathlessness as his distrustful eyes began to fill with tears. Suddenly, the doorway and the bright day-lit world outside began to spin out of control as a mixture of breathlessness and shock came over him. Ronnie held onto the door for balance but his weak arms couldn't take his weight and he fumbled with the woodwork for something to hold onto. The sudden increase in gravity overwhelmed him and pulled him to the floor. He landed heavily on the old Persian rug, his head slamming on the floorboards beneath. His vision flickered before him, fighting a losing battle to remain conscious.

The last thing he saw before the black veil fell over him was the ghostly silhouette of the stranger stepping into the hallway. As Ronnie Fletcher drifted off into the blackness, he had the strange sensation that he was in the presence of something evil.

As soon as his eyes opened and his wits returned, Ronnie Fletcher knew he wasn't alone. He was sitting in his wheelchair but how he'd got there was a mystery to him. Then the image of the silhouette in the doorway came creeping back into his mind's eye together with an overwhelming feeling of dread. He looked around him, his living room looked as it always did. He spun the wheelchair around the darkened room peering into the darkness as if searching for some kind of weird insect that had somehow crept into the house. He *saw* nothing but he knew the man was there, he could smell him. The man's clothes had once been sprayed with expensive aftershave or deodorant but the once-attractive perfume had now long since dissipated and its olfactory delicacy had faded, drowned beneath the unmistakable sickly-sweet stink of male body odour.

"You gave me away, didn't you?"

The words made Ronnie jump. He spun towards the sound. The man was sitting in an armchair in the corner of the room, just an outline in the darkness. In truth the old man had forgotten the chair was there at all, so long had it been since he'd sat in any of the chairs in the house apart from his wheelchair. He couldn't see the man. He was sitting in one of the long shadows cast through the dirty, lace curtains that spread across the room from one of the yellow streetlights on the road outside. Whether the man had chosen the spot for its hidden position, Ronnie couldn't tell.

"W . . . w . . . what?" the old man's voice was raspy due to being dehydrated. The man answered without hesitation.

"You gave me away, *didn't* you?"

"Gave you away?" Ronnie's reply seemed to make the man agitated and the shadow in the armchair shuffled uncomfortably.

"Do you even know who I am?"

Ronnie shook his head.

"No!" He said blinking in to the darkness. "I haven't got a fucking clue!"

I'm Daniel, your *son*!"

Ronnie flinched at the name.

"That's impossible, my son died years ago!"

More fidgeting from the leather armchair in the shadows.

"No, he didn't die, he . . . "

Ronnie interrupted the man.

"Yes, he did. He's dead and you ain't him, you're some sick cunt that's here to rip off an old man. You ain't fooling anyone!" Fletcher laughed to himself. It wasn't really a show of humour, more a well-rehearsed chuckle to hide the fact that the old detective was grasping in the dark and didn't want to face what was rapidly becoming a bizarre twist of reality.

The shadow rose from the chair and crossed the room with astonishing speed. He closed in on the wheelchair quicker than Ronnie could react. Daniel slapped his open hand around the old man's cheek. *Thwack!* Ronnie's head flew to his right with the power of the blow. The pain in his jaw unimaginable, sending what appeared to the old man to be a shower of meteorites shooting off in all directions into the darkened room.

As the stars in his head dissipated Fletcher instinctively hunkered down into his wheelchair for protection. He closed his eyes, waiting for another blow but it never came. He could see himself in his mind's eye, as if he were floating somewhere in the room above them both watching the proceedings like a lost spirit, but Ronnie didn't need any supernatural spirit to know what was coming. He'd seen this little scene countless times before, in the police interrogation offices and jail cells. Only back then it had been *him* doing the thumping and some other poor fucker sat in the chair taking the cocktail of punches, kicks and psychological torture DCI Fletcher could come up with on the spur of the moment. Any irony was lost on Daniel. He was more concerned sudden awakening of venomous black spider inside his head. His eyes still tightly shut, awaiting the next blow Fletcher could smell the man's breath. He could feel warm air from the other man's nostrils and he knew that the visitor was close. Fletcher raised his head a little and slowly opened his sleep caked eye lids, only millimetres, just enough to see around him. There he was, the blonde gaunt man, crouched in front of his wheelchair, leaning in, his face only inches from the Detective's. His breath had a touch of halitosis that made Ronnie want to gag.

"You gave me away to *Jarvis*!" Daniel could barely bring himself to say the name and so whispered it instead. Fletcher opened his eyes fully at the sound of the name. He shook his head, trying to recall where he'd heard it before. It was familiar to him but he couldn't recall why.

"Jarvis?" Ronnie asked. Saying the name brought with it connotations of perversion and suddenly Fletcher knew, the red-haired queer from way back in the day. The sick stories he'd heard of the Meat Market Mob's lieutenant, Toddy Burns' right hand man. The police reports of male rape, a Birmingham paedophile ring and kids snatched off the street and at the epicentre of all of these tales was the name. "*Duncan Jarvis*!"

Ronnie said the name again, only this time it wasn't a question, it was an answer to a question. A question he'd been asking himself for over thirty odd years. Ronnie suddenly knew who that man had been so many years ago. The thin figure in the bright red Father Christmas costume walking freely amongst the hoy-ploy of Birmingham at the Bermuda club back in 1961. The images ran through his mind like an old horror film. Ronnie could suddenly see himself and little Daniel standing at the edge of the Bermuda Club dance floor, watching the pack of excited kids gathering around Santa Claus, he could feel the softness of his son's blonde hair once again as he ran his fingers over the boy's scalp with a father's loving caress. Then he recalled pushing the kid through the pack so *his* little boy would be the first one on Santa's knee.

Unconsciously, Ronnie raised his hand to the kneeling man in front of him and ran his fingers through the man's dirty blonde hair and although the hair was unwashed and a little greasy. Ronnie knew that this man in front of him was his long-lost son. The tears were instant. Emotion overwhelmed the detective as he gave up any thought of trying to conceal his feelings. The poker face he'd so stubbornly wore for the last fifty years, fell from him like a mask of cut-glass, smashing into a thousand pieces on his tear-stained trousers and Ronnie Fletcher, the maverick and hard man with the stone cold heart, the head of the infamous West Midlands Serious Crime Squad broke down completely.

Daniel stood again. He watched over the sobbing man in front of him with a mixture of emotions he'd never felt before. The spider in a sudden frenzy inside his head. The room was dark and silent except for the sobbing man. Daniel looked about him. The decor in the house was old, at least twenty years out of fashion, maybe older, not that Daniel would've known what was in fashion in interior design anyway. All he knew was that this place was better than the shit hole he'd crawled out of in London. He made a decision to stay there for a couple of days, at least until he'd finished what he'd come here to do. He turned back to the sobbing man who for all intents and purposes had withdrawn into a world of his own.

The blubbering was beginning to irritate Daniel. He crossed the room to the hallway and go into the kitchen. Ronnie heard the man rummaging beneath the kitchen sink for a minute or two before returning. The younger man stood in front of him and produced a roll of grey duct tape from behind his back. Ronnie could see the man was looking for the start of the roll with his fingers. The blubbering stopped. His initial thoughts that his long lost son had returned for some kind of loving reunion, suddenly vanished amidst a stream of images of duct taped torture that he'd indulged in over his thirty odd years as a detective, and he also knew that the presence of duct tape at a moment like this was never a good sign. On seeing that things were about to go sideways for him, Ronnie Fletcher's natural survival instincts kicked in. He recognised that his usual aggressive tactics wouldn't work here, the man was too young and fit for an old man to deal with.

"Daniel, you've come home to your old dad at last!" he said between sobs, trying not to sound too desperate. "I only wish your mother was alive to see . . . "

"You gave me away . . . *dad*!" Due to the lack of any previous emotion from the visitor, the last word was said with such venom that it sounded as if it were spat from a cobra.

"Gave you away? No, no that's not true Danny my boy. I didn't know that the Father Christmas was Duncan Jarvis did I? I mean you can hardly blame . . . "

"Do you want me to tell you what he did to me?"

For once Ronnie didn't know what to say. He just sat staring at the man, blinking away his tears. Finally, after a short silence he muttered.

"We don't have to talk about that if you don't want to."

Daniel wasn't listening. He shook his head trying to dislodge the insect inside his head but far from calming the imaginary anthropoid, the black spider began to vibrate in a dance of spiteful ecstasy.

"Oh he raped me, over and over again . . . " He turned to look at the old man in the eye. "I can't recall exactly how many times as I was only eight years old when you handed me to that animal."

Ronnie couldn't disguise his feelings of disgust but Daniel had only just started.

" He was raping the other kids too, *Dad*. Yeah, my older brother Tigger got his fair share of *Uncle* Jarvis. I only had to suffer a month or two before he stopped coming around and we found Tigger's Dad dead in his armchair."

Ronnie shook his head in confusion.

"Tigger's dad?"

"Toddy, Toddy Burns that was Tigger's dad, he acted as if he were my dad but he never got it right. He's the one that killed Uncle Jarvis, at least that's what mother told us."

Fletcher recalled the reports of Toddy Burns' death and the reports of Duncan Jarvis's disappearance back in 1961 but had never put two and two together.

"Did he, Toddy Burns, you know?" Ronnie tried to broach the subject of the Birmingham paedophile ring he'd heard about as a young copper. Daniel shook his head.

"*No*, not Toddy, he knew about it though but did nothing, which I suppose is just as bad if you think about it."

Ronnie couldn't stomach the normality of the conversation. As if the young man were talking about the weather. Daniel continued.

"Jarvis was the ring leader though. He was the one that took me around to the big houses on the back of his scooter to the parties. He got me to drink alcohol and then sat back and watched as I was shared around the other men, Jarvis's friends."

Ronnie began to cry again, this time with tears of anger rather than sorrow.

"Those filthy fucking bastards, you were just an innocent little boy."

Daniel nodded, still playing with the roll duct tape in his hands.

"Ha!" he replied. "I wasn't so innocent after a couple of weeks of that, *Dad*!"

Now the spite had returned to his voice as he tore a twelve inch strip of tape from the roll. The spider shivered with a new level of pleasure.

"Oh, is it making you angry *Dad?* Because that's not even the worst of it, you see Jarvis was only the first. He stopped raping me after a few weeks. After Toddy died mother took us to live in London and that's where my step-brother Tigger took over where Uncle Jarvis and his friends had left off."

Ronnie didn't want to hear anymore, even for the old detective it was just too painful to comprehend and he felt as if he would be sick. He could hear the rage in the visitor's voice simmering just beneath the surface, barely noticeable but there nonetheless. He looked at the gaunt man who was now tearing off other strips of the duct tape and carefully laying them on the coffee table. Ronnie watched with a growing dread and tried to change the subject.

"Well, you're home now son, back where you can be loved and taken care of. We can go to see a shrink if ya like, they'll help you to deal with your demons. God knows you must have plenty of them running around your head."

Ronnie smiled at the man, stalling for time. "Anyway I'm glad you found me son, I really ... " his mind still on tearing the strips of duct tape into similar lengths Daniel interrupted him.

"Even though he was a few years older than me, Tigger was far more creative when it came to pain. You see ... " Turning towards his father Daniel looked for the right words as he approached the wheelchair, one of the strips of tape in hand.

" ... rape is something that you can learn to live with and God knows I learnt young, but I never got used to the pain, Tigger wouldn't let me. He was a bright lad my brother ... very ... *imaginative*, although in reality we both know he wasn't really my brother, he was my ... " the words trailed off as he came alongside the wheelchair with the grey duct tape stretched out between his hands, " ... well I don't suppose it matters what he was now does it, he's dead and gone and I'm all alone."

Ronnie saw his chance.

"*No*, you're not alone son, *I'm* here for you, we can live here together, just the two of us, it'll be . . . "

The emotionlessness had returned to the visitor's face once more. Ronnie looked up at him and at the moment the realisation that there was good chance that he was likely to die today finally dawned on him. In truth, Ronnie Fletcher had always known it would end like this, to be killed by another's hand. After all he'd made so many enemies over the years that he'd always presumed that at some point in his police career, some faceless villain would step out of the shadows and put a bullet in the back of his head. There had been points in his life where he'd prayed for someone would do it, but never in a thousand years would he have thought he'd die at the hand of his own long lost son.

"I've never talked to anyone like this before!" Daniel spoke in a soft, almost apologetic tone. "I didn't get a chance to talk much when Tigger was around. If I did, he'd beat me, and if mother stuck up for me, he'd beat her too."

"But she wasn't your *real* mother Danny my boy, she was just as bad as the bastards that stole you . . . "

Daniel shook his head.

"No she wasn't bad, she was just weak, the same as I was . . . *am* . . . weak!"

Daniel's lips creased at the corners, in a resigned smile but the expression dropped as quickly as it had appeared, replaced by the cold blank mask he'd worn since arriving.

"You're not weak Danny, you can't blame yourself for what those fuckers did to you. It's not your fault that . . . "

Ronnie's outburst caught Daniel by surprise.

"Oh, I don't blame myself, how could I, I was just a little boy, if there's any blame, then it lays firmly at your feet *Dad*."

The melancholy that had haunted the man's words had vanished in a heartbeat, replaced once more by the bitterness that bubbled inside the visitor.

"*Me*, you can't blame me, I had nothing to do with Jarvis taking you, I was as much a victim as . . . "

"*You* gave me to Jarvis!" Daniel snarled.

The fury inside the man had simmered long enough. Thirty years of abuse, rape and mental torture now spewed from the visitor as he vented his spleen at the old man.

"You were the *big* detective weren't you, I can remember that much about you, you never stopped talking about your job, but you never solved this little mystery, did you? The detective who couldn't even find his *own* son, how pathetic!"

Now the visitor's mask had fallen completely and Ronnie could see the depth of pain in the man's face clearly. The old detective had seen enough brutalised faces over the years to recognise even a trace of anguish, but never had he seen such hopelessness and fear as he saw in the face of his own son that day. Daniel's dilated irises glistened like black polished stones, menacing and evil in the semi-darkness of the living room and Fletcher could see the demon inside that promised to overwhelm the situation if he didn't turn this interview around in his favour.

"I, I waited for years but you never came to to get me!"

The gaunt man continued as if talking to himself. Ronnie's survival instincts set in once more and his mind raced as he looked for someone else to blame.

"*It was Eddie Fewtrell's fault!*" he blurted. "*He* was the one that said he'd organised Father Christmas. He said he knew who it was but he didn't did he? He was lying!"

The name caught the visitor's attention.

"Fewtrell?" Daniel repeated.

Ronnie grasped at the lifeline.

"Yeah, Eddie Fewtrell, he's the one that caused all this to happen, he probably planned it all along to get at me!"

Ronnie took a breath, rasping in the air to his damaged lungs as he began to construct more half-truths in his head.

"He's the one that sent his boys out looking for you the night you were taken. When they came back to the Bermuda club empty-handed, your mother and I were heartbroken. They said they'd talked to Duncan Jarvis *and* Toddy Burns in the Market

Tavern and that neither of them had anything to do with your abduction!"

He looked into the younger man's face to see if his words were finding root in his psyche. The exertion of his outburst sent Ronnie into a coughing fit and he sat exhausted, wheezing in and out.

"Don't you get it son?" He forced himself to continue. "We've both been duped all along, by that fucker Fewtrell!" Ronnie decided the half-truths had run their course and now it was time for full-blown lies. "Eddie Fewtrell had you abducted in order to get at me, because I refused to take his bribes, he was probably helped by a bent copper that was hanging around called Chris Dixon, they're still friends from what I've heard."

Ronnie had lied enough over the years to know that sticking as close to the truth as one could, was always the best place to plant a lie, and so he continued.

"Fewtrell is probably at the office of one of his clubs, either that or he uses a casino on the Hagley Road called the Wheel Club . . . it's not far, I can take ya if ya like!"

Ronnie felt as if he were in control of the situation now that he was back on his home turf of lies.

His hatred for his old nemesis had never died. If anything the years that had passed since his last run in with the nightclub owner back in the 1980s, had allowed his loathing to mutate like some sort of tumour, eating away at him as he relived countless lost chances to destroy Eddie Fewtrell. Over the last eight years he had virtually revelled in the misery he'd created in his mind's eye, as he sat in a trance like state watching the blank television screen in his lounge happy in his madness, and then, as if by magic, this blonde avenging angel had appeared from nowhere.

This wraith had turned up at his door to seek revenge for a life time of abuse. The visitor had laid the blame firmly at *his* feet, but if there was one thing DCI Ronnie Fletcher had learned from his fifty years in the force, it was how to shift the blame away from himself and onto some other poor soul's shoulders.

"Have you eaten Daniel? I've got food here. Why don't you sit down and I'll get something on the stove? Then we can talk about getting pay back on Fewtrell, if ya like son?"

Daniel showed no signs that he was taking in a word that came from the ex-detective's mouth. Instead he took four of the long strips of tape and softly stuck them to the front of his suit jacket lapels. He crossed to the seated man and reached down to his right wrist and grabbed it tightly. Ronnie was slow to react and instead tried to pry the man's fingers off with his left hand. However, Daniel's grip was vice like and the old man was too weak to resist.

"What are you doing son? There's no need for this, is there? I'm trying to help you!"

Daniel didn't react to the plea, instead he pulled one of the strips of tape from his jacket lapel and wrapped it tightly around Ronnie's wrist and the arm of the wheelchair incapacitating the old man's right arm. Ronnie began to fumble at the tape with his left but just as quickly as he'd taped the right wrist, Daniel did the same with the left until both the old man's arms were held in place by the thick grey duct tape.

The visitor then pulled a further two strips from his jacket and wrapped them further up the forearm, pinning the man uncomfortably to his wheelchair. The old man struggled as best he could for a few minutes before exhaustion came over him and he slumped into the chair, resigned to the situation. Daniel stood back and looked over his handy work. For the first time since turning up Ronnie saw him smile. A broad mischievous grin spread across the chiseled face which sent a shiver down Ronnie's spine.

"Look, I told you the truth Danny, son. Eddie Fewtrell is the one you want he's . . . "

Daniel tore the last strip from his lapel and taped it across the old man's mouth. The action caught Ronnie by surprise and he shook his head from side to side, trying to dislodge the tape somehow, all the time screaming illegible obscenities toward the younger man in front of him, until a lack of oxygen to the lungs forced him to stop his tirade. The old man's mind was racing, as he desperately tried to draw what little oxygen he could into his lungs through his bloody nose. He forced himself to control his rising panic, trying to gather himself together as he searched for a way out of this situation.

Ronnie glanced at the old clock above the fire place. It had been hanging there since the 1970s and he hated the thing for reminding him of the hours that passed by so slowly. However, today he was glad of it as it reminded him that the social worker who cared for him usually turned up around 4pm Monday to Friday. It was now nearly 4am and he'd only have to hold out until the doorbell rang and the promise of rescue from his damaged jailor. If Ronnie didn't answer the door, then the social worker would assume that something had happened to him, which it had, and call the police to get access to the house. All he had to do was hold on for twelve more hours.

Daniel turned and crossed to the television and switched the dial of the old set to on. The black screen crackled into life and Ronnie sat exhausted and enthralled in equal measure watching the small white dot in the centre of the screen slowly widen until it filled the whole screen. The old man couldn't remember the last time he'd actually seen the television screen turned on. A colourful picture of a hairy rock band filled the screen, all bowl haircuts and gurning faces. A bug eyed man stood to the side of the band shaking a pair of maracas. Ronnie could see the dancer was obviously out of his mind on some sort of drug, as he threw bizarre shapes at the edge of the stage. Thankfully the volume was turned down and the rock band strutted and danced silently. The screens light flickered around the darkened room, making the shadows dance across the walls as crazily as the bug eyed junkie in the band.

Daniel left the room and went through to the kitchen. The old man could hear him rummaging around through the cupboards and fridge looking for food. Ronnie heard the sound of a tin being opened before the ping of the microwave oven being started. He tried to control his breathing.

"Only twelve hours!" he thought to himself. "I can do that!"

Then he listened as the visitor left the kitchen and went up stairs. He could here the man's footfall in the master bedroom above him as Daniel went through the wardrobes searching for a new set of clothes.

The music TV show had come to an end, its credits rolled up the screen superimposed over the top of the hairy rock band who were still performing their song in silence. Ronnie looked back towards the kitchen. He could see the visitor's shadow moving around and he began to relax, knowing that it was only a matter of time before his rescue. His eye was drawn back to the television screen where a pretty female presenter was saying something to him. With the volume turned down, he watched the red lipstick on her lips as her mouth opened and closed like some sort of beautified gaping goldfish, as he tried to lip read her words. He couldn't make out anything she was saying and so just waited until the next show to start. He breathed as best as he could through his bloody nose. However, each breath had to be fought for and even then, the little bit of air he was pulling in was only enough to half fill his lungs. The effort of this would have been difficult enough even when he'd been a young man, but with his lungs and heart being as damaged as they were, each gasp had to be drawn in with an Olympian effort.

A new show began on the TV and Ronnie was relieved to see it was the local news. He couldn't remember the last time he'd seen the news. If truth be told, until tonight's little drama, he hadn't been the least bit interested in what was happening outside his front door but now he was a prisoner, he had a desperate urge to run into the street and scream that he was alive. He visualised himself walking amongst his neighbours, chatting and smiling like some latter day Scrooge, brought back to life after the vision of Christmas to come. Ronnie's daydream was broken by the sudden *ping* of the microwave in the kitchen as it finished its timed cycle. The visitor re-entered the room carrying a plate of something, a small cloud of steam rising from the plate, illuminated in the televisions light. He sat in a chair opposite and began to eat greedily, all the time never taking his eyes from the man in the wheelchair. Ronnie wasn't interested in the visitor anymore. Ronnie was watching the news presenter, well' actually he was watching the screen behind the presenter. Images of Birmingham city centre flashed before him displaying what was happening in the city over the weekend. *The weekend.*

The realisation hit the old man like a sledgehammer. Today was Saturday, meaning that the social worker and his potential rescue wouldn't be happening for at least another thirty six hours. He didn't think he could hold out that long. Panic seized the old man making him gasp for air. Ronnie began to desperately pull oxygen in and out of his blocked bloody nose causing him to hyperventilate. Daniel just sat watching with a bemused smile on his face. He had everything he'd come for thanks to the old man's willingness to drop the blame on someone else's shoulders. All he had to do now was watch the old man die, and judging by the look on his purple face, it shouldn't take too long.

The old detective began to panic, struggling against his bonds, his feet kicking wildly out in front of him, his head swinging this way and that. Daniel watched the man thrashings as if he were an animal caught in a snare, which to all intents and purposes he was. The thrashing became more animated as the tiny amounts of breath he sucked through his bloody nose failed to supply his heart and brain with the vital oxygen they needed to survive. This fight for life went on for nearly two hours and Daniel's meal of Heinz hoola hoops had formed an orange skin over it by the time the final death throws settled over the old man.

As Ronnie's chest heaved in and out, Daniel mulled over the old man's words.

"Eddie Fewtrell . . . the Wheel Club."

As he said the words he suddenly knew what his next step on this road of revenge would be.

CHAPTER 22

Dover Sole

1995

"Dad, this is Davey, Davey this is my Dad, Eddie!" Abi stood back and watched with some concern, as the two most important men in her life met for the first time. The Irishman stepped forward, his hand held out in front of him. Eddie stood, smiling he leant across his desk and took the young man's hand and shook it firmly.

"Have a seat our kid." he said pointing at one of the office chairs. "Abi tells me your a singer?"

Davey turned to Abi and smiled nervously.

"Yeah that's right, been singing professionally since I was twenty-two Mr Fewtrell."

"Call me Eddie!" He leant across to the phone handset and pushed a button. "Becs, bring in some tea, will ya bab!" Without waiting for a reply to his request he let go the button and began talking to the pair on the other side of his desk. "So you're are a *professional* then." he said emphasising the word with a nod of his head. "What kind of music is it you sing, Rock, Reggae?"

"Irish!"

Eddie raised his eyebrows, slightly confused by the reply. He'd never come across traditional Irish music and could only go by what he'd seen on one of the variety shows on TV.

"What, Foster and Allan, that type of stuff?" he said laughing.

Abi and Davey joined his laughter.

"Eh . . . no Eddie, my music's a little livelier than those pair of antiques!"

"Well, as long as it ain't that bleeding Punk Rock, that racket gives me a bleeding headache."

The door opened behind them and the chubby office assistant stepped into the office with three mugs of tea. She crossed the room and placed them on the desk. She smiled at the blonde Irishman before breaking into a red cheeked blush and backing out of the office. Eddie saw her flushed face and broke into another laugh.

"You're the talk of the office Davey. Most of our Abi's blokes usually get the once over from the staff and judging by Bec's blush, you've been approved!" Without warning Eddie stood and clapped his hands together. "Have you pair had lunch yet?"

Abi smiled to herself. She knew her father's ways and she also knew that this offer of lunch was something her father did when he liked someone. Something that had only ever happened once before with one of her other boyfriends many years ago.

"*Starving* dad!" she said.

Eddie came from behind his desk and clapped Davey on the shoulder.

"Come on then you pair, we'll go to the Wheel Club, I'll treat ya to a nice lunch."

Abi stood.

"Thanks Dad that'd be lovely."

"Do you like Dover sole, Dave?" Eddie asked.

Davey having never tasted Dover sole nodded.

"Yeah, I love it, Eddie!"

"Call me Ed, Dave, call me Ed!"

Abi had never heard her father tell anyone but family to call him Ed, thus much to her joy, the approval of his daughter's choice in boyfriend was given its final confirmation.

"Come on then you pair, I got someone I want Dave to meet!"

****

The Wheel Club was situated in a large Victorian house along the old Hagley Road. The restaurant and casino had been a regular haunt for many of the Birmingham faces since its opening and, for Eddie, it was a home from home.

As Eddie swung the jet black 7-litre Mercedes Brabus onto the driveway of the club, Davey stared through the tinted windows at the rather shabby looking building and was struck by how colonial the place looked. Wooden slatted shutters hung from every window, their paint cracked and peeling to show the bleached timber beneath. Victorian gothic designs had been carved into the sand stone lintels above the front door and windows, each layered with over a hundred years of dust, grime and pigeon shit. The Wheel Club had a beautiful old-world shabbiness about it, rundown but with that unmistakable aura of old school wealth hidden in its distressed elegance.

A huge weeping willow tree had been left to grow wild on a small patch of grass towards the front of the building, its branches spreading wide and thick, throwing the whole frontage of the mansion into shadow, and if it weren't for the trundling of buses and nonstop passing traffic, one would have sworn that they had stepped into the pages of some American civil war classic of the 1850s.

As Eddie parked the car Davey caught sight of a man in his late 50s leaning against a silver Ford Sierra Cosworth, a cigarette hanging from the corner of his mouth. Although the man couldn't see who was traveling in the car, due to the tinted one way glass of the Brabus, he was nevertheless paying a lot of attention to the large black car reversing into its parking space with what was either a thin smile or an impatient scowl. It was hard to tell which. However, it was obvious that the man had been awaiting the arrival of the car and at the sight of him Davey felt a sudden emptiness in the pit of his stomach. A void that had little to do with thought of Dover sole and everything to do with the little canvas bag of cash from the Brazen Maiden he had secreted back on his narrowboat.

The man glanced at his watch before taking the fag from his mouth and flicking it into the flower beds at the front of the club. He crossed to the car and, as Eddie killed the engine, he grabbed the passenger door handle and pulled the door open. The daylight illuminated the interior of the vehicle, making Davey suddenly feel vulnerable. The expression on the man's face changed into a broad smile and he held his open hand out the Irishman in a gesture of friendliness.

"Hello son, my name's Detective inspector Chris Dixon, you must be Davey the singer?"

The sentence wasn't a question, it was a statement and Davey could tell that this character knew exactly who was in the car. The man's smile grew wider but far from putting the Irishman's mind at ease, it only made the hollow feeling in his stomach worsen. Davey took the man's hand and gave it the best handshake he could muster under the circumstances.

"Hello Inspector Dixon, very pleased to meet ... "

"Nah, forget all that copper shit, my friends call me Dixie!"

As he said the words, Abi, who had climbed out of the rear passenger door of the car stepped into Davey's field of vision, threw her arms around the policeman and gave the man a kiss on the cheek.

"Uncle Dixie!"

Dixie turned away from Davey and hugged the girl.

"Abi?" he said mockingly. "Nah it can't be, last time I saw you, you were only about three feet high and just a little girl!" He unwrapped himself from Abi's arms and stood back to give her the once over. "My God girl ... " he said, shocked at the change in the girl's appearance, " ... you're all grown up, look at ya, you ain't the little caterpillar anymore are ya, you've blossomed into a beautiful butterfly!"

Abi laughed, embarrassed by the attention. Eddie joined them.

"Come on you lot, I'm bleeding starving." he said impatiently. Without looking to see if they were following him, he crossed to the front door of the club and vanished inside. Seeing this, Dixie grabbed Abi's arm and led her towards the doorway, following Eddie. The sight of the depth of friendship between the two helping to settle the rising panic in the singer somewhat. He followed the pair close behind, listening to the small talk as they entered the Wheel Club.

The club was split into two main rooms. The restaurant area towards the front of the building and the casino with its gaming tables and large roulette table at its centre in the adjoining room, towards the rear of the building. The place was empty except for one or two businessmen talking in low tones at the bar. Eddie acknowledged the men with a short nod as he walked passed them and into the restaurant room, joined by Dixie, who had broken away from Abi to point out to Eddie his favourite table in the bay window of the property. Davey took Abi by the arm and pulled her gently to a halt just outside the doorway to the restaurant.

"So this bloke is your uncle?"

Abi, who had been to the Wheel Club many times, and therefore felt almost at home as her father, saw the concern in her boyfriend's face. She turned to face him and leant towards him and planted a reassuring kiss on his face.

"Don't worry about Dixie, he's one of us!"

"Your uncle?" Davey said, pressing for an answer to his question.

Abi laughed.

"No, not a *real* uncle, I've always called him Uncle Dixie since I was a little kid. I dunno why, just have." She shrugged, trying to put the Irishman's mind at ease. "Don't worry, he may be a copper but he's also a very old family friend. Him and my Dad have been through a lot together over the years." The words didn't have the effect of reassuring the Irish man. "Why, what's the problem are you feeling guilty about something?"

Davey laughed nervously.

"*Me,* guilty nah. I just like to know who I'm talking to is all!"

"Well, come on then, you ain't tasted Dover Sole until you've eaten it here!" Abi turned and stepped into the bright room with its huge bay windows and crossed to the table where Eddie and Dixie were already busy in conversation. Davey went to follow but stopped at the threshold to the doorway. A thought came to mind, something troubling deep in his subconscious told him that if he were to step into this room and take his seat at the table next to these two powerful men, it would somehow change his life forever and once across the threshold he would never be able to return to his previous carefree life ever again. He stood in the doorway for a few seconds not knowing what to do. Abi turned towards him and gave him a puzzled expression. She gestured with her hands.

"Come on!" she said quietly. "They ain't gonna eat ya!"

Davey looked at the woman's beautiful face and for a heartbeat he hesitated. She gestured with her head that he should follow her.

Taking a deep breath and throwing caution to the wind, Davey stepped across the threshold of the doorway and into the lion's den.

****

As the four sat and talked lightheartedly in the daylight shining through the huge Victorian bay window, none of the party noticed the tall blonde man in the unusual diesel blue three buttoned suit standing on the far side of the road watching their every move. Every so often the man shook his head to the left, as if trying to dislodge something immovable and irritating from inside his ear.

CHAPTER 23

Sausage Roll

1995

D avey unfolded the newspaper that had been slid under the door to his room at the Edgbaston Palace Hotel. He walked back into the room and sat on the edge of the bed the newspaper in hand. It had been a sleepless night and not all of it caused by Abi, who was still lying across the bed in a tangle of bedsheets and long, blonde hair.

The night had been spent running over the conversation with Eddie and Dixie at the Wheel Club. To say it had been a real eye opener for the Irishman was the understatement of the year. He liked Eddie and more importantly, Eddie seemed to like him. Dixie on the other hand was harder to read but he seemed to be on Davey's side too. Whether this was due to the fact that Dixie was just a fair guy, or he was just going through the motions because Eddie Fewtrell liked him wasn't clear. Either way, Davey, rightly or wrongly, was off the old Bill's hook. Dixie had escorted Davey into one of the private offices at the Wheel Club and showed him the CCTV footage of the robbery at the Irish Centre and the Brazen Maiden on one of the clubs small TV monitors. He had flushed in shock at the sight of himself in the grainy images, picking up the cash bag and making his escape from the little Irish Pub followed by another image of the kiss with Abi at the back of the Irish Centre stage. He glanced at the detective who on seeing his guilty expression, leant forward and pressed the fast forward until the image of the singer taking the cash was no longer on the screen.

"Don't worry about that son ... " he said, " ... anyone in your situation would have picked up that bag, it's a natural reaction," Davey raised his eyebrows, shocked at the casualness of the policeman. "How much was in there by the way?" Dixie asked.

Davey shrugged.

"Around twelve grand." he replied with a guilty sigh, "I've still got most of it. I was gonna take it back but ... "

" ... nah, there's no need for that, son. You keep the cash and take Abi out and buy her a treat or something." Dixie said laughing. "As I said, we're not interested in a few grand here and there, so you're no longer of interest to us "

"Us?" the singer enquired.

"Us. The West Midlands police." Dixie answered.

"Thank God for that." Davey sighed.

"Oh, if only it were that simple!" The Irishman looked at the detective with an expression of concern. "You see ... " Dixie continued, " ... we ain't the only people looking for ya, are we? You see whoever was responsible for the murder at the Brazen Maiden a few weeks ago, was also the same team that robbed the Irish Centre, *and* by robbing the Irish centre, they've unwittingly trodden on the toes of the Birmingham IRA. Which, I'm sure you'll agree, is not a good place to find yourself, *unless* that is, you've got someone else who'll take the fall for you. Hence, why these two ... " Dixie tapped the screen of the television, " ... are more than happy to lay the blame at *your* feet!"

The revelation sent a shiver down Davey's spine as images of IRA executions he'd seen in newspapers and on TV ran through his mind. He knew the detective was right when he suggested that he should reach out to one of his Irish contacts and perhaps try and make contact with the IRA in order to explain the situation and get his name off their lips. He also knew, this would be easier said than done. Oh, he was sure he could find someone who *said* they were IRA. After all, to some of the young, second-generation, Brummie-Irish who wanted to prove their Irish roots, being connected to the organisation was almost some kind of sick, badge of honour.

Davey knew he could sit for hours explaining himself to the wrong person, only to have Chinese whispers make matters worse in the long run. He also knew that these type of men didn't like complications and that they would be more than happy to sort things out with a bullet to the back of the head. Nevertheless, playing Irish music had a way of opening doors that would otherwise slam in your face. Davey made a mental note as he ran through the names of the prominent Birmingham Irishmen he knew who were most likely candidates for this dreaded future conversation.

The *interview*, had lasted for nearly an hour before the pair returned to Abi and her father in the casino. Both were leant over the roulette table lost on a winning streak.

"All sorted?" Eddie asked without taking his eyes off the wheel.

Davey opened his mouth to answer but Dixie beat him to it.

"Yeah, all sorted Eddie!" Dixie patted the young man's shoulder with a smile.

Eddie turned away from the spinning wheel for a second.

"Maybe you pair should get out of town for a couple of days." he said to his daughter, "I'll ask around some of the duck eggs I know and see what I can find out."

Davey gave Abi a quick glance and when he saw her smile back at him he gave Eddie a quick nod of approval.

"Good, that's sorted then." Eddie said, turning back to the slowing roulette wheel he continued, "Now, let's win some bleeding cash!"

The afternoon slowly turned into night. After Eddie's win on the gambling table, Eddie and Dixie sat either side of the Irishman and the storytelling began in earnest, each tale getting taller and interspersed with laughter, drink and one-up-man-ship.

They talked of the old days, a time before law, order, health and safety had turned the city into a nanny state. Davey listened with interest, fascinated by this window into Birmingham's past. However, as Davey sat on the edge of the hotel bed twelve hours later, he was having difficulty recalling any of the stories in detail due to his dreadful hangover.

He flopped the newspaper open over his knee and was instantly captured by the bizarre headlines. *Death at the Mop,* he went on to read about how two gay lovers had somehow been killed in a freak accident at the Mop Fair in Kings Norton. Apparently, one of the gay men had fallen into the machinery of a fairground ride, dragged into the machinery by his long, golden frock. His lover had leapt to his transvestite boyfriend's assistance, only to be killed by the very same machinery himself. The only way the lovers could be recognised was from a wallet found in what was left of the boyfriends raincoat.

"A tale of true love. The ultimate sacrifice." The headlines read, the irony to the reality to the backstory lost on the reader. Already bored by the newspaper Davey dropped it on the floor and climbed back into the bed next to the sleeping woman. He ran his fingers through her hair, pondering the mixture of excitement and gravity it meant to be dating Eddie Fewtrell's daughter. It would be a difficult tightrope walk between falling in with Eddie's expectations of a future son-in-law, and maintaining some level of self-identity under the Fewtrell family umbrella. Eddie liked straight talking, that was for sure and he had obviously seen and done a few things, and even if he enjoyed a bit of exaggeration when telling a tale, Davey knew the nightclub owner had been correct about one thing.

"Get out of town for a few days until the dust settles!" Knowing that this was coming from a man who had had his fair share of close shaves, he was only too happy to take Eddie's advice.

****

McBride and the Fox stood atop the bridge above Gas Street Basin looking down over the waterway watching the little community of boat-dwellers and water gypsies. The scene was a pleasant one, especially on a clear day like this. The deep blue sky reflecting in the canal water took away some of its normally brown hue turning it to a muted diesel blue.

Since discovering the whereabouts of what they assumed was the Irish singer's canal boat, the pair had been standing like inner-city sentinels watching for any movement around the narrowboat with the shamrock in the window. Their watch over the last few days had only been broken by the occasional styrofoam cupped coffee, fags and plenty of amphetamine, and to say both men were now strung out would be a major understatement.

"For fuck's sake Foxy, this is a waste of time, the cunt ain't coming back here anytime soon, especially if he knows the IRA are after him!"

The Fox turned away from the view and sighed.

"You know what we used to call people like you in Dublin?"

McBride shook his head.

"No but I'm sure you gonna enlighten me!" he said sarcastically.

"A dead man walking!"

McBride laughed trying to hide the mixture of anger and concern at the statement from the Dublin hitman. The Fox turned to face the Brummie-Irish doorman.

"No, seriously, when I worked for the General we used to *off* gobshites like ye all the time. As a matter of fact, any sort of complaining could end up with a trip down to the Dublin docks *or* if the General liked ye, ye might get a shallow grave with a view over the Dublin mountains." The hitman began to laugh. "Every time I think about those dumb American tourists coming over to Ireland to find their *roots*, wandering around the hills taking photos of the view. I think to myself, little do they know they're taking pictures of Ireland's biggest fucking graveyard."

McBride snorted.

"Yeah, well them days are over ain't they Foxy!" The doorman stood tall and took his hands from the pockets of his black MA1 jacket. "The General's dead and if you keep barking like you do. I'm gonna have to teach the little fox pup a lesson in . . . "

The other man raised his hand.

"Shh . . ."

He pointed towards the tow path beneath them. McBride didn't move. Instead he was priming himself for a swift punch to the Dublin man's jaw. The Fox turned his head and gave him a dismissive look.

"You ain't too clever are ye McBride?" he said with a laugh. "You only see the man in front of ye, ye don't see the hundred men that stand behind me. If anything happens to me then you'll find out just how many men are willing to take my place."

He let the words sink in for a few seconds.

"And if you're in any doubt about what I'm saying, just ask the British army, if the IRA can beat those bastards, then I'm sure we'll have no problem making a fat arsehole like you disappear."

McBride's angry scowl fell from his face as his testosterone filled balls began to shrink to the size of hazelnuts in the face of the IRA hitman's deadly warning.

"Now stick to the fucking job at hand."

The Fox pointed down the tow path towards two figures in the distance.

"Seems like our bait has drawn out another couple of rats, *look*!"

McBride was glad of the distraction and he turned towards the area where the Fox was pointing.

There were two men walking along the two path, which in itself was nothing unusual. The canal system cross-crossed the city in all manner of directions and for many, it was the fastest way to get where they were going to without having to walk around entire blocks of office buildings as the canals simply ran underneath the streets in long straight lines. For anyone that knew their way around the spider's web of waterways, this was a god send when it came to commuting to work in the rush hour or struggling home with a day's shopping from the rag market or Bull Ring.

However, this pair were no commuters or lazy shoppers. To the Fox, who it must be said, had spent most of his life in the busy back streets of Ireland's capital city, either following his victims or being followed by the Garda Siochana and thus knew a thing or two about people watching, it was blatantly obvious that this pair were searching for something or someone.

"Looks like our singer boy has pissed someone *else* off?" he said.

McBride watched the two men below him with suspicion. The tall dark haired man was slowly walking along the cobbled path. He bent and began looking in the windows of each of the canal boats. The other man, short and stocky with a brutal face and a bald tattooed head walked ahead and did the same. The bouncer and hitman watched from their post with a growing interest.

"Lets go down there and ask em who they're looking for!" McBride said in a whisper.

The Fox turned and looked at him as if he were mad.

"*You* ain't going fucking anywhere pal, least of all down there." he said angrily. "All we're gonna do is watch and wait and see what happens next."

The thin Irishman began to laugh to himself.

"What's so funny?" McBride said quietly.

"You don't need to whisper McBride, they can't see us, never mind hear us." He shook his head at the doorman's embarrassed expression. "Tell ya what, if ye wanna go anywhere . . . " Fox nodded down the street, " . . . and go down to the rendezvous cafe and get us both a cup of coffee, I'll stay here a keep and eye on Pinky and Perky down there."

McBride didn't move, the Fox turned to him with a smile. "Go on ya soft lummox, fuck off !" With that the large bouncer turned and began walking down the street back towards the city centre and the greasy spoon cafe where he had been buying styrofoam cups of coffee for the past two days. He was happy to get away from his perch next to the Dublin man. Over the last few days he'd begun to ask himself why he was even involved with any of this. He wasn't a member of the IRA, so why should he give a shit about the collections to the cause? The only reason he could find was his friendship with Declan O'Dwyer, his boss, and that was strained to say the least. As the doorman trod the pavement away from the Fox, he experienced an overwhelming moment of clarity.

"Fuck this shit . . . " he said to himself, " . . . none of this is my problem, I'm stood here like a prick letting that little twat talk to me as if I'm a . . . "

He didn't finish his sentence, something caught his eye, or at least *someone* caught his eye. A beautiful blonde girl was climbing from a black cab fifty yards ahead of him. The rant stopped abruptly as he continued to walk towards where the blonde was now standing on the pavement awaiting the other passenger to pay the cabbie and climb out. He didn't know why but the hair on the back of his neck rose like spines at the sight of the cab, his instincts telling him that this was who he'd been waiting for the past forty-eight hours. He stopped and stared through the window of a random shop, hands in the pockets of his nylon jacket trying to look casual, all the time keeping one eye on the cab in the windows reflection. Eventually, the other passenger stepped out on to the pavement. The blonde man turned and paid the driver, took the girl's hand crossing the pavement and stepping inside the Rendezvous cafe and out of sight.

"*Fuck*!" McBride said aloud recognising the Irish singer. "It's him!"

He stood frozen for a second, pondering the situation. The singer certainly didn't look like he was in hiding or worried about being found. The doorman stood on the side of Broad Street inwardly wrestling between a quick sprint back to inform the Fox or stay where he was and keep an eye on the two new arrivals. He decided on the former.

The Fox was still leaning over the railings to the bridge watching the two men below who were totally unaware they being watched. He turned to see the burly bouncer sprinting as best he could along the wide pavement towards him. His mean face broke into a smirk as McBride drew near.

"Ye forgot the coffee ye gob-shite!"

"He's *here*!" McBride shouted.

"Who?" Fox replied.

"The fucking singer ... *Keogh*!"

The answer caught the Fox by surprise and he flustered for a second, turning his head this way and that between the bouncer and the two men on the tow path below. He saw that the men had grown bored of their search and had begun to cross one of the low wrought iron bridges that spanned the canal.

"Come on, he's in the cafe with some blonde tart, we can corner him in there and ..."

The Fox was already sprinting down the street, past the doorman towards the cafe as fast as his spindly legs could carry him.

****

"Black coffee and a cappuccino please, darlin'!"

Davey laid a ten pound note on the counter without taking in the person behind it.

The elderly Greek woman on the other side of the formica top recognised him instantly and broke into a broad smile.

"Ahh Davey da Mod, it-sa-been-a-long-a-time, why you no come-a see me no more?"

The Irishman laughed at the way the woman had turned a friendly greeting into a guilt-ridden question. He opened his mouth to speak but she wasn't finished.

"You-a all grown up now, Davey." She eyed his shoulder-length blonde hair. "What, you ain't-a Mod no more? I thought you said you was always-a-gonna be a Mod!"

She burst into laughter and peered over his shoulder towards Abi who had taken one of the window seats and was enjoying seeing her boyfriend's embarrassment.

"My God you've got some memory on ya!" Davey exclaimed, barely able to remember the woman never mind the conversation about being a mod back in the days of the 1980s Mod revival.

The Rendezvous and Acropolis cafe two doors down had been regular haunts with the young scooterists and Mods during the 1980s and Davey, being a 16 year old Modernist peacock virtually lived there day and night. The cafe was busy with shoppers, commuters and the odd builder taking a tea and fag break and the Greek woman's fuss had drawn attention from the other customers. Davey pulled the two cups of coffee towards him across the formica counter before slapping a ten pound note down in front of the heavily made-up woman.

"Keep the change, love." he said trying to extricate himself from the reunion. "Nice to see ya again after all these years!"

He smiled and picked up the cups.

"What, no sausage rolls?" The woman exclaimed in her thick accent. "Dot-cha-want-a-one-a-ma sausage-rolls?"

The words were joined together as if it were one long singular word. Davey stood in front of the woman holding the overfilled coffee cups in front of him.

"Pardon?" he said, shaking his head, unable to decipher the woman's speedy sentence.

"Aww, Davey, don't ta-tell-a-me you-a-forgot about-ta-ma sausage rolls, you-all-a-ways-a love-a-ma-sausauge rolls."

The woman's expression changed from her initial friendly smile to one of heartbreaking sorrow. The change of expression caught the Irishman by surprise.

"I eh ... I ... " he stuttered, " ... I did?"

The other customers were beginning to enjoy the conversation now, with the odd stifled laugh breaking through the background noise of chewing, traffic and the tinny sound of a radio blaring pop music from somewhere in the kitchen behind the counter. She nodded.

"Yeah you-a-did, you used to come-a in here with all the other little Mod boys and say, *Mama I like a bit a sausage*!"

A loud guffaw of laughter spread around the smokey cafe, Davey felt his cheeks burning. He turned towards Abi only to find she was laughing too. He shook his head, mouthing the words, *no, I didn't,* silently whilst trying to smile to hide his growing embarrassment. Unfortunately, the Greek cafe owner saw him do this, the sight of which seemed to shift her recollection up a gear. Now she began to address the whole cafe.

"Oh-a yes-a you did Davey, don't-a tell-a lies! You used to come in-a here with your big green coat and hush puppies and say-a. Mama Nikolopoulos, where's-a ma big-a sausage in-a da roll-a!"

By now the whole cafe was openly laughing at the blonde man with the bright red face holding the cups.

"I tell-a ya what, I-a give-a you da sausage on-a da house!" the woman continued.

She turned and vanished into kitchen area at the rear of the rear of the building, calling out. "Mr. Nikolopoulos, little Davey wants-a sausage, a big-a thick-a sausage!"

The singer took advantage of the woman's exit to escape the embarrassment at the counter. He picked his way through the packed cafe towards the table in the window where Abi was still laughing.

"Here mate!" Davey turned towards a group of scruffy scaffolders who were huddled around one of the booth tables smoking and drinking tea. A large man in a day glow yellow vest was looking directly toward him.

"Ain't ya gonna wait for Mr. Nikolopoulos' big thick sausage?"

The group burst into laughter. Davey felt his face flush a deeper shade of red and scurried past the group with a self-conscious smile.

"I heard you like a bit of Cumberland!" another of the builders called behind him.

The Irishman ignored the jibe and sat down at the window table opposite his hysterical girlfriend only too happy to join the other seated customers. He looked at her pretty face and saw her eyeliner had smudged into thick black lines beneath her eyes smeared by tears of laughter.

"Very funny!" he said matter of factly.

"Oh my God, she's hilarious!" Abi said, dabbing a napkin around the skin beneath her eyes.

The Irishman sighed.

"Hilarious ain't a word I would have chosen!"

As he spoke his eye was drawn to the large glass door to the cafe opening behind Abi. Two men stepped inside the smokey cafe, one he recognised instantly as a doorman from the Dublin Barrel, a venue he'd played at several times before over the past few years and had become friendly with many of the door staff including this fellow. The other, the thin man with the spiteful face, he didn't.

He saw the thin man glance in his direction followed by the doorman. The glance seemed odd to Davey, especially when he nodded back towards them, who obviously recognised him but seemed to be avoiding his gaze. Davey recalled talking to the bouncer a few months before and how he'd even stepped in to help the doorman when a fight had broken out between the staff and a group of Irish travellers.

Although he couldn't recall the doorman's name, he remembered that they had become friendly after that. So why was the man avoiding his acknowledgement now? Abi was talking but Davey wasn't paying attention. For some reason he couldn't explain, his eye was drawn to these two men who had just entered and were now taking their seats at the far end of the cafe. Strangely, they sat side by side on the long booth seat instead of opposite each other as most people would have. Abi was still making fun of Davey over the incident with the Greek cafe owner and although he was looking directly at her face, his eyes couldn't help but stare over her shoulder, though her long blonde hair.

There it was again, a quick glance from the thin man towards him followed by another by the doorman. Davey smiled and nodded again but the bouncer wouldn't meet his stare. Then the penny dropped. Well, penny wasn't really the right word, bowling ball was a far better analogy to describe the feeling Davey felt in the pit of his stomach. The realisation that this bouncer who he couldn't recall the name of, was definitely connected to Declan O'Dwyer, owner of the Dublin Barrel, a fully-fledged Irish republican *and*, as far as he knew, an active member of the Birmingham IRA. The previous night's conversation with detective Dixie re-ran through his mind. The sudden realisation that the IRA had found *him* before he could reach out to *them* and explain his innocence in connection with the Irish Centre robbery, sent a jolt through him. He tried to reason with himself that the odd couple may just be another couple of customers in need of a cuppa. However, another shifty glance in his direction by the red-headed man with the spiteful face soon put a stop to any thought that this was going to play out favourably.

"Are you ok?" Davey's attention came back to the girl in front of him. "You've gone as white as a sheet!" she said with a concerned smile.

Davey opened his mouth to explain the situation but couldn't find the words.

"We have to go!" he finally said under his breath.

Abi's smile turned into a bemused scowl.

"For God's sake Davey, she was only taking the piss, it was funny . . ."

"No, it's something else, we have to leave!" Abi's expression didn't change, and Davey knew he wasn't making sense. "It was something I was talking to Dixie about last night, a . . ." he searched for a description of his situation, " . . . a problem."

"Problem?" she repeated.

"Yeah a problem that's getting worse by the minute," he glanced absently over her shoulder as he said the words. Abi, on seeing this began to turn her head in the direction of the two men.

"*Don't*!"

He placed his hand upon her's lest she think he was being aggressive.

"Don't go staring or you'll make the problem worse than it already is."

It was Abi's face that now lost its colour.

"Shall I call my Dad? If you're in trouble he can sort it out!"

Davey tried to smile.

"Thanks Abi but I'm afraid even your old fella can't deal with *these* people."

Abi shook her head.

"Are you joking, Dad can deal with anyone . . ."

He squeezed her hand softly.

"No, these fuckers have given the British Army a run for their money. This is out of his league I'm afraid."

Abi went to turn once more, trying to see what her boyfriend was talking about. Just as she did they were joined at the table by the cafe owner who blocked her view of the two men Davey was referring to.

"Here you-a are, on-a da house. Mr Nickolopulos's big-a sausage roll!" the woman said at the top of her voice as she placed a white plate with the longest sausage roll either of the lovers had ever seen in on the table front of them.

A cheer from the other watching customers went up around the cafe and the Greek woman stood back for a second to admire the pastry.

"I must admit . . . " she continued, " . . . I do-a like-a bit-o sausage myself every now and-a then."

Another burst of laughter followed, along with a small round of applause and cheering from the builders and scaffolders on the bench seats as the woman unconsciously made one double-entendre after another.

Davey gave her a quick smile before standing and snatching the sixteen inch long sausage roll and grabbing Abi's hand, who rose with him to leave. He then leant into the Greek cafe owner and planted a kiss on her cheek.

"I'll have it to go, thanks love!"

****

By the time Fox and McBride realised what was happening the lovers had exited the cafe and were already running down an alleyway behind the building towards Gas Street Basin and Davey's narrowboat. McBride sprung to his feet just as the Greek cafe owner approached their table. The woman blocked the aisle for a few seconds as both men tried to extricate themselves from the long bench seat in the booth in which they were seated.

"Get the fuck out of the way you silly *bitch!*" McBride shouted as he watched his prey escape through the front door.

However, his words didn't have the effect he wanted and far from being cowered and stepping aside, Mrs. Nickolopoulos exploded into a tantrum of her own. Strange sounding obscenities filled the room as she swore at the men in her pigeon English and native greek. The commotion caused an even longer delay as the woman refused to budge an inch until the burley doorman had apologised for his remark. McBride's unbridled aggression, brought about by three days without sleep, finally got the better of him and he screamed into the woman's face. This time she folded her arms in a buffalo stance and continued to babble Greek obscenities back at him.

The table of scaffolders and builders began to stir. The young men didn't like what they were seeing, and although the bouncer looked like he could handle himself, there were eight of them, which was more than enough for the big guy in the black jacket and his scrawny pal. The largest of the scaffolders stood and approached the altercation. He tapped the woman's shoulder.

"Don't worry love, I'll deal with this."

He pushed the woman softly but firmly to one side and stepped into her place right in front of McBride. The Fox saw that the other builders had begun to stand now, ready to join their leader.

"We ain't got time for this, McBride!" he said under his breath. "Just say sorry to the lady and we'll fuck off!" The doorman heard the words but his rage had already consumed him.

"Fuck that!" he snarled into the scaffolder's face. "You got a problem big boy?"

The builder, who was as big as the doorman didn't answer, instead he brought his fist up in what should have been a lightning blow to McBride's jaw. However, the bouncer had already anticipated the move and simply turned his head an inch to the left and let the fist sail past his jaw into thin air. In reaction the doorman brought his own fist up with as much speed and force as he could muster where it met the scaffolder's chin with an explosion of energy, lifting the fifteen stone builder off the floor smashing his jaw with a crunch of teeth.

Crack! The sound of the bone in the man's face breaking was clearly audible to all in the cafe and as if in slow motion, the huge day-glo clad scaffolder flew backwards across the table he'd just left, scattering tea cups and plates here and there, in a shower of blood, teeth and Tetley's.

If testicles made a sound every time they got smaller, then the sound of balls shrinking inside the cafe would have been deafening. Suddenly, the scaffolder's weren't too sure about their fighting prowess now that their champion had gone down like a Led Zeppelin. McBride had seen this a hundred times before at the Dublin Barrel, as had the Fox at the rough drinking spots in Dublin and both men began to push their way through the packed aisle towards the front door of the cafe and back onto the pavement of Broad Street, where they burst into a sprint back towards their sentinel spot on the bridge.

✦ ╬╫╪╫╪

Davey held Abi's hand tightly as he helped her step onto the rear deck area of the boat. She was still in some confusion as to what was happening but realised that this wasn't a time for questions and just went along with the panic. Davey checked around him to see if the two men in the cafe had followed them.

"You open her up and I'll untie the bow line!" he said tossing a set of keys towards the girl.

She caught the keys but didn't move.

"Who are you running from Davey? What's going . . . "

The Irishman had jumped from the boat and had begun to walk down the cobbles towards the bow where the thick rope had been tied in a bowknot through a cast iron hoop in the old tow path.

"I'll explain everything Abi . . . " he called over his shoulder, " . . . but for the moment let's just get out of here!"

As he bent to untie the rope, something caught his eye on the far side of the canal. Sitting on an old cast iron bench were two men watching him. He instantly recognised Abi's ex-boyfriend

270

Dez as one of them but couldn't place the other thick-set, brutal-looking man next to him.

Suddenly, Davey knew where he'd seen the swallow and star tattoo before. It had been on the hand of the dark-haired man who was now rising from his seat on the opposite side of the canal and tugging on the sleeve of the thug sat next to him. Neither man made any secret that they were after the singer as they both burst into action, running along the canal, back towards the narrow pedestrian bridge that joined both sides of the canal. Davey watched them as they closed in on the bridge. Panic set in to his fingers as he tried unsuccessfully to untie the rope in the old metal hoop. He daren't take his eyes off his assailants for a second but he must if he was to untie the bow rope. Turning his attention to the knot he fumbled with shaking hands to release the slipknot. *Clang, clang, clang,* he could now hear their heeled shoes clomping on the metal bridge and still the knot wouldn't release.

"*Fuck*!" he cried trying to control his panic.

He let a long breath of air escape his lungs and drew his nerves together. He held the rope in his hand and wondered why the knot wouldn't release, after all he'd done this a thousand times before. *Clang clang clang.* Now there were two sets of feet on the bridge. He tried to breathe slowly.

"Ok, get your shit together Davey!" he said to himself.

Holding the loop in the palm of his hand he suddenly realised that he had been holding the knotted rope upside down and had been tightening the bow rope instead of releasing it. He turned the rope and pulled. The knot released itself through the loop easily and fell to the floor. He quickly shot a look towards the men and was shocked to see that they were just turning the corner of the bridge and were now running along the cobbles towards him at speed. It would only be seconds before they cleared the one hundred or so yards between the bridge and boat and then Davey knew by the looks on their vicious faces, it would be game over.

Gathering the rope he threw it in a pile on the forward deck and ran back along the tow path. He pushed the side of the canal boat until it started to drift away from the dockside and into the middle of the canal and leapt onboard before it went too far. The bow was the last part of the boat to leave the stone wall it had been tied to and Dez and Bull were closing in sharply.

Abi had gone below and was unaware of the commotion that was happening on the tow path above. Davey stepped towards the controls to the boat and pressed the large green button beneath the throttle. The huge Lister engine began to rumble in the engine compartment beneath the decking under his feet. He began to pray silently that the old engine would start from cold without its normal fuss. The engine turned over with a grind of cogs. Davey watched as the men raced towards him.

"Come on *come on* you bastard, start!" he said aloud. He could see the look of triumph Dez's mean face clearly now as the men cleared the fifty or so yards between them. He took his finger from the button and forced himself to count to three. A trick the previous owner of the boat had shown him on the day he'd purchased it.

"One, two . . . ," he said to himself, all the while watching the pair close in, " . . . three!" He pressed again. This time the engine burst into life with a cloud of blue diesel smoke emanating from its exhaust. Davey sighed with relief as he pulled the throttle backwards sending the boat into reverse. There was a few second's delay as the boat's propeller gathered enough water to drive the little boat backwards. All the time the man drew closer and were now only twenty yards away. The Irishman watched as the bow slowly cleared the dockside. Inch by inch it crept away from its mooring and Davey knew that if he didn't clear the gap, then the men could easily jump aboard the boat from the dockside, especially at the speed they were running.

A plume of white water bubbled up behind the little boat as he reversed from the mooring and the propeller started to find its momentum. One, two, three feet now separated the bow and the dockside. He saw the brutal-looking, bald man burst into a sprint as he set himself up to leap across the divide and land on the bow of the boat.

"Come on *come on!*" he said under his breath again as he pulled the throttle lever as far back as it would go.

The action caught him by surprise as the minute movement in the lever seemed to kick the engine into another gear. The boat lurched backwards just as Bull's feet left the dockside. As if in slow motion the big man sailed through the air as the boat continued its backwards momentum. Then, *thud!* The man's feet found a purchase on the edge of the thick ledge surrounding the bow area. The weight of the man sent a shiver through the boat causing it to waddle sideways in the water as it continued backwards. Bull smiled to himself as he balanced on the ledge watching the blonde man at the far end of the narrowboat pulling hard on the throttle with a horrified expression on his face.

If Bull had stepped aboard properly at that point the lovers would have been trapped like rats in a barrel . . . However, he didn't. Instead the big man was too busy congratulating himself on his leap of faith and tidy landing on the boat's edge. Davey saw this and with a quick pull of the tiller the canal boat suddenly changed direction unbalancing Bull for a second. It was enough. The boat had cleared its moorings now and was completely afloat in the middle of the cut. Davey swung the tiller the other way. The action caused the boat to rock in the water and the big man on the front began to wave his arms around wildly as he fought for his balance. Their eyes crossed for a split second. Now Davey could see the triumph on the tattooed face vanish, replaced with one of panic as the two men swapped expressions. Still flailing his arms in windmills around him, Bull fell backwards into the filthy, canal water with an angry shriek and a splash of brown, oily water.

The Irishman threw the throttle into its forward position and the boat's backwards movement slowed for a second before the boat began to travel forwards down the canal. Dez watched helplessly from the tow path as Bull splashed about in the canal and his *Patsy* escaped at the snail's pace of the narrowboat. Bull surfaced from the murky water with a gasp, spitting the water from his mouth and yelled his rage at the passing boat.

"You fucking bastard, I'm gonna . . . !"

The man's rage was brought to a halt by the sixteen inch sausage roll hitting him square in the face. Davey turned to see Abi behind him. She had picked the pastry from the deck where Davey had dropped it, and had launched Mrs. Nickolopolous's pride and joy towards the man's bald head with as much force as she could. It landed with a loud slap on his forehead, some of it coming to rest in Bull's open mouth, which brought the vocal abuse to a sudden stop, replacing the rage with a coughing fit instead. Bull coughed, spluttered and choked on the pastry as he splashed around.

There was a moment's silence before both on the narrowboat burst out laughing at the ridiculousness of the bizarre situation. The laughter soon stopped though as Davey caught sight of Dez glaring at him from the tow path. The dark man was walking at a slightly slower speed than the canal boat so kept up with it for a short distance. He said nothing, only glared at the couple on the deck with a burning vengeance that left no one in any doubt that this little debacle would be paid for at some point in the very near future. As the boat gathered speed it moved down the basin towards the Broad Street bridge, both passengers watched the man in the water swim towards the dockside until he was clumsily helped out by his associate. Davey and Abi watched the pair with growing relief as the little canalboat chugged along the waterway making its escape to the countryside.

He turned around and took Abi's hand. She was still laughing. He could see it was a nervous laughter and he knew that underneath this show of bravado, she was scared. He pulled her towards him and kissed her square on her full lips.

"As long as I live, I'll never forget what you did with that sausage roll!" he said trying to stifle a nervous laugh of his own.

"Are you going to tell me what's going on now?" Abi asked, with more than a touch of anger in her voice. "Why is Dez after you and who were the two men in the cafe?"

As if on cue the pair's attention was drawn to some commotion happening on the bridge overhead. For just at that moment

McBride and the Fox appeared at the handrail to the bridge, the two of them panting from the sprint along Broad Street. McBride opened his mouth to say something but the Fox placed his hand on the doorman's broad forearm and stopped him. The four people watched each other suspiciously for nearly a minute as the boat passed under the bridge at its top speed of five miles per hour. Slowly the narrowboat sank into the shadows of the bridge and each group lost sight of one another.

****

"We've lost em!" McBride said angrily. "We could always run up the canal side and try and stop em further up the . . . !"

"Nah!" The Fox stopped him. "We don't need to do that."

McBride turned to the Dublin man and saw he was watching the other two men on the canal side. Without taking his eyes from the men, the Fox asked McBride a question.

"You said you've met that singer before, didn't you?"

McBride nodded.

"Yeah, when he's played at the Dublin Barrel," the doorman replied, a bemused expression replacing the angry one he'd had since the confrontation in the cafe, "Why?"

"Does he know about Declan's connections to the I.R.A.?"

McBride shrugged.

"I don't know for sure, probably. Even if he doesn't, he *does* know you don't fuck with a bloke like Declan!"

"Well did he look like he was *scared* of us?"

McBride shook his head.

"Not really, no!"

The Fox raised his eyebrows, still staring at the men on the tow path who were oblivious they were being watched.

"*Exactly*, he didn't try and hide from us, far from it, in fact, as soon as he saw you, he smiled and nodded."

The bouncer seemed confused.

"Yeah, so what if he did?"

"Well, if you were guilty of robbing the I.R.A. and you knew that the men who had just followed you in to a cafe were somehow connected to the I.R.A., then would you be smiling and nodding at them to get their attention?"

The doorman suddenly clicked.

"No, you fucking wouldn't, you'd be hiding your face so as not to be seen but why did he do a runner?"

The Fox turned to McBride and gave him a little punch in the chest.

"Sure look at the size of ya! If you were sat staring at me with your ugly puss, I'd do a fucking runner, it's only natural."

McBride shook his head.

"So you're saying he's not involved?"

"Oh no, he's involved somewhere along the line but whether he actually did the robbery or not seems doubtful to me, he might just be a stooge to throw us and the pigs off the scent!" The bouncer's face screwed into a confused scowl.

The Fox continued.

"Those pair on the other hand." He nodded towards the men on the tow path who were now walking back across the metal pedestrian bridge at pace towards a parked up black BMW. "Now those two look far more likely to have been involved in the shenanigans at the Irish Centre than our singer and his pretty girlfriend."

McBride watched as the pair stopped at the car. The dark-haired man began to climb into the driver's side but stopped as he did. He noticed the two men on the bridge staring towards him. He stared back for a second before climbing into the car. The tattooed bald man stood at the rear of the car. He opened the trunk and took off his soaked jacket, screwing it in a ball he threw the garment into the boot. He started to dry himself off with an old grey blanket he found inside.

"If there's one thing a fox is good at, it's smelling a rat and I got a feeling that if we follow them . . ." Fox said as he watched the little scene, " . . . *they'll* lead us to the singer and with a few questions asked in the right way," the Fox made the shape of a pistol with his hand, "I'm certain we'll get to the bottom of bloody mess once and for all!"

"And what if the singer and his bird *are* involved?"

"Well, it'll be four bullets instead of two, won't it?" the Fox said coldly.

McBride slapped the metal handrail of the bridge with his open hands before spinning on his heel and waving down one of the black cabs along Broad street. The car stopped and he threw the rear door open. Calling back across the pavement to the Dublin hitman.

"Come on then, Foxy!" he said sternly. The hitman turned from the railing just as Bull was climbing in the BMW. In a half-trot he crossed the pavement and pointed towards the black car.

"Follow that car!" he said laughing. McBride gave him a puzzled look. The Fox raised his eyebrows excitedly.

"I've always wanted to say that!"

CHAPTER 24

The Balti Belt

1995

The journey to Davey's overgrown hideout in Lapworth seemed to fly by as they talked earnestly about the men who had chased them. Slowly, the little boat found its way out of the city and into the countryside and against a backdrop of overhanging trees and country tow paths, the lovers tried to work out what their next move should be.

The further away from the city they sailed, the calmer they became. Each slow chug of the diesel engine took them further down the brown river until finally the panic that had initially gripped them following the chase had subsided altogether. Davey navigated the canal boat into the sunset, through the growing evening mist, delicately pulling and pushing the tiller arm until at long last they came-to on the hidden mooring of the long forgotten creek. The boat brushed aside the tall water reeds until the bow of the boat nudged the grass covered bank delicately with a soft thud. Arrival at the tranquil setting seemed to revive the pair as if the events earlier that morning were some distant memory and no longer mattered. Neither passenger could have guessed that far from escaping into a mist-shrouded sanctuary they had just sailed into the very heart of darkness.

****

Meanwhile, somewhere back in the city, a black BMW wound its way through the streets towards the old Stratford road. The traffic around the Mermaid Pub, situated about halfway along the road was at a standstill due to Birmingham city council's decision to cut back the huge, oak trees that stood either side of the busy road. The oak trees had been planted there the same year that General George Custer had come to his grizzly end at the battle of the Little Big Horn in the mid 1800s and since then had grown so large that during the summer months, the trees, which were staggered along the pavements on opposite sides of the road, often formed a gargantuan green canopy overhead, giving the impression that one was travelling through a long green tunnel.

However, since the 1970s the area had become heavily populated by Indian and Pakistani immigrants, many of whom owned businesses along the stretch of road beneath the canopy. The custom in their far off homelands was to array their goods along the pavements outside their shops which was exactly what they did when setting up business along this historic British highway. Unfortunately for them, the huge English oak trees created havoc on the pavements below. In the spring, a fresh layer of sticky seedlings and freshly-hatched chicks fell from upon high onto whatever lay on the stalls beneath. In the summer, so much shade was cast by the huge branches that it left most of the pavement and goods in a dark shadow and during the autumn and winter months things got even worse, with the slightest breeze sending a never ending shower of falling leaves, twigs and bird's nests from the highest branches, covering the stalls and goods beneath in a layer of wet squelchy mush.

Of course it wasn't long before the very vocal population of the Sparkhill area of the city, demanded something be done and so down they came. Much to the delight of the merchants and much to the annoyance of the city's commuters.

"For fuck's sake Dez how much longer are we gonna sit here!" Bull finally blew his top. "It'd be faster to fucking walk!" He wound his window down and leant out.

"Come on you lazy cunts, we got somewhere to fucking be!" He screamed at a team of day-glow clad workmen further along the road who were busy cutting the lower lying branches on one of the huge trees.

Dez laughed.

"Calm down Bull! You're gonna give yourself a bloody heart attack."

A group of old Pakistani men turned to see what the commotion was about. Bull saw them looking at him and began to vent his spleen towards them instead.

"What you lot fucking looking at?"

Inside the car Dez sighed, knowing what was coming.

"Why don't you Paki cunts fuck off back where ya came from?"

The old men began to mutter amongst themselves.

"Yeah that's right, yap, yap, yap, that's all you cunts are good for! Why don't ya get a fucking job instead of standing around here claiming ya fucking dole money you shower of camel-shaggers?"

"For Gods sake Bull!"

"What?"

"What . . . *what*?" Dez turned to look at the big man next to him. "You're leaning out the window of my fucking car shouting bloody murder at a bunch of old Paki blokes."

"So what?" Bull said shrugging.

"You're drawing attention to us!"

Bull looked at his boss, incredulous.

"Yeah so what? They're only a bunch of old blokes, what ya scarred of?"

Dez sighed again, then as if speaking to a child he explained.

"How fast are we going?"

"What?"

"I said, how fast are we going?"

Bull looked around him.

"We ain't moving, boss." he pointed at the long line of stationary traffic in front of their car, "We've been sat here nearly and hour and a half, that's why I'm giving these Paki's some stick, I'm bored!"

"Yeah, we ain't going nowhere and even if I could get out of this traffic, which I can't by the way, unless I drive along the pavement, we ain't going anywhere fast."

Bull nodded.

"Yeah, that's what I just said."

"So knowing that we're stuck here, you decide to go winding up the locals!"

Bull laughed.

"For fuck's sake boss, they're *old blokes*, one of my farts would blow em *all* over!"

Dez shook his head.

"You ain't the brightest of sparks, are ya Bull?" He pointed towards a group of ten or so younger Pakistani men, who had started to take notice of the black BMW. "*They* might be old farts but those bastards looking at us, look pretty mean to me."

Bull followed the line of Dez's finger. As he caught sight of the gang he unconsciously swallowed nervously.

"Nah, they're just Paki's too, we'd hammer em!" he said, trying to sound confident.

"You assume you're harder than them because they're skin's a different colour than yours?"

Bull didn't know how to reply.

"Nah . . . I ehhh!"

"Because . . . " Dez continued, " . . . those fuckers will be carrying, I fucking guarantee it and if you think I'm gonna get out of my car and take on . . . " he began to count the men, who had started to walk towards the car, " . . . *nine* of those fuckers, just because you're fucking bored, well, you got another thing coming, pal."

"But they're just Pakis boss, *sand* niggers!" Bull exclaimed loudly. "They ain't hard men like us, are they? They might be tooled up but they won't be anything against a bit of British beef me old son!"

"British beef?" Dez shook his head in disbelief. "How old are you, *twelve?*"

Bull huffed to himself and turned to stare back out of his window, trying to hide his embarrassment. Dez pressed a small button on the door of the car to lower driver's window. He poked his head out of the gap and scanned the packed road in front and behind. The long line of traffic was nose to tail as far as he could see. He saw faces of the other drivers behind their steering wheels. Car horns beeped and engines revved as the trapped drivers grew more and more impatient. Dez's eye was drawn to a taxi in the jam, three cars behind his own. He couldn't be sure but he had a suspicion the black cab had been following them since they had left the canal side. He decided to find out one way or the other.

He looked back towards the growing group of angry young Pakistani men who were still walking along the pavement towards him. They had reached the group of older men, the victims of Bull's outburst. He could see them talking earnestly amongst themselves in raised voices in their own language. The old men began to point towards the BMW and suddenly it was clear what was about to happen. The gang of Pakistani's began to approach the car en masse, violent looks on their faces and the odd flash of a silver blade in their hands. Dez smiled to himself mischievously as he turned the car key, igniting the engine.

"There ya go Bull, I told you they'd be carrying, didn't I?"

Without waiting for an answer, he pressed his foot to the floor on the throttle pedal. The BMW's exhaust roared high above the idling engines of the other cars in the traffic jam. The sound brought the group of Pakistani men to a standstill, their angry expressions replaced with ones of concern that their prey was about to escape.

"Put ya seatbelt on, Bull!"

"But if there's gonna be a scrap we'll need to get out of the car . . ."

"Just put your *fucking* belt on!" Dez ordered as he revved the engine once more.

Bull suddenly understood what Dez had in mind. The Pakistani men began to run towards the car along the pavement, blades in hand. With another loud rev, Dez spun the wheel towards them and released the clutch. The powerful car sprung to life as if it were a black panther, leaping towards its prey. With a deafening screech of rubber on tarmac, the car lurched onto the pavement towards the gang of angry men. It crossed the space in the blink of an eye, hitting the first of the group at around thirty miles per hour. The skinny Pakistani fellow spun off in the air on impact, flying over the car's roof like a rag doll, landing in a crumpled mess of dumbfounded concussion and broken bones on the pavement behind the car. Bull slapped the dashboard laughing.

"Ha ha, ten points for that one boss!"

Dez wasn't listening, he was busy concentrating on steering the car with surgical precision between the stationary traffic, the street lights and shop fronts.

The Pakistani men had nowhere to go. Their escape routes blocked by the stalls of goods lined along the pavement. On seeing the fate of their unfortunate comrade, a panic took over the group and they began to throw themselves over the tabletops full of goods trying escape the oncoming car. The car smashed into the first stall with a sickening thud, sending the fruit that had been piled on the counters high into the air. The man sheltering behind the flimsy stall didn't stand a chance. The wooden counter and aluminium frame collapsed under the weight of the car as if it were made of paper. His legs instantly caught beneath the driver's wheel shattering the bone from toe to hip. The tyre tread pulled him beneath the BMW's chassis like a meat grinder before spitting him out behind the car in a ball of torn rags and gristle.

Dez paid no attention to the chaos around him, instead he felt a surge of energy tingling through his limbs as he drove the car along the pavement towards a side road and his escape route. He felt the massive power of the car as if it were part of his own body, enjoying the sensation of unbridled cruelty. He was the centre of the storm, a God of mayhem on four wheels.

****

The Fox saw the black-haired man's head poking from the car window and even though the black cab he was seated in was three cars behind the BMW, he instinctively ducked his own head so as not to be seen. They watched the little drama unfolding in silent fascination as the Pakistani gang began to approach the black car in front of them. Then without warning the BMW mounted the pavement.

"What the fuck is he doing?" McBride said, astonished as he watched the spectacle of the black BMW racing along the pavement crashing into shop stalls, tossing pedestrians aside as if they were nothing more than a child's toy. He and the Fox sat openmouthed in the rear seat of the black cab. However, the Fox was already wise to Dez's ruse.

"He's heading for that side road. He must've seen me!" he snarled. "Hey!" he leant forward and slapped the glass behind the taxi driver's shoulder, "Follow that BMW!" The driver, a plump tattooed Black-Country man in his fifties turned in his seat.

"Yow wha?"

"You heard me, follow that car!" the Fox shouted into the small money hole in the plexiglass window.

The man stared through the spittle-covered glass at the odd couple in the back of his cab for a few seconds, trying to weigh up the situation. McBride was taking no notice of the driver, instead he watched as the BMW cornered the road and vanished behind the Balti house on the corner of the street.

"We're gonna lose him, Foxy!"

The Fox slammed the glass with his fist.

"What are ye waiting for fatty, follow that fucking car *now*!"

"I ain't driving on the bleeding pavement for no one, I'll lose me bloody license!"

The Fox put his face to the money hole, filling it with his features and snarled a yellow-toothed threat at the driver.

"You'll lose more than your fucking license if ye don't!"

He pulled his filleting knife from his pocket. In less than the the blink of an eye, he had withdrawn his face from the hole and replaced it with his outstretched arm, knife in hand, bringing the razor-sharp blade up at lightning speed, until its point lay directly beneath the taxi driver's double-chin.

"Am I making myself clear sunshine? Follow the car or I'll shank ye right here and now and take the cab anyway!"

The colour from the driver's normally gammon pink face fell from him in an instant. He hesitated for a split second, not knowing what to do. Foxy prodded the blade into his flabby skin.

"Don't even think about dicking me around! Just do as your told and follow that fucking car . . . *now!*"

McBride wrapped the plexiglass with his knuckles, frustrated that the chase was taking so long to get started.

"Do as he says mate . . . " he gestured towards the Fox with his head, " . . . or I swear he'll gut you right here, in the middle of the street."

The taxi-driver stared into his rearview mirror where his eyes darted between the desperate faces staring back at him. Whether it was McBride's warning words or the sight of two such violent looking men in the back of his cab, or indeed, the twelve inch filleting blade jabbing into his stubbly chin, we'll never know, but whatever it was, the driver pushed the gear lever into first and floored the throttle of the old diesel cab and took up the chase. The whole incident had taken less than a minute and on seeing the driver's reaction, Foxy withdrew his knife and tried to reassure the him.

"Don't worry big man, ye'll be getting a good drink out of this when we catch up with that car."

The taxi mounted the pavement with a thud. What the taxi lacked in fineness, it more than made up with torque and weight, pushing the metal-framed stalls aside as it followed the same path that the BMW had taken a minute or so before. The injured pedestrians who were just beginning to gather themselves together after the initial hit and run, now found themselves in the sights

285

of a much larger heavier vehicle speeding along the sidewalk towards them. Once again, almost comically they began to throw themselves aside wherever they could to escape the oncoming cab.

The two men in the back of the cab couldn't help but chuckle at the ridiculous sight of grown men flying here and there across the pavement as the taxi caught one after the other with its wings and bonnet. McBride instinctively looked behind him out of the rear window at the trail of disaster they had left in their wake. Shop stalls and goods lay everywhere burying the Pakistani gang members who had been caught by the first car.

People who had been caught in the traffic jam were now standing beside their cars, watching the spectacle, and to McBride's surprise, some were climbing back into their cars and pulling up onto the pavement, following their path in order to escape the traffic jam themselves. He turned back just as the cab left the pavement and pulled into the same side of the road the BMW had taken. Although the road had parked cars lined along either side, it was clear, and McBride could see the BMW at the far end of the road blocked by an oncoming car. Due to the cars parked so tightly either side of the road there was nowhere for either car to pass. As the taxi raced towards it as fast as the driver dared, both McBride and the Fox stared through the scratched plexiglass window towards the car at the other end of the road, each of them praying silently that they would reach it before it had a chance to escape.

****

It came as some surprise to Dez and Bull when the twelve inch filleting knife suddenly appeared through the open window of the trapped BMW. Dez gripped the steering wheel tightly, waiting for the cold steel to piece his throat. Bull reacted and made a grab for the knife but as he did the passenger door of the car flew open and he was grabbed by his thick set arm and pulled through the open door by the burly doorman McBride. Bull turned instinctively to see who had hold of him and as his head came through the gap in the open door, McBride slammed his huge fist into the ex-con's face with a scream of anger. The man's already-broken nose exploded into a fountain of claret as McBride smashed his fist into the man's face several times until Bull's tattooed head swung back into the car and he fell unconscious onto Dez's lap.

Dez froze at the sudden violence. His usual spiteful bravado nowhere to be found in the face of such aggression, replaced with shock and confusion as he recognised the pair from earlier that day.

"You're, you're the two on the bridge at Gas Street basin . . ." he stuttered, "We thought you were a pair of homeless tramps or something. Who the fuck are you, old Bill?"

He hoped they were police but in reality he knew the answer to his question even before the words had left his mouth. These two weren't the Old Bill, that much he was certain of and when the Fox answered his question in his thick Dublin brogue, his deepest fear that the game was up was confirmed.

"I . . . R . . . A." Foxy said with a malicious grin.

Dez gulped deeply at the sound of the three letters. His mind raced through various escape scenarios as he tried to figure out how he could talk this way out of this sudden change of situation but nothing came to mind and besides, that knife was still at his throat. Unable to move his head due to the blade, he just stared ahead at the other driver in the car that had been blocking his path, who, it must be said, on seeing the flash of a knife blade had suddenly found his reverse gear and was busy backing out into the busy traffic on Stoney Lane High Street. He heard the passenger door slam and then the rear nearside door open. He glanced in his rear view mirror just as McBride climbed into the car's back seat.

The doorman took the knife from Fox's hand and held it in place whilst the Dublin hitman climbed in his side of the car.

"Ok pal . . ." the Fox said, " . . . you're gonna drive and we're all gonna have a little chat while you do."

Dez nodded gently so as not to cut himself on the knife.

"Yeah and none of your Nikki Lauder shit either!" McBride said referring to the carnage on the pavement on the Stratford road only a few minutes before.

Dez pushed the gear lever into first gear and the car began to roll forward.

"Ok, where do you want me to drive to?" Dez asked softly.

"Just fucking drive!"

An idea of how he might talk his way out of this situation came to mind as he pulled out onto the main road.

"I was on my way to get the bloke that's been stealing all the money from the Irish pubs. I take it that's what this is all about?"

This openness caught the Fox and McBride by surprise. Normally men in Dez's position talked about anything and everything *except* the situation at hand. But now the initial shock had worn off, this guy was as cool as a cucumber.

"You mean the singer?" McBride asked.

Dez nodded,

"Yeah, the singer!"

"Ok, well, that's good then, cos we wanna talk to the singer too!" McBride said sternly.

"How do you know where he is?" Foxy asked.

"Oh, I know where he is alright, he's got himself a little hideout in the countryside." Dez answered, the spite in his voice returning now that he had these two men in the back of his car on the hook.

"Is that where he takes the blonde bird for a dirty getaway?" McBride asked with a mischievous snigger.

Dez gripped the leather steering wheel tightly as he tried to control his jealousy about losing Abi Fewtrell to the blond Irishman.

"Yeah," he muttered, "that's where he takes the blonde bird for a dirty getaway, only this time, they ain't gonna get away, are they?"

And just like that, all of them, except for Bull who was still out cold, suddenly had the same agenda, find the singer. The IRA wanted to *question* him about the robberies. Dez had other ideas.

The car travelled through the back streets of Birmingham avoiding the busy traffic jams until it reached the outskirts of the city and crossed the M42 motorway. They had left the city limits and were now in the Warwickshire countryside. As they travelled, they talked. Dez trying to extricate himself from suspicion and lay the blame for the stolen money fully at Davey Keogh's feet. The Fox and McBride sat in the rear of the car listening, both agreeing with everything the driver said but neither convinced by his explanations. Happy to just let events take their deadly course.

CHAPTER 25

Confrontation

1995

Daniel's weekend was spent snacking on what was left in his father's fridge and watching the stubborn old bastard in the wheelchair slowly suffocating. The pair sat in silence, watching each other until Ronnie Fletcher, fallen hero of the West Midlands Serious Crime Squad finally lost consciousness and passed away around 4am on Monday morning.

Daniel, who for the first time in years felt some relief from the spider, had fallen asleep himself. He was awoken by his father's final death throws and as the old man's chest heaved in and out, and as his tobacco blackened lungs beneath fought for oxygen.

He watched from the armchair opposite with a macabre fascination until the old man became still. Then as if nothing had happened he fell back to sleep again until the bright morning sunlight shone through the gap between the curtains. He rose from the armchair, made some instant coffee and toast. He sat in back the armchair opposite Ronnie Fletcher's corpse and chomped on his toast as he studied the dead man. Ronnie still taped to his chair had already started to succumb to the early stages of rigor mortis and his head hung forward over his chest revealing the flaky skin on his balding head.

As Daniel stared at the man's scalp, he suddenly felt a deep satisfaction at finally getting some 'justice' from the man who had, in his mind simply *given* him away to that sick pervert Duncan Jarvis. He sat back in his chair and polished off his toast, swirling the bread around his mouth before slurping at the coffee and swallowing it. Inwardly he began congratulating himself on his shrewdness.

"You didn't see this coming, did ya *Dad?*" he asked the corpse. "Not such a great detective now, are ya?" he said with a spiteful snigger.

However, beneath his smugness, he could already feel the seeds of disappointment growing and like some sort of cruel child who enjoys torturing a puppy or kitten, he now wished he'd kept the old man alive a little longer in order to make him suffer a little more. Given himself a little more time to enjoy the power he'd held over the man's life and death.

Daniel tried to push the feelings out of his mind. Congratulating himself on his self-control. After all, he'd let the old man die peacefully compared to what he'd done to the poor businessman on the train. He could have been much crueler if he'd wanted to be, if he'd given it a little more thought. Then suddenly he felt cheated, as if the agony that he'd wanted to bestow on his victim had been somehow denied him by his own stupid negligence.

He stood and crossed to the dead man, his mind overflowing in a battle of emotions as he stood over him. He pressed his groin into Ronnie's head, as if somehow showing the dead man who was in charge here, displaying his dominance over him.

And then he raised his fist and brought it down hard onto the back of the old man's head with a sickening thud. He stood above the corpse swaying as his head spun with a rising rage. Daniel raised his other hand and once again brought his fist down hard on the same spot. His punch broke the already dry skin, splitting it. The sight of the blood sent Daniel into a frenzy of violence. *Bam bam, bam,* he reigned down his fists clenched like hammers on to Ronnie's head as if he were a blacksmith smashing his rage into his anvil until it was little more than a bloody pulp.

The attack on the corpse lasted almost an hour, leaving the room looking more like an abattoir than a lounge and leaving Daniel covered in his father's blood and brain matter.

He stepped back from the corpse, panting deeply. He looked at his bloody hands and felt a rush of orgasmic power surging through his body. He stood there in his own private abattoir for a full ten minutes enjoying the sensation before gathering himself together.

He left the room, climbed the stairs towards the bathroom and stepped fully-clothed into the shower. The water was cold but energising. He watched the blood draining from him with a childlike fascination as it flowed over the white porcelain and down the plug hole. Stepping from the shower he left it running and took off his soaked suit and dropped it to the floor.

Daniel walked into his father's bedroom and slid a wardrobe door open and smiled. Inside was a line of his father's suits. He ran his fingers across the line of clothes until he came to a diesel-blue mohair suit, lifting it from the hanger he lay it on the bed. He didn't know why but the suit seemed familiar to him, as if he'd seen it before somewhere, he didn't know why but the sight of the blue shiny mohair suit with its 1960's three-button, small lapels, somehow made him feel like everything would turn out ok, and so began to dress himself in it.

The irony was lost on the man as he pulled on the suit his father had worn on the very night he had been abducted. After dressing, Daniel stood in front of the full-length mirror on the wardrobe door. Amazingly, this was one of the first times he'd actually seen himself in a mirror. Yes he'd seen the distorted reflection on the blood-speckled stainless steel mirror train but this was different, this was a high definition reflection that left nothing to the imagination. He saw the blond man staring back at him and once more, just like the moment on the train, he was pleased with what he saw. He admired himself for a long time, turning left and right checking the line of the suit against his figure. He was handsome, he concluded. Daniel turned his mouth up either side of his face as he'd seen other people do when happy with something. Yet he felt no pleasure in his smile, like everything in his existence, it too was filled with an inescapable pain. A feeling of disgust began to rise in the man as he admired himself and so he turned from his reflection and set out to find The Wheel Club and Eddie Fewtrell.

A few hours later he found himself standing like a blond sentinel, expressionless and silent across the road from and old Victorian mansion with a small faded brass sign screwed to its limestone entrance, *The Wheel Club*, blocking the way of the odd pedestrian who happened to cross his path on the narrow pavement, forcing them to step into the gutter to get around him. His large, blue eyes watched the window like a hawk, just as he had watched the Black Brabus pulling into the car park of the casino earlier.

He hadn't missed any details about the people who got out of the car. Firstly the man who was there to greet them. He noticed the hidden blue lights beneath the grill of the Ford Sierra and assumed it was an unmarked police car. Then the man in the passenger seat wearing a three-button, black leather jacket and blonde hair. He was followed by a beautiful girl who had climbed out of the rear seat to hug the policeman. Then finally, an older man, in his late fifties with neat, almost white hair and the tailored suit. Daniel felt a familiar stirring in his ear. He pictured the spider awakening, its shiny jet black body shimmering like some sort of Devilish jewel, its eight needle thin pin sharp legs dancing across his brain. Eight black, gleaming eyes, like tiny discs of evil within it's head. Daniel spoke the name out loud, as if by doing so it would placate the insect inside him.

"Eddie Fewtrell." Daniel muttered to himself as he watched them go inside the old building. "Eddie . . . Fewtrell."

He made his calculations as to who was who. The daughter, the policeman and Eddie Fewtrell himself. The only person that didn't fit was the blond man. He couldn't work out who that was at all.

"Maybe his son?" he asked himself softly. He levelled his cold stare on the window and watched the group within as they ate and talked.

Now that he had found Eddie Fewtrell, he wasn't going to let him out of his sight.

CHAPTER 26

Jobbo's Big Day

1995

J obbo's wedding plans had fallen apart as soon as he'd reached the wedding reception venue on Broad Street. If the argument with the management wasn't enough to ruin the party then the fight that followed certainly did.

It wouldn't have happened at all if the wedding party had been allowed into the function room above O'Neill's Irish pub as arranged. However, thanks to a certain someone's insistence and Dixie's threat of council and police harassment, the management had decided that it was just too much hassle, and so the fifty or so wedding guests were left standing on the pavement, confetti in hand, shouting abuse at the door staff, who in turn began shouting back.

Of course it wasn't long before the bride was crying and the groom was red with rage. Jobbo, still in top hat and tails, became incandescent with anger and in a moment of unbridled rage, chinned the nearest doorman with his prized right hook. His fist slammed into the bouncer's chin with all the power the skinny cellar man could muster. The effect was incredible. Not it must be said because it floored the burly doorman, because it didn't, as a matter of fact, the blow had no effect on him at all. Jobbo's knuckles smashed into the man's stubbled chin with a pathetic slap that hurt the attacker more than its victim. Everything froze for a second. The whole group, wedding party *and* door staff, stopped their shouting and yelling and turned to look at the cellar man as he danced about the pavement, clutching his right fist with his left hand, wincing with the pain of his broken knuckles, top hat balancing at a weird angle on his head as if he were some kind of demented aristocrat. The poor doorman who in all honestly hadn't felt a thing, rubbed his chin with a puzzled expression.

"Did he just punch me?" he said to the bouncer next to him.

"Yeah, well I don't think you could call it a punch mate!" he said stifling a laugh.

The chinned doorman stepped from the doorway of the pub onto the pavement.

"*Oi* . . . !" he shouted pointing at the dancing aristocrat, "What did you do that for?"

All eyes were on the little scene as it played out. The doorman, began trying to reason with Jobbo, stepped away from the shelter of the pub doorway and closer to the groom. Then, without warning, a fifteen stone, four-foot high vision in white appeared from nowhere.

Like an avenging angel, the bride crossed the space between her newlywed husband and the doorman in the blink of an eye. Above her head was a huge, plastic rubbish bin she had pulled from the door of the restaurant next door. The rotund woman hurled the bin with what can only be described as 'Herculean strength' straight at the bouncer's head and what Jobbo's fist had failed to do, the wild bride's projectile did with ease. The plastic bin smashed into the side of the doorman's head like a litter-filled meteorite.

To the onlookers, it was as if they were witnessing something from the pages of a Marvel comic, where the superhero picks up an unfeasibly large object and hurls it at their evil super-foe. Only instead of superwoman lifting a car above her head, it was

Tracy from Dudley hurling a plastic Birmingham City Council litter bin.

BONK!

The sound of the bin hitting the back of the doorman's head was almost laughable. However, he fell in an instant like a sack of potatoes in a heap on the pavement on Broad Street, semi-conscious and covered in the foul, stinking contents of the bin. He lay moaning surrounded by half-eaten burgers and fag butts.

The short silence ended with the sound of the poor man's head hitting the pavement followed by what can only be described as pandemonium. The door staff stepped from the doorway as one, throwing punches left right and centre joined by the customers inside who had been watching the proceedings through the windows and were already streaming out of the pub in order to join the affray on the side of the outnumbered door men.

In the midst of the chaos, stood Jobbo's bride, dressed in a bridal gown that was far too big for her and made her look like an oversized blancmange, swinging left and right hooks like Mike Tyson in a wedding dress. Jobbo standing behind her, pointing out who should be her next victim. Within fifteen minutes, the argument over a cancelled wedding booking, had now turned into a full scale riot with mounted police, blue flashing lights and paddy wagons racing here and there. Jobbo, his new wife and most of his wedding party, were carted off to Steel House lane police station to be booked for affray.

As that was happening, Eddie Fewtrell stood at the door to XL's night club two hundred yards up the road, looking at his watch and cursing his cellar man, wondering what time the wedding party would arrive.

It was around midnight that Eddie got the call from the station.

"Alright Eddie, it's Jobbo!"

The line went silent for a second and the cellar man could hear the thump of the night club's sound system in the background.

"Where the fuck have you been, Jobbo? I've been stood here like a prize prick, waiting for you and your wedding lot since ten o'clock?" Eddie wasn't holding back.

"I've been arrested Eddie!"

"What?"

"Arrested!"

"On ya bleeding wedding night?" Eddie burst into laughter.

"Yeah some bastard cancelled my booking at O'Neill's and it all kicked off!"

Eddie's laughter stopped abruptly.

"Ahem, eh, well who would have done something like that?" Eddie asked as nonchalantly as he could.

"I dunno . . . ," Jobbo snarled, " . . . but when I find out I'll fucking kill em, Ed!"

"Oh there are some right bastards out there, our kid. They're probably jealous that you got yourself a good-looking bird son."

The fact that he'd never laid eyes on the cellar man's new wife didn't stop Eddie from trying to cover his tracks. "It was probably her ex-fella!"

Jobbo took the bait.

"Yeah, probably Eddie, I'll bleeding *kill* him when I catch up with the bastard!"

Eddie looked around himself at the half-empty nightclub.

"Look Jobbo, it's only just gone midnight, the night's still young. I'll come and pick you up in me Rolla and bring you up here for a few drinks on the house. How does that sound, our kid?"

The line went quiet as the cellar man turned to talk to someone in the background. Finally, after nearly a minute Jobbo spoke.

"That'd be amazing Eddie, the only problem is, there's about fifty of us down at the nick. How we gonna get to you at Five ways? It's too far to walk."

Eddie could hear the sound of a cash till ringing in his head.

"Nah, don't worry ya-self about details son. I'll pick you and your Mrs. up in me Rolls Royce and the rest can jump on one of my happy buses that I use for the clubs."

Eddie was referring to the two Ford Transit, seventeen-seater ex-mental home minibuses he used to steal customers from the queues of his competitor's nightclubs and ship them up to XL's nightclub or one of his other clubs around the town.

"See you in five, Steelhouse Lane nick . . . tootle pip!"

CHAPTER 27

Shadows on the tow path

1995

The meal wasn't the best they had tasted but with the help of a few drinks it went down well nonetheless. The bell sounded behind the bar announcing last orders and the ten or so customers who were still drinking began to slurp up the dregs of their pints and begin the stagger back home.

Abi and Davey watched from their table at the fireside as the locals pulled on their coats and began to leave under the landlord's watchful eye. Davey stood unsteadily and held Abi's coat open so she could put it on. The conversation over dinner had been about the day's events and had been a heavy one but as the night wore on and more alcohol had been consumed it had eventually turned into a cheerfully romantic affair with both of the lovers anticipating what lay in store for them back at the secluded mooring on the riverside.

As the pair stepped out of the old inn doorway and into the evening, Davey noticed that the brief warm spell they had enjoyed on their trip along the canal had ended and the night had the beginnings of a bitter coldness to it.

"It's gonna get really cold in the wee hours, we'll have to keep the log burner going all night."

"Oh my God, it's so foggy out here!" Abi said, amazed at how fast the mist had risen from the river.

"It's always like that around here for some reason. Some people don't like it but I do, somewhere to hide away, where no one can find you!"

Abi laughed nervously as they stepped from the light of the pub doorway towards the path that ran back to the river.

"It's too spooky for me, like something from a Hammer House of Horror film!"

Davey laughed.

"Well, I can assure you *Christopher Lee* isn't going to jump out the reeds and bite you on the neck . . . !" He pulled her towards him," . . . but I might, w*oahahahaha*!", Davey shouted in a caricature Dracula voice before sinking his face into the soft skin of her neck and giving her a playful bite.

"Get off me, you prat!" Abi pushed him away with a serious look on her face. "If you're gonna try and scare me I'll just get a taxi back into town!"

He laughed it off and took her hand in his and for the first time that day they had totally forgotten the incident at Gas Street Basin earlier that morning.

Neither lover noticed the four men watching their every move from the black BMW car parked beneath the overhang of a large willow tree in the pub's carpark.

"Come on, I'll get the log burner going and we'll have a glass of something back on the boat."

The pair picked their way through the darkness, walking along the stone wall frontage of the pub until it led to a narrow alleyway which in turn, led them towards the river behind the pub and onto the narrow tow path. They walked blindly into the pitch-black mist. As they passed, they set off a sensor on one of the pub's security lights triggering a bright halogen lamp which illuminated the tow path in its white light. Abi jumped.

"There ya go . . . " Davey said cheerfully, " . . . ain't so spooky now is it?"

He felt Abi's hand tighten in his.

"*What*! It's even *more* creepy now the security lights have come on, now you can actually see just how thick this mist is!"

They continued down the tow path illuminated by the powerful beam of light, their shadows dancing across the misty water in front of them. Davey could just make out the flickering oil lamp he'd left on the bow of the boat burning in the distance. After a minute the security light switched itself off, plunging the lovers back into pitch blackness once again. Abi stopped in her tracks. Davey sensed her panic and tugged her hand.

"Come on, it's ok, I know where I'm going." He came in close to reassure her. "There . . . " He pointed towards the soft glow in the distance, " . . . you see that light, that's the oil lamp I lit before we left the boat. Just keep walking towards it, that's where the boat's moored. If you keep that directly in front of you, then you'll stay on the tow path and won't fall in the soup." He laughed but sensing her discomfort at being out on such a night, Davey squeezed her hand softly. "Come on Abi, we'll be fine."

He stepped ahead of her, leading the way until they reached the little canal boat, which rocked gently in the ebb and flow of the river. The water lapping around the hull of the boat was the only sound in the dark night. Davey stepped onto the edge of the boat and caught the handrail. Pulling himself on board he turned and helped Abi aboard. Unlocking the cabin hatch they climbed down into the interior of the boat where Davey lit another oil lamp and began to prepare the log burner. "There's some wine in the fridge if you fancy a drink, otherwise stick the kettle on and I'll make us both a cuppa once I get this old girl fired up."

Abi gave the little black stove a once over.

"Will it take long? It's bloody freezing in here."

"Nah, five minutes and it'll be toast and once you put the kettle on the gas burner it'll warm the place up straight away."

"So you want tea?"

Davey laughed.

"You decide!"

He turned his attention back to the log burner. He noticed the stack of logs he usually kept next to the fire had been depleted down to three or four small logs and so turned to back to the steps leading the rear deck area where he always kept a stack of wood beneath one of the bench seats on the rear decking area. Davey stepped into the blackness of the night once more and knelt down next to the pile of wood. He began to fumble beneath the bench, trying to make a small stack of wood in the nook of his elbow, whilst grabbing one log at a time. Behind him a light came on and he assumed that Abi had found the electric light switch in the forward cabin and living area.

"You'd better turn that light back off . . . " he called over his shoulder, " . . . if it's left on too long it'll drain the battery and we won't be able to start the engine tomorrow morning!"

"What?" Abi called from the galley.

"It'll drain the battery!" Davey said, trying to balance the pile of wood in one arm whilst pressing his chin down on the top of the wood so it wouldn't spill from his grasp.

"What'll drain the battery?" Abi replied, suddenly appearing at the cabin hatch.

Davey turned as best he could.

"The electric lights will, they get their power from the main battery and we'll need all the power we have tomorrow in order to start the engine on such a cold morn . . . "

" . . . but I haven't used any electric lights?"

Davey smiled at the girl who was silhouetted in the cabin's doorway.

"Yeah you've probably done it by mistake, I do it all the time, it just a . . . " he stopped talking abruptly and stared past his lover into the cabin, " . . . habit."

His words trailed off. He could see the electric light inside wasn't on. Only the soft glow from the oil lamps he'd lit earlier were illuminating the canal boat with their flickering flames. Something else was lighting up the boat, something further up the canal tow path. Davey stood up from the bench, the little pile of wood still balanced under his chin. From the elevated rear deck of the boat, he could see the security lamp at the Inn had been activated. He stared into its white halogen beam, which, even though it was over three hundred yards away, was still blinding in the relative darkness of its surroundings. He watched the tow path with concern.

"Something must have set off that light." he said to himself.

Time seemed to stand still. Even the soft lapping of the river against the boat's hull faded to nothing as he watched the illuminated scene further up the river bank with growing unease. The gentle breeze blowing the soft mist across the surface of the river drifted silently across his field of vision as he waited to see what had triggered the light. Abi saw the look of concern on his face.

"What's wrong?" she asked, alarm in her voice.

Davey didn't answer, instead he raised a finger to his lips with his free hand.

"Shh . . ."

The feeling of dread he'd experienced earlier that day after the chase at Gas Street Basin returned, leaving a hollow in his stomach and a sudden dryness in his throat. He swallowed, trying to hide the fear in his voice.

"It's probably just a fox." re replied, completely unaware of the irony . . .

Abi climbed the steps to the deck and joined her lover. The silence of the night was suddenly deafening as the two stared into the distant light. Then something stirred. A dark silhouette of a man stepped from the shadows, followed by another. Then two more silhouettes stepped into the light. The lovers stood in silent shock for a second, watching the black outlines of four men striding down the tow path towards them.

The security light glistened from the bald head of one of the men and Davey recognised him from earlier that day.

"*Fuck!*" he said dropping the logs to the deck.

Abi gasped as she also saw that these were the same men who had chased them along the canal side in Birmingham city centre.

"Get below and dowse those oil lamps." Davey turned to the tiller and slipped the hooped rope which held it in place from its hook. "We gotta get out of here!" He turned back towards Abi who hadn't moved. "Come on girl, we ain't got much time, go put those lamps out!"

Abi seemed to be in a trance. Davey ignored her and leapt from the deck onto the riverside in order to untie the mooring lines. He raced down the boat side until he reached a rotted wooden stump where he'd tied off the boat. He looked down the tow path towards the oncoming men. He could see they had picked up their pace now and had started to walk faster. His heart thumped in his chest as he desperately tried to untangle the knot of the thick blue nylon rope.

"Fuck, fuck, *fuck*. Come on, you bastard!" he snarled under his breath.

The rope was caught on an old nail. He shook the stump which swayed from side to side in the soft mud of the river bank. Realising there was no way he could untangle the rope in the darkness he left it tied and returned to the rear deck. He grabbed the rear mooring rope and followed it to a tree stump on which he'd lashed it. Much to his relief this knot fell apart with the slightest of tugs. He rolled the rope around his arm and climbed back on the deck of the boat.

As he did he caught sight of the four men breaking into a run along the tow path. Davey noticed that Abi had gone below and had already extinguished the oil lamp on the bow and was doing the same to the one in the galley. He watched as the silhouettes of the men continued to run towards his boat. Suddenly, the timer on the security lamp kicked in, turning the light off and pitching the whole tow path into dense blackness. Only the single oil lamp in the galley below shone into the night on which to give their pursuers a point of reference on which to aim their vengeance. Abi turned the tiny wheel on the side of the lamp and she watched with satisfaction as the wick was drawn down into the lamps wheels thus extinguishing it completely. A sudden blackness enveloped her leaving only a thin line of red glowing embers along the wick's edge.

Davey stood on the pitch-black deck in silence, knowing that the men on the towpath would be as blind in the darkness as he was. He shuffled across the deck trying to find the tiller, almost tripping on the log pile he'd dropped earlier. His hands searched around him, trying to find a hand hold to give him some bearing in the night. He could hear the thump of feet on the tow path as they men raced towards him. Just as his hand fell across the brass handle of the tiller, he heard a splash of water from along the river bank followed by a shower of expletives and he knew one of them had either lost his footing or his bearings and had fallen into the reeds at the side of the river.

"*Fucking hell* . . . !" the voice was a thick Dublin accent, " . . . get me out of here you gob-shites!" The sound of the Irishman's voice chilled Davey to the bone.

"The . . . IRA!" he muttered fearfully under his breath.

He could hear the other men continue to run down the path towards him ignoring their associate's plea for help to free him from the thick mud of the bank. Although he couldn't see her, Davey heard Abi climbing the steps from the cabin and stepping onto the deck.

"Abi?" he called into the darkness.

"Yeah, I'm here."

He could hear the alarm in her voice.

"Be careful now, I'm holding my hand out, walk towards my voice and try and find it!"

Abi stepped away from the cabin doorway into the pitch black of the night knowing that if she lost her bearings she could end up stepping off the boat's deck and falling into the river. If that happened she knew that Davey would never find her in the darkness, especially when the oncoming men reached them.

"Come on, this way . . . " Davey whispered, " . . . I'm right here."

She held her hands out in front of her as she followed his voice, all the time she could hear the Irishman further up the river cursing his associates as he struggled from the sticky mud on the river bank. The sound was causing her to panic and she froze midway across the deck.

Davey could sense her panic and knew he must do something. He was standing next to the throttle controls and he had an idea. He flicked a small switch on the boat's control panel which was used to prime the engine by warming the diesel engine's glow plugs. Instantly a tiny red LED light came on. Although the light was tiny, to Abi it shone like a beacon.

"Walk towards the light, Abi!" Davey ordered. He held his hand out again and a second later he felt her soft hand clenching his. "There ya go . . . " he guided her hand down to the handrail behind the tiller arm, " . . . hold that and don't let go, whatever happens!"

Suddenly, they could hear the sound of feet pounding across the muddy tow path towards them. The two lovers froze as the footsteps grew louder until the men were so close the pair could hear grunts of exertion from their sprint along the path. Davey drew a deep breath knowing that this was it, a confrontation with the IRA. Abi, who had come in close beside him felt Davey brace himself for the inevitable clash.

Much to their surprise, the pounding feet on the tow path simply carried on past them.

The lovers stood for a second wondering what was going on until Abi whispered.

"They can't see us in the dark!"

She felt her lover release a deep sigh of relief. They listened as the footsteps faded as the men ran up the tow path. Then the sound of running stopped. The whole scene was thrown into a deafening silence once more. Davey lent into Abi's ear and, barely audible whispered, "They've realised their mistake!"

Without warning he pressed the ignition key to the boat. *Brrrrrummmmm!* The old *Lister* engine burst into life with what seemed in the relative silence, a deafening roar, *brrrrrrrrummmm!*

Davey pushed the throttle to make sure the engine wasn't going to stall and when sure it wasn't, he threw the gear lever into reverse and pushed the chrome throttle handle down once more. The engine began to do its job, slowly pulling the rear of the boat away from the riverbank and out on to the river. The sound of pounding feet were drowned out now but that didn't mean they weren't there.

As the boat drifted out on to the river it was caught by the ebbing tide which dragged it further away from the bank. Suddenly, the bow rope that Davey had been unable to untangle sprung taut. It was still attached to its mooring stump and caught the boat's rearward momentum bringing it to a sudden halt midway across the river at a dangerous angle to the flow of the water. The little canal boat's engine struggled to keep its position and due to the ebb of the river, now found itself at a ninety degree angle to the bank. Davey knew this was a precarious position to be in and if they remained there too long, the boat would be overwhelmed by the oncoming pressure of the water and could even capsize. He held the tiller in a position that kept the boat balanced but he could already feel the mighty pressure of the water building along the port-side of the vessel and knew that he had two choices, either bring the boat back into shore or somehow shake off the trapped bow line. He felt the flat-bottomed canal boat begin to lean starboard.

"We've gotta shake off that bow line or it'll capsize us. Hold this!" he ordered Abi, guiding her hand to the tiller arm. "Whatever you do don't let go or it'll flip us over."

"What? . . . I . . . " Abi protested, " . . . I don't know anything about boats." Panic finally gripping her.

"What happens if the boat flips over?" Davey asked.

"We, we sink?" Abi said, more a question than a statement.

"There ya go, that's all you need to know about boats. Now hold on to that tiller as if your life depended on it!"

"Where are you going?"

"I'm gonna cut that bow line at the front of the boat!"

They could hear inaudible shouting from the river bank now as the aggressive thugs began to organise themselves. Davey stepped down into the cabin and walked through the galley. He grabbed at a knife on his way through and hoped it would be sharp enough to cut the tough blue nylon rope. He reached the cabin doors at the foremost part of the cabin and climbed onto the small foredeck. A chrome, directional spotlight was positioned to his right and he flicked it on. The powerful lamp illuminated the whole of the riverbank in front of the boat and the sight he saw in its yellow glow made him shiver.

For there, only a few feet away from him, were three of the most violent men he'd ever seen. The light's glow brought silence to the men on the riverbank who raised their hands as one to shield their eyes from the blinding searchlight. Davey recognised Dez instantly, he also recognised the doorman from the Dublin Barrel, as well as the other bald brute who had been hit on the head with the sausage roll earlier that day.

Forgetting the bow rope for a second Davey called out, "What the fuck do you want?"

"You! Dead!" Dez shouted.

"What! Why because I'm seeing Abi?"

The man laughed spitefully.

"No I don't give a fuck about that Fewtrell bitch, you stole our money!"

McBride, who had until now known nothing about the involvement of any of the Fewtrell family turned to Dez.

"Fewtrell, did he just say Fewtrell?"

Dez shrugged it off.

"Yeah, Fewtrell so what?"

"What have the Fewtrell's got to do with any of this?"

"Never mind the Fewtrells!" Dez pointed towards Davey's figure on the boat, hidden in the shadow of the bright light, "It's that cunt we wanna be concentrating on!"

Suddenly Davey saw the doorman's expression change from anger to confusion.

"No, hold on, *we* don't fuck with the Fewtrell family." He turned back to face the light and called to Davey. "Which Fewtrell is it?"

He could see now that these men were in some sort of disagreement about something and so he decided to exploit it as best he could.

"It's Abi Fewtrell, Eddie's daughter, you know who she is McBride and you know the shit-storm he'll cause if you fuck with his daughter!"

The doorman was surprised to hear his name being used.

"You know me too mate, we've spoken loads of times at the Dublin Barrel whenever I've played there."

McBride nodded.

"Yeah I know ya, Davey but this is business, this bloke reckons you're responsible for ripping off the I.R.A and we both know what that means!"

He gestured over his shoulder towards Dez.

"He is . . . " Dez shouted angrily, " . . . he's the one that stole the money from you!"

Davey shook his head.

"For fuck's sake McBride, you know better than that?"

The bouncer shook his head.

"These pair say you stole £140,000 from us at the Irish centre?"

"What?" McBride could just make out the shock in the singer's face in the shadows. "What the fuck are ye talking about?"

Davey continued. "I took a few grand from the Brazen Maiden on the night it was robbed, it was just left there by the door and I took it. I wished I had never seen the fucking bag of cash but I just happened to be in the wrong place at the wrong time. I swear, there was just over ten grand in that bag, nothing more!"

"*Brazen Maiden*? No, I'm talking about the *Irish Centre*, you were playing there the night the place got rolled. You were handing out the leprechaun masks to cover the robbers' escape. " McBride shouted.

"Yeah I was there and so was *he!*" Davey stepped from the shadows and pointed directly at Dez. "*He's* the one that gave me the bloody masks."

McBride shook his head.

"How do you know if it was him? Both robbers were wearing the same masks that night!"

Dez stepped close to McBride.

"Don't listen to him, he's trying to talk his way out of . . . "

"*Shut the fuck up!*" The doorman snarled at Dez. "I wanna hear what he's got to say!" Without hesitation Davey answered.

"Yeah, I *couldn't* see his face but I did see his *tattoo* . . . " He pointed towards Dez, who had started to back away from the beam the light, " . . . the one on his hand, go one McBride, take a look for yourself, it's a swallow and stars. I'd seen it somewhere before at one of my gigs but couldn't remember which one, then I recalled it was at the Brazen Maiden." Davey raised his voice, "On the night it was *robbed*. It took me a while but then I finally figured out who it was. It was him, *Dez*, I only know him because he was Abi Fewtrell's ex boyfriend, he's the bastard that ripped you off McBride, not me!"

The doorman could hear by the desperation in the man's voice that he wasn't lying and what was more, everything he'd just said was beginning to make sense but McBride needed more persuasion.

"So *how come you* were you present at so many of these robberies if you weren't involved?"

"Cos my gigs are always busy, you know that McBride and a busy gig means big take at the bar. That's why he's been following me around robbing the pubs I'm playing at, trying to lay the blame for all these Irish pub robberies on my shoulders with the I.R.A *and* the Old Bill to cover his tracks."

He could see McBride was mulling it over. Dez and Bull on the other hand had both stepped out of the spotlight and were standing off to the side in the shadows talking closely.

"Look McBride, I'm an Irish singer, singing in Irish pubs. Why the fuck would I bite the hand that feeds me?" he pleaded. "Not only that but what kind of nutter rips off the I.R.A. and expects to get away with it?"

The doorman's mind was made up. He nodded towards Davey.

"You two had best be on your way." He wasn't sure but Davey thought he saw the big bouncer wink. "You're no longer of any interest to the I.R.A." He said officially.

The words were music to the singer's ears. "Go on . . ." McBride continued, " . . . cut the rope and get out of here otherwise you'll witness something you wished you hadn't!"

Davey didn't need to be asked twice. He stepped forward and grabbed the thick blue rope and began to saw at it with the kitchen knife. However, the blade was blunt and barely made any mark on the tough rope. Out the corner of his eye he saw McBride turn towards the other men on the bank and for the first time that night he saw Dez and Bull clearly. Both had fearful looks on their faces, Bull's distorted tattooed face, bizarre in the searchlight, Dez's normally handsome features twisted in fear at the prospect of tackling the doorman.

As McBride turned, both Dez and Bull were on him as one. Davey watched the scene in the misty pool of light as if he were in the stall seats at a cheap theatre watching a Shakespearian stage fight. Bull's massive fist caught the doorman unaware, knocking him into the reeds and out of sight where the thug threw himself on the prostrate bouncer who was caught in the slimy mud on the riverside.

"*Hurry up!* I can't hold this much longer!" Abi yelled from the back of the boat, until that moment Davey hadn't noticed that the canal boat had listed to the left by about a thirty five degree angle. He knew if it went over anymore, it would surely capsize and drown them both in the freezing water. He sawed harder on the rope but in the dim light he couldn't see if he was making any headway.

"Just hold on," he called over his shoulder, "it's nearly there!" he lied, trying not to panic her any more than she already was. On the riverbank he could hear McBride moaning and grunting as he was pounded viciously with punches and kicks from his two assailants. Now Dez was shouting too, venting his rage at the escaping Irishman.

"Hey *singer*, you pair ain't going nowhere . . . " he pointed towards Abi at the rear of the boat " . . . you and that *bitch* are gonna be getting what's coming to ya as soon as we've dealt with this cunt!"

The boat was nearly at a forty degree angle now and it was just a matter of seconds before the water pressure along its port side tipped the vessel completely. Davey blindly felt the rope where he'd been sawing with his hand. His heart dropped when he found that his knife had barely made a mark.

"Shit."

He shook his head, as it finally dawned on him that the boat was lost.

"That's it, it's over!"

He stopped sawing and made a move backwards away from the bow line to help Abi abandon the boat before it capsized. As he did so he saw something moving on the riverbank, something dark in the shadows. At first he thought it was an animal from the river, a long brown thing clawing its way through the mud and thick reeds. The thing, whatever it was, was way too big to be a mammal like an otter or badger. Davey stood dumbfounded trying to work out what it was when it suddenly turned its gaze to him. To his astonishment, he could see two large blue human-like eyes staring back at him illuminated by the searchlight and to his shock the brown sludgy animal smiled at him. A flash of steel shone in the searchlight for a second and without a word, the Fox, who had finally freed himself from the slime of the riverbank, whipped out his filleting knife and slashed it across Davey's face. The knife was so sharp that the singer didn't feel the cold steel as it cut a long straight scar into his cheek just below the left eye.

"That's something to remember me by *singer*!" he said coldly. Then with one quick flick of the wrist, the razor-sharp blade cut through the blue nylon rope as if it were butter, releasing the boat and sending it splashing back on its flat bottom, righting the vessel instantly. The canal boat rocked violently in the water, nearly throwing Abi from the tiller arm. As the boat was caught by the ebbing river it pulled the bow away from the bank, and so the searchlight that had seconds before been illuminating the violent attack on McBride, now swung down the bank until the bright beam of light now rested on the Fox. Davey and the Dublin hitman stood only feet apart from each other, separated by the black water. Davey felt the sensation of warm blood flowing down his cheek and onto his neck.

The Fox spoke again.

"We came here to find out the truth and now we know it, so do yourself a favour and get her out of here!"

He gestured with his head towards the confused girl at the back of the boat. Davey nodded towards the man who was covered from head to toe in a thick brown sludge.

"I, I will . . ." he stuttered.

"And every time you see that scar on your face, you'll remember your little run in with the *Fox*!" he said with a laugh, before turning and stepping from the circle of light and into the pitch blackness of the night.

All of this had happened in an instant, too fast to comprehend and before Davey or Abi knew what was happening, they were fifty, then a hundred, then a hundred and fifty yards down river as the boat was caught in the tide, drawing it along into the misty night.

Behind them, they heard the faint but unmistakable sound of men screaming.

CHAPTER 28

One too many guests

1995

Jobbo's motley crew arrived at XL's nightclub en masse twenty minutes after Eddie's phone call; forty five or so guests, covered in cuts, bruises, black eyes and busted lips, their cheap suits and dresses ripped to shreds after the almighty punch-up outside O'Neill's Irish pub on Broad Street.

They stumbled and fell, already drunk, out of the club owner's happy buses onto the pavement at Five Ways roundabout where they were greeted with bemused sniggers by the nightclub door staff. They gathered at the pavement's edge in a large group awaiting the arrival of the happy couple who were being chauffeured by the man himself, Eddie Fewtrell.

Jobbo and his new wife sat like a royal couple in the back of the plush Rolls Royce waving at their guests as the huge car pulled up to the kerb. Eddie jumped from the driver's seat and came around the car. He pulled on the large chrome handle and the heavy door swung open with a luxurious swoosh.

"Ladies and Gentlemen . . . " Eddie announced loudly, " . . . I give you Mr. and Mrs. . . . "

It suddenly dawned on him that he didn't even know his employee's real name.

"I . . . give you . . ." he stuttered, trying to figure out what to say, finally settling for, " . . . Mr. and Mrs. *Jobbo!*"

Everyone there, including the door staff, knew Bob's nickname and so burst into a mixture of cheering, laughter and applause. Jobbo stepped from the luxury of the car and bowed as if he were some sort of dandy pop star. He held out his hand where it was clasped tightly by the bride, who, with an almost athletic leap, almost fell through the car door, champagne in hand, a drunken smile on her face and mascara-smudged black around her eyes. Jobbo beamed with pride at Eddie who gave him a wink.

"You've got a keeper there, kiddo!"

"Nice one boss, yam saved the day, yow did!" he gushed in a thick Black Country brogue.

"It's nothing our kid, now you pair get inside. I've reserved the V.I.P. suite in the main room upstairs." he said referring to a small area partitioned off from the main dance floor. He patted the cellar man's shoulder. "Go on then, Jobbo, it's ya big night son!"

The cellar man pulled his young wife's hand and the pair set off at the front of their friends and guests into the nightclub. Eddie watched from the pavement as the group vanished through the double doors and upstairs to the club. He watched the last of the revellers step inside the club before noticing a tall, gaunt-looking man standing in one of the doorways watching him. Eddie assumed, by the way he was dressed in a blue mohair, three-button suit that he was one of the wedding party and so called out to him.

"Better get up there mate or they'll drink all the bubbly before you get a chance to get any!"

The man remained silent, returning the nightclub owner's remark with an expressionless stare. Eddie's eyebrows furrowed as he watched the man, who seemed for some unknown reason, to be trying to stare him out. Eddie's eye was again drawn to the man's suit. Unlike the other wedding guests, who all seemed to be wearing cheap, off-the-shelf, ill-fitting suits, *this* suit, with its three buttons and small lapels seemed to be a much finer tailored item of clothing. He could see the detailing around the lapels, five inch vents and buttoned cuffs. This was a real bespoke suit from the 1960s.

The sight of it triggered something in his memory and for some reason he recalled his first meeting back in the early days at the Bermuda Club with his old nemesis Ronnie Fletcher. The more he looked at the man in the shop doorway, the more he realised just how much this man resembled him, thinner yes, and with a full head of hair instead of the bald patch but there was a definite likeness. The memory wasn't a pleasant one and so Eddie shrugged it off, pushing it to the back of his mind.

However, he couldn't resist commenting on the cut of the man's clothes as he locked the Rolls Royce.

"That's a nice set of togs ya got there, our kid, reminds me of someone I used to know, he had a suit exactly the same as that."

The gaunt man didn't reply and Eddie assumed he was too drunk to answer. Leaving his car on the double yellow lines of Five Ways, he crossed to the man and held his hand out, coupling the gesture with his trademark smile.

"I'm Eddie."

Daniel looked at the open hand for a second before taking it and shaking it weakly. He forced his mouth to crease up either side, but inwardly, he tingled from head to toe with a heady cocktail of fear and nervous anticipation as he visualised in his mind's eye, the revenge he had planned for the club owner.

"Come on son, I'll show you the way upstairs." Eddie coaxed.

Inside the club the music boomed from the array of speaker cabinets which hung from the ceiling of the club as the resident DJ played the chart hits of the day. A myriad of lighting effects reflected across the mirrored walls, bouncing every colour in the spectrum around the room in a chaotic mishmash, synchronising with the beat of the music at the DJ's command. The light show reached into the darkest recesses of the nightclub where Daniel Fletcher stood alone with his vengeance against a backdrop of matt black paint and red velvet.

He watched Eddie from afar as the white-haired club owner sat at the end of the bar drinking a small glass of Irish whisky, spinning yarns and telling tall tales from his infamous past to the group gathered around him. The women fawning and sexual, the men trying their best to act like villains and gangsters. Daniel fumbled in his trouser pocket. His fingers ran over the short bladed knife with its razor-shape blade. He congratulated himself on getting the knife into the club at all but in reality, it had been Eddie himself who had ushered him past the door staff.

Daniel had taken the knife from a drawer in Ronnie Fletcher's kitchen with the intention of finishing his quest for revenge on the men he blamed for the abuse he had suffered as a child. He would fulfil his destiny by plunging the blade deep into the heart of the man who his father had named as the person responsible for his abduction. The fact that Ronnie Fletcher, one of the most corrupt cops ever to have worn the badge had been lying in order to save himself a violent death didn't even occur to Daniel. Only vengeance mattered now.

The spider twitched.

"So there I was, doing the doors, the bar and collecting glasses!" Eddie said loudly over the beat of the music. "I was rushed off me feet, when I got a tap on the shoulder!"

The group around Eddie already knew the story. After all, it had been circulating around the Birmingham city since the early 1960s and had now become a firm part of the second city's folklore. The story of the infamous London gangsters, Ronnie and Reggie Kray, and how, back in 1961 they had come to Birmingham heavy-handed to take over the city's clubland by any means necessary only to be driven out of the city by the Don of the Brummie mafia, Eddie Fewtrell.

The group of partygoers listened intently as the club owner relived the tale. Each of them knowing that they were hearing it from the horse's mouth so to speak and thrilled to be in the company of a *real* gangster, just like the ones on television or the movies.

Of course Eddie didn't consider himself a gangster and never had. To Eddie, it was all business, nothing more and certainly nothing less. If he had to re-tell the story a thousand times more he would, as long as they kept buying drinks and coming to his clubs to hear the tale, he would keep repeating it as if it were the first time he'd ever recounted it.

"Then this cockney bloke said," Eddie puffed himself up to look tougher and put on his best London accent "This is Ronnie and Reggie Kray, they're two brothers from London, fighters and hard men, they could help you, Eddie!" The small group listened with baited breath for the next part of the story. Their favourite part. The part where the Brummie underdog told the heads of one of the most vicious gangs in Britain to go do one and "*Fuck of back to the smoke you pair of Cockney ponces!*"

Eddie delivered the lines perfectly. He'd said them so many times that these days, he honestly believed them himself. Of course the story could have been true and things might have happened exactly the way Eddie had told it except for the fact that his estranged brothers all had a different slant on the incident and the Kray twins and their henchmen all denied that the meeting ever happened at all. There was no doubt that the Fewtrells and the Birmingham Whizz Mob had had a run-in with 'The Firm' as the Kray twins gang were called. However, whether it had all fallen on Eddie Fewtrell's shoulders to *save* Birmingham from the terror of the London underworld or not, we'll never know for sure. But that didn't matter to Eddie who was mid-flow through his story when he was approached by the gaunt man in the blue, mohair suit.

Eddie turned to the man and without hesitation said.

"*Ronnie Fletcher!*"

The words just fell from his mouth and now the man was closer he could see that far from being a smart brand-new set of clothes, the suit, even with its sharp lines and Mod cut, was old and natty. The mohair had lost its sheen in places and there were clumps of fluff around the back of the neckline.

"*Ronnie Fletcher*!" Eddie repeated abruptly. "That's who that suit belonged to!"

He raised his hand and felt the lapel. Daniel flinched but Eddie continued. He rubbed the material between his fingers for a second, a frown growing on his face.

"It can't be the same suit, can it?" He raised his face to Daniel's. "Any relation to Ronnie Fletcher?"

Eddie's words, more of an accusation than a question. Daniel's fingers fumbled with the knife in his trouser pocket, ready to pull it out and use it on the man in front of him. However, the question threw him for a second and Eddie, who had spent a lifetime studying people and their reactions knew that the man meant him harm.

The conversation with Dixie he'd had in his office a few weeks ago, about a man asking questions about the night DCI Fletcher's son went missing suddenly made sense. In the blink of an eye Eddie Fewtrell knew who this man in the natty suit was and more importantly, why he was there.

"You're him, ain't ya?" he asked, trying to hide his unease, "You're Ronnie Fletcher's son."

The words hit Daniel as if they were a slap around his face. The spider who had until then been growing in size since entering the club, now in the face of its prey, began to scuttle backwards in fear, back into the shadows of Daniel's mind. Daniel could feel its fear and it was infectious.

His normal expressionless face lost what little colour it had. He opened his mouth to answer but found he couldn't. Eddie stood from the bar stool to face him.

"What was your name again?" Eddie asked but Daniel didn't answer, instead he backed away, his hand still in his pocket, ready to use the blade at any moment. Eddie stepped towards him, a thousand questions running through his mind. "Come on son, you're him, ain't ya?" he asked again. "The kid that went missing that night all those years ago!" He tried to recall the kid's name but it escaped him. "There's no doubt about who's son you are though. You're the spitting image of your old man. I just hope you're not as much an arsehole as your dad!" Eddie said spitefully. "How is your old dad by the way? Have you been to see him? Well, obviously you have." He said pointing at the suit. "More's to the point, is that why you're here tonight? Did Ronnie Fletcher tell you to come here?"

Eddie watched the man as a boxer watches his opponent, he took in his whole figure, the arms, the legs, the way the man's eyes moved in his head, they were all indicators as to what his next move would be. In a lifetime spent protecting his business and family from people who had come to do him harm, he weighed Daniel up in seconds, just liked he'd weighed up scores of other people over the last thirty five years in his nightclubs. He saw the left arm hanging by his side and the right hand in his pocket, fumbling and he instinctively knew what the man was hiding.

"Did your old dad tell you to come down here and have it out with me? Is that what this is . . . *revenge*?" He pointed at Daniel's right hand. "Well, are you gonna use that knife in your pocket or are you just gonna stand there looking stupid in your Dad's old suit?"

For Daniel the room went silent. A mixture of shock and confusion washed over him as he tried to work out how this old man could know his violent intentions, even before he knew them himself. The spider's eyes glimmered with malevolence from the darkest recesses of the gaunt man's mind.

"*Y . . . you!*" he stuttered as he pulled the knife from his pocket. "Y . . . *you* had me abducted to hurt my father cos he wouldn't take your bribes."

Eddie saw the blade but didn't react, knowing that if he showed any fear at all, then it would only encourage him. Instead, Eddie burst out laughing. His reaction caught Daniel by surprise and he scowled at the white-haired man in front of him. Eddie made a point of glancing towards the knife which Daniel was now brandishing openly in front of him and shaking his head in pity.

"For God's sake son, who told ya that load of old bollocks, your old man Ronnie?" Eddie tutted, his voice losing its mocking tone. "You see son, your old man was one of the biggest cunts that ever walked the streets of Birmingham. He lied to everyone he came into contact with, he fucked over *everyone* he knew in the police force and in the criminal world and in the end, in a town like this, you end up running out of people to fuck over and that's what happened to your Dad."

Eddie held his open hands up in front of his face. To Daniel it was a gesture of submission but in reality it was a defensive trick Eddie had learned in his national service days back in the late 1950s.

"I assume you've already paid a visit to your old man with your knife and now you intend to do the same to me?"

Daniel nodded affirming Eddie's suspicions that Ronnie Fletcher may already be dead, killed at the hands of his own son. Even though he'd predicted it, the affirmation came as a shock to the club owner who, for a split second let his pokerface fall. The spider finally scuttled from the shadows, its fangs dripping with deadly venom, its eyes gleaming with hatred.

Daniel saw his chance and thrust the weapon towards Eddie's throat.

****

The Gas Street Basin was deathly still as the canal boat chugged towards it mooring. The lovers held each other, entwined in the coldness of the early hours of the morning. Only the starlight and the dim yellowish light from a Victorian streetlamp lit the blackness of the basin but Davey's eyes had grown accustomed to the darkness perfectly on the long trip back along the river to the city centre. Both passengers knew that they had to get away from the carnage they'd escaped on the riverbank and back to the relative security of Eddie Fewtrell's wing.

They worked as a team, mooring the longboat in the darkness and Davey shut off the engine with his free hand. His other hand held a blood-soaked towel firmly pressed against his left cheek in order to stem the blood flow from the deep gash left on his face by the Fox's blade. The silence that followed only lasted seconds before they heard the telltale sounds of the city above them. The chatter from a thousand voices along the strip on Broad Street, the nonstop hum of traffic as it trundled its way through the city centre. It was as if they had stepped out of a nightmarish silence and back into reality, as the buzz of the city shrouded the pair in sound, creating a blanket of security under which they were only too happy to hide.

The brisk walk from Gas Street to Five Ways only took around five minutes, each giving fearful glances over their shoulders to see if they were being followed. When they saw they weren't and as they drew nearer to Eddie's XL's nightclub, the terror that had seized both of them since their deadly confrontation a few hours earlier now slowly, started to dissipate. Abi held her boyfriend's hand as she guided him through the doors to the club.

"I'll get Dad to take you to the hospital and get some stitches in that wound!" Davey protested.

"No, it'll be ok." Abi stopped walking and stood in front of the Irishman. She carefully peeled back the towel to reveal the deep wound beneath.

"No!" she said squeamishly, "That won't heal by itself. It's almost gone right through to your jawbone!" She replaced the towel and turned back along the pavement again. "Come on, we're nearly there!"she said pointing towards the large illuminated sign reading XL's nightclub.

She stopped in the foyer. The door staff and receptionists who usually congregated around the entrance were nowhere to be seen.

"Something's wrong." Abi said under her breath.

"Well the music's still playing!" Davey stated, gesturing his head as best he could towards the mirrored staircase and the heavy thumping bass beat of a Manchester rave tune seeping through the concrete ceiling above them.

"Yeah, but there's normally people here." Abi swept her hand around her at the deserted entrance foyer. "Maybe something's happened here too?"

Now it was Davey's turn to lead the way. He pulled Abi's hand, leading her to the foot of the long stairwell.

****

The slash was lightning fast, the silver blade glinting neon blue in the disco lights which whizzed and spun overhead. Daniel threw himself into the attack but Eddie, with his open-handed gesture of submission was ready and he blocked the thrust easily.

The razor-sharp blade made contact with Eddie's sleeve, ripping it open, leaving a long tear along the forearm from wrist to elbow. The sleeve fell apart as if it were paper and to Eddie and the group of onlookers around the bar, there was now no mistaking as to what the gaunt blonde stranger had come to do. Eddie stepped away from the man, his face ashen grey and bravado as tattered as his suit. He examined the sleeve as the fabric rolled down about his elbow, perfectly cut by the blade. He turned his eye back towards his attacker just as the next attack came, this time aimed at his heart. Daniel leant into the thrust, his whole body weight body behind the point of the knife, desperate to shove the eight inch long, cold steel deep into the heart of the club owner and man he blamed for the years of sexual abuse he'd suffered as a child.

"This is it!" he thought as he threw himself into the attack, the moment he would be free from the nightmares and memories that plagued him. This was the moment he would feed the arachnid in his brain. Daniel saw the faces of those responsible in his mind's eye, flashing across his field of vision in a stroboscopic slide show only he could see; the spiteful cruelty of Duncan Jarvis, the brutish menace of Toddy Burns, Tigger's sadistic torture, the pathetic excuses of his down-beaten stepmother. Even the long-buried memories of the night he'd been abducted came to him in this moment of unfettered madness. The faces of his father Ronnie Fletcher and birth mother came flooding like a tsunami into his mind. He saw them as a little boy of eight once more, holding his father's hand at the edge of the dance floor at the Bermuda club.

The images were so vivid he could smell the thick fog of cigarette smoke that always hung in the air, even the softness of his father's grip seemed real to him at that moment. In the intensity of that final thrust of death, in the millisecond it took to stretch out his arm, blade in hand, aimed perfectly at Eddie Fewtrell's heart.

Daniel Fletcher, the abducted and abused child, the lost soul and now the murderer was transported back to the moment of his abduction with such clarity that it was as if time had stood still. He was standing at the edge of the Bermuda dance floor scanning the faces of the watching crowd as 'Father Christmas' organised himself. Duncan Jarvis placed the heavy sack in front of himself and gestured to the children to come and sit on Father Christmas's knee. To the side a beautiful, dark-haired woman was smiling at him. She was holding her husband's hand and the look on her face was without doubt one of love and happiness for the child but also one of longing for a child of her own. The man next to her was a lean, tough but handsome, a thirty year old Eddie Fewtrell and in this subconscious moment, Daniel's memories flowed as clear as spring water.

He saw now that the woman next to Eddie was his wife Hazel and he could also see that the couple were deeply in love with each other. They smiled at him as if he were their very own child and at that point Daniel Fletcher knew in his heart, that his father *had* been lying, just as Eddie Fewtrell had said he had been. These people had nothing to do with his abduction. Now he could feel the press of his father's fingers wrapped around his shoulders and he turned his gaze upon his father once more. The man looked down on him with a broad, proud grin. The sheen from his blue mohair suit catching the light as he did, and behind him, in perfect detail, Daniel saw his mother, watching from his father's shoulder with a loving smile across her face as her husband coerced their son to the front of the pack of children in order to be the first child on Santa's lap.

Daniel realised all too late that all his life he'd been wrong about these people. The ghosts from his past, that he'd gone to such lengths to bury so deeply in his subconscious mind, weren't the monsters he had convinced himself they were and more importantly, none of his misfortune had happened through hate, perversion or spite, as he'd thought it had, but through love. A simple gesture of love that had been taken advantage of by a predator who had just happened by. *They* weren't to blame for his abuse and *he* hadn't been the only victim at the hands of the sick paedophile Duncan Jarvis.

In this frozen state of time, Daniel could now see the sorrow in his mother and father's eyes. He could see the confusion in the Fewtrell's faces too, especially Hazel Fewtrell and the more he saw, the smaller the spider grew and the less its pin-sharp legs pricked at his mind as the insect was forced into the shadows of Daniel's mind once and for all. All of these images and feelings ran through his confused brain in the blink of an eye, and as he awakened from his dream state, Daniel realised too late that he'd committed himself totally to the thrust of the knife, which at that moment was only milliseconds from piecing the heart of the man in front of him and just as the blade touched the club owner's breast . . .

BAM! , , ,

The sucker-punch came from nowhere and took the attacker totally by surprise. It caught him from behind under his ear on the right jaw, shattering it instantly and sending him to the floor a dead weight. By the time Daniel's head hit the beer stinking carpet he was already unconscious. Eddie followed the man's descent until he lay at his feet, broken in body and mind. He stood there for a second frozen in shock, still awaiting the killer blow that would never come. A macabre fascination overwhelmed him as he stared down on his would-be attackers body as it twitched and spasmed on the beer-soaked floor. Eddie slowly raised his eyes to find a four foot high woman dressed in a bridal dress standing in front of him, her eyes wide and wild, her breast panting deeply, her fists clenched and the knuckles on her right hand red raw and already swelling from the scrap outside O'Neill's earlier that night and the sucker punch she'd just landed.

Jobbo suddenly appeared at his bride's side and placed his hands softly on her shoulders. He smiled meekly at the club owner.

"Sorry Eddie, I hope he wasn't anyone important . . . " He patted his new wife's shoulder with his hand. "She gets a bit emotional, you see!" He steered the bride back towards the dance floor. She obeyed him as if in a trance and as they turned, Jobbo stepped in close to Eddie and whispered. "It's her time of the month!" as if that would explain the crumpled mess of a man at their feet. The two looked at each other for a few seconds until Abi stepped between them to hug her father.

"Oh God. Dad, are you alright?" she blurted.

On hearing his daughter's voice, Eddie regained his composure and put his pokerface firmly back in place. He smiled over Abi's shoulder at Davey and gave a wink, as if nothing out of the ordinary had happened.

"What happened to your face our kid? Are you okay?" he said on seeing the bloody towel.

"I thought you pair had gone away for some peace and quiet and you turn up like something from a *Freddie Kruger* film." Eddie said with a scowl.

Davey stood transfixed by the scene, unable to comprehend how his future father-in-law was able act as if there wasn't an unconscious man with a large kitchen knife still in his hand at his feet.

"He needs stitches." Abi said to her father who instantly took charge of the situation. He clicked his fingers at two of the door staff that had been listening to his stories at the bar. Pointing towards Daniel Fletcher on the floor he ordered them to pick him up.

"Get him out of here!"

The men obeyed instantly.

"What shall we do with him, boss?"

"I don't give a flying fuck what you do with him, just get rid of him!" Davey watched as the two burly bouncers carried the unconscious man from the floor.

"Who is he Eddie, a villain?"

Eddie shook his head.

"Him, a villain? *Nah*, he's just a blast from the past son, a blast from the past!"

CHAPTER 29

Sweet Goodbyes & Porky Pies
1995

The story of the battle on the riverbank spread through Birmingham's underworld like a dose of French clap. Within hours anyone who was connected in some form or other to the, shall we say, shadier style of life within the city, knew that there had been a reckoning of some sort and in the days that followed, various groups of criminals throughout Birmingham felt a prickle of cold sweat climbing their spines as they awaited for the newspaper to release the names of the dead. Arses twitched and phones were left unanswered as the criminal fraternity awaited to see if they were somehow involved in a new turf war. The Evening Mail didn't help matters by running with the story as if it *were* a gangland, drug-related turf war.

Riverbank Blood Bath

As the days rolled on, so the story gathered momentum. Another body was found, this time two miles further down river, floating face down, bloated and fit to burst with noxious gasses and the same unusual stab wounds. The local police were stumped by what appeared to be a senseless massacre of three unrelated men. The first, a well-known and well *liked* doorman who worked the city's Irish quarter of Digbeth, James McBride. His connections with the underworld were not known but what *was* known about him was his very vocal support for the I.R.A and so the police began to follow this path of enquiry. However, the other man found next to McBride wasn't known to the police at all, a *John Doe*, no police records, no fingerprints, no facial recognition, or at least what was left of his face, could be recognised at all, early to mid-thirties, six foot tall with a shock of dark hair. His face mutilated beyond recognition by the attack, as if the attacker hadn't been able to see what he was doing and so slashed out nonsensically in the dark.

What was clear was that both men had been murdered on the riverbank in a frenzied, prolonged attack. Their throats finally slit so cleanly it looked to the police forensics team as if a surgeon had performed the final death stroke. What the men were doing on the riverbank in the middle of the night was still a mystery. Then there was the floater found down river. The third man, a well-known Brummie boy, who'd spent years in and out of *Winson Green* prison. This man was a well-known con who went by the nickname of 'Bull' easily identified by his face and neck tattoos, stabbed with the same blade as the others, his throat slit from ear to ear making what was left of his corpse by the ever-hungry river rats, looking like some sort of bizarre circus clown.

D.C.I. John Dixon, head of Birmingham's homicide division was given the job of connecting these three dots together, men who on the surface came from different worlds yet had all ended up gutted on this sleepy riverbank in the dead of night.

The John Doe would have to be identified by his dental records, which thanks to government police cutbacks could take weeks. The other two on the other hand, were easier or so it first appeared. In fact, the more Dixie peered into their murky lives of these cadavers, the muddier the waters became. For instance, on the day D.C.I. Dixon went to visit McBride's last employer at the Dublin Barrel, Birmingham's toughest Irish pub in the heart of the Irish Quarter to interview Declan O'Dwyer, landlord and publican, the man seemed unusually pensive, as if he were hiding something. Nothing unusual there you might say. Irishmen will sing and dance at the drop of a hat but try to make them talk, now that's a different matter altogether.

Dixie questioned the man but found him fearful for some reason. He'd met Declan before on several occasions for one reason or another and always found him either overly friendly or heavily aggressive. However, on this occasion, the big man seemed truly afraid and acted as if he didn't want the detective to leave, offering him several drinks on order to make him hang around, which he did for nearly two hours, pressing the Irishman for any kid of detail that would shed light on his former employee's untimely death. Dixie left the pub none the wiser, O'Dwyer following him to the door of the pub. Declan opened his mouth to speak but was stopped by the sound of another man calling his name from the rear of the pub. Dixie looked over the big man's shoulder but only saw the back of a red-haired man in the darkness of the office.

"Well, Declan, if you can think of something or hear anything to help us understand what happened to McBride please feel free to call me."

He handed the landlord a business card, knowing full well that he would never call.

He gave him a short nod and walked away and that would have been that, had it not been for the burning car found blazing in the carpark to the Dublin Barrel only three days later. A flurry of blue flashing lights and a short firefight later, Declan O'Dwyer's body was discovered curled in a foetal position in the trunk of the car where he'd been trapped and burned alive. The only clue to the murder was the grainy CCTV footage showing a wiry red-haired man leaving the premises via a back door creeping away like a midnight city fox, heading to the taxi rank on the opposite side of the street. The taxi company records showed that the man had been taken to Birmingham airport where he had boarded an Aer Lingus flight to Dublin. When Dixie tried to identify the red-haired man at passport control, he was informed that the Irish flights were still classed as internal flights thus, no passport was required to board a flight to the Republic of Ireland and so, Dixie had to admit that, with no irony intended, the fox had fled the coop, leaving only dead chickens in his wake.

Bull's death revealed even less answers than McBride's had. The man was a loner, only having one real friend, if you could call him that. Another ex-con who, coincidentally had died at the Kings Norton Mop trying to save his transgender lover from the grip of a fairground ride machinery in which she/he had become entangled. Even in Dixie's overworked imagination, these two events couldn't be connected and so he awaited the return of the dental records for our John Doe. Once again nothing except a name. Derrick Hanlon. A police record of criminal activity found that he'd spent a short time in prison only a year before hand.

Dixie payed a visit to Winson Green prison to establish what type of inmate he'd been, to see if it would cast any light on the man before his death. Once again he found nothing at first until a comment by the deputy chief of the prison who told him that Hanlon had been taken under the wing of an old lag. Nothing unusual there you might say. Older prisoners often take younger offenders under their wings to help them get through their sentences. All good there then, except for one strange detail, Derrick Hanlon had shared a cell and friendship with the very same man who had been killed in the fairground accident a short time before his own death. The very same man who had been the one and only friend of ex-con 'Bull' who had been found floating down the same river on which Mr. Hanlon had found himself murdered. Like everything else in this case, the prison visit turned up more questions than answers and so, with great relief, a next of kin was tracked down and Dixie decided to go break the bad news himself. He found Neil Hanlon's office easily and called to make sure the man would be there when he arrived.

"I'd like to talk to Neil Hanlon, please." he said into the crackly line.

"Who calling?" a bright, female voice answered.

"My name is D.C.I. John Dixon, I'm calling in connection with Mr Hanlon's brother Derrick."

A short silence followed before the sound of a hand being placed over the receiver and a muffled voice.

"I'm sorry he's ... " Dixie could hear a man in the background giving the woman prompts. "He's not here, he ... doesn't work here anymore!"

"He doesn't work there anymore?" Dixie asked, his suspicions aroused. "Well who was that you talking to? Can I talk to that person instead, please?"

Another short silence then the phone line went dead. In the time it took Dixie to race over to the offices on the industrial estate across town, blue lights on the Ford Sierra Cosworth flashing to clear his way, the girl he'd spoken to and the mystery man in the background had vanished. The detective cornered an old security guard at the industrial estate who assured Dixie that it *had* been the deceased man's brother who had been in his office that morning.

Neither the girl nor Hanlon were ever seen or heard of again.

****

A thick blanket of white fog shrouded the old structure of the Severn bridge. It connected England to Wales, spanning the turbulent currents of the River Severn one hundred and twenty feet below since the mid 1960s. The place was a favourite spot for sightseers.

Daniel Fletcher had checked himself out of the hospital to come here specifically for one reason and one reason only. With his broken jawbone wired into place and unable to answer the questions he'd been asked by the uniformed policemen he'd awoken to at his bedside. The man had mumbled incoherently until the copper had gotten bored and sauntered away none the wiser as to how he'd ended up with a broken jaw in the first place. He'd dressed himself, ignoring the pain of his jarring jawbone and left the hospital not really knowing where he was going or why he was going there. A few hours wandering the streets of the second city led him to the Old Bristol road and a sign saying

M5 South West. Without any further thought he turned ninety degrees to the pavement and stuck his thumb out.

Six hours later he was dropped off at the Severn Bridge services in the early hours of Sunday morning. The fog clung to the huge concrete pillars that rose from the river bed to a height of nearly one hundred and forty meters. The company that ran the collections for the bridge were always told to watch out for suicides on one of the many CCTVs that lined the walls of the control office on the English side of the bridge. However, with the fog being so thick that morning the small television screens were worse than useless, showing only white screens and no images at all.

Daniel walked along the concrete walkway until he reached the centre of the span. He looked through the grated fencing that separated him from the thin air and the edge of the bridge. He scanned the waters below but could see nothing through the drifting white mist. Without hesitation he began to climb the cold metal cage that had been put there to stop would-be jumpers. His hand holds were fine but he couldn't find any foothold on the fence so climbed back down and took his shoes and socks off and tried again. This time he scaled the grid fencing all too easily until he sat precariously balanced atop of the thin metal fencing, his feet dangling into thin air. A bitter breeze had started up and blew through the thin material of his father's old mohair suit. The breeze stirred the fog beneath him and he caught a glimpse of sunlight reflecting on the brackish waters of the ancient river a hundred and twenty feet below him.

Since his epiphany at the nightclub, he'd been unable to shake the images from his mind. The look of love in his mother's eye and the proud face of his father as he'd held his hand all those years ago. Now both parents were dead and Daniel decided he wanted to see them once more. The spider hadn't shown itself since that night but he knew that it was just a matter of time before the creature's spindly legs crept across his brain once more.

And so without anything more than a resigned sigh, Daniel Fletcher let go of the wire fence and vanished into the white fog forever, leaving behind him only a scruffy pair of size nines to prove he'd ever existence.

****

"So there I was on me own and these two Cockney lads are stood in front of me!" Davey took a sip of brick red tea Eddie had given him as he sat on a tall stool in Eddie's kitchen. "I'm Reggie and this is me brother Ronnie ... " Eddie said, "we're the Kray twins from London and we can help ya."

Davey had heard the story before but could happily listen to it a thousand times more. He'd won a place in Eddie's heart since the night at XL's night club, a rare thing for anyone these days, let alone one of Abi's boyfriends. Over the three months since the attack in the nightclub, the pair had talked nonstop about about Eddie's rise from Aston guttersnipe back in the 1950s, to his current status as Birmingham's *King of Clubland*

The battle on the riverbank, the attack in the nightclub, Daniel Fletcher, the I.R.A and the Irish-themed pub robberies were never mentioned again. The only thing to remind them that the events had occurred at all was the six inch long scar on Davey's cheek left by the ever-elusive Fox. Both Abi and her father were in agreement that the scar gave the Irishman an almost romantic, roguish appearance and Eddie assured him that once he'd gotten used to the scar, it would be something that he would wear like a badge of honour.

Over breakfast and the next few hours the Irishman picked Eddie's brain for snippets of information about the early days in clubland. He wasn't sure why he was so interested in Eddie's beginnings and these larger-than-life characters he had spoken about. Long forgotten people with the most bizarre nicknames, who had peddled their trades on the grimy streets of Brum back in the late 1950s. Most of these people were long dead and gone, along with their trades *and* rackets and so maybe, somewhere at the back of his mind, Davey felt a responsibility to somehow document a time that had passed and was never to return. Anyway, Eddie loved to talk and Davey loved to listen.

After breakfast the pair walked through the hayfields on Eddie's farm on the Welsh borders. Eddie was telling him about another, particularly vicious battle with two enforcers from London called the Lambrianous brothers and how he had had to step in and put a stop to their collection rackets in Birmingham.

Suddenly Davey stopped walking, turning to face his future father-in-law and asked.

"You really *were* a gangster then?"

Eddie stopped walking and gave a wry smile.

"A gangster . . . ?" he mulled the word over for a few seconds as if by doing so it would add a touch of drama to the conversation. "Nah, I was never a gangster our kid, I was a businessman that's all, if I ever acted like a gangster then it was by *accident!*"

Davey laughed, shaking his head at the explanation.

"An accidental gangster?" Davey asked incredulously,

Eddie raised his eyebrows and still smiling Eddie replied.

"Yeah, that's me son. The Accidental Gangster!"

EPILOGUE

The Rolls Royce braked suddenly in the middle of Harborne High Street. The screech of tyres catching many of the pedestrians by surprise. They stopped to see what they assumed was an accident. However, instead of seeing a fender-bender they saw a white-haired man in his early sixties, climbing from his car and standing in the middle of the road. The man began to shout obscenities at the driver of the car behind him.

"Hodgy . . . .*Hodgy*!"

He began to walk down the side of his luxury car to the small hatchback behind. On reaching it he slammed his fists down on the bonnet of the car with a metal crumpling thud.

"Hodgy . . . I know you're in there, you *fucker*!"

The shocked driver wound his window down.

"What the fuck is your problem, granddad?" the twenty-something shouted. He wished he hadn't. If the old man looked crazed before now he looked virtually demonic.

"You tell Hodgy, I'm gonna fucking kill him! *Understand?* Fucking *killlll himmmm*!"

He dragged out the last two words to emphasise his incandescent rage. A crust of white foam had formed at the corners of his mouth making him look like a wild, rabid dog. In an instant that caught the young driver by surprise, he crossed to the driver's window and began dragging the unsuspecting man from his seat. The twenty something froze in fear of his life. Instinctively he grabbed at his steering wheel in order to stop the old man dragging him completely out of the driver's window.

"Stop it! What the hell do you want you crazy old twat!" the man screamed.

"I want fucking Hodgy."

"Who the fuck is Hodgy?"

The words seemed to confuse the old man and on seeing this the twenty-something continued.

"I'm not Hodgy, I don't know who Hodgy is?"

Suddenly the man's hand was around the younger man's throat. He began to squeeze. The twenty-something was shocked at the old man's power and he let go of the steering wheel and grabbed his assailant's hand.

"Where *is* Hodgy then, you ponce?"

The old man's words grew more vehement with each passing second. The young man panicked.

"He's .... in ... " he stuttered, trying to draw breath. "He's ... in the boot!"

He didn't know why he'd said that, the only thing in the trunk of the little car was some old washing he was about to drop around to his mum's. Nevertheless it worked. The old man let go of his throat and spun on his heel and walked to the back of the car. As he fumbled with the lock, the younger man made his escape into the mass of pedestrians who had begun to gather on the sidewalk. The old man found the boot-latch and pulled the trunk of the car open. He stood there for a second trying to comprehend what he was looking at. Leaning into the small boot space he began to fumble through the pile of dirty clothes.

"Come on Hodgy, you wife-stealing bastard. I know you're hiding in here somewhere." He began to toss the clothes onto the road around him. "You can't hide from me forever ... I'm the King of Clubland!"

****

Hazel Fewtrell had noticed a change in her ex-husband's behaviour over the last few days. He'd developed a manic look in his eye that she'd never noticed before. To most people he looked and acted the same as he always had but Hazel, who had known him intimately for over forty years, recognised the subtle changes in him. She could see something hidden to most, a dark and unpredictable thing in the shadows.

Even Eddie's normal manic highs and lows couldn't camouflage this to Hazel, and she had wondered how long it would be before the first threads of sanity began to unravel. Hazel had put it down to the stress of the sale of his nightclub empire to Ansells Brewery. The landmark deal had been going on in the wings over the last few months and now he'd pulled it off, it had netted Eddie a considerable sum in the region of £15,000000.

He had visited her on several occasions over the last few weeks on the build-up to signing off on the deal. He'd spilled his heart out to her about his new relationship with a six foot blonde. Hazel knew all about the girl and had her own opinions of her. The blonde had once been an au-pair for a friend of the family before jumping ship and backstabbing Eddie and Hazel's relationship and finally sinking her claws into the flesh of Eddie's mid-life crisis. She could see it even if her ex-husband couldn't. However much Hazel blamed the girl, she couldn't fault her timing. The blonde had timed it perfectly, what with the Fewtrell fortune hanging by a thread and Eddie without anyone around him to tell him the truth instead of the sycophantic ramblings he wanted to hear. She had stepped into the fray and whispered the sweet nothings that young women like her always seem to whisper into the ears of men as rich as Eddie and as far as Hazel was concerned, the gold digger had not only stolen her husband's heart but most of his money too.

No matter whether it was the deal or the spiel, the end result was the same. Eddie Fewtrell, *King of Clubland* was in the midst of a nervous breakdown and it was only a matter of time until one flew over the cuckoo's nest.

Hazel pushed the button on the phone receiver and put it in her jacket pocket. She looked down at the little bottle of blue pills she held in her other hand and sighed. She had crushed three of the Valium pills into Eddie's tea the night before in an attempt to control his extremely manic behaviour. However, from what she'd just been told about her ex-husband's antics on Harborne High Street by the police only an hour before, the pills had had the opposite effect and instead of calming him, had sent him totally over the edge.

"Where's your gold digger now then Eddie?" she muttered under her breath.

Bam! Bam! Bam!

The noise made Hazel jump and she dropped the bottle of Valium onto the floor where it smashed sending the little blue pills spilling across the granite surface of the kitchen in all directions.

Bam! Bam! Bam!

There it was again. A thunderous knocking from the front door. It could only be one person. Hazel crept to the hallway and peered around the door. She could see Eddie's silhouette behind the stained glass of the front door. Eddie saw a movement in the hallway through the stained glass window and began banging his fist against the door with fresh energy.

"Open up Hazel! Is Hodgy in there with you?" He screamed blindly into the glass panelling. Hazel froze.

Bam! Bam! Bam!

"Open this fucking door Hazel or I swear I'll smash it down!"

There was no way in a month of Sundays she was going to open that door. She turned and went back through the kitchen to the rear stairs and climbing two at a time up through the back of the house until she was standing against the hall window on the first floor directly above the front door. She opened the latch and leant out of the window.

"He's in there ain't he? That marriage-wrecking bastard! Hodgson . . . *HODGSON*!"

Eddie had bent down now and was screaming through the letterbox. Hazel looked down at the top of her ex-husband's white hair with its pink little bald patch. For some reason it reminded her of a rabbit she'd owned as a child. She watched the white rabbit below her with a macabre fascination as it bounced around in a fury screaming at the front door.

"Hooodgyyy . . . I'm gonna kill y . . . "

"He ain't bleeding here, Ed!" she called down.

Eddie stopped his ranting and looked around him as if he'd heard the word of God.

"Hodgy ain't here!" she repeated. Eddie couldn't tell if the voice was real or one of the voices he'd begun to hear in his head over the last few days. "I told ya months ago, I ain't seen Hodgy in a couple of years!"

Eddie held his hands to his ears, trying to block the voice from his mind. He looked around himself, searching for the source of the words, an expression of terror spreading across his face. Hazel continued to watch him, enjoying the moment of confusion she had created in the man below. She could see he was no longer the charismatic powerhouse that had ruled her life for the last forty years. Now, he was more like a lost child, who couldn't differentiate between the real world and the paranoid fantasy inside his head, and suddenly Hazel felt the Catholic guilt she thought she'd discarded years before, return with a vengeance. The emotion washed over her as she watched her ex-husband below. She decided to put the white rabbit out of its misery.

"I'm up here Ed!"

Eddie spun towards the sound of her voice, his hand still over his ears. He craned his neck upwards to see her, walking backwards as he did. She gave him a little wave accompanied by a nervous smile. He continued to walk backwards until his heel caught the edging stone of the footpath and he fell backwards into a bloom of rhododendrons with a pathetic yelp, his arms flailing around in circles as he tried to catch his fall. Hazel couldn't help herself and burst out laughing at the spectacle of Birmingham's most powerful businessman disappearing into the flowerbed. She watched for a few seconds, waiting for Eddie to reappear.

"Are you okay Ed ... Ed?" she called from her casement window.

Suddenly Eddie Fewtrell sprung from the bushes looking like an extra from a *Midsummer Night's dream.* His face and shirt covered in mud and green leaves and twigs caught in his hair. Hazel placed her hand to her mouth and stifled another laugh.

"Where is he Haze?" he said, his face set in a dark scowl. "I know he's in there ... *let me in*!" He began to climb out of the bushes and back onto the pavement where he began to bang on the front door with his fists once more.

"You ain't coming in here Ed, not like this!" She shouted. Eddie stepped back from the door and looked up at her. He could see her smile had dropped from her and was replaced with a look of real fear.

"It's my fucking house! I bought it and I wanna come in *now*!" Hazel shook her head.

"No, it ain't your house Ed, it's mine, remember?" His eyebrows raised as he tried to comprehend her words. "We're divorced Ed, you got the money, I got the house, the kids got a eighty grand each, the judge ordered it, as plain as day."

"Fuck the judge, this is my fucking house!"

"Not anymore it ain't. So piss off or I'll call the old Bill!" The mention of the police sent the nightclub owner into another level of fury. His face turning from an already flushed red into a deep purple.

"Call the fucking police, you bitch! You think I care about the old Bill? You let me in or I'll ... "

"Why do you wanna come in?" The question seemed to catch Eddie by surprise. He opened his mouth to answer but the words never came, his mouth just hung open as he suffered a sensory overload and had a fleeting moment of clarity. In that moment he saw himself standing at his old house, a question on his lips but for the life of him, he couldn't recall what the question was *or* why he was there. As quickly as the fog of madness had cleared, the veil of confusion returned.

"I . . . I . . . wanna talk to Hodgy!" he stuttered, unsure as to why he wanted to talk to Hazel's ex-lover.

"Well he ain't here, so fuck off!"

Hazel's insult stoked the fire of Eddie's madness and he began to kick at the front door with all his might. He began screaming bloody murder at the top of his voice as his mental breakdown became complete. Hazel knew that if the door came in, and it *would* judging by the power of Eddie's kicks, that her ex-husband wouldn't be reasoned with and this would end very badly for her. She reached into her pocket for the mobile house phone with a shaking hand and a feeling of overwhelming dread in her heart.

Bam, bam, boom!

She could hear the doorframe begin to splinter below.

"I'm calling the police, Ed!" She shouted from the window. Suddenly, the banging stopped.

She could see Eddie leaving the front door and stepping onto the lawn at the front of the house. Their eyes crossed for a second, hers dark concern, his blue pools of madness. Eddie broke his gaze and he sprinted out of sight around the side of the house. The phone line buzzed a couple of times before a familiar voice answered.

"Hello. D.C.I. Dixon."

"Dixie, it's Hazel Fewtrell here, you gotta come here quickly! Eddie's gone totally berserk!"

"What?" Dixie said unsure if he'd heard the words properly.

"Eddie, he's gone mad! He's gonna kill me. I'm sure of it." He recognised Hazel's voice but still didn't register what she was telling him.

"Eddie's gone mad?" he repeated.

"He's trying to break into the house screaming how he's gonna kill Hodgy, honestly he's having some kind of breakdown!"

"Ok, Hazel, I'm on my way. I'll be there in five minutes." The telephone line went dead just as a loud clanging came from the front of the house.

Her attention was drawn to the noise of metal clanging coming from the front of the house. Hazel leant out the window just in time to see her ex-husband bringing down the telephone line with the top of a long set of ladders. The cable fell around his feet as he placed the ladder directly beneath her window. Hazel's heart skipped a beat when she realised his intentions.

"Don't you dare!" she said under her breath.

"Ha! Now who's fucking laughing?" Eddie said to himself with a spiteful laugh. He turned to see Hazel peering from the window, a look of pure fear on her face.

"What's the matter, Haze? Someone taken the jam out of ya doughnut?"

He burst into a manic snigger, then without anymore ado he began to climb, all the while talking under his breath to himself.

"Yeah, you ain't so mouthy now, are ya Hazel? I'll deal with you *and* that bleeding wife-stealing fucker you're shagging!"

Hazel watched with a growing terror as he drew closer to her window, his spiteful smirk morphing into a violent grimace with each rung of the ladder.

"Don't you dare Eddie! Don't you *dare*!" she warned him as he climbed but it made no difference, Eddie's fragile mind had already drifted.

Faces from the past came flooding back; gangsters, villains, coppers, living, dead, all of them had a strip to tear from Eddie's soul and all the time his mutterings grew more and more distressing to hear. Finally after what seemed like an age, he reached her window. Eddie's ramblings came to a sudden halt and he stood atop the ladder, face to face with his ex-wife. The divorcees stared at each other for a few seconds in silence and right at that moment Eddie had another fleeting moment of clarity.

"Alright bab!" he said breaking into a broad grin. Hazel, openmouthed didn't reply. Instead she looked into Eddie's eyes and was dismayed when she saw the depth of his confusion. "How are ya Haze?" he asked.

She stared back at him, incredulously.

"I'll be better when you've climbed back down that ladder and pissed off back where you came from, you crazy bastard!"

Her words seemed to wake him from his fantasy and for the first time since setting foot on the aluminium ladder, it dawned on Eddie that he was standing over twenty feet above the ground. Hazel was flushed with a desire to punish him for the spitefulness she'd suffered at his hands over the years.

The sound of police and ambulance sirens broke the silence, shattering the peacefulness of the leafy suburb as Dixie's Sierra Cosworth screeched around the corner of the road, followed closely behind by an ambulance. The siren, triggered a response in Hazel that she would never be able to explain later in life.

As the police car drew nearer she grabbed the top of the ladder and pushed as hard as she could. Now it was Eddie's turn to be filled with terror. Hazel strained to lift her husband's weight from the window ledge. Eddie saw her intentions and started to try and slap her hands on the ladder. The slight woman put her whole weight behind the push and finally the ladder left its perch and gravity took hold. Eddie felt the ladder stand vertically for a few seconds. He pushed himself backwards and forwards trying to prolong the moment of gravity defiance before the ladder would start its inevitable fall backwards to Earth. The petrified nightclub owner gripped the rung in front of him for all he was worth. His blue, watery eyes wide with shock, hers dark circles of revenge. For a millisecond the ladder stood tall and the ex-lovers stared intently into each other's souls. Hazel saw Eddie's little boy lost expression and met it with a mischievous smirk.

"Hazel . . . ?" Eddie said pathetically.

Hazel raised her eyebrows and smiled spitefully.

"Enjoy ya trip, Ed!"

Then Eddie's moment of soul-searching was over as the ladder swung backwards in a long, sweeping arch carrying its unwitting passenger, Birmingham's No.1 club owner descending with a childlike yelp before crashing into the huge privet hedge at the end of the garden. Hazel watched as her ex-husband vanished into the thick hedge still clinging to the aluminium ladder and couldn't help but chuckle nervously.

Suddenly, the street was full of screeching of tyres, blue flashing lights and sirens as Dixie arrived followed closely by the ambulance. He leapt from the car just as the ladder carrying Eddie crashed into the hedge. Dixie's stood horrified as he stared at the scene of domestic violence and he wondered if his old friend had survived the fall. He turned just in time to see Hazel closing the window on the first floor. He caught her eye and she stopped.

She leaned out the window and gestured towards the large hole in the top of the privet hedge with a nod of her head.

"He's your problem now, Dix!"

Without further ado she closed the window and vanished into the house. Dixie walked across the lawn to where the ladder had landed, its end, with the nightclub owner still attached lay unseen moaning and mumbling nonsensically in the thicket. The detective was joined on the lawn by two panting ambulance men.

"What the fuck's happened here?" the larger of the two medics shouted on a high-pitched Birmingham brogue.

"I've seen Evil Knievel have better landings than that!" said the other with typical Brummie gallows humour.

Dixie shook his head and sighed. Thoughts of the years he'd spent with the Fewtrell family, especially Eddie, danced through his mind. He'd witnessed the upwards spiral of the second city's very own Godfather. A cartoon-like film of ups, downs and sideways shenanigans he'd witnessed over the last thirty-five years played out in his mind.

He'd been right at Eddie Fewtrell's side at the start of his rising-star ascent to success back in 1961. It was only fitting Dixie thought to himself that he should be here now, when the rising star finally plummeted back to Earth. He put his hands in his jacket pockets like a bored schoolboy, shook his head and turned to leave.

"You're gonna need a straight jacket for this one lads!" he said over his shoulder to the medics.

They turned away from their victim and watched with bemused expressions as Dixie washed his hands of the situation and simply walked away. They watched him leave just as the first heavy drops of rain began to patter on the leaves of the privet hedge and trees. Both men noticed a sudden change in the air pressure around them and on the slightest breezes, there hung the distinct odour of an electrical charge.

A storm was coming.

Printed in Great Britain
by Amazon